Acclaim for Jay VanLandingham's

Sentient

"VanLandingham forges a powerful story of three characters who seek to create safe lives for themselves and their loved ones, whether human or animal… Sentient's ability to call into question the survival tactics of a disparate society makes it a hard-hitting, action-packed story that combines well with a teen coming-of-age backdrop to appeal to both teen and adult readers of dystopian sci-fi."

     -D. Donovan, Senior Reviewer, Midwest Book Review

"Sentient will take you on a roller coaster of adventure through the eyes of both humans and animals. Feel what the animals feel, strive to take down those who keep you captive, stop the revolt, and desire to be listened to. Learn from this story, though we are all different, every life is important."

     —Felisha Antonette, Author of the Separation Trilogy and The Sephlem Trials.

Dedicated to my mom, Debbie. Thanks for thirty-five years of support while I wrote stories. This one is for you.

Katie
Thank you so much for you support

Chapter One

Bray

United States, Year 2040

Bray Hoffman watched as they slit Alice's throat.

It was a recurring nightmare, of course, but it was more real than anything in her waking life. Any interaction with Alice was the most real thing she'd ever experienced-and so to lose her would feel like losing a part of herself.

The end was coming, and far sooner than she feared.

Bray sat up in bed. Sweat gathered along the back of her neck and on her forehead. Her hair stuck to the sides of her face. She pushed it away and took a deep breath. These nightmares would never leave her. Then she noticed her throat was sore, tender and in pain. Shaken, she ran her fingers down the

.

front of her neck. She felt nothing there.

Closing her eyes, she connected with her best friend, Alice. She had to warn her.

A view of the factory farm in which Alice was confined came to Bray's mind. She had the ability to see everything from above, as if she were in the room. When she located Alice's gestation crate, one of the workers stood beside it.

"Alice...they're going to take you away," Bray said.

"How do you know?" Alice asked.

"I can see it. They spray painted the number four on your back," Bray replied, sitting still in her bed. "It means you have four days left."

Bray watched as the man stood behind Alice, just outside the bars of the gestation crate. Alice lifted her hind legs. She kicked backwards. Her hooves punched him in the gut. The man let out an "umph," and fell backwards, nearly into the crate behind him.

Bray flinched, then smirked. That's what

you get, she thought.

The man disappeared out of sight. He returned seconds later with an electric prod.

"Oh no," Bray whispered to herself. There was nothing she could do to stop him.

The prod struck Alice in the back just above her tail. An electric shock coursed through Bray's back. Both she and Alice convulsed, simultaneously. The man pulled the prod away, laughed.

Then Bray felt a sudden, sharp burn in her lower back.

"Ah!" she let out a scream, then quickly covered her mouth. If the nurses heard her, they'd come running.

The sting sharpened, shot up her spine again. Her body shivered. She fell forward in bed. It became hard to breathe. Reaching around, she felt along her back. It was hot to the touch.

"What the..." she whispered, pulling her hand away.

She didn't know what to think. With her

eyes now open wide, staring straight ahead at the bare wall, she'd disconnected from Alice. Further communication would have to happen later. Bray was too shocked and in too much pain to talk to anyone.

Even her closest friend.

She picked up a journal from the bedside table and opened to the next blank page where a pen sat waiting. Picking up the pen to write, she heard a knock at the door. Startled, Bray turned to look at it, hoping they didn't hear her scream.

A second later the door clicked open. A nurse entered, pushing a metal cart dressed full of medications.

"You ready for your medication?" The nurse entered. If Bray had a favorite nurse, it would be this one. Her name was Bethany. She was short like Bray and had this calming energy that made Bray feel safe. Truth be told Bray was attracted to the woman. She'd always known she was a lesbian, but she'd never been with another girl. Not yet. Maybe not ever.

"Do I have a choice?" Bray asked in resignation.

Bethany did not answer. She held out a clear, plastic cup and gave Bray a half smile.

Bray had been in the Denver Health youth psychiatric unit for days. She took the cup and cringed. It sat nearly weightless in her hand. Three pills rolled around inside. She was the tiny, round white one. That was the antidepressant. It was overpowered by a blue capsule, the antipsychotic. That one was her mother. An oval-shaped one the color of maple syrup hid at the other end. Vitamin D. That would be her dad, for sure.

She lifted the cup to her mouth and stopped just before tossing the pills in. Her gag reflex was already triggered, a muscle memory that had been building up since she was given her first antidepressants when she was just a child. It all began at age five when Bray began showing symptoms of schizophrenia. Of course they didn't diagnose kids that young, but she'd complained of hearing animals' voices calling out to her. Once she told her parents she was also having visions, and that's when they grew concerned. It caused her considerable distress, and sleepless nights, and frequently she would spend time alone in her room. She had trouble making friends. The psychiatrist initially diagnosed her with depression. The "early-onset schizophrenia" diagnosis came one year ago. If she had known as a child what she knew now, she never would have told her parents what was happening. She would have kept more of it to herself.

Years of being on these medications had caused numbness. If you really want to know what a zombie apocalypse is like, Bray thought now, come here. It's not all that exciting.

"C'mon girl, I don't have all day," Bethany said.

Bray tossed the pills in her mouth. Bethany handed her a cup of water and she swallowed them down. Letting them sit in her mouth for too long would just worsen the gag reflex. Bray tossed both cups into a nearby trash can and Bethany turned for the door. For a moment Bray wished she would stay. She could use someone to talk to other than herself and Alice.

"By the way, those are your last set of pills," Bethany spoke, stopping at the door.

"What?"

"They're switching you to an injection, starting tomorrow. And your parents are coming today, for a care conference."

The door clicked shut and Bray stood up, feeling a sharp pain in her bones from the burn. The floor was cold and impenetrable beneath her bare feet. She hobbled into the bathroom, cringing from the pain. She pulled her hair back away from her face and stepped up to the toilet. Bending over, she took a deep breath and closed her eyes. She pushed two fingers into her mouth. Her eyes watered, and she folded over further. Just as she did during every visit to this place, she forced herself to throw up.

She scanned the contents of the bowl. One...two...three pills. It had worked, again. There, that'll show them. She quickly rinsed her mouth out in the sink and then stopped when she noticed herself in the mirror. Her brown hair scattered down to her shoulders in clumps. Her eyes were low and her cheeks seemed to sag.

She sat back down on her bed and thought about what the nurse said.

An injection? No, no, no. She buried her head in her hands. There was no way to purge an injection. What was she going to do? This was clearly her mom's doing. She'd have to tell Alice right away.

"Alice?" she said, closing her eyes.

"Yes?"

"You and I may not be able to connect as much," she said, her shoulders slumping.

"How come?"

"It's hard to explain. They are giving me this...medication. It's going to stop my abilities." She paused, checking whether Alice understood. She sensed some confusion and continued. "You remember when they stuck you with that painful, sharp object, when they made you pregnant?"

"Yes," Alice said, her voice waning.

"I'm being stuck with something painful, but it's going to take away my ability to talk to you."

"I understand."

Suddenly an ache throbbed in Bray's heart. Everything went silent.

"Alice?" she called.

Nothing. Bray held her breath and froze. She turned and stared at the ceiling. Rubbing her fingers together, she remembered she had a worry stone in her coat pocket that her grandfather had made for her out of burl, cottonwood and walnut. He had to order the wood special just to make it, as trees like that rarely grew anymore. On it he had engraved the words: *Love ALL beings, equally*.

Bray slid out of bed and walked over to a small table and chair. There, the boho coat her dad had gifted her hung over the chair with all its weight. Bray searched the pockets until she found the worry stone, and then she returned to the bed with it, curling up under the covers in fetal position.

Squeezing and pressing her fingers into the stone, she closed her eyes and tried Alice again.

Ever since Bray and Alice met, they connected every day. But the connections were interrupted whenever Bray was placed on medication. Being in and out of a psych ward since childhood made it nearly impossible to have any friends at all. Bray felt lonely much of the time, but with Alice the loneliness was less severe. Now Bray was seventeen. Alice was four. Bray had read once that sows only live four or five years in captivity.

Alice's days were very numbered indeed.

Now that Bray had experienced Alice's injury first hand, she began to wonder if her days were numbered, as well.

Bray's body shivered. Not because it was

cold or because of anything on her end. No, this shivering was coming from Alice. It was a strange, unfamiliar feeling, to feel what Alice was going through.

"Alice, I'm afraid," Bray said.

"What of?" Alice responded. This was often Alice's response when Bray expressed fear. Alice didn't understand perceived fear, the fear of something that hadn't yet happened.

"Just, the next four days, I guess."

"I don't understand time the way you do. But if I did, I imagine I'd feel the same."

Then another set of knocks hit the door. Bray's eyes shot open. When the door opened she saw Bethany.

"Bray, c'mon," Bethany said, waving her to the door.

"What for?" she asked, frustrated.

"It's time for your care conference."

"Already?"

"It's one o'clock," Bethany said, glancing down at her watch.

"How's that possible?" Bray whispered.

"What?"

"Nothing. I-I'm coming."

Bray wiped the sweat from her face and combed her hands through her hair. She didn't want to look a complete mess to her parents. She wanted them to see she could take care of herself, that she didn't need to be in here. She thought about Alice, whispered in her mind, while getting out of bed, that she'd be right back, to hold on. She pushed the worry stone into her pocket and started for the door.

The hallway walls of this place were muted and colorless. Long corridors of naked loneliness. She passed the rooms of other young souls. They were nothing short of anger, confusion, and most times, a silence blinding to the mind.

A female security guard stood short and stout beside the front desk, a gun holstered on her side. A hat bearing the word Security covered her eyes. She glared down the hall, motionless.

And there, across from the front desk, was

the glass door that led to the conference room. Bray stopped and stared at it. The door's shades were down and so she could not see inside. Why they called this meeting a "care conference" baffled her. There was no care in places like this.

She opened the door and stood there. A glossy, wood table took up the entire room. Leather office chairs surrounded it. Leather came from cow hides. She knew this, and it made her stomach turn. She walked over to the corner across from her dad and stood there. Sitting wasn't going to help the pain in her back anyway, and she needed to hide it.

"You're not going to sit?" her dad, Cole, asked.

He wore these flashy ties he always thought were so cool. Today it was a yellow one with gray, squiggly lines and patterns in the shape of teardrops. She had to admit the tie did look very...unique. The yellow of it matched his hair. The rest of his suit was gray and quite plain. His eyes were soft as always, same brown as her mom's, but there was more warmth in them. She liked to believe she had her dad's eyes.

"All I do is sit," Bray responded, feigning a smile.

From down the hall came a clapping sound. Clash, clash, clash against the tile floors. Bray pulled out the worry stone and squeezed it tight. Her muscles tightened with it. She breathed deeply, feeling the edge of panic.

Then, the door opened. There stood her mother, Dianna.

"Bray," she said, shutting the door and taking a seat beside Cole. She grinned a kind of soulless, drooping grin. One that should've actually turned upside down, but didn't. "Hope you're ready for this."

Chapter Two

Kage

Kage Zair felt himself imprisoned, though there stood no walls around him. Instead, he sat on his knees in the back garden, pulling weeds. The soil was wet with morning dew and from the water drain that led into the garden from a nearby stream. His eyes followed the drain pipe out of the garden, past the chicken-wire fences and into the pack of trees behind the garden. What lay beyond this acre of land on which he'd lived these past twelve years he only knew little of.

He rose to his feet. Stepping along the narrow walkway of bare ground between rows of growing vegetables and fruit, he stopped at the fence and looked out into the woods. From here he could hear the trickling of the creek, but he could not see it. Just like he knew there was more out there despite the fact he hadn't seen what was left of the country since he was sixteen.

"Kage," his uncle Trevor called him from the kitchen door. "Breakfast is ready."

Kage turned back to the house. This place was the same, every day. That's what made it feel like a prison. Breakfast, lunch, dinner, always at the same time every day. Tasks were monotonous. The only hobby he really had other than playing his hand drum was tinkering with his motorcycle, which rested beside Trevor's Jeep in the front yard.

As he exited the garden, he remembered what life was like before he ended up here. When he was a kid and always felt uncomfortable in his skin. Having the wrong body parts kept him in a kind of prison until he realized at age ten that he was trans.

Kage entered the house through the back, where the door led into the kitchen. Faded, blue paint lined the door frames and banisters along the walls. This place hadn't been painted in years, and it showed. But it also added a kind of character, a feeling that even though the place was aged, it was wise. Along the walls were painted canvases of farm animals. The white cabinets along the right side of the kitchen looked down on a marble countertop, which led to a white sink. There, a pile of dishes waited. He'd be expected to wash them after.

The scent of sage, maple from the nearby trees, and baked vegetables wafted in from the dining room. Kage followed it in to find everyone sitting at the table. It was a mahogany table Ethan had made himself way back in his twenties. Its deep-brown legs were shaky but sturdy nonetheless. The table took up the center of the room, and over against the wall a china cabinet held dishes and cups.

Kage sat down between Emily and Dennis. Before him, an empty plate, silverware. Bowls of fresh fruit, jam made by Dennis, and toast sat between plates of sweet potatoes, spinach and steaming broccoli. By far the food here was the freshest and healthiest he'd ever eaten.

And sometimes all he wanted was a vegan burger.

"You get very far?" Ethan asked Kage, sitting across the table from him.

"No," Kage replied, picking up a bowl of strawberries and plopping them onto his plate with a spoon.

"That's all right, I'll get out there after we eat," Ethan replied.

Ethan and Kage were not related, yet Kage looked up to Ethan as a grandfather. He was in his mid-seventies, bald, with a gnarly tattoo of a chicken's talon gripping his head as if to lift him up into the sky. Not to mention back in the early twenty-teens he was the leader of the Animal Rights Movement. But no one would know it these days.

"Kage can finish it today, right Kage?" Trevor asked from the head of the table.

Kage set the bowl down and dropped his spoon on his plate. Frustrated, he shot a glance at Trevor.

"I'm twenty-eight. I really wish you'd stop treating me like a teenager," he replied.

"Okay," Trevor said. "If you're an adult then you'll take responsibility for your projects and finish the weeding."

"Can you please cool it at the table, guys?" Emily said.

Kage quieted himself. His heart and chest bubbled with resentment. As much as he appreciated Trevor for saving him all those years ago, the constant nit-picking was getting old.

Kage wanted out of here, and that was the truth. A window called to Kage from behind Virgil, who sat beside Ethan. Kage looked out at the tall corn stalks. He couldn't see past them. They'd grown as a kind of protective layer between the house and the rest of the world. Just corn and blue sky.

Each time he looked out a window, he thought about his parents. Truth be told he thought of them all the time. Where were they? What happened to them? After the fallout of the Animal Rights Movement in the late 2020s, they were supposed to come here, to this rural town of Meeteetse, Wyoming. They were supposed to come live here with Kage and Trevor and everyone else.

But they never had.

Kage set his eyes to his plate and rushed through breakfast. The others relaxed into conversation about the day. The lack of newness was evident in every moment of every day, save the change of seasons and crops.

Kage stood up quietly and walked his empty plate into the kitchen. As he washed the dishes with a concoction of lavender and mint oil that Emily had made, his eyes carried back out the window. The view from here showed a bit more of Wyoming. He was curious how the world got on since he had left it.

He dried the dishes with a towel and set them in the cabinets above the sink. He thought about his parents. Twelve years had passed and even still, he'd learned nothing new of their disappearance. As long as he remained here, he never would. Another ten years would disappear. Then twenty, then thirty. Then he'd be like Trevor and-not that Trevor was a bad person to be-he'd have lost his fire for all the things that made life worth living.

"You okay?" Trevor's voice leapt in from behind.

Kage jumped, not realizing Trevor had been standing beside the dining room entrance.

"Fine. It's just..." he replied, his words trailing off. He wanted to talk to Trevor about his desire to leave, but he knew Trevor wouldn't hear it.

"What?"

"Don't you ever wonder what happened to them?"

"Every day," Trevor said, stepping up to stand beside Kage. He turned on the water. "I think about my brother every day."

"Then why don't we do something?" Kage asked, feeling a sense of purpose rise up within him.

"Like what?" Trevor said, stepping back.

"Like find out what happened."

"And how do you suggest we do that?"

"I don't know, but we're never going to if we just stay here the rest of our lives."

"Kage, we've talked about this. There's no place out there for us," Trevor replied. He crossed his arms. "Besides, they were supposed to come here. That was the agreement. That they never did tells us they are probably, well, you know."

Kage could see Trevor was losing his patience, but he went on.

"We don't know that. It's been twelve years. Maybe they're still out there."

Ethan entered the room, placed his plate down on the counter beside Kage. Turning, he quietly exited out the back door.

"Even so, I can't spend the whole rest of my life in this house. I'll go mad. When you brought me here, you couldn't possibly have thought this would be the end for me."

"We were running for our lives. I wasn't

thinking about the future back then," Trevor said.

"We're not running, anymore. I really want to get out there, for myself. See if I can find anything, or maybe just live my own life."

"We'll talk about it later."

"You always say that and then-"

"Just not right now, okay," Trevor said. He shot a sharp look at Kage and turned for the dining room.

"Fine," Kage said. He stomped out the back door, allowing the screen door to slam behind him.

In the garden, Ethan was pruning the Canadice grape vines along the back fence. Kage approached him and eyed the vines. It was too soon for grapes, with it being only April and winter still not edging off of the garden.

"I heard you two talking," Ethan said, his gray eyes remaining on the grapes. His aged hands graced and felt along the vines with ease, like they knew just what to do.

Ethan always knew just what to do.

"Yeah, well it never goes anywhere," Kage replied.

"What never goes anywhere?"

"Talking about leaving. He always puts me off. Tells me we can talk about it later."

"He's just scared. He doesn't want anything happening to you. You're his only family, you know?"

"Yes, I know," Kage replied, rolling his eyes. He hated how Ethan tried to get him to see things from Trevor's point of view. "But what about me? I've been here forever and I still don't know where my parents are. Even if it is dangerous, I'll die inside if I don't do something."

"I hear you. I'd probably feel that way if I were your age," Ethan said. He pulled away from the grapes and motioned for Kage to follow him. "Come help me down in the cellar."

Kage followed Ethan over to a patch of grass that hid the cellar door. Ethan flipped the patch over to reveal the steel door. He pulled a hatch and the door pulled open. They stepped down a narrow ladder into a dark room. There, the stone-built walls held shelves of canned goods, pickled vegetables, potatoes, grains. An extra barrel of water sat over in the corner on the hard, earthen floor. It was colder down here than outside, and Kage shivered.

Ethan flipped on a flashlight that rested on a nearby barrel of water.

"I think you should go," Ethan said.

Kage's ears lifted in surprise, and he was near speechless.

"Really?"

"Yes. And I'm going to help you," Ethan said, turning. He walked back into the far corner and pulled out a black, steel box with a lock on it. His fingers slid a code into the lock and the box popped open. There, Kage noticed a couple wads of cash. He couldn't believe it.

"Here's some money to get you started. Should be enough to find a place, get gas, whatever."

"Are you sure about this? Trevor'll be pissed," Kage said, hesitantly taking the cash.

"Look. I'm seventy-five. I've got plenty of life left in me. But not like you do. I can't sit around and watch you slowly go off here. I can tell you're not happy, haven't been for some time. You'll always regret it if you don't go. And some day, Trevor will, too."

Ethan searched the box and pulled out a paper map and a face mask. He dusted off the mask and handed them both to Kage.

"Here, it's a road map of the US. Should come in handy. You just have to be sure to learn where checkpoints are, and stay away from them. And please wear a mask. You'll stand out too much if you don't."

Kage quietly nodded. He pushed the cash and map into his back pocket.

Ethan hid the box back behind a shelf on the floor. He turned back to Kage.

"Is the bike good?" He asked.

Kage thought about his motorcycle. It was his dad's, the only thing he had been able to take from the house when they left. That's when he realized exactly where he needed to go first.

"Yes," he replied, feeling an aliveness in his chest.

"Good. Then leave tonight, after everyone's gone to sleep."

"But what about Trevor? He'll never forgive me."

"Leave him to me. Write a note, leave it on the dining room table. Make sure to grab some food before you go," Ethan said.

Kage and Ethan returned back up to the surface. Ethan closed up the cellar, stood up, and winked at Kage. He started back for the fences.

"Ethan," Kage called out.

Ethan stopped and turned. Kage walked up and hugged him. He buried his head in Ethan's chest. Ethan wrapped his arms around Kage. His chin set on the top of Kage's head.

"You stay safe out there, man. I love you," Ethan said, his voice shaking.

The tears hit Kage's eyes with sudden velocity. He held them back as best he could, so Trevor wouldn't notice he'd been crying. He pulled back from Ethan, smiled, and nodded his head.

They parted. Kage wiped his face clear. He returned to the house, taking a deep breath before entering.

Tonight, he would start his search for his parents.

And he was ready.

Chapter Three

Bray

"I hate you both." That's what she wanted to say, deep down inside. But she held back, sat there staring at her mother.

Dianna was the complete opposite of Bray's dad. She seemed to have no emotions, none that Bray ever saw. Every movement was so controlled, exact, like she had everything thought out in advance. Even her hair up in that tight ponytail made her face pull back and her expression look like she needed to take a shit but felt it too improper. From around her neck hung a peridot stone, a gift Bray had gotten her one year for her birthday.

Dr. Howard, the scrawny psychiatrist, entered the room. His curly black hair reminded Bray of a bird's nest on the top of his head. You could stick pens in there and they'd stay put.

"You want to have a seat, Bray?" he asked.

"I'll stand, thanks," she said. Everyone had taken enough freedom from her as it was.

"Then let's get started," he said, shutting the door and taking a seat across from Cole. "We have something we want to try."

"An injection?" Bray guessed.

"Yes. There'll be fewer side effects. And it's monthly. No more pills to swallow."

"Okay," Bray said, still choosing her words carefully.

"We'll have to keep you here for the first month, to see how it goes."

"What? C'mon," Bray begged, flinging her hands in the air and then crossing her arms.

"Sorry, but it's procedure," Dr. Howard said, frowning.

Procedure my ass, she thought.

Bray looked over at her dad. He had a few extra wrinkles—"chicken talons" were what he called them—crawling out from the corners of his eyes. He rubbed his hands together and leaned back in his chair. His silence was a sign that he agreed with what was happening. She wished he'd say something. Surely he cared about her. Of course he disappeared to DC all the time to work on his presidential campaign bid, but she still loved him more than she did her mom.

"Doctor, what are your thoughts on keeping Bray here until she is eighteen?" Dianna spoke.

"Mom," Bray pleaded, then stopped. The word mom felt so far from the truth. Dianna was more like a stranger, a roommate whenever Bray got to come home. These two people in the room were becoming more and more like acquaintances every day even though she very much wanted to know her dad, and wanted him to know her.

"There wouldn't be a need for that once she's stable on the medication-"

"Would you guys please stop talking like I'm not in the room?" Bray interrupted. She dropped her hands to her sides.

"Once you're an adult and have shown some responsibility managing your illness," Dianna replied.

Bray coiled back. She would've disappeared into the wall if she could. Tears welled up in her eyes. She looked over at Cole for help, but he did nothing.

"I want to discuss obtaining legal guardianship of Bray when she turns eighteen," Dianna continued, turning back to Dr. Howard.

"What?" Bray said. "You can't do that."

"I can. You have a very severe mental illness, and someone needs to care for you."

"If she continues to improve and adhere to medications on her own, that may not be necessary," Dr. Howard replied.

She stood and watched them. It was as though they were playing some strategic game and Bray's entrapment was the prize. She thought about Alice, wished she could talk to her right about now. Alice felt more like family than her own parents did.

"She'll never completely adhere to her

medications, trust me. She'll always find a way, even with an injection. We've still got nine months to see, but for now, just keep it in the back of your mind. I'll need you to sign off on it."

"I can't believe this," Bray said, crossing her arms. The pain in her back was making it harder to stand still.

"See what I mean?" Dianna replied, pointing at Bray while eyeing Dr. Howard.

Bray glanced over at her dad. He was sweating. His thinning, blonde hair was slicked back with gel, giving it an almost colorless look. He loosened the tie around his neck and crossed his arms. Bray could tell he was uncomfortable with all of this. If only she could read his mind right about now.

"All I really want is to go back home," Bray admitted, looking Cole in the eye. "I miss you. I just want a normal life again. Will you please let me come home?"

Cole leaned toward her and smiled. He took her hand in his. "If you agree to be seen by

an at-home nurse, twenty-four seven, then
I'm sure we can see about bringing you
home."

"I'll do anything it takes."

"I'm not signing her out of this place
until she's had a few of those injections. A
few months of proving to us that you'll take
the injection, then we can bring you home,"
Dianna replied.

"The doctor said just one month," Bray
insisted, gritting her teeth.

"You know, I can't really keep her here if
she's not a harm to herself or anyone else,"
Dr. Howard replied.

"Remember the agreement we made?" Dianna
snarled at Dr. Howard.

He quietly nodded his head and then
shrugged his shoulders. "Sorry Bray, since
you are under eighteen, your parents still
decide what happens with you."

Bray looked at Cole, but again he said
nothing. His shoulders slumped and he looked
past her, out into the hallway. He was
checking out, just like he always did the

moment things got hard. Instead of standing up for her or sharing his opinion, he would just shut down and disappear.

The feeling of these two people being her parents had long since gone.

It was over after that. Her parents left the facility without much goodbye. She really hated her mom now, and she grew increasingly frustrated with her dad for doing nothing. His silence was more powerful than any of her mom's actions. She always wanted her dad's acceptance more than her mom's, and all she ever wanted was for him to believe her. Feeling completely betrayed, she started down the hall to her room.

Halfway to her room, her back suddenly stalled out on her. The pain from the burn wound became so severe she couldn't walk. Pressing her hands against the cold, hard wall, she cringed. Dizziness brought her to her knees. The hallway spun. She closed her eyes, wishing desperately to pull herself together and get back to her room before someone noticed her.

The burning sensation pulsed even through her head and inside her ears. Tears developed in the corners of her eyes. This, this burn. How could this have happened? How could she so suddenly get this burn, and from a simple link with Alice?

But that link wasn't so simple. It wasn't safe to assume that. The risk in passing this off as coincidence meant Alice's death, and then her own. Slaughter. Bray didn't know what that was like for animals, but she feared she was going to find out in a few days. Four days, and here she was, trapped in this psych ward.

She had to find a way...her thoughts crowded and her vision blurred...she'd have to get...get out...the walls spun...around and around and went...all she'd known...blackness crept in around her eyes...there had to be something she could...do...

The pain grew so immense that she had no choice but to scream.

Chapter Four

Bertan

Bertan Duarte often had his head in a book. If he wasn't at work, he was glaring at the screen of his tablet, where he could stop thinking about the constant stress of his life. Today he was on page 266 of a post-apocalyptic novel called *Civilization*. He was sitting in his 2030 Nissan Leaf, passing time before his shift at the processing plant.

His phone rang.

"Carmen?" he answered quickly. He'd been waiting days to hear from her.

"Yes, how are you?"

"Bien. You?" he asked. He closed the book and set it on the passenger seat.

"Well, Gabriella and I really miss you."

"I know. I miss you, too."

"It's too hard here, without you," she said. Her voice sounded mechanical, like she was speaking from her head. "I'm taking Gabriella to go stay with family in San Pedro."

"Why?" he asked, leaning forward. His eyes glanced over at the glove box, where a bottle of vodka hid inside.

"It's getting dangerous here. Campesinos are being threatened, and now Medina is threatening us for fighting back. More and more are disappearing. Then we find them dead weeks later. We have to leave."

"Then go, yes," he said. He felt frustrated that Carmen continued to work with the campesinos-to try to help them stand up to the nation's main agriculture corporation. Of all people, Bertan knew how dangerous Medina was. He knew what they did to campesinos just to get their land. He could only imagine what they would do to his wife and child.

"Please will you come home?" she asked.

Bertan's heart stopped at the thought. There was nothing more he wanted than to be reunited with his family. But he was scared. If he returned home and Medina found out, then the three of them would be even less safe.

"It's not that simple. I don't have that kind of cash to get to the border." He paused. "And there's no telling if Medina could find me again."

"That's unlikely now, don't you think? It's been so long."

"I don't know," he replied, and stopped. He didn't know what else to say.

"Do you know how hard it is to wait here for you, years and years? I don't know how much longer I can go, just waiting. And Gabriella is really struggling. I just want you here."

"I thought we agreed I'd save up money to have you and Gab come up here," he replied. A heat was rising into his head.

"I don't want to come to the U.S. This is our home, amor. Please."

Her words dropped onto him like heavy rain. The kind of painful rain that stings and pelts. The kind only found here in Idaho where the weather was all fucked up.

"If you don't come home soon, I'm not sure what's going to happen," Carmen said.

"What does that mean?"

"Right now, I don't know. I'm just telling you we're leaving. I can call you once I get to San Pedro Sula, but really if you can't come home then we need to make a decision."

"A decision?" he asked. Now his heart was starting to drop down into his stomach.

"About us."

And that was it. Bertan had a tendency to shut down whenever things got difficult, and he did it now, on the phone. He was so upset and distraught that he couldn't voice it. He didn't know what to say.

The pain was real inside him now.

"Fuck!" Bertan shouted. He threw the phone against the windshield. His fists punched at the steering wheel. Picking up the phone frantically, he checked to make sure he hadn't broken it. It had hit the window head on, yet somehow did not crack or show any signs of damage.

Bertan stepped out of his car and took a breath of the night air. His head spun. Sweat grew along his upper lip. Was she going to leave him? Sounded that way. Not being physically there with her just compounded the confusion.

Sitting back down in the Nissan's driver's seat, he waited for his head to stop spinning. He pulled the phone up and checked it again. Just a frozen lock screen with a photo of his wife and child standing side by side outside their farm in Bajo Aguan. He saw that it was 9:20 p.m. He had five minutes. He could hardly focus, uncertain as to what was going to happen with his family. But if he didn't at least go inside and clock in, they'd fire him in an instant.

Outside, the Idaho landscape was nothing but darkness. He could barely make out the barren hills of dirt that lined the horizon. He took a breath and shifted in his seat, pulling the bottle of vodka from the glove

box. He took a swig, another, and then a
third, and returned the bottle to its home.
The sounds of whistling winds slid along the
car windows. The creatures of the night had
come out. Wolves yelped.

From a distance, the processing plant was
silent and foreboding. Its single-level
building lay flat, waiting for hundreds of
beefs to die on the inside. The lights that
lined its tight corners were all that could
be seen. Everything else was dark.

Bertan grabbed the cell phone—an S-Corp-
issued Samsung crapster, he called it-and
stepped out of the car. He spent the next
five minutes sliding into his uniform. There
was no one around so he dropped his pants
and removed the diaper he'd been wearing all
day.

The managers made them all wear diapers to
work. No bathroom breaks permitted.
Sometimes he could tell who was relieving
themselves by their crying. They'd stop
working for a moment, stand there, and quiet

tears would roll down their faces. Usually it was the new workers who cried. He never did. Eventually the diaper became a part of him, like an extra limb. Walking around in it was beyond humiliating, and chafing scars lined the insides of his thighs, but at least every worker was in the same boat.

He pulled on a pair of dark gray pants, buttoned his shirt and tied a black tie around his neck...the pressure of S-Corp upon him. He was tired. He'd been working this shitty security job for three years. So many years, and where did time go? Down the sanitation drains and out to the waste pond. Time went there and stuck with all the decay, unmoving yet unreachable and dead. He felt himself older every moment though he was only thirty-eight.

Bertan hurried along the quarter-mile of deadened ground surrounding the processing plant, checking the property just as he was trained. He listened for anything unusual. He carried himself in a meek posture, his shoulders slumping forward and his head down as he stepped carefully through the night.

He approached the door. He pulled a set of burdensome keys from his side pocket and unlocked it. The place was dark and smelled of shit. Bertan flipped on the lights, hearing the buzz of florescent bulbs that hung from the eight-foot-high structure. He noticed the motionless, industrial-sized ceiling fans and wished he could turn them on to get the air moving in here. Everything felt stuck.

The beefs rustled and grunted as he rushed past them. The three holding pens to his right were stuffed with well over 300 beefs, he surmised. The two pens to his left held perhaps another 300. Each beef had their hind legs shackled to prevent workers from being kicked.

The beefs stared at him and he looked away.

Turning, he moved through the Kill Floor. Dried blood splashed the walls with the remains of lives gone by. He heard a crunch and lifted his foot. The slime of a cockroach's body nestled into the contours of his boot's sole. He scraped his boot along the steel leg of the Cattle Scale until the bug's remains slid off.

He passed by the Squeeze Pen and stopped at the Knock Box.

The Knock Box.

He stared at it for a moment. Its cylindrical, metal tunnel sat and waited for the beefs. This was where death began for them. He tapped the back of his flashlight against the metal box and nodded. It was all too familiar.

Moving onward, he climbed up a flight of stairs to the Maintenance and Surveillance office. He unlocked the door and stepped inside. Sitting down at the desk, he faced a stack of monitors displaying various parts of the plant. He used one of the laptops to clock himself in, just as he did every night. He did this by punching in a six digit passcode that was his and his alone. Each worker was given one when they were hired. That way if anyone tried to breach the system, S-Corp would know exactly who it was.

Now what to do about his family? Should he try to get back home? His eyes scrolled the security monitors as he thought. The black-and-white videos showed an ominous exterior. Everything was so still it was almost frightening. The indoor cameras only saw the Clean Side. There were no cameras on this side of the facility, a good way for someone to hide what they didn't want others to see.

He had to do something, or he'd lose his family for good.

Chapter Five

Kage

The stinging dust winds that scratched at his face gave him the freedom he'd been yearning for. His black boots pressed hard into either side of the 2018 Ducati Monster. Gloved hands squeezed the handle bars.

The motorcycle raced down WY-201 East to avoid any major highways. He'd never been this far south before. He'd only left the house to go on runs for gas, some food and supplies. And only at times it was safe to leave home, according to Trevor.

As the bike meandered along the western edge of Wyoming, the expansive, green prairies and miles of untouched land were guideposts of possibility, of unknown adventure.

He smiled.

Kage had left in the night, to make it

easier on everyone. Maybe it would make it harder when they found just a note. Trevor, his uncle, would be most upset, but hopefully Ethan would make him understand.

A chill of cold morning followed Kage, even as day came. It was the chill of Trevor, of his disapproval. He'd told Kage not to leave, that there was nothing out in the world for people like them.

Kage glanced backwards, and he was not being followed. He knew he was alone. He could feel it. He'd felt this deep knowing inside himself since he was sixteen. He liked to call it instinct, that thing in the pit of his stomach that guided his decisions like a compass. And the longer he remained hidden in that house, the fewer decisions he had to make. Life wasn't hard. There was no challenge, no adventure. Remaining in hiding all his life was making him weak, numb, bored. It was dulling that very instinct that made him feel alive.

The motorcycle continued on along the border. Kage observed the blueing sky, knowing that drones could be circling the border, but saw none. He thought about hidden things, like secrets, how the truth hid under such convenient veils that S-Corp had built up over the years. Kage had never seen a factory farm himself, only heard about them through the stories Ethan, Trevor and Emily told.

Now Kage edged so close to the border that he had to slow the bike, and stop. Taken aback by what he saw coming at him in the distance, he stepped off the bike and stared. Miles and miles of dust and dry earth lay before him. The way the sun hung low in the sky turned the atmosphere a strange yellow brown, like the color of the sand itself. The color of the sun nearly matched the earth, and it was not beautiful. Kage turned back, seeing the rolling valleys of green edging away behind him, into the liveliness of Wyoming.

But now as he turned toward Utah, his home state, this he did not expect. It had been twelve years since he'd left this place, but he had not thought that this would be what was left when he returned.

What did this mean for his home in Salt Lake? Kage jumped back on the bike. He checked the gas level. It held steady at half a tank. He had placed some gas reserves in the bike's back compartment before he left.

Revving the engine, Kage started down a now-dusty path—Utah 16 North—once traveled regularly but now so covered in dust he wondered who ever came through here anymore, and when they last might've.

Once the bike had been consumed by surrounding dust and dead earth, Kage assumed he'd arrived in Utah. Trevor said that Utah had become uninhabitable due to drought, but he didn't actually—couldn't actually—know what that meant.

Now it was dropped out before him like the dying of leaves in fall. But all this earth had died ages ago and was never coming back. The trees were naked, and those that remained standing seemed to only because their deaths were so hard they died in place. Their branches appeared to have reached up for rain and then crumpled into dead ends. Those that had fallen lay like bodies along the road. Kage shifted the bike around them and, as he got closer to Salt Lake, he slowed once again.

From this distance he could see the Great Salt Lake, or what must have been the Great Salk Lake. Still three miles away, he could see a great cavern of deep ridges and vast air where water was supposed to be.

He continued on, and when he arrived at the lake, he stopped and gasped. Now seventy-four miles of dust had replaced the waters in which he once swam as a child. And at the bottom he saw rock and more cracked earth, even the bones of creatures that once swam the waters, now trapped in the hard earth. His eyes teared up.

A faint hum caught his attention. He glanced around but saw nothing for miles in each direction. The sky was now fully clear, no clouds, no drones. So it seemed. It was best to move on, not stay in one spot for too long.

Kage drove down into the city, where suburban houses decayed from dust storms, their siding faded and browned, windows cracked or blown out completely. This is what had been left behind during the 2030 Migration.

As Kage passed through downtown Salt Lake, the buildings remained strong; however, after ten years of lacking human connection they had taken on a foreboding zombie-apocalypse feel. The city buildings were ever present and therefore all the more quiet, which made Kage's hairs stand on end. His chest tightened as he slowed along the empty streets. There was rarely a parked car anywhere. When people left, they had done so in a planned manner. They must have all known what to do and where they were supposed to go. This realization was way more frightening than any zombie apocalypse show he'd watched as a child. The organization of it all, how the buildings still sat waiting for humans to return, how sands nestled into the sidewalks from the most recent storm, how any sign of humanity had packed up and abandoned the place he once roamed when he was young. His heart dropped a level in his chest. A strange feeling came over him as memories of his past flooded his eyes. He wished he had never had to leave, that none of this had ever happened. A part of him had clung to the magical thought that if he came back here, he could somehow get some semblance of his old life back again. Maybe even see his parents hiding in the house, and then he could get back to something like who he was before the world stopped.

Kage shivered. This place gave him the creeps, so he quickly exited the downtown area and raced to Fruit Heights, where his childhood house stood on the corner of Eagle Way and Bogey Drive, the house not recognizing him at all now as he pulled up onto its sidewalk.

He stared at the two-level house. It didn't bother staring back. The upstairs windows had been blown out. The garage door was still open. Their Toyota Mirai was missing. On the garage floor rested a black motorcycle cover, the one he and Trevor removed when Kage begged to take the bike with them. Seeing it now, the memory hit him...

"Take the bike," Kage's dad, Todd, said.

Valerie, Kage's mom, was standing in the corner of the garage, crying. Her hand was over her mouth and the tears spilled down onto her fingers. She had just handed him her favorite jacket, told him to hold on, to wait for them.

"Why can't you guys just come with us now?" Kage asked. He stood beside the bike, his dad on the other side, separated not only by some machine, but now by a distance that Kage knew in that instant was never going to change.

"They're on to us, Kage. This is to protect you. Please. Take the bike, and go."

Trevor walked up to Kage and placed his hand on Kage's shoulder.

"Come on, bud. We need to go, now."

And that was it. Kage remembered getting on the bike, a resentment growing in his chest, and starting the engine. He remembered watching his mom and dad stand in the driveway watching him as he followed Trevor away.

Now Kage lifted his mom's charcoal jacket to his mouth. He wore it every day, despite the hot temperatures of summer. He used to smell her scent on it, but that had long since disappeared.

Kage stepped off the bike and left it there on the sidewalk, beside the rusty mailbox. He walked up the drive and into the garage.

Walking over to the door, he turned the knob. As the door swung open, a wave of pain rushed at him. He took a step back, turned and breathed, and then entered the house.

He stopped right there in the kitchen. Everything was dark. Sunlight entered the one window over the sink across from him, leaving a square of lonely light on the tile floor. The air was stale, holding the scent of old life. The beige countertops were covered in a film of dust and grime. The lack of sound was the worst. He opened the refrigerator. The power was out, and the fridge was empty. He slammed the door shut, confused. A heavy feeling weighed on him as he walked slowly through the kitchen and into the front room.

On some level, he had hoped his parents would be here, hiding. To see that they weren't created a stillness in his body, and not the kind that brought comfort.

A chocolate couch stood across from him, beneath a bay window that had somehow maintained itself. Kage glanced out at the motorcycle, wondered if he should hide it.

When he looked up the stairwell, he stalled. He didn't want to go up there, but he needed to. With his last bit of remaining hope, he opened his mouth and called out for them.

"Mom?"

Nothing.

"Todd? Valerie?" he screamed up the stairwell.

The silence screamed back. His hairs stood on end. He stood there and stared up at the empty hall. He waited. It felt like hours passed. Finally, he decided to move.

His boots felt heavy as he made his way up. The stairs creaked beneath his weight. A narrow light entered the upstairs hall as he approached it. He ignored the family photos along the wall to his left. If he looked at them, he'd surely break. He needed his wits and he also couldn't stay here long.

At the top of the stairs, he turned and faced his old room. He took a deep breath, his hands now shaking, and he walked in. Paintings of goats and mountains covered the palm-green walls. Kage once loved goats. Everything in the room stopped at age sixteen, and in many ways, so had he.

Kage turned and walked back out into the hall. Flashes of himself at sixteen passing

through this very space popped on and off in
his mind. Inside he felt as though he'd
never really left.

His parents' bedroom was down the hall
from his. The door was open, slightly ajar.
The bed was neat, made. That meant they had
control over when and how they left. No
signs of forced entry or kidnapping. Kage
stood in the doorway, wondering what had
happened.

Kage searched the room. On his dad's
nightstand was a black lamp, his reading
glasses, and that was all. No evidence,
nothing.

Discouraged, Kage turned to leave.

Then, he heard a click.

Then a door closing.

He froze.

The downstairs floor moaned again.
Footsteps came close to the stairwell, then
stopped.

When Kage turned for an escape, something
fell from the nightstand. There on the floor
he saw a black and red flash drive. He

grabbed it and put it in his pocket. He ran
over to the windows. They'd both been blown
out, and beneath them a twenty-foot drop
ended at a cracked concrete patio.

Kage saw the back yard and froze in
distress. The once lively and tall bamboo
his dad planted had died, bent and fallen.
The grass was replaced with sand. And over
in the far corner of the yard, a child's
climbing wall was covered in dead ivy. Kage
used to climb on that thing every day. His
eyes fixed on it, and he was thinking how
sometimes he just couldn't leave his past,
even while the footsteps came up the
stairwell. If he jumped from here he'd break
a leg, or worse. He couldn't remember the
code to his parent's safe room, not that it
would work anymore.

He quickly turned to duck below the bed.
If he had to fight someone, then so be it.
He felt for the knife he'd hidden away
inside his jacket pocket. As he went to
slide under the bed, he saw someone enter
the room.

Jay VanLandingham

And it wasn't just someone.

Chapter Six

Bray

They had her on the floor.

Bray lay on her stomach. Two nurses, one male, one female, both in their twenties, knelt on either side of her. The female lifted Bray's shirt.

"Holy shit, Bray," the nurse said, staring at her back. "What the hell did you do? And how?"

"Nothing!" Bray shouted, the pain now excruciating. "Just stop it!"

They were in the hall. Other nurses began crowding around her. Even through the pain, Bray sensed her lack of privacy and wished for more.

"How did this even happen?" the male nurse asked, looking down at the burn.

"No clue," the other responded. They called into their radio, something about taking Bray downstairs.

Bray began to sweat. Her mind screamed for relief. And then she felt a coolness against the burn. The female nurse had covered the wound with a wet rag.

"We need to get you downstairs," the male nurse said. He stood up and disappeared down the hall.

The pain subsided and Bray exhaled. Now that she could breathe, she could think. They said something about taking her downstairs. The emergency room was downstairs. Must've been what they meant. Bray closed her eyes. She pictured it in her mind. The elevator. The tile floors that led to the Dialysis Unit. The ER was to the left of the elevator and down the hall. She'd frequented this hospital enough times to know.

The exit was also downstairs.

"How on earth, Bray?" the female nurse asked, disturbing her thought process.

Bray said nothing. Anything could incriminate her, could land her in even more trouble with her parents. Probably would anyway.

Bray's head was turned away. A shadow approached the wall, and her eyes shifted downward. The male nurse had returned with the wheelchair.

Together, the two nurses carefully lifted Bray into the wheelchair. The cool rag was removed and the wound began to throb.

"Rag, please?" Bray begged.

The male nurse looked at the female nurse.

"I've got to get to my rounds. Think you can take her down?" he asked.

"I'd rather do this than my rounds, so sure thing," she replied, stepping behind the wheelchair.

"Here you go," she said, bringing her hand around and placing the rag on the wound. "You'll have to hold it there for me."

Bray brought her hand around and placed it on the rag. She leaned back in the wheelchair, cringing.

As the nurse wheeled her down the hall, Bray felt sweat break out on her brow. Her

teeth clenched as the pain seemed to turn up
like the volume on a stereo. It came on
suddenly. Like the coming of morning after
deep sleep. It just showed up, appeared. Was
Alice being shocked by an electric prod
again?

Alice had been shocked by electric prods
countless times in her life. It had never
previously affected Bray physically. So why
now?

Bray's eyes watered. She cringed. It felt
like sweat was covering her whole body, yet
she felt cold.

Then the elevator slid open. The nurse
pulled the wheelchair in, turning it so Bray
faced the doors.

The doors closed. Bray saw her reflection
in the bare, frigid metal before her. A
bloated image of a body looked back at her,
faceless but with a head full of brown hair
that had hardened like overcooked spaghetti.
She looked mentally unstable, but she
couldn't be. This was real. Alice must have
been shocked and then Bray burned in the

same location. Even the nurses saw it. She wasn't making it up in her mind. When that man hurt Alice, it hurt her.

What would that mean when Alice went to slaughter?

#

As the elevator dropped quietly to the first floor, the nurse leaned against the wall, tapping away at her phone. Distracted. Once these doors opened, Bray would be facing the exit. The Dialysis Unit would be on the right, gift shop on the left. Right in front of her, the doors. An opening. A start, launch, forward.

A moment later, the elevator rolled to a stop. There was a ding. Bray braced herself, leaned a little forward. The doors slid open. There, just a couple hundred feet away, stood the glass entrance, and exit. People walked in and out, not thinking how lucky there were to be free to go where they wanted, when they wanted.

The nurse approached the wheelchair handles. Bray's feet touched the floor.

Leaning forward a bit more, she felt her back scream. But this was it. If she didn't run now, she would not have another chance.

Bray stood.

"What are you doing?" the nurse asked.

"I think I can walk the rest of the way," Bray replied.

She stepped out of the elevator. Her mouth watered with thirst for the outside. When her feet touched the tile floor, they awoke. In that moment, the doors freed themselves of people. Outside, the sun was already starting to disappear for the night. It was time to go.

Bray ran for the door. Her bare feet clapped against the floor. People in the gift shop stopped and watched.

"Hey!" the nurse yelled.

Behind her, Bray heard the nurse call for security. Her outstretched arms smacked into the exit door. It pushed open and she was out, out in the evening of real world.

But she couldn't stop. She couldn't embrace the fact that she was out until she was really out. Behind her, a perp gained on her. Perp was a derogatory term for a drone, the things that followed people everywhere, watched everything they were doing, without their permission.

As the sun touched the lower tips of the Rocky Mountains in the distance, Bray ran along Delaware street. The pain in her back amplified now that the rag was gone. It must have fallen somewhere near the elevator. She wobbled and hobbled along the sidewalk. Passersby gave her twisted looks with their eyes, their mouths hidden behind cloth masks. It didn't help that she had worn the same clothes for weeks and her pants had lines on them from the fading of fabric.

She turned to look back. Two perps were following just above the back of her head. Volocopters buzzed back and forth through the sky, taxying people to their destinations. Bray picked up her pace. The uneven concrete poked up at her feet, scratching her delicate toes.

To her left, Sunken Gardens Park came into

view just past the Denver Health building.
Bray ran into the park, turned every which
way looking for a place to hide. Artificial
trees lined an open field of fake grass.
When Bray stepped into it, its prickly green
blades tickled her feet. The sun peeked out
behind her. She wished it would go away for
the night now. The perps buzzed above her
head. Soon, Marshals would arrive.

Just to the right of the line of trees,
gardens of artificial flowers-lilies, irises,
roses-glittered the ground. Bray ran over to
them and dropped into one of the patches of
flowers. Since everything was artificial,
there was no concern for creepy crawly bugs
or stinging bees. She just lay there,
holding her breath in hopes that the
Marshals would not find her. It was a stupid
idea, she knew, as the perps hummed above
her body in midair, but she needed this time
to come up with a better plan.

Then, one of the perps lowered itself
toward her. The bottom of its body-a metal,

convex circle with four legs popping out, two on each side-blinked with a tiny, red light. Bray watched it slowly drop to just inches above her face. A slight, warm breeze stirred from its propellers. She could feel it against her cheeks and forehead. Goosebumps developed along her arms. Holding her breath and closing her eyes, Bray wished it away. A thought occurred to call on a nearby animal for help, but there were no animals here. Maybe a few rats. The only animals in this city a person had to pay to own or pay to see.

The perp held itself just above the tip of her nose. Bray's eyes opened hesitantly. She didn't want to look at it, but she had to find out what it was doing. Suddenly her forearm warmed. She looked down at it. The implant her mother had forced her to have surgically inserted just below her skin now blinked red. The perp beeped back. A red light from the perp met her eyes. It was blinding. She closed her eyes again. Her heart racing, she searched along the ground with her hand.

Only a matter of time before the Marshals arrived.

Bray felt something hard beneath her fingers. Something concrete. She reached her hand around it, gripped the rectangular object in her palm. The perp hovered in midair above her.

Bray lifted the heavy object into the air. She used its heaviness to build momentum as her hand brought it across her body. It met the side of the perp with a thunk. The perp dropped to Bray's side but then began to rise back up. The second perp dropped down closer. Bray sat up, turned. She slammed the concrete brick into the perp. It fell into the grass, still buzzing, its propellers rapidly spinning. Bray sat up over it and brought the brick down onto its body, smashing it again and again and again. She felt satisfaction from it, seeing it fall apart, its body parts now the ones exposed and violated, dead.

"Take that, you pervert," she said.

Sirens whirred behind her. The second perp circled her head. She'd have to ignore it, find somewhere else to hide.

Standing up, Bray ran. Now the sun could only be seen bouncing its remaining light along the windows of apartment buildings that lined Elati street.

Across the street from the park, a Mennonite church stood with gray, concrete walls and a strange, triangular roof. It was one of those more modern churches. She approached its glass doors. Lights were on inside. It was probably the only place she could get into this time of day. And maybe it had a kitchen. She needed a knife.

The remaining perp followed her across the street. The Marshal vehicles remained in the park's lot but wouldn't for long.

Bray pulled the door open and ran inside, stopping cold in the empty sanctuary. The lights were all off, save those that lit up a cross above the hardwood stage. The sound of footsteps approached. Bray jumped in between a row of pews and crawled beneath one.

A door slammed shut. The sound of a turning key caused her to slide out and peek. No one in sight. Whoever had been in the building must've left for the night. Now all lights were off save a subtle illumination on the wood cross as it hung on a sparse, white wall. Maybe a cross was all these people needed, but for Bray, believing in a god made no sense in a world where animals were treated in such demeaning ways.

Bray slid out from under the pew and stood up. She approached the cross and, standing below it, sighed. Its wood shape to her was nothing but a hollow, empty, man-made structure where life ought to be but was not.

The sound of more sirens alerted her. She ran to a side door and opened it. A sign for the kitchen pointed down a flight of wooden stairs. She ran down them, feeling each step pulse the wound in her back.

The kitchen sat open across from the

stairwell. Half the wall was sectioned out
to expose the inside of the kitchen. Two
metal tables stood side by side in the
center of the room. A sink and white
cabinets stood behind them. The doorway on
the far left was open, void of any door. She
ran into the kitchen and glanced around. She
searched the cabinets for a first-aid kit.
Turning, she saw one hanging on the wall by
the doorway. She yanked it open and the
contents fell out onto the floor. Carefully
coming down onto her knees, she scrummaged
through Band-Aids and gauze to find a packet
of burn cream. She pulled it open and rubbed
the cream into the wound, taking a deep
breath of relief.

A set of sirens neared the building. Bray
froze, listened. The sirens stopped. They
were here. Bray's heart jumped into her
throat. She yanked open drawers until she
found them. A set of shiny knives called for
her. She grabbed one and eyed it, cringing.

Setting the first-aid kit down beside her
feet, she stood over the sink and placed the

knife's blade on her forearm. She knew the
location of the implant, never had to guess.
She could feel it, so unnatural beneath her
skin.

No time, she whispered to herself.

Bray punctured her skin with the blade.
Carefully sliding it along, she made sure
not to cut too deep. The pain sounded loud
in her ears. It moved from her back into her
arm and fingers. She dropped the knife into
the sink. It clashed against steel, landed
above the drain. Blood splattered up and
onto the faucet.

Taking a deep breath, Bray stuck two
fingers into the open cut. Her fingertips
felt a touch of hard metal.

The sound of doors pulling open upstairs
caused her fingers to slide back out.

"Shit," she said, the pain mounting.

The Marshals were inside the building. She
heard their footsteps.

Bray slid her forefinger and thumb into
the cut, gripped the slippery implant. She
pulled at it, and it came out.

"Bray Hoffman," a male voice shouted. It came from the top of the stairwell.

The implant fell out of her fingers and onto the floor. Bray bent down and grabbed the first-aid kit. Blood dripped from her arm. When she stood, she grew dizzy. A round light bounced along the wall. Bray turned and ran out of the kitchen. She pushed on the first door she saw and found that it opened to a back alley. She nearly tripped down a set of concrete stairs. She turned and ran up the alley, where all light was absent and the coming of night reached in and hid her beneath a set of apartment buildings.

She decided it best to keep moving, so she made a run for it. Her arm bled down, covering her hand in a warm, crimson blanket of shaking and dripping pain. The first-aid kit trembled in her other hand. Concrete cut into the arches of her feet. The wound on her back vibrated into her bones, but she kept on. Now that the implant was gone, no perps followed.

The sun was now gone.

Chapter Seven

The Knocker

Everything happened automatically. That was how the Knocker made sense of it. The beefs came through in a frenzied line. Confused, their eyes black and growing. As the beefs approached the serpentine—a narrow path only wide enough to fit one beef at a time—the pen workers beat them with electric prods, stabbing them in the sides and in their faces repeatedly to force them up the shoot and into the knock box.

The sounds entering the Knocker's ears ranged from grunts, shouts, laughter...to the howls of beefs as they tried with all their power not to move to their inevitable deaths.

Every ten seconds, Serpentine—a slinky

Guatemalan with shoulder-length black hair—
would force one into the knock box with his
electric prod. He had his own system, where
he used his belt to whip the beefs in the
hind until they were red and bleeding. Once
their overweight bodies neared the knock
box, he'd use the electric prod and stick it
right up their asses. They'd jump in
response and before he knew it, they'd
jumped themselves right into the knock box.
A metal door trapped them inside the
darkness.

The Knocker had been at this job for ten
years and had developed a system, too.
First, the cow, or beef, as he called it,
was automatically sprayed with a mist gun
located at the top of the box. Its body now
on a conveyor, the beef's belly was lifted
and its legs suspended in air to prevent
movement. The Knocker then pressed a button.
The beef's head was pushed forward on the
conveyor, and the job was his.

The Knocker wiped his forehead clear of

sweat and pulled a metallic gun over,
pressing it against the beef's head just
above its eyes. He concentrated on that spot
and pulled the trigger. Beef brains
splattered across the Knocker's face as
globs of blood rolled slowly down between
the creature's eyes. The Knocker watched as
the beef's head successfully dropped and hit
the conveyor.

Done.

Always he made sure not to have direct
contact with the beef. It was in, shoot, and
then on to the next one. There was no
thinking, only doing. Automatic, for twelve
hours a day.

Easy.

Pushing another button, the Knocker wiped
blood and brain matter from his goggles. The
beef's body was pushed onward and lifted
upside down by a metal hook that the
Shackler twisted around its leg.

The day went on like this, with everyone
in their proper places, doing their separate
jobs and at a speed of 360 beefs per hour.

If everything ran smoothly, he would knock
over 4,000 by the end of the day.

One of the Prodders stepped up to relieve
the Knocker for his only fifteen-minute
break of the day. He handed the knock gun
over and nodded to Serpentine, who also
stopped for break. All the men on the Kill
Floor had real names that no one used here.
Instead, they called each other by the
positions they held. Serpentine's job was to
push the beefs up the Serpentine. The
Knocker's, to knock beefs unconscious. Some
of the workers, like Teet Puller, hated
their given nicknames, but no one much cared
how anybody felt in a place like this.

"I'm hungry as a dick," Serpentine
commented as he followed behind the Knocker.

The Knocker grinned but said nothing. He
stepped up the Decline, turned right at the
Cooler doors and headed down the hall,
passing supervisors and Clean Side workers.
They all stared at him. He looked like
death. The blood stuck to his smock, and the
heat of the Kill Floor made him smell of

dried sweat.

The Clean Side workers had it easy, and that wasn't saying much. The facility was separated into three sections. The first they all called Heaven, which was at the front of the building, where only white people worked. They were the ones who ran the place and never saw what went on in the back. Next in line was the Clean Side—which they called Purgatory—where the USDA offices, the manager office, the "clean men's lunch room," knife-sharpening area and locker rooms were located. Those in Purgatory could swing back and forth between both sides with ease. And then the Dirty Side, which they called Hell, was downstairs where the beefs were knocked on the Kill Floor, dismembered and then sent to the Cooler and Fabrication department to become someone's steak.

The Knocker stopped into the Dirty Side restroom. In the one empty stall he removed a diaper full of urine and tossed it in the

can beside the toilet. Hanging on the door
was a tin box with fresh diapers inside. He
pulled one out and looked at it. Just then,
he heard a man in the stall beside him,
whimpering.

"What's going on, man?" the Knocker called
over.

"I cut myself on the line. It won't stop
bleeding and I know they're going to send me
home."

The Knocker did not reply. These stories
were common around here. The workers made so
little money as it was. If anyone injured
himself, they got sent home without pay. And
often times they were replaced the very next
day, and that was it.

Escaping the bathroom, he turned back down
the hall to the locker room. Once inside,
the Knocker ripped off his smock and tossed
it in the trash. There was no time for
formality.

"What did you bring me for lunch today,
man?" Serpentine asked the Knocker.

"I didn't bring you shit," the Knocker

replied. He pulled off his goggles and hair cap and tossed them inside his locker. He grabbed a bag of chips from the vending machine and sat down.

"I can't believe you've been at this knock job for so long," Serpentine said as he sat down beside him. "You've stayed the longest out of all of them."

"It's not a big deal," the Knocker replied.

"I'd lose my mind."

"I'm used to it," he said with a shrug.

"No one gets used to that shit, man. I've seen so many tough men go through that job and end up dead on the inside. You do it like it's second nature."

"It is. I've tortured and killed men. These are just beefs," the Knocker said. Deep down he wasn't proud of killing, but he was not in touch with any guilt. No, he used his past experiences to get through this job-and to show the other men around here that he was not to be messed with.

It was best this way.

Serpentine stopped and looked at him, then took a bite from his sandwich.

"Killing who, man?" Serpentine asked.

"I can't tell you that."

"Or what? You gonna kill me?" Serpentine said, smiling.

"Maybe," the Knocker said pointedly.

Serpentine quieted.

Suddenly uneasy, the Knocker stood up and dropped the empty chip bag into the garbage bin. He was on edge whenever he worked this job, and today was no different. He waved to Serpentine and left the room.

Chapter Eight

Kage

Trevor Zair was Todd's twin brother. The both of them worked as animal activists for years. When President Walker was assassinated back in 2028 and animal activists' lives were being threatened, Todd had said the family was in danger. He and Trevor had come up with a plan: Trevor was to take Kage and go stay with Ethan.

Todd and Valerie were supposed to be right behind.

But Trevor and Kage never saw them again.

From under the bed, Kage recognized Trevor's sneakers, worn and caked with mud. They had been a forest green color with white trim. Now the white was brown and black in places.

"Kage?" Trevor called out.

Kage pulled himself out and stood up. There by the door stood Trevor, arms crossed. His shoulder-length black hair lined his face like a cloak. His cobalt eyes narrowed with the shape of his mouth. Kage could tell Trevor was not impressed.

"What do you think you're doing, leaving a note like that and coming all the way out here? I had to hear from Ethan why you'd left."

"I had to," Kage said, sitting down on the bed. The climbing wall caught his eye again.

"Did you find what you were looking for?" Trevor asked, walking over to him.

"Not yet. But I will," Kage replied, thinking of the flash drive in his jacket.

He stood up again, now feeling uneasy.

"How'd you find me so easily?" Kage asked.

"It was pretty obvious where you'd be."

"Am I that predictable?" Kage asked, grinning.

"I want you to come back home," Trevor said, quickly moving on.

"I know you do, but I can't."

"Why?"

"I feel trapped there. And I have to find

out about mom and dad. They were supposed to come meet us. Maybe I can find out..."

"You're not going to find out about them," Trevor interrupted. "They're gone. If you try, Marshals won't be far behind."

Kage started to speak and Trevor lifted his hand up to stop him. He turned his head as if he heard something.

"Sounds like they're on their way," Trevor said. "We need to go."

Kage stood there, confused. He hadn't heard anything. Trevor hurried back to the door and then turned to Kage.

That's when Kage heard it. The very faint, drawn rise of a siren.

"They're coming. Let's go," Trevor yelled.

But Kage stopped. He looked at Trevor, thought about the bike, the Jeep outside. He suddenly had an idea.

"You go."

"What?"

"Take my bike, and get out fast. I'll stay behind, distract them."

"I'm not doing that."

Sirens neared the house. Kage ran downstairs. Trevor followed. He unlocked the front door and ran outside. There was no sign of Marshals, but the sirens were coming closer and closer.

He pulled the keys from his pocket, threw them to Trevor. Trevor caught them and looked up at Kage.

"Go dammit, now!" Kage yelled. He felt himself near tears.

"No!" Trevor yelled back. He went for Kage, his arms reaching for Kage's shoulders. Kage could not allow Trevor to get caught. It was his decision to leave, and he had to follow through with it. So he drew back and then swung at Trevor, punching him in the side of the head.

Trevor stumbled backwards, a look of shock showing on his face.

"Here," Kage yelled, pushing the flash drive into Trevor's hand. "Take this."

Kage ran for the Jeep, then turned and stopped, glancing back at Trevor.

"We can't afford to both get caught," Kage

yelled. "They'll find out about Meeteetse. Trust me! Now get out of here!"

Trevor glanced back at the street, got on the bike, and raced off up the road.

Moments later, he turned a corner and disappeared from sight.

That was when the Marshal vehicle turned the opposite corner and stopped behind Kage.

"And now here we are," Kage whispered.

The Marshal stepped out of the vehicle. She wore a black uniform with American flag insignias on either shirt sleeve. A black mask covered the bottom half of her face. She held a gun at Kage.

"Don't move!" she screamed.

Kage stood there, waiting. He hadn't done anything wrong.

"What did I do wrong, officer?" he asked innocently.

"This state is uninhabitable. You can't come in here. It's illegal."

"Well, I didn't know that."

He thought to make a run for it, but three drones circled above the house. He wouldn't get far. Hopefully Trevor had disappeared without the Marshal seeing him.

The Marshal took one hand away from her gun and reached for Kage's wrist. She pulled him into her from behind, brought the gun around and pointed it up at him. He was stuck in her grip. By instinct he knew that now was not the time to run.

The Marshal handcuffed him and pushed him into the back of the car. The inside was spacious and cold, with leather seating that made Kage's skin crawl. She pulled a light-blue mask from a box on the floor and strapped it around his ears.

"And you're supposed to be wearing a mask," she replied. "I could get you for that, too."

This world was not at all turning out to be what he had expected.

#

Now the sun was hiding somewhere above

them. The Marshal steered the vehicle northward, most likely to Cheyenne.

"Weren't you supposed to read me my rights back there?" Kage asked.

"Rights? I already told you what you were arrested for. You'll get a lawyer appointed to you if you don't have your own. Something tells me you know the drill," she replied, glaring back at his face.

But he didn't. He didn't know how any of this worked. He only knew the thing about reading rights from watching tv.

Soon enough it didn't matter, as Kage's attention moved to the sights outside his window. They neared Cheyenne, and its high-rise buildings transfixed him. He hadn't been to one of the main cities since the migration. They were all comfortably far away from his home in Meeteetse.

As they approached the city, the highway filled with more cars. Kage grew claustrophobic. He sat back in his seat to avoid being seen by passing drivers. There were so many tall buildings, like a forest

of them, rising hundreds of feet, separated
by concrete and asphalt streets. They housed
the state's citizens. Ethan had described
this development to Kage several years ago.
Now that suburban living was no longer a
thing, people lived in these enormous
cities, most of them squeezed into
apartments and suites. The poorer ones lived
just on the outskirts in broken-down
apartment buildings built in the early 2000s
before climate change demanded more
sophisticated architecture. The steel,
concrete and brick and glass buildings of
the past could not stand up against dust
storms, super storms and the like.

The 2030 Migration was a direct result of
a terrorist attack on US soil, so they said.
Kage knew better. Nonetheless, the drought
that came after that migration left a string
of states uninhabitable, and climate change
had only worsened since then.

Now, these newer buildings that Kage had
to bend his neck just to see were made

mostly with wood and glass-able to withstand harsh winds, intense heat, sun and dust.

The Marshal vehicle pulled into a parking lot. The Marshal got out and came around to Kage's door.

"Come on out, ma'am," she said, waiving him out into a lot full of cars and people.

"It's sir," Kage replied angrily. He hated that his voice still sounded feminine. He never got the chance to start hormone replacement therapy. "I'm not a woman."

"Sorry," she replied dryly, and led him toward a brown, windowless building. The sign above the entrance read: CHEYENNE JUSTICE CENTER.

No justice here. Kage laughed at the sign. The Marshal ignored him, brought him inside where they passed through a series of metal detectors and down a dull hallway. His boots clapped against a gray concrete floor. Fluorescent lights shone down on him as if laughing. Everyone they passed in the hallways wore masks, leaving Kage with an even deeper feeling of unease.

"They sure make you want to stay here, don't they?" he asked.

Again, the Marshal remained silent.

Two guards came up behind him. The Marshal stopped at a black, steel door. One of the guards unlocked it, and the Marshal waved him inside.

"You'll stay here until we get your paperwork set up," she said.

"What about my phone call?" Kage asked, not that he had anyone to call.

"You'll get one later."

The door shut.

Once again, he found himself imprisoned.

Maybe he should never have left home.

Chapter Nine

Bray

There was blood everywhere. On her sweat pants, shirt, even her feet had little red splatters of blood on pale skin. But at least she had been able to clean and bandage the cut with the contents of the first-aid kit, which found its new home in the dumpster beside her.

Night came full on. The streets surrounding this block of apartment buildings bustled with the life of young people, taxi drivers, food delivery cars. Perps floated through the air, creating their own traffic, but they would not find Bray. Not now.

This particular building she hid behind was a one-hundred-story ugly gray-and-crimson-colored building with sheets of glass running down its four sides like a white line down a skunk's back. It was one

of a dozen or so apartment buildings in
Denver that made Bray feel like gagging, but
this was where everyone lived these days—
unless you were the daughter of someone
important, like she was.

The building's rear entrance was not
locked. With her gait measured to avoid
drawing attention, Bray slipped inside and
climbed the stairs to the fifth floor. The
apartment she wanted, number 502, stood at
the end of the hall, past a set of silver
elevators where a table and two chairs sat
alone, waiting for someone to come sit with
them.

Bray approached the door quickly and with
excitement. She knocked. A shadow slid along
the peephole above her head. A series of
locks clicked and the door opened.

When she saw him, his full eyebrows rose
to his forehead, where lines of surprise
crossed like straight rivers. He grinned,
but only slightly. A black mole hung below
his left eye and just beside his nose, a

birthmark from his mom, he once told her. His skin was a dark shade of brown, nearly black. His dreadlocks were longer than when she last saw them. He had on a blinding white shirt that held the chest muscles of a well-framed athlete. A white jacket hung over the shirt, so clean she could eat off it.

"Bray. What the hell? Get in here." Elliott pulled her into his apartment. He glanced down the hall and then swiftly shut the door and locked it.

She turned to him and he pulled her into his broad chest. His hugs always felt like home. She hadn't seen Elliott in so long that she burst into sudden tears. He pulled away and looked down at her.

"You okay, kiddo?" he asked, looking down at her arm.

"Yes," she said, wiping the tears away and laughing in relief.

"How did you get out? Anyone follow you?" he asked.

He ran over to the windows. His dreadlocks

slapped against his back as he shifted his head to look down at the street. That's when she noticed: the whole apartment was empty. His couch, his entertainment center, tables, lamps, all gone. There was nothing but the hardwood floors and his backpack, which waited at full capacity beside the door.

It made her feel empty, confused, even...angry. How could he just pick up and go without telling her? They were best friends. Clearly he was planning to leave and never come back. What if she hadn't escaped? She'd never have known where he went, maybe never have seen him again.

"I was injured," she said, feeling the sudden pulse of pain in her back now that the adrenaline was wearing off.

Elliott continued staring out the windows. He was distracted, anxious. There was something else going on here.

"What's going on?" she asked. "Your stuff's all gone."

"I'm leaving," he replied, stepping away from the windows.

"Where're you going?" she asked, crossing her arms. She was afraid of him leaving. He was her only refuge.

"Red Lodge. In Montana."

"What's in Montana?"

"Can't say right now," he said. He looked down at her. "You okay? You're wincing."

"I got shocked in the back," she lied.

"What? You mean they shocked you?"

"Something like that."

"Show me."

Bray turned, lifted her shirt and lowered her pants to reveal the festering wound. She didn't mind Elliott seeing her panties. They'd been friends since they were kids. She found Elliott attractive, but she had never wanted anything more from him than a friendship. That was another indication that she was very, very gay. Not to mention he was twenty-two and only saw her as a little sister, which she found endearing.

Bray met Elliott when she was six years old. She was forced to attend a weekly group for kids with depression, and Elliott was in

the same group. His parents had died in the
2027 terrorist attack. To address his
logical sadness, his grandparents had him
placed in the group.

"Geez," he said.

"I need the bathroom," Bray replied,
dropping her shirt.

She wobbled down the hall and into the
bathroom. Closing the door, she sat down on
the toilet. Now that she was safe, she
thought about Alice. With it being night,
that meant Alice had only three more full
days. Maybe that was true for Bray, too. How
would she know for sure? She'd know soon
enough, and what could she possibly do about
it? On the one hand, she didn't fully
believe it, that she could die if Alice
died. There was no evidence but the burn
wound. This was one of those "wait and see"
situations.

"You okay in there?" Elliott yelled back
to her.

"I'm fine," she replied.

Bray closed her eyes and called for Alice.

Nothing.

It was at the age of thirteen that Bray first met Alice. She'd been begging her parents for years on end for a pet, or to at least visit a farm so she could connect with animals. Secretly she wanted learn more about her curious ability to hear their voices.

So one day her mother took her to visit an S-Corp facility. It was "Bring Your Daughter to Work Day." This facility was located just outside of Denver and held over 300 sows. The sows had just birthed piglets, and Dianna took Bray to see them. It was a rare experience for Bray to spend any alone time with her mom.

While at the facility, Bray was left alone in a fenced spot outside while her mother interacted with the plant manager. More than twenty piglets ran around the enclosure, snorting and playing with each other. One in particular, a pure, pink-skinned one with a hankering in its eyes for Bray's shoestrings, gave Bray a weird kind of sense. A sense of laughter and ease. Bray picked the piglet up and it allowed her to hold it in her lap. They sat there for the remainder of Bray's visit. Other piglets came and went on to play amongst themselves, but this one did not stray from her.

Ever since that day, Bray could link in her mind with the piglet, who was female. She named her Alice after her grandmother, and they were inseparable even from a distance and across species. To this day, Bray could not understand why she was able to link so deeply with Alice, yet couldn't do it with any other animal.

Bray didn't want to die, but this was such a hellish life already. What kind of life could she have, repeatedly locked away and forced to take medications she didn't want? Her biggest dream was to be a writer and to live alone out on a big farm where animals could be free. Where Alice could be free. The mere thought of Alice being slaughtered violently just so someone could have her for dinner angered Bray.

In Elliott's bathroom, she stood up, paced the floor.

"Alice?" she called again.

Still nothing.

What was she supposed to do? Her friend was about to die in a matter of days. Her only other friend was leaving town. And Bray had no clue where Alice even was. It felt like she had no choice but to just give up, go into hiding forever. It wasn't like she could help Alice or save her. She had a gift, sure, but that was all. She could talk to animals, not save them.

Bray pressed her forehead against the bathroom wall. She closed her eyes. Tiredness set in. The darkness behind her eyes invited her to nod off, pass out, let hopelessness take her.

Then a series of images rolled through her mind like slot machines at a casino. Except, instead of cherries, the first image was a sign: *Welcome to Wyoming-Forever West*, in bright yellow letters. That was followed by an image of a man on a horse with mountains in the background.

Strange, Bray thought. She wasn't one to have images just randomly pop up in her head.

Then another: a team of wild horses running along open prairies, up and over hills, their manes flashing like gold strands of light.

Then it stopped. Went black again.

"Bray, you sure you're okay?" Elliott said, now just outside the door.

Bray's eyes popped open.

"I'm good," she said, wondering about the images she had seen.

She took a deep breath and opened the door. Elliott smiled, then turned and walked back into the living room, where he stopped by the windows. She went over and stood across from him. His eyes were busy, looking down at the street and then back to Bray, then to his watch.

"So tell me again how you got out?" he asked.

"They had me in a wheelchair, on the elevator. When it opened I just made a run for it."

"And that was it?"

"Yep." She shrugged.

"Hmm," he said, looking back out the window.

Elliott was always quite paranoid. But maybe he needed to be. He'd been arrested a couple of times for hacking, but there was never enough proof to charge him, so he went free both times.

"Can I come with you?" she suddenly asked, not knowing where else to go.

"I don't know. You're only seventeen. Your parents are going to be looking for you. If you come with me, I'll become an accomplice. I'm already in enough trouble as it is."

Then, he pulled out his phone from his back pocket. He typed into it and put it away.

"Please? I can't go back to that psych ward, and you know that's exactly where they'll put me, again. My mom wants to get

legal guardianship over me when I turn
eighteen."

Elliott looked into her eyes.

"I'm sorry. Your parents really do suck,"
he said. He bit at his lower lip. He always
did this when he was thinking. Maybe he was
changing his mind. Surely he'd take her with
him, especially now that he knew she had
escaped and clearly had nowhere else to go.

"No, sorry. I just can't."

"But why?" Bray asked, raising her hands
in the air.

"I don't have to give you a reason."

"Come on. Where the hell am I supposed to
go? I just escaped a psych ward."

"You should've thought of that before you
escaped."

Bray's mouth dropped open. She couldn't
believe what he just said.

"How dare you," she replied. "I thought we
were friends. All I'm asking is to come with
you."

If Elliott wouldn't help her, it would
only be a matter of time before she ended up

back in the psych ward. She began to cry.

"Oh, come on," he said, reaching out to her.

Bray pulled away, turned her back on him. She wiped the tears away with forceful fingers. She didn't want him seeing her exposed, scared for herself. Then she felt his hand on her shoulder.

"Look," he started, then the air went dead.

Bray turned to look at him. He was staring down at the street.

"What?" she asked.

He said nothing, just nodded his head down at the road.

Bray looked down. A thousand feet below, Marshal vehicles had lined up outside the building. One Lincoln Navigator sat with its engine running.

Her parents had found her.

Chapter Ten

Dianna

Dianna Hoffman sat in the back of a Lincoln Navigator, remembering all over again why she seriously disliked Bray's father. The Lincoln stopped at a red light on the corner of 8th and Fox Street, where people sat at tables outside the Pierogi Dumpling Shoppe. Her eyes searched there for Bray even though she knew this was the last place she'd see her vegan daughter.

The light changed. The Lincoln rolled onward through the city. Cole sat beside her, fidgeting. In normal circumstances, he would be in DC, working on his bid for the next presidential election. He had returned home to Denver for this care conference with Bray, his time here extended now that she had escaped.

It was the only reason he'd returned home.

He had a knack for appearing as the good guy. He came when he was needed, but never actually spent time with Bray. Not like he used to when Bray was a child. Of course, neither did Dianna, but someone had to work to pay for Bray's care. Someone had to be here for her.

"I can't believe you," Dianna said to him.

He remained silent and glared out the window. A series of notifications popped up on his forearm. He looked down at them.

"It's your fault she's gone," Dianna continued. She was scared. If Bray went too long without her medications, there was no telling what could happen to her.

"How on earth is it my fault?" he responded.

"You should never have suggested she could come home. She got all these thoughts in her head about getting out, which probably led her to trying to escape."

"Everything's always my fault."

"I don't have time for this." Dianna yanked her purse from the floor and pulled out a cell phone. "She can't be out there roaming the streets alone."

She pulled up a number for the Chief of Denver Marshals and waited while it rang.

The psych ward definitely wasn't a place Dianna would ever want to be, but she knew Bray was unstable. She'd be even more so now that she'd escaped. Dianna's eyes darted along the streets as she wondered where her daughter could possibly have gone.

The Chief didn't answer.

"Of course not," she said aloud, and then spoke into his voicemail. "Chief Thomas, will you please give me a call? It's about Bray. She escaped and I need your help."

She hung up and looked over at Cole. He was sweating.

"Are you alright?" she said to him, glancing down at his arm. He had a list of health problems, heart issues being the main one. The indictor on his forearm was probably a notice about his blood pressure.

"Fine." He waved her off, pulling the sleeve up on his shirt to hide the notice.

Dianna returned her attention to the streets. She didn't know how to have a conversation with Cole anymore. Their fundamental disagreements were always about Bray. He didn't want her in the psych ward. Dianna did. He wanted her at home, but when she was home she never adhered to her medications. Often times Dianna felt as though Cole didn't even believe Bray was sick.

"You have any idea where she might've gone?" Dianna asked him, finally.

"Uh..." Cole's voice trailed off.

Dianna took a moment to think. Where would Bray go? She didn't have many friends, not that Dianna was aware.

"There is one place," Cole admitted. "But if I tell you, you can't get the Marshals involved. This needs to remain between the three of us. I want to be able to talk to her, for us to make a decision as a family, not just throw her back in the hospital."

"Cole, she's mentally ill. She is not capable of thinking clearly. Obviously, she just escaped a psych ward." Dianna turned to the window and then shifted back to Cole. "There's no family discussion to be had. She needs to be in the psych ward so she can be stabilized. Don't you see that's best for her right now?"

Cole did not respond.

"Where is she?" Dianna asked. She paused and thought. There was one person she'd go to. "It's Elliott, isn't it? Of course. Why hadn't I thought of that."

She pulled her cell phone back out of her purse. Cole reached over and put his hand on the phone.

"Please, don't call the Marshals. Maybe we can go talk with her and convince her to go back without getting authorities involved."

"Does she have you brainwashed or something? We're not going to convince her to return to a place she just ran away from. You don't seem to be thinking clearly." Dianna's eyes traced his face. "Are you sure you're okay? You don't look so well."

"I'm fine." He pulled back.

Dianna looked at him for a moment. His consistent denial of his health issues concerned her. This caused the aggravation in her chest to grow even more.

She made another call to Chief Thomas. This time, he answered.

"What is it, Dianna?" he asked.

Dianna had a long history with the Denver Marshals, dating back to when she first started as S-Corp's Western Regional President in 2035. The Marshals worked with S-Corp to keep protesters at bay. More recently, there'd been a resurgence of animal activists posing as S-Corp workers to get video of S-Corp's animal agriculture facilities. None of these activists had yet been caught, but they would soon enough.

"I just need an address: Elliott Bansfield," she replied.

It took only a moment and she hung up the phone.

"Driver," she called into an intercom in the ceiling of the car. "Please get us to West Ninth Street."

As the Lincoln pulled off down the road, Dianna saw Cole shake his head out of the corner of her eye. But she didn't respond. Cole could pout all he wanted, but Dianna knew what Bray needed. At least one of her parents tried to do what was best for her rather than disappear for ages at a time.

The Lincoln stopped outside one of dozens of high-rise buildings. They all looked the same, inside and out. Concrete blocks, like Legos, with varying colors. Gray next to crimson then back to gray again. And the windows were made of environmental protective plexiglass. They were black tinted and made the buildings appear dark even in the daylight.

Two Marshal vehicles had already arrived, their lights flashing a blinding white in Dianna's eyes as she got out of the car. Cole followed. She wished he wasn't here with her, but she decided it didn't really matter. He had no power in this situation. The Marshals were here, and once they found Bray, she'd be taken back to Denver Health.

A pair of Marshals walked into the building with her, then Cole behind. They took the elevator to the fifth floor. When they arrived at apartment 502, Dianna stopped.

"Let me knock," she said. "The two of you stay back. I want to try to talk to her first."

The two Marshals glanced at each other.

Cole stepped up and looked over at Dianna. They both equaled in height.

"Maybe you should let me, just to be safe," Cole said.

"Sh," she replied, turning to the door.

"She could be dangerous, ma'am."

"She's not dangerous to others, just herself," Dianna said, rolling her eyes and knocking.

No answer.

"Bray? You in there?" she called as she pressed her ear against the door.

No sound came from the place. If they had caught on, they might already be gone.

"Break the door down," Dianna said, losing

patience.

One of the Marshals approached the door. From his belt loop he pulled out some kind of remote unlock mechanism. The Marshal pressed a metal strike plate against the door where the handle was. Attached to it was a narrow, black square that the Marshal clicked. Then, the door popped open.

The Marshal pulled his gun and entered.

The place was empty.

Dianna walked in behind him. No furniture, nothing. Even the walls were empty.

Elliott had planned an escape long before Bray arrived.

Or had Bray been plotting this somehow, all along?

Chapter Eleven

Bertan

Returning home to Honduras was a lot to consider. If he got himself deported, that could be the easiest way. But then he'd have deportation on his record with little hope of returning to the US in the future. It had been hard enough to get over here the first time. Even then, he had to kill a few men to get into Texas from Mexico. So the only other thing he could think to do now was ask for money. He had already taken a second job as a Knocker at the plant, but it wasn't enough.

Bertan hurried through the Kill Floor and ran upstairs to the plant manager's office. He had ten minutes left on his break. Maybe they could give him some kind of raise. Serpentine did have a point, that he'd managed to work here so long without losing it. That had to say something.

The door to the office was open. Ruben, the plant manager, was sitting inside. He had his head turned down to look at a paper on the desk. Bertan stood in the doorway and cleared his throat. Ruben looked up.

"Hey man, what's up?" he asked, looking at Bertan. His frown shifted into a gentle smile.

Ruben was Mexican, looked to be in his mid-fifties, with curly black hair that matched the polo shirt he wore. His full beard hid his scarred face, and a pair of round glasses rested on a notch in his nose. Beside him, a desk was hooked into the wall. Two laptops sat on either end. A line of shelves hung above the desk, on them a row of tablets revealing security video.

To Bertan's right, a pair of filing cabinets peered at him. He always wondered what was inside.

"You want to take a seat?" Ruben asked, his eyes pointing at the empty chair between him and Bertan.

Bertan stepped in and took a seat in

the steel folding chair. He would rather be doing his job than sitting here. Deciding to take on a second job to help his family was hard enough to sit with.

"I need a favor," Bertan started.

"What's that?"

"I need a raise."

Ruben stiffened in his chair. His eyebrows raised. The two of them had a pretty good relationship, Bertan thought. They often talked on their breaks, and Ruben was always kind to him. So it didn't feel intimidating to ask for more money.

"I can ask, but unfortunately I have no control over the wages here. I answer to el jefe like you do."

"So what do I do to get more money?" Bertan asked.

"What's going on? Everything okay? I thought this knocker job was helping you out."

"Carmen and Gabriella are in some danger. Because of Medina."

"That's the food corporation down in

Honduras, right?" Ruben asked.

"Yes. They threaten and murder the campesinos for land. And because Carmen works to help the campesinos, she's at risk. So she's taking Gabriella to San Pedro Sula." Bertan paused for a moment. This was the most he would tell anyone about his situation. His trust of Ruben was natural enough that he didn't think twice to hold back. "I think she's going to leave me."

"What makes you say that?" Ruben asked. His shoulders visually slumped. Bertan could tell Ruben was disheartened by this.

"She said. It's been ten years and she wants me to come back home."

"And so you want a raise so you can get back?"

"Yes. But please don't tell anyone. I don't want to lose my jobs here. I haven't decided if I'm really going back."

"I get it. Your jobs are safe. You're a good worker and those are hard to come by. I know I can trust you."

Bertan rubbed at his hands. His leg

shook.

"You okay?" Ruben asked.

"Fine," Bertan said, shrugging.

"You seem uneasy." Ruben paused. "How is the knocking job going, by the way?"

"Fine. Why?" Bertan asked, growing annoyed. Carmen's name spun around in circles in his head and would not stop.

"I'm just curious if the knocking job ever gets to you."

"Gets to me?"

"Yeah. Is it hard for you to knock cows?"

"I don't think about it. And besides, they're not cows, they're beefs. Is it hard for you when you crave a steak?" he replied with a bitter tone.

"I don't eat meat," Ruben said.

"Look, are we done here?" Bertan asked. He didn't like where this was going. He needed to get back to figuring out what he was going to do about getting back home.

"I'm sorry about that, Bertan." Ruben took a breath. "I just know that knock job hasn't been easy for others. I care about you, is all."

Bertan looked at Ruben. They eyed one another for a moment that felt permanent. The way Ruben looked him in the eye, wasn't afraid to look him in the eye, impressed Bertan. Not many men could look at him once they found out beefs weren't the only things he had killed.

"I have to get back to work," Bertan said, standing up. "Can you please ask about a raise?"

"Sure," Ruben replied, but the tone of his voice was uncertain.

Bertan turned for the door.

"Bertan," Ruben called.

"Huh?" He turned back to Ruben.

"What's that on your neck?"

Bertan brought his fingers up to the side of his neck and rubbed along the one-inch scar just below his jawline.

"This?" He tapped his finger against it.

"Yeah. I never noticed it before."

"It's a scar. From when I was trying to choke a guy and he slit my throat."

"Hmm. And did you succeed?"

"I always do," Bertan replied, eyeing Ruben and then exiting the office.

Chapter Twelve

Kage

The holding cell was half full, or half
empty, depending on how one looked at it.
Kage looked at it with anxiety. He hadn't
been around strangers in so long he forgot
what it felt like. Strange. He walked over
to the farthest bench and sat down. The
bench was metal and cold, even through his
jeans. He shivered.

The women in the cell paced around, stood
alone or stood talking to one another. Most
were white, around Kage's age. One Black
woman sat in the corner, chewing something.
She stared at Kage. Kage turned and looked
at the door. Then he glanced around the
room, looking for a way out. But the walls
were concrete, thick. No windows. The
ceiling was also concrete. He was silly to
think there was a way out of this place.

The Black woman stood up quickly, came closer. She sat down on a bench along the opposite wall. Kage guessed her to be in her thirties or forties. She had short hair, curly. Her clothes were all black. Her shoes were covered in mud. Kage wondered what the woman was in for. She nodded at him, and he quickly looked away.

Kage's leg shook impatiently. He rubbed his palms together. The air was freezing. Maybe to keep everyone calm.

The Black woman got up again. She walked over to Kage, sat down a foot or so away.

"What's on the front of your jacket?" the woman asked.

Kage looked over at her, and then down at the jacket. She must've meant the insignia that his mom had sewn onto the upper left chest.

"You mean this?" Kage asked, pointing at it.

"Yep," the woman replied, moving something white around in her mouth.

"I don't know," Kage said. "I stole the

jacket off someone."

"You lie," the woman replied, smiling.

Kage stood up and walked over to the opposite wall and leaned against it. He didn't need people asking questions. He was in enough trouble as it was. Along with cutting his long hair, he thought maybe he should burn the insignia off the jacket. It was an Animal Rights Movement symbol, a dead giveaway to anyone who recognized it. It never mattered at home, but out here he was constantly being reminded of all the ways he needed to remain anonymous.

The door opened. A name was called. One of the women laughed and exited. Kage approached the door, watched it close. No one was coming to get him, nor should they. By now, Trevor should've made it back to Meeteetse. Now all Kage had to do was find a way out. He stood a few feet from the door, and put his thoughts together.

But nothing came. Each way out he thought of would only end in him getting caught again. There had to be something he wasn't thinking of.

The door opened again. Kage turned and looked out. There standing in the hall beside one of the guards was a woman in black dress pants and a black suit jacket. Kage met her eyes and they held him in place the way the moon holds the ocean, the way it moves the ocean. His breath stopped, yet he felt moved.

"Tori Banks?" the guard called into the room, standing by the door.

Kage continued to stare at the woman in the hall. She was clearly no Marshal. Maybe a lawyer? The way she stood commanded the hallway, commanded Kage. He hadn't seen such a beautiful woman in all his life. Even with her mouth and nose hidden beneath a purple-patterned mask. He'd seen more women today than in the last twelve years combined.

Another reason he needed to leave home.

The Black woman approached Kage. As she walked, she pulled something from her pocket. She stopped before Kage and slid a white card into his hand.

"There's others like you," she whispered, and turned to exit the cell.

The door closed. Kage glanced down at the card:

TORI BANKS

Toraba@ai.email.com

Kage recognized this as an email address, but was curious what the ai stood for. Whatever it was, it didn't matter. The card offered no other indication of who the woman was. What did she mean about there being others like him?

Kage knew there weren't other activists, so the woman probably confused him for someone else, thought Kage to be someone he wasn't.

Hours later, the door opened again. Kage sat back in the corner of the room. The guard came in and stood above him.

"You're coming with me," the guard said.

"Where?" Kage asked, remaining seated.

"Time to answer some questions," the guard replied. He grabbed Kage by the arm and walked him out of the cell.

They turned away from the front and walked farther down the halls. Not knowing what was happening, Kage felt a bit nervous. He wanted to resist the guard but willed himself not to.

The guard stopped at another door, this one black but with a square window looking in at an empty table and chair.

The guard unlocked the door and pulled Kage in, sitting him down in the chair. Handcuffs were locked around both his wrists, the other ends linked to a set of chains melded into the table. The guard stepped back and stood beside the door, silent and hard as a wall.

Moments later, a tall man in a button-up pink shirt and jeans entered the room.

I hope this guy's not my lawyer, Kage thought to himself.

The man sat down across from Kage and placed a manilla folder on the table.

The guard closed the door. Kage stiffened.

The man silently opened the folder and set out a series of photos. They were black-and-white images of Kage on his bike, Kage at his parent's home. Trevor on the bike.

Shit, he thought. Now he had no way of knowing whether Trevor made it or not.

The man read Kage his rights. While he did so, Kage's eyes looked at the photo of him at the house. He felt disgusted that drones could do this now, that they could follow anyone anywhere.

"First off, where's your partner?" Pink Shirt asked.

"What partner?" Kage replied.

Pink Shirt pointed at the photo of Trevor.

Then Kage remembered his rights, and he said nothing. He was relieved, as this meant Trevor must've gotten away.

"Get me a lawyer," he said, the handcuffs hanging hard on his wrists.

Pink Shirt rolled his eyes, stood up.

"Get her fingerprints and photo," he said to the guard.

Kage cringed. He opened his mouth to correct the man on his gender, but before he could, the man spoke again.

"And one more thing," he said, reaching over and grabbing Kage's arm.

"Hey," Kage said, trying to pull his arm away. But Pink Shirt's grip was too strong. He pushed Kage's arm down onto the table and pushed back the jacket sleeve to expose Kage's skin.

"No implant. Interesting," he said. "Get her set up for one of those, too."

"It's he," Kage yelled. "And I'm not getting any implant without a lawyer."

Pink Shirt turned and glared down at Kage. His black, tiny eyes narrowed. Kage gritted his teeth, his anger fueling the blood in his veins.

Challenge me again, fucker, Kage said to himself.

But Pink Shirt left the room, and the guard followed.

Kage glanced around at the walls. No windows to escape out of. There wouldn't be, in a place like this.

Suddenly he stood up, walked over to the door. He banged on it several times.

"Hey," he yelled, hitting the door with his fists.

Finally, the guard opened the door a crack.

"I want my phone call now," Kage said. Except, instead of a phone call, he was hoping for a laptop, some way to get hold of that Tori woman. Maybe her attractive lawyer could help him out of this place, too.

The guard slammed the door and walked away.

Kage yelled again, and then kicked at the door in frustration.

Getting out of this place would be near impossible.

Chapter Thirteen

Bray

"You sure that's them?" Elliott asked.

Bray eyed the Lincoln Navigator. It used
to be the "family" vehicle, before Cole went
off to half-live in DC. It was hard to tell
from here whether her dad was inside. For
some reason, she hoped he was. Maybe it
would mean he was trying, for once.

"Yep," she replied.

"Then let's go, now."

Elliott pulled out his phone, sent
another message. He ran over to the door and
pulled on the backpack. He slid a light blue
mask over his face and handed an extra to
Bray. Inside the psych ward she wasn't
required to wear a mask. She'd even
forgotten she wasn't wearing one. She put it
on and braced herself for a run, praying her
back would hold up.

They exited the apartment and disappeared

down the exit-only stairs. Bray felt her
wound pound at her lower back as they
descended down, down, down to the garage.
She followed Elliott out of the stairway
into the dark, cool, concrete parking
garage.

Elliott ran up a slight incline where cars
were lined up on either side. There, she
watched him run out into the street. She
hesitated, fearing her mom would see her.

"Bray, c'mon," Elliott's voice echoed back
into the garage.

She didn't have much choice. She ran
outside. Parked on the street was a two-door
Mini Cooper. Elliott opened the passenger
door and waved her in. Without looking
toward the Lincoln Navigator, she quickly
slid into the back seat and sat down, the
wound throbbing momentarily.

Elliott sat down in the passenger seat.
Beside him, a young, white guy, close to
Elliott's age, glared back at Bray.

"Not what we planned, man," the driver
said to Elliott.

"Will you just go?" Elliott yelled.

The driver shifted gears and drove off.

"Bray, this is my friend, Bishop." Elliott glanced back at her.

Bishop glanced at her in the rearview mirror. In the dark of night it was hard to make out the color of his eyes, but he had a buzz cut of blonde hair with thick blonde eyebrows to match. A white mask covered the rest of his face.

"He's gonna help us get past the border," Elliott added.

"Us?" Bishop asked. Bray sensed very quickly that Bishop did not want her here.

"It's a long story," Elliott said, turning to face the highway. "She's in a lot of trouble herself, so let's at least get her into Wyoming..."

Wyoming, Bray thought to herself. The rest of what Elliott said trailed off somewhere. The image of the Wyoming sign popped up in her head again. Maybe it was the border sign.

But there was a problem. Ever since

Martial Law was enacted, the state borders crawled with checkpoints. Cross-country travel was a thing of the past, and to get across the border required a work permit or other identification.

"I don't have ID," Bray said.

Bishop shook his head, turned and grimaced at Elliott.

"Can't we just hide her in the trunk?" Elliott asked, shrugging.

"Dude, you're really screwing up this plan."

"Come on. She's my best friend," Elliott said. Bray smiled, sat back in her seat.

"Fine," Bishop replied.

That's when it dawned on her: Elliott really did have his own plan, without her, and Bishop was clearly a part of it. Especially since he was white. Now that the US police force had devolved into a militarized unit, race relations had only grown worse. There was no way Elliott would get over the border on his own unless he had a work permit.

Up ahead, a rest stop stood on the side of the highway. Bishop pulled the car off the highway and parked at the far end of the building near some trees. Real trees. Bray hadn't seen real trees before. They all got out and she walked over to one, touched the leaves.

They weren't glossy like the leaves on the artificial trees back home. This one she felt with her forefinger and thumb. Its veins were like hard muscles. Or were they more like the veins of a human body, sending life into these leaves? Bray shrugged at the realization that she didn't know. She didn't know anything about something as simple as a tree.

"Let's go. No time for sight-seeing," Elliott called to her.

Bray let out an exhale of disappointment and walked over to him as he stood beside the car.

"You wouldn't happen to have an extra pair of socks, would you?" she asked, looking down at her bare feet.

"Oh man, I forgot you had no shoes on," he
replied. He stepped over to the trunk where
Bishop was moving his belongings out and
into the back seat.

Elliott opened his backpack, took out a
pair of socks, and handed them to her.

"Don't say I never gave you anything," he
said, winking.

"Thanks," she replied, quickly pulling
them on over her now tired and very scraped
feet. The air out here was cool, making her
wish for sleep. She glanced into the now-
empty trunk and figured this was her only
chance to catch up on rest.

Bishop had disappeared into the restroom.
Elliott sat quietly against the bumper,
looking out into the open fields across from
the highway. Bray turned and sat beside him.

"I've never seen so much land before," she
said.

"Amazing, isn't it?" he replied.

"Yeah," she said, but she couldn't say
what she really thought, which was how all
this land could've been used for farm

animals.

There was so much openness. Vast prairies of dried grass, trees dotting the fields in little dark specks. Then, she saw movement. A group of shadows danced beneath the light of the stars. From here, Bray could see waving manes flow from their heads.

"Are those...horses?" Bray asked, pointing at the animals.

"Yep. Wild horses," Bishop said, approaching the car. "They're probably migrating."

Bray stood up slowly. Her eyes set on them, watering in amazement. She felt them slow to a walk. Peering more closely, she saw they bore a striking resemblance to the horses in her vision.

"Wild horses," she whispered.

"Yep. Now get in," Bishop interrupted, gesturing into the trunk.

"Can I breathe in there?" she asked, a bit frightened.

"Yes. It won't be long," Bishop replied.

Bray took a deep breath and crawled in,

lying down on the scratchy, black material.
She lay on her side, turned facing out.
Bishop slowly closed the trunk.

Everything went black. Starting to panic,
Bray closed her eyes. She pulled off her
mask. Inhaling, exhaling, over and over
again, she managed to calm her heart. She
then did the one next thing that always
calmed her down.

She called for Alice.

Alice made her presence known. They
remained in silence. It was enough to just
feel Alice nearby. The hum and vibration of
the car beneath her brought the thoughts in
on a steady stream. What was going to happen
once they crossed the border? It was clear
to her now that Elliott was going on his
own, or maybe with Bishop. She was not
invited. Turning slightly, she looked up,
pretending to see the blue sky as Alice sat
beside her.

"Alice?" she said, breaking the silence.

"Yes?" Alice replied, looking up at her.

"I escaped the psych ward."

"You did?"

"Yep. Now I don't know what to do."

"You are free now. You can do anything."

"I wish that was true," Bray said.

"Is it not?"

"If my mom finds me, she'll take me back. I'd have to spend the rest of my life in hiding and—" she said, then stopping. She thought about the burn wound, how it might've gotten there. "And I just don't understand how I got burned when you did."

"You think you will die when I die," Alice commented.

"How did you know?"

"I sensed it."

"I just feel, lost," Bray admitted.

Alice said nothing. She laid her head on Bray's thigh. Bray placed her hand on Alice's head, wished she was really touching it.

"I wish I could find you," Bray said.

"Can you?" Alice asked, sounding hopeful.

"I'm not sure how. I'm all alone. My

friend Elliott will help me get into
Wyoming, but-"

"What is Wyoming?"

"It's a state. A place near my home."

"I don't understand."

"It's not important. What I'm saying is
that I don't have anyone to help me. And I
don't know where you are."

"I feel you are close," Alice said.
"Closer than you've ever been."

"I hope that's true," Bray said, but she
didn't believe it. Alice could be anywhere.
And Bray was no closer to finding her, and
time was running out. Soon she might have to
decide how she wanted her life to end, if
the end was indeed coming.

"Can you ask your friend to help?" Alice
asked.

"No," Bray said. "Besides, he doesn't know
about us."

"How come?"

"I don't know. I'm afraid of what he'll
say. And he's got his own plans. I'm not

sure that where he's going is where I'm supposed to go. I just don't know what to do."

She felt the car slowing. Her body pushed forward as the car came to a stop. It rolled forward, then stopped again. The third time, it stopped and remained that way. She recognized Bishop's voice as it vibrated into the trunk. She gulped, her mouth dry.

They had arrived at the checkpoint.

Chapter Fourteen

Bertan

La Bestia was a Mexican freight train that ran through Mexico. Bertan had been riding for two days now. He was starving and sleep deprived. No one sleeps on La Bestia. Sleep and wake up dead.

It was night. Bertan sat on the top of one of the cars. Tree branches smacked at the countless piles of people who crowded the roof with him. No one spoke. They only moved their heads in unison as tree branches came down upon them when they passed. Bertan had been told it was safer to remain inside, but he disagreed. Inside it was pitch black, and on the first night he nearly fell asleep and woke suddenly to a man reaching down his pants. Most likely he was looking for hidden drugs or money, but it freaked Bertan out.

Now the moon was wide and close. It stared

at him. Below its light a pair of men stood and walked in his direction. He diverted his eyes, looking away at a passing house. The men came closer. He felt them looking at him. He kept trying to look away, but the moon pulled his head in their direction. They approached, smiling. One bent down before him. A knife swiped up to his throat and waited there. Bertan felt it graze his skin. The other man walked around and stood behind him, put a gun to his head. Unfortunate for them, Bertan knew combat, knew how to defend himself.

He was quick. He grabbed the hand that held the knife. Simultaneously, he kicked backwards into the man behind him, right in the groin. It was so sudden and swift that the man fell backwards, off the train. A scream and then the sound of crunching bones punctured the quiet night.

The man with the knife pulled back, freeing himself from Bertan's grip. Bertan, now down on his hands and knees, glared up at the man. His eyes focused on the blade of *the knife. The man leapt at his face with the knife. Bertan shifted to one side and the man fell forward. As he stumbled, Bertan's hand grabbed onto the knife's blade. It was painful, how it cut into his palm, but he managed to yank the knife away. The two of them faced one another. Bertan showed the man his bleeding hand and he laughed. A second later he punched the knife into the man's throat.*

Bertan jumped up. Sweating, he rubbed the scar on his palm. His heart squeezed. He panicked. He bounced out of bed and pulled off his shirt, threw it on the floor. He began to sob.

"You okay?" one of his roommates, Merced, called over to him.

Bertan nodded in the dark, sat back down in bed. He pushed away the tears.

"I can't do it," he whispered to himself. "I can't do it. I can't do it."

He cried again. Carmen and Gabriella came to the forefront of his mind and his heart ached for them. How he could ever return home, he wasn't sure. It was all he wanted to do now that Carmen had asked, but how could he go back to what haunted him?

A chain hung around his neck. It was a thumbprint piece Gabriella had given him right before he left for the United States. He picked it up in his fingers and rubbed his finger into the indent. He'd rubbed it so much over the years a hole was developing in the center. And he loved it.

The other men in the housing unit were asleep. Merced must've fallen back to sleep also. Bertan quietly bent down and reached under his bed. Glancing around the room to ensure no one was watching him, not that he could really tell in the dark, he pulled out a locked, metal box. The contents consisted of a few family photographs, a pistol, bullets, and a roll of cash. Bertan counted the cash: $500. Maybe he did have enough to get back home.

But now he wasn't so sure he could go through with it.

Before leaving the unit, Bertan searched a

box beside his bed for a clean pair of jeans and a t-shirt. Though he wore a smock while doing the knocking job, he never got away from the stench. A metallic smell, and a smell of piss and feces and rotting flesh, latched onto his clothes and even seeped into his pores and stayed with him like the past. No matter how many showers he took or how many times he changed his clothes, it would never leave.

When he pulled off his shirt, he looked down at the tattoo. It was unavoidable. The name MEDINA scrolled across his collar bone in black ink. The letters, written in a block cursive font, stood for a name that was not his own, a name he believed he'd been brainwashed to love. Scars from old cuts jutted along the letters: all the times he tried cutting himself to get the name to go away.

He found a white t-shirt and quickly slid it on to hide the tattoo. The shirt had short sleeves and so exposed a falcon tattoo on his upper left arm. That one he got when he turned twenty-two and became a squad worker for Medina Corporation.

Bertan turned away from the tattoo and pulled on the clean pair of jeans. His phone was lying beside his pillow. He grabbed it and left the unit on tiptoes, careful not to wake the others. They could sleep through anything, but Bertan—especially now that he was having nightmares—was not going to get sleep any time soon.

#

Stepping out into the parking lot of the hostel, Bertan unlocked his cell phone. He sat down on the walkway that led to several other units. The hostel was one of twenty S-Corp housing units in which he and several other undocumented workers lived. It was free housing, but he had to share it with five other men. Something he didn't mind since they mostly left him alone.

The air was balmy. It reminded him of Honduras. If only he had never left. Maybe he should've just stayed there. But he couldn't. There really was no other way to get away from Medina, to get away from what he'd done.

Bertan dialed Carmen and waited for her to pick up. One thing he did like about being in Idaho was that there was no time difference between here and home.

"Alo?" Carmen answered. He could tell she'd been sleeping.

"Sorry to wake you," he replied.

"It's okay. What's wrong?"

"Nothing. Just wanted to hear your voice," he said. He was delaying the thing he really needed to say. "When do you leave?"

"Tomorrow night."

"How are you getting there?" he asked. Everything in Honduras was precarious these days, especially for a woman and her teenage daughter.

Often times he forgot he had a teenage daughter. He deeply regretted this.

"Bus," she replied.

Bertan went silent. A series of thoughts went through his head, things he could say or should say, but didn't.

"Did you think anymore about coming home?" she asked.

And there it was, dropped like a beef's head after a knock.

"Yes," he said, and then he paused. "What if I can't do it?"

"Why can't you? If it's the money, my cousin can probably send you some to help."

"No. It's not the money," he admitted. "I checked and I have enough."

"Then what?" she asked. Now her voice was sounding very much awake. He could hear the sheets shifting around in her bed. He wished he was there beside her.

"I'm afraid it's all going to come back."

"What is, love?"

"The past. The stuff with Medina. Maybe you're right that they'd never know I was there. But I would know I was there, and there's so much I did wrong. And I don't know what I might have to do to get across the border, to get back to Honduras."

"Like you'd have to hurt someone?" she

asked.

"Yes. Like I had to on *La Bestia*."

Carmen went silent. The humidity in the air stuck to Bertan's skin. His forehead burned. His heart was beating fast. He was afraid of her response. He felt like a coward. A man who knocks beefs all day and has killed other men now can't even get himself across the border to be with his family.

He was sick of himself. He would never admit it to Carmen, but this was the real reason he felt he could never go back home.

"I don't know what to do with this," she said finally. "If you don't come home, then I can't go on together. I have to move on. For Gabriella's sake, too. She has had such a hard time without you."

The words hit him in the stomach, made him nauseous. He hated knowing that Gabriella was struggling because of him.

"Just give me some time. You get on the bus and get yourselves to San Pedro Sula. Then we'll talk when you get settled and are safe."

"Okay."

"Please be safe. Please call me if you need anything. I'll be waiting to hear from you again."

"Yes," she replied.

"I love you," he said, near tears.

"I love you, too. Do what you need to do to get yourself home. Whatever we need to do, my love," Carmen replied, and hung up the phone.

Bertan stood up and paced the parking lot. His hand squeezed the phone so much his forearm throbbed so he pushed the phone into his jeans pocket. Truth was, he was angry. Angry at himself, yes. But also at Carmen. Why couldn't she understand? Why did she have to give him such an impossible ultimatum? Couldn't she see that he was here to take care of them? The original plan was for them to come here, not for him to go back home.

His head began to spin with a heavy barrage of thoughts and scenarios. He couldn't see a way back home without having to do something he'd later regret. He'd come here to get away from all of that. Going home felt both like a dream and a nightmare. And he believed only the latter would come true.

Chapter Fifteen

Kage

They gave him his phone call, but it didn't matter. He needed a tablet, but they laughed when he requested one. And once they took his mugshot and got his fingerprints, they discovered him as the child of Todd and Valerie Zair. Two "ecoterrorists" in a time when "ecoterrorism" had nearly taken down the agribusiness industry.

And so they sat him down and tried to get him to talk.

"What's your address?" Pink Shirt asked as he sat across from Kage.

"Don't have one. Now get me a lawyer," Kage replied.

"Lawyer's on his way," Pink Shirt huffed. "But that's not going to change the fact that we need your address. You're not leaving here till we get it."

"I'm homeless," Kage said.

Kage didn't know how the law worked. He didn't know how much Pink Shirt was lying, so he lied back. He'd buy time until the lawyer arrived.

"I know you're lying, which implies you're hiding something. This implicates you further. You realize that, right?" Pink Shirt said, looking plainly at Kage.

Kage knew the man was right. But he didn't even know his own address. He only knew how to get there, on instinct and sense of direction. So, he did the only next thing that made sense.

"The last place I lived, was a long time ago. I actually don't remember the address," he said.

Pink Shirt made eye contact with the guard, then he looked back at Kage.

"How would you not know the address? And why don't you have an ID?" Pink Shirt added.

Kage started to sweat, but thankfully only under his arms and against his back. Places they couldn't see.

"I have ID, I just lost it back in Salt Lake."

"We didn't find you registered in the system. So yet another lie."

Kage had been holding his breath. He sighed, looked down at the floor.

A knock rapped at the door. The guard opened it. In walked a man in a plain suit, with thick-framed glasses, a bald head and a healthy paunch popping out of his shirt. He reminded Kage a bit of Ethan.

"Hey Jim," Pink Shirt said, leaning back in his chair.

"Hi. I'm Jim Chambers," the bald man said, nodding to Kage. He was holding a tablet, which Kage desperately wanted to get his hands on.

"What's going on here?" he asked as he stood beside Kage and rested the tablet on the table. "Some kind of trespassing charge?"

"Yep. Found this one down in Utah, sneaking around her—sorry, his parents' old home."

"Okay. So what's the big deal? Why you
still holding my client?"

Yeah, Kage thought, smiling inwardly.

"Because your client won't give us
her-dammit. His address."

"Can you give us a moment to chat?" Jim
asked.

Pink Shirt stood up and left the room with
the guard.

"You want to tell me what's going on
here?" Jim asked as if they'd known each
other for years. He walked around the table
and sat down in Pink Shirt's chair.

"Depends. Do you keep everything I say
confidential?"

"Yes, mostly. Unless you say you've
murdered or are planning to murder or hurt
someone, including yourself."

"I didn't know it was a crime to go visit
my old home. I'm from Wyoming, but I am
roaming, homeless at the moment."

"Well, you need to at least tell them

you're from Wyoming. Give them something.
Here, let's look it up—" Jim reached for the
tablet.

"No," Kage interrupted, placing his hand
on the tablet.

"What are you hiding?" Jim asked.

Kage sat back. He didn't know what to say.
He'd already said too much.

Jim opened the tablet and put in a six-
digit code. This tablet didn't look much
different from the ones Kage used over
twelve years ago. Either this guy didn't
make much money, or Kage wasn't the only
thing that had frozen in time.

"Where did you last have residence?" Jim
asked, pulling up a Quest Earth app.

"Here...in Cheyenne," Kage said quickly.
All he had to do was give them something,
enough to get back out on the road.

"Great. Where exactly?"

"Can I?" Kage asked, pointing at the
tablet.

"Sure," Jim replied, pulling his hands

away and sitting back.

Kage pulled the tablet toward him. He typed in Cheyenne, and the map pulled him into a visual image of the city. He widened the span of the map and moved along the city, to the outskirts, and found an older apartment building.

"Here," he said. "That building on Powerhouse Road."

"Okay. Apartment number?"

"Four," Kage guessed. What apartment building wouldn't have a number four?

Jim wrote down the address, alongside Kage's name, then looked over at Kage.

"How old are you?"

"Twenty-eight."

"How come you don't know your address?"

Kage stared at the building, a red brick structure that stood a couple stories tall. Its flat roof held a few empty chairs and a table.

"Because I never left home before," he said. "Isn't that how it is these days? I just set myself up there when I was eighteen, and never left. My parents disappeared, as I'm sure the pink shirt dude will tell you. When they disappeared, my life just kind of stopped. I got really scared and just holed myself up."

"Then what made you decide to go out?"

"I was losing my mind. Online friends started to notice. And the more I isolated, the more I forgot things, like my address and my age. Maybe some things I meant to forget, I don't know. So I finally hit a breaking point. I thought, if I don't leave and go try to find out about my parents, I might hurt myself."

"Okay. Well, at least for now I can give them this. I'll get your court date set and be right back," Jim said, closing up the tablet and standing up.

"Court date?" Kage asked. If he was going to continue living out here, he would have to learn a few things about the law.

"Yep. You still have charges. We'll go to court and try getting you cleared, but it's unlikely."

"Then what?"

"You'll do some time," Jim said, and he shrugged.

Kage looked at him, lost.

"You'll go to prison. For a year or more."

"Aren't you supposed to make sure that doesn't happen?"

"I can try. Odds are stacked against you," Jim said, knocking at the door to summon the guard. He disappeared down the hall and the door slammed shut.

Kage realized he was going to have to disappear himself. He couldn't go back home, not now. Maybe not ever. He couldn't risk being followed. And his bike was gone, so now he had no way around, no money. Then he pulled out that card and looked at it. He turned it over in his hand, noticed a tiny inscription in the lower right corner that he hadn't noticed before. He brought the card up to his eyes for a closer look.

Then the door clicked open. Kage pushed the card back into his pocket. Jim entered the room again.

"You're free to go," he said, setting a paper down on the table. "And you need to get an implant before your court date. Location and appointment are on this paper."

"I'm not getting an implant," Kage replied.

The guard walked in and asked for Kage's hands. Kage raised his hands up onto the table, and the guard removed his cuffs. Kage rubbed his red and raw wrists.

"As your lawyer I advise you to get one. It'll show that you're abiding by the law," Jim said, watching the guard exit the room. "That's your only case, that you just didn't know you were trespassing. Besides, if you don't do it, they'll just give you one the moment you get to prison."

Kage shuddered at the thought of going to prison. Worse than if he had just stayed home. But he wasn't getting any implant. He'd disappear out of this city and then decide what to do next.

"You coming, or what?" Jim asked. He was standing by the door.

Kage grabbed the paper and walked up to him.

As Kage stepped out into the night, he was free but very much stuck. No bike, no food. Everything, including the wad of cash Ethan had given him, was with the motorcycle. And now the only proof he had as to what might've happened to his parents was with Trevor. He'd have to go back home if he was ever going to know what was on that flash drive. But he couldn't go home now and risk the Marshals finding the Meeteetse house.

He had to disappear, and fast.

Chapter Sixteen

Bray

The Marshals had them.

She could tell by the sounds. The car was stopped. Engine running. A door slammed. Voices, one she didn't recognize. A pause. In the car's trunk, Bray began to sweat. She rushed to put her mask back on.

Then she heard Elliott's voice. A second door opened and shut. She felt the impact in the sting of her burn wound. Having never crossed a border in her life, Bray wasn't sure if this was normal protocol. It didn't feel right.

Following the 2030 Migration, the government set up checkpoints along major highways of each state. Every driver entered and exited the checkpoints, forced by law to provide identification. Some pulled to the side, their cars inspected at random. In addition, Marshals were required to have implants, and perps heavily monitored the area.

Suddenly a light jumped in at her from above. The trunk had popped open. She turned her head toward a blinding flashlight. Bray's eyes took a moment to adjust to the light.

"Would you look at that," a Marshal said, looking down at her. "Get out."

Behind him, Bishop and Elliott stood silently. Bray sat up. The Marshal reached down and helped her step out and onto the highway. They all stood outside the Mini Cooper, rows of cars behind and across from them, each awaiting its turn at the checkpoint.

Another Marshal jumped into the car and pulled it over to the side of the highway. There, a detainment center stood near the checkpoint like a small jail.

"Identification?" the Marshal asked Bray.

"I don't have any," she admitted.

"Come with me, then. We'll need to call your parents."

No! Her mind shouted. If they called her parents, this whole thing would be over. She'd be sent straight back to the psych ward, put on even heavier medication, maybe restraints to ensure she wouldn't be able to try to escape again.

"Please, officer," she begged. "We're just headed to Cheyenne, and coming right back to Denver."

"Then what were you doing hiding in the trunk?"

"Don't answer that," Bishop said to her.

The Marshal suddenly turned, stepped over to Bishop. He yanked a pair of handcuffs out and snapped them around Bishop's wrists.

"Not another word," The Marshal said. "You three are coming with me."

Inside the detainment center, Bray and Elliott sat down in some empty chairs beside the door. Her eyes wide, Bray glanced around the room at all the desks and computers. Down a hall she noticed a series of offices, doors closed, probably where people were questioned and then detained—Bishop being one of them.

The Marshal stepped around a desk and sat down. The desk sat across from Bray and faced her with piles of documents that left her feeling suffocated.

"What's your mom's name?" he called over to her.

Bray hesitated.

"Dianna Hoffman," she said, more sweat building on her palms.

"No shit," said another Marshal who stopped, mid-typing, and looked over at her.

"*The* Dianna Hoffman?" asked the Marshal who had brought her in.

"Yes," she said under her voice. Elliott glanced at her and rolled his eyes.

She hated telling people who her mother was. Anyone who was someone knew Dianna Hoffman, and this was never a good thing. It had never helped Bray get out of any situations. It wasn't like her mom was some famous actress who, when people learned of

her, got Bray free tickets or free dinners
or anything of that kind.

No. It only made things worse for Bray.

"Let's give her a call," the Marshal said,
smiling. He picked up a cell phone and
entered a number.

Her hands started sweating. Down the
hall, Bishop was still in one of the
offices. She assumed Elliott would be next.

She couldn't just sit there, do nothing.
She overheard the Marshal on the phone,
describing Bray, how he'd found her.

"Yes, come and get her. She's here with a
young man, Black...oh, you want me to bring
him in, too? Sure thing...I'll hold them
both till you arrive."

And that was it. The Marshal stepped up to
the door and stopped beside her.

"Your mom's on her way," he said.

Bray closed her eyes. It would take her
mom about a half hour to get there,
depending on where she was. Probably she
would leave her dad out of it, not even tell
him, as was her standard. She'd come get

Bray, and then any chance Bray had of going free would be lost. Her friendship with Alice would be lost, too. That was the truly unbearable part. She'd spent so many years with Alice that she feared the concept of living without her. Only three days, she gathered. Time was just passing without any resolution. She didn't know what to do, even so. There had to be some way out. She'd gotten this far, but she wouldn't have without Elliott's help. She looked over at him and grinned.

Glancing outside, she thought about making a run for it. Marshals surrounded the place, as did a busy highway ahead and behind. Perps circled the place like vultures hovering over a dead animal. That wasn't going to work. It wasn't a resolution, only a Band-Aid on an age-old wound—the one that stood between her and her mother and festered with blisters whenever her dad left her to deal with it on her own. And now Elliott was stuck. Even more so because he was Black. She wished for a way to help them both out of this, but nothing came.

Bray was frustrated as a flower in need of rain.

One Marshal called to another from across the room.

"Just got another heads-up from Cheyenne about those damn wild horses," he spoke.

"What they saying?" the other asked.

"Be on the lookout. It's spring and they'll be migrating north again. Remember last year, how many there were?"

"Yeah, man. Amazing. I hope we get to see them again. Not often we get to see wild animals."

Wild horses. The animals she saw back at the rest stop. If Bishop was right and they were migrating north, then maybe they were headed this way. There were hundreds of them. Enough to stir up some serious confusion if they happened to run through here.

If they came close enough, maybe she could connect with them. She thought back to an

incident when she was ten, at the aquarium
with her parents. The place was huge. While
in the penguin area, she felt very strongly
the presence of a hammerhead shark. The
shark exhibit was clear on the other side of
the building. Bray had leaned against the
glass of the penguin exhibit and closed her
eyes. The hammerhead had quite the busy
mind, and she connected with it and within
seconds, felt it swimming back and forth,
back and forth. She felt anxious and knew it
wasn't her anxiety, but something to do with
the shark. She wanted to help it calm down,
so she suggested the shark just break the
glass, try to get out. Moments later she
heard people screaming. A crack had
developed in the glass over at the shark
exhibit, shutting the entire place down.

So maybe if Bray could connect to some
nearby wild horses, ask for help, maybe
something could come of it. There was really
no other option at this point. She closed
her eyes, centered herself. Breathing
deeply, she called out. Her mind focused on

an image of horses. She envisioned the open fields of Wyoming that spread out beyond the highway. She focused and searched. As her breathing deepened, she rose above herself in her mind, looked down onto herself and then down onto the building. Gaining distance, she was now looking down onto the highway and the fields that spread out to the mountains in the distance. She hung above everything, and she waited.

Chapter Seventeen

Kage

Kage started for the street. Night blanketed the city. Who knew what time it was, not that it mattered. Now that he was free, he was starving. But freedom was a shamble out here, just as it was back home. He had no idea where to go, but he needed to get off the street.

As Kage walked the streets of Cheyenne, each person he passed was wearing a face mask. This was no surprise. Mask wearing in public had become mandated in 2022, after the COVID-19 endemic ravaged the world and put the US economy into a recession. The one he was wearing had began to rub at the backs of his ears.

The hum of drones passed by above him. He'd forgotten what all this was like— wearing a mask and hearing drones dancing around as if their presence were somehow normal.

His home in Meeteetse was completely off the grid. They lived entirely off the land, he and the others. It really had been a peaceful existence, and the peace eventually bored him out of his mind. It wasn't entirely untrue, what he told that lawyer. If he hadn't left, he may very well have taken his own life. He may as well have, seeing as he already felt dead. At least out here things were just uncertain enough to keep his blood moving, to keep him engaged. And at least now that he was out, he really could find out about his parents.

As he observed the grotesque apartment buildings, the fake trees with white lights dancing and flickering through their leaves as they stood along the sidewalks, a volocopter caught his eye. They taxied passengers through the city. And even twelve years ago when they were starting to become a thing back in Salt Lake, they also had free WiFi.

He only needed to get into one.

Kage turned down a busy street and picked up his pace. The April air was chilly and he was grateful for the jacket. The scent of Indian spices mixed with cooking meat would've made him more hungry, but he hadn't smelled burning flesh in so long it made his stomach turn. He quickened past a series of street-side shops and restaurants. The places were empty aside from the occasional person who walked in and then walked out a moment later with a bag of food. No one was sitting inside and eating. This city life was becoming stranger and stranger by the minute.

Soon he came upon a parking garage. He entered through a green side door and took the stairs to the roof level. There, the roof opened to a lot dotted with a handful of cars. Kage stepped up to the wall that stood between himself and the street below.

He watched the skies. He was now at eye level with most of the drones. The rest were flying low, closer to the street. Of course, they'd catch him jumping onto a volocopter, but he paid it little mind. His knowledge of fixing cars did not extend to knowing how to steal them, so this was his only option.

A volocopter approached from the left. Lights flashed on its four wings that stretched out, two on either side, like a small airplane. The volocopter was white, the size of a tiny car with space for two passengers in the back. There was no driver, just an automated screen in the front dash where the passenger voiced their destination and paid with their finger.

At least that's how Kage remembered it.

The volocopter floated near. Kage stepped up onto the concrete wall. As it came within four feet of him, he did not hesitate.

He jumped, arms outstretched. His hands touched a wing and grabbed on. It was slippery. His hands slid down and caught onto a piece of the wing that pointed upward for aerodynamics. The volocopter leaned harshly from Kage's weight. Kage nearly slipped off again. He swung his legs up onto the padded, narrow platform. The volocopter

beeped and its lights flashed. Kage heard a
yell from inside the car. He kept his focus
on his hands while he reached over to the
door handle and grabbed it. He was over
thirty feet in the air. Fall now and it
would be a clear death.

But with his grip on the locked handle, he
managed to pull himself up onto the side of
the copter. It regained its balance. Kage
peered at the man inside.

"Unlock the door, now!" he shouted through
the window.

The man shook his head, his face
shivering.

"I said now or I'll fall!" Kage yelled
again, his hands holding tight onto the
small handle. "You want me to die?"

His palms sweated. The wetness was causing
his fingers to slip from the handle. He was
beginning to panic, a feeling he was not too
familiar with. A drone was headed his
direction, surely coming for him.

Suddenly the door clicked. Kage looked in
and saw that the man had scooted to the

other side of the copter. Kage slid his feet slowly over to the edge of the platform. His heart was now beating into his throat. His mouth was dry. He took a breath and pulled the door open. The force of the wind blew it shut. He slipped, banged his head against the door. He held onto the handle for dear life. His feet swung out into the air. The drone buzzed toward him. The door pulled open as his feet slipped off the platform. He was now swinging in the air, the drone buzzing closer. But the door swung open so suddenly the drone did not have time to move, and its body smashed into the door. Its metal pieces shot up into the sky and fell to the street below. One piece hit Kage in the forehead. One of his hands slipped. The man reached out and pulled him up into the back seat. Kage quickly slammed the door shut, shivering.

"Thanks," he said, looking at the man, who was dressed in business attire.

"I'm calling the Marshals," the man replied.

"Don't bother. I just need a ride and internet and I'll be out of here. I'm not dangerous, just poor."

The man pulled out his phone and dialed some numbers.

Kage yanked the phone out of the man's hand and threw it into the windshield. The phone cracked and dropped to the floor. A hole opened in the windshield.

"Mother fucker!" the man yelled.

"If you'd just left me alone everything'd be fine!" Kage yelled, growing increasingly angry.

In front of him, a blank screen hung from the ceiling. He turned it on. He pulled the card out of his pocket and turned it over in his hand. The two tiny letters in the lower right corner, ai, meant something.

"What's this mean?" he asked the man, pointing to the tiny inscription in the corner.

"Not saying," the man said.

Kage turned back to the screen and noticed the familiar Quest search engine. He grinned.

So not much has changed, he thought.

He typed the letters in the search engine. Nothing.

"Ha," the man laughed, watching Kage.

Kage sat back and thought. Before the country went to hell twenty years ago, animal activists used encrypted email to communicate. This was a part of Tori's email address, but then why didn't it come up in the search? Not knowing what else to do, he created a Quest email account, started a new message, and put in Tori's address.

"Ha," Kage laughed back at the man, giving him the finger. The man rolled his eyes but said nothing.

Kage typed:

HI. WE MET IN CHEYENNE JUSTICE CENTER LAST NIGHT. YOU GAVE ME A CARD. I HAD THE JACKET WITH ARM INSIGNIA ON IT. I GOT OUT. CAN WE MEET? I NEED HELP.

Kage stopped again, looked over at the dashboard. They were nearing West Lincolnway, the volocopter's final destination. Kage typed it in as his location, omitted his real name, and sent the message. Probably nothing would come of it, but he had to try.

The volocopter dropped like an elevator to the sidewalk. The man got out, slamming the door. Kage got out and quickly ran into a dark alley across the street.

"Hey. I'm calling the Marshals, you fucker," the man yelled out into the dark. He turned and entered a bar. Kage ran and, at the end of the alley, turned the corner. He needed a nearby place to hide, to wait and see if Tori actually came to meet him.

One block up, a subway entrance beckoned. Kage ran over and down into the subway tunnel. He found a bench in a corner and sat down. A crowd of people entered on and off the platform and onto the train. It disappeared down a dark tunnel. As Kage watched it, he thought about his parents. What in the hell had happened? They were supposed to have been right behind him and Trevor. Something definitely happened. A physical pain twisted in his chest. He still felt their loss in his heart, even after all these years. If he knew for sure they were dead, it would be a different feeling. Maybe a sense of acceptance would've come by now. But the uncertainty was like looking down that dark tunnel and expecting something to move backwards, expecting time to do what it couldn't.

Chapter Eighteen

Bray

Bray lost all track of time when she connected with an animal. It was hard to know whether minutes passed, or hours. Now, she was still hanging above herself, looking down at the broad and exposed land of Wyoming. The moon sat there like a dulled-down coin in the sky. Never had she seen anything like this—except, of course, in picture books.

And then they came. She had been calling out for help, looking for the horses, and there they were. From afar, a band of them danced into view, a wave of bronze approaching from the west. In her chest, she felt a thu-dump, thu-dump, thu-dump as their hooves advanced against the hard ground. There were hundreds of them.

"Looks like your mom's here," a man's voice intruded on her vision.

My mom, she said to herself. *Dump is here.*
Dump, as she and Elliott so "affectionately" called her, had arrived.

Bray turned and looked at Elliott. She leaned over to him and whispered in his ear.

"Follow my lead."

He pulled away, eyebrows raised. He nodded at her.

The door opened beside Bray and the sudden, cold air forced her eyes open. There, standing above her, was her mother.

"Thought you could just run off?" Dianna asked, her hands pressed firmly into her hips.

Bray said nothing.

"Where'd you think you were going?" Dianna asked, chuckling.

Suddenly the thu-dump, thu-dump returned to Bray's chest. She closed her eyes, ignored her mom. Then the thu-dump sped into a trill, a thu-du-du-duh, thu-du-du-duh. They were coming closer. Bray felt the wind of their velocity inside her. She felt herself trampled, yet open and running.

Rising above herself again, in her mind, she saw the wild horses. Only now they were just feet away from I-25 North.

Bray's eyes opened. Her mind couldn't fathom what was happening. There was no time. She stood up and turned, looked outside.

"Bray, are you listening to me?" Dianna said.

Out beyond the lines of cars at the checkpoint, the heads of the horses came into view. Bray could barely make out the lines of their faces in the dark.

"Would you look at that?" Bray said, stunned and also relieved that her plan seemed to have worked.

She pushed past her mom and ran outside.

"Hey!" Dianna yelled.

A row of horses leapt over the guardrails. They were running right toward her. Elliott ran out of the detainment center and stopped beside her.

"Elliott, run!" she screamed.

Now the horses sprinted across the

highway. People ducked or jumped back into their cars. The horses jumped clear over car hoods to make their way to the other side. In the beams of the cars' headlights, Bray saw Elliott running alongside them, his hands covering his head and his backpack bouncing behind him. Smiling, Bray turned and ran in the same direction, following the horses, Elliott just up ahead.

The horses surrounded her and Elliott. Another guardrail stood blocking her way. The horses naturally jumped the guardrail as if it weren't even there. Bray had to stop and bring one leg over, then the other. But there were enough horses around her and behind that it did not matter. They all broke free of the highway and were now in the grass, in the real grass, running. Free.

The horses stayed with them far past the highway. Behind her, the Marshals yelled and chased after them. Up ahead, Elliott had somehow managed to get on one of the horses and was riding it. Bray couldn't believe what she was seeing. But then one of the horses ahead of her stopped cold, knelt down, and waited. As Bray reached it, she carefully got on and gripped its skin with her hands, afraid she'd hurt it. The horse stood up and ran. The bumping hurt between Bray's legs. Frigid wind slapped her in the face and she couldn't breathe. She glanced over her shoulders and saw that the Marshals had fallen behind. Bray turned away, grinning.

In the darkness, she couldn't see out in front of her, only the hard terrain a few feet ahead at a time. The horse bounced along the ground, absorbing much of the shock from hard earth. What couldn't be absorbed hit Bray in her burn wound. She cringed.

Above her, a perp buzzed. The band of horses shifted direction and moved in a line toward the mountains. Bray sensed that Elliott was still holding on a few horses ahead. The perp followed. If there was any chance of getting away from the Marshals, they'd have to ditch the perp somehow.

The horses picked up their pace. The perp kept up, but Bray sensed the horses had some kind of plan. As they neared the mountain range, the terrain became a series of hills. More hills, more up and down, more pain between Bray's legs and along the wound on her back. But the horses were gentle in their movements, so much so that eventually the pain dulled.

Hours passed. Daybreak came, and then the sun rose above Bray's shoulders. Its rays were fast approaching the top of her head. When she looked up, she could hardly see the perp, its body blinded out by the sunlight. The sun warmed her face and her exposed skin and she felt things, good things, she'd never felt before. Her heart awakened to a feeling she might call joy, relief, a kind of calm she hardly recognized.

As the mountains drew near, exposed rock in mixed shades of blinding oranges and reds jutted out of the sprouting foliage that dotted the mountainsides. They came up onto a hill and rolled down into a valley of trees and grass and occasional rock. The perp was still keeping pace, but suddenly it beeped, beeped again, and then pulled backward and disappeared back west.

The horses slowed just below the first mountain. The band of them stopped, and Bray jumped off and ran over to Elliott.

"Holy fucking shit," Elliott said, wiping away tears from his face. He dropped to the ground, pulled off his backpack, lay down, and covered his face with his hands.

"You okay?" Bray asked. Suddenly she felt dizzy. She came to sit beside him. She noticed her mask had flown off somewhere along the way. So had Elliott's.

"My mind's just been fucked."

"Mine too," she said, smiling.

The horses spread out and began eating at the nearby trees and grass. They said nothing to Bray, just went about their business. Bray was in the midst of trying to understand what just happened, how it happened. Had the horses really come because she called for them? She could ask, but she didn't want to interrupt their meal. Though she never doubted her ability to connect with animals, she'd never been able to do anything like this before.

"Did you see how that perp just flew away?" she asked.

"No, can't say I noticed," Elliott replied, pulling his hands away from his face and dropping them to his sides.

"It followed us for hours, and when we got to the mountains, it just...left."

"Perps run on connectivity. A mountain range would probably stop them from accessing satellite power. Kind of like how there's no radio frequencies outside the city limits," Elliott replied, kneeling down while rubbing sweat away from his forehead. "Oh, no."

"What?"

"We left Bishop," he said, looking back in the direction of the checkpoint.

"I know. I'm sorry. We can't really go back and get him," she replied. She wasn't all that impressed with Bishop, so going back for him wasn't exactly on her to-do list.

"No. It just puts him in a shitty situation, that's all."

Bray nodded and lay down beside Elliott and closed her eyes. The feeling of fresh earth beneath her was so grounding. Kind of how she felt whenever she was free of medication.

Once her head stopped spinning, she called out for Alice. This time, the link was immediate.

"Alice?"

"Yes, I am here."

"You won't believe what just happened," Bray said, her eyes watering in disbelief.

"What?"

"My friend and I were nearly caught. I called for help from some nearby horses, and they helped us get free."

"I'm so glad," Alice said. "You feel even closer now."

Bray stopped and thought. There was truth in that image she received back in Elliott's bathroom. The horses, the Wyoming border. And how on earth did she get these horses to help them? Was that just coincidence? Her vision and the events that followed were too closely linked to be random. She went back and forth about it in her mind, sensing Alice there, waiting.

Perhaps the visions she'd received were just extensions of her gift. Now that she was off medications, anything was possible. But to think at this point it was more than coincidence was, for her, a kind of blasphemy. Her gift was just getting stronger because her senses were cleared.

So what could that mean for Alice?

"When you say I'm closer, do you mean I'm physically closer to you?" she asked.

"Yes."

"How do you know, though?"

"I don't know. I feel."

Suddenly Elliott's voice edged in.

"How the hell did all that happen?" he said.

Bray opened her eyes and turned to him. He

was looking up at the sky.

"You wouldn't believe me if I told you."

"What do you mean?" he asked. He sat up on one side and faced her.

"I called for them. In my mind. I overheard the Marshals talking about horse migrations, and I tried asking for help."

"And they just came?"

"Pretty much."

Elliott rolled his eyes and lay back down.

"Maybe you really are crazy and I need to take you back to the hospital."

"Whatever," she said and slapped his arm. "How else can you explain all this? And why would they bring us here, to the mountains, where that perp couldn't follow?"

"I don't know. Coincidence."

"Coincidence? Is that your answer for everything?" she replied, her annoyance rising. But some part of her wondered...was her annoyance with Elliott, or was it with herself, for not wanting to see past what she called coincidences in her own mind?

"I'm hungry," Elliott said, sitting up. He

pulled the backpack over and opened it. "You want some water, a snack?"

"Sure," she said, wishing he'd be quiet so she could talk to Alice. She never could figure out how to communicate with Alice and humans simultaneously. It gave her a headache to try. It was like having too many voices in her head.

Elliott handed her a bottle of water and a protein bar. Bray read the ingredients and then handed the bar back.

"I'll just take some water for now."

"You're not going to eat it?"

"It has dairy in it."

"Here's some raisins then," he said, throwing a box into her lap.

Bray sat up and opened the small box and began chewing. She thought about how these raisins weren't even real. They were grown in an underground S-Corp lab somewhere.

Nothing was real anymore. Nothing but this hard ground beneath her, the air against her face, these mountains. She'd never seen anything more real since she was a kid. This could be a place to live...some day.

"How are you going to go through all of life without eating animal products?" he asked. "You just going to eat salads and rice?"

"Yes, I'll eat salads and rice. What's the big deal?"

"It's not healthy, for one thing. You need protein."

"I'll eat beans," she refuted.

"Look, I get that animals are probably intelligent, even that they feel pain. But they're here for us to eat. What the hell else are we supposed to do, eat dirt?" he replied.

"No, of course not."

"Don't turn down food just because it has animal products in it. You die then you aren't here to help any animals."

"I just have to believe there's a way for us to not eat animals. They did it in the past, so why can't we get there again?"

"Because people love meat."

"Then S-Corp can make lab-grown meat. You

know they're capable," Bray said.

"True. But people aren't going to stop eating animals. Sorry, kiddo," he said to her and lay back down. "Besides, if you got these horses to help us, then isn't it kind of hypocritical to use them to save yourself and then turn around and say we shouldn't be using animals?"

Bray glared at him.

"I need to get some rest," she said, and lay down and turned her back to him. There was no hope for getting people to stop eating animals if she couldn't even convince her best friend.

Things between them went silent. Bray closed her eyes, listened to the horses chewing, to the soft breezes through the trees. To the nothing and everything around her.

The thoughts in her mind were louder than an oncoming train. What Elliott said had stung. Was she using animals when she shouldn't be? Was he right? She hated thinking that she, too, was doing what everyone else did—just using animals to her own benefit. But she had asked for help. It wasn't like she forced the horses to do something they didn't want to do. That was different. It was next to impossible to live in a world where she was the only one who could communicate with animals and then know how deeply they felt things, too.

Bray turned and looked up at the stars. They reached down to her from time, from beyond time. Would they still reach her if she died? Where would she end up? Her eyes searched the sky for the emptiness she equated with death and found none. Only the silent spaces between the stars' light, the way it would feel to lose Alice.

Maybe now that she was out here, she could try to find Alice, but then what?

Chapter Nineteen

Dianna

"What the hell just happened?" Dianna said to no one in particular.

She had run outside to chase after Bray. Either she was also mentally unstable or she just watched her daughter ride off on a wild horse??

A whole group of drones had gone after Bray and Elliott. The Marshals wouldn't be far behind.

All the while, Dianna stood and watched the wild horses run toward the mountains. And Bray and Elliott were with them.

What the hell? she thought again.

"Did I just see..." said one of the Marshals, a twenty-something Asian man. He was standing beside Dianna.

Dianna traversed her mind for some explanation, but nothing came. She told herself not to worry, as the drones would track them down. At least she was on their tail and knew exactly what to do next.

"I want Elliott arrested for kidnapping," she said to the Marshal. "And for hacking."

"No offense ma'am, but looks to me like your daughter was happy to go off with the guy. Not sure we can get him on kidnapping. And hacking, why?"

Dianna turned and went back inside the building. She'd wait here until Bray and Elliott were detained. The Marshal followed her inside.

"Elliott once worked for S-Corp," Dianna said, sitting down in the chair she'd found her daughter in only a short while ago. "He got fired for breaking code. He was looking for info on his parents."

"What info?" the Marshal asked, taking notes on his smart phone.

"They died in the terrorist attack. I think he thinks we somehow caused it."

"How so?" the Marshal asked. His face crinkled as if Dianna was the one needing interrogation.

"I don't need to answer that. Just get them back here," she said, standing up again.

She turned and looked outside. Suddenly she remembered seeing dry blood on Bray's shirt and pants. Her forearm had been bandaged.

She must've cut out her implant.

Smart girl, taking after her mother.

Dianna's phone rang.

"This is Dianna," she answered swiftly.

"Everything's set. First extraction was good," said Lewis, the S-Corp West Water District Manager.

"Great. And were you able to set up where we agreed?"

"Yep."

"And you understand this is to remain completely covert," she said. Excitement and anxiety swelled up inside her.

"Yes. Of course."

Dianna thanked Lewis and hung up. She was too distracted to work right now. She looked at the time on her phone.

"What's the status on Bray?" she asked. When no one answered, she turned toward the desks, which were empty. The Marshal had disappeared outside. Of course they were busy doing checks, but Bray had proven herself to be quite slippery. If they let her get too far, she could get away again.

Whenever things didn't go the way Dianna needed them to, it was because someone else was in charge. It was time she took matters into her own hands. So she lifted her phone and called Dan, the head of S-Corp West Security.

"I have a job for you," she said quietly. She needed to be quick, while the Marshals were out of the room.

If the media found out about Bray, found out that she had schizophrenia, it could ruin Dianna's image as S-Corp's regional president. She'd been aiming for a new CEO position for the last three years. She couldn't let something like this be the reason for not moving up in her career.

"Shoot," he replied.

"My daughter escaped from Denver Health last night. She's with a young man by the name of Elliott Bansfield, who used to work for S-Corp IT. They were last seen crossing the border into Wyoming. They're on foot. I need you to use whatever resources you have to find them both. Have Elliott detained. Bring Bray to me."

"We're on it."

Dianna hung up the phone and her mind continued its busy fervor. How to fix this thing with Bray before it really became a thing. The best way to manage the media was to get out ahead of it.

So she made one last call, to the press, to announce Bray's kidnapping. It was key to beat Cole to the punch on this one—and to ensure the story never got out that Bray had chosen to escape the psych ward. This move was the only way to secure a future not only for herself, but also for Bray. Bray needed protection, and Dianna was the only one able to protect her.

Chapter Twenty

Cole

Cole's phone vibrated promptly at 5 a.m. He turned in his bed and slapped at the phone as if that would stop the buzzing. He grabbed it, shut the alarm off, and tossed the phone onto the covers near his feet. No one else was in the room, as usual.

He climbed out of bed with a headache that felt like a spider climbing through his head, its eight legs digging and sliding into different parts of his brain. He entered the bathroom, and the light streamed on. His headache just got worse.

Naked, he stepped into the shower. A monitor installed in the far wall announced the water levels available for the day. Due to the current water crisis, each individual American was allotted twenty gallons of water per day, and usage was monitored by each city's water company. Because he had a "family," Cole had access to forty gallons per day. *No family here right now*, he thought.

He turned the nozzle to cold, just the way he liked it. His ten-minute shower woke him up, but did not ease the headache.

After drying off, he considered what to wear. He had to wear suits for obvious reasons, and he hated it. Suits were way too stiff, especially now that he'd developed a distinguished paunch. So he wore distinct ties and flashy shirts to set himself apart. It was one area in his life where he felt he could be a bit playful and show some personality. And so today he put on his favorite tie, a silk paisley in red, white and blue. A cardinal-red shirt popped out from behind the tie, and the charcoal black suit he slid on helped him appear thinner than he was. Dressing this way made him feel energetic, even attractive.

His hair, a sunny blonde reflective of his German descent, stood out on the sides and back of his head at a precise one-quarter inch. The top was finely textured and stood at one inch, making him look young. He needed all the help he could get. While standing in front of the mirror, he slicked the hair back with a styling gel he didn't really need—but again, he was getting insecure about his age, so he wasn't past using products to make him appear younger.

Below the mirror, he eyed the square, black box on the dresser. It stared back at him. It was an exclusive Embedicare triggering sensor, used to turn his implant on and off as he pleased. Not everyone who had an implant had one of these. They were expensive, still costing hundreds of dollars, but incredibly worth it for someone who didn't want to be woken up by alerts throughout the night.

Cole rolled up his shirt sleeve and turned his forearm to face the machine. A red light flashed, followed by a beep, indicating the implant had been turned on for the day. Cole pulled his arm away and glanced down at it.

He thought about Bray, wondered if she'd had an implant. He wouldn't know. Dianna wouldn't ever tell him these things. Just another way to control their daughter.

The skin implant, a microscopic computer chip the size of a mustard seed, was surgically injected into the user's forearm with a hypodermic needle and embedded just beneath the skin. The chip used radio-frequency identification, or RFID, to pick up satellite signals in order to alert the user of important notifications like Amber Alerts, criminal activity and other dangers. The chip also contained sensors to track heart rate, blood sugar levels and blood pressure. The newest model, which Cole had embedded two years ago, included an entertainment component that set off shocks and various sensations to give the user a 4-D experience when watching television shows and movies.

Cole made his way downstairs. The air was crisp with bitter air-conditioning. On the kitchen counter sat a framed photograph of

Bray. She would have been five years old in
this picture. In her smile, her teeth were
missing from the bottom front of her mouth.
She was holding a pair of drumsticks. The
photo cut off half of the bass drum that
rested on the basement floor. She would
pretend to play drums with him back then. He
made her wear headphones—too large for her

head—to protect her hearing. He stared at
the photo now while setting his favorite
coffee cup below the instant coffee maker.
The coffee pissed into the cup and he popped
a few Ibuprofen with the hot liquid.

He sat down at the dining room table. Six
empty chairs sat around him. The table's
glossy finish showed him a reflection of a
man he hardly knew anymore. His laptop had
been waiting on the table for him all night,
and he pulled it toward him to cover the
reflection. The screensaver was another old
photo of his daughter. Bray was about eight
in this picture. She was holding a ferret
they had encountered at a pet store. She

wanted it, but their lives had no room for
pets. He worried about her, wondered where
she was.

That led him to check his messages, which
he could do with his implant. The image of a
screen popped up on his arm and displayed a
"home screen" with various apps for news,
email, messages and more. He had twenty
messages. He opened them to reveal that a
majority were from his campaign manager back
in DC. That would have to wait. He couldn't
return to DC without first finding Bray.

There was a message from Dianna to check
the news.

Cole opened a news app on his arm and saw
a list of headlines about the water crisis
and continuing protests and riots throughout
the country. As much as he thought S-Corp to
be the solution to the water crisis, he
equally doubted its effectiveness. So far it
had achieved little in solving the nation's
water shortages, and now more and more
states were nearing drought at alarming
rates.

This was not something he could ignore.

Then, he saw the headline: MINOR KIDNAPPED FROM HOSPITAL, KIDNAPPER CONSIDERED ARMED AND DANGEROUS.

What? Kidnapped? Armed and dangerous?

Cole opened the article and began reading. According to its source, which could only be Dianna, Elliott kidnapped Bray and took her across the border into Wyoming. Cole was pretty certain that Bray got herself into that Mini Cooper. There was no kidnapping involved.

The article also named Bray as Senator Cole Hoffman's daughter.

"Damn it," he said aloud.

Standing up, Cole walked over to the kitchen counter and pulled his phone off its charger. He called Dianna.

"Yes, Cole?" she answered.

"What the hell is this news article? You and I both know that Elliott did not kidnap Bray."

"It was a kidnapping, end of story. Besides, you just got back in town. Don't try to get involved now."

"Elliott isn't going to hurt Bray," he said, ignoring her comment about his absence.

"Fine, don't believe me. I'm doing what I can to find her, which is more than I can say for you."

That stung. He clenched his teeth, kept quiet when he really felt like screaming. Instead, he hung up. Cole stood there, staring at the phone. There was a time when he would pledge such obedience to Dianna, mostly because he was afraid of how she would react if he went against her in any way. He hated to admit it, but it was true. It got so bad that it made him sexually impotent. They hadn't had sex in years.

But he hated seeing Bray in that psych ward. It ate at him every time she had to be readmitted. Though he believed it was for the best, he always hoped for something better. And when Dianna said no to allowing her to come home, he was devastated.

He looked over again at the photograph of

his daughter. Tears rose in his eyes and he swallowed the grief back down. He had missed her for years, and now he was scared to death for her safety. He didn't believe for a second that Elliott was any danger to her. Elliott was her only friend. He had seen that first hand when he watched her escape down the road with Elliott. They were in on this together. He hated that she was gone, but maybe it was best for her. He remembered how it felt to watch her get away, outside Elliott's apartment building, the surprising sense of freedom it gave him to see his daughter finally freed from Dianna's control.

If only there was something he could do to make things right for her to come home again. There had to be a way for her to both be home and be free, and to get the mental healthcare she needed. All these years he'd travelled back and forth between Denver and DC and barely saw his daughter. Often times he'd sit and bite at his lower lip, wondering if things would've been different for her had he been around more. He couldn't change that now, but he could change things moving forward.

His forearm vibrated with a reminder that 9 a.m. session would begin in thirty minutes.

"Shoot," he said, shutting off his laptop and carrying it with him to the front door. He'd have to grab coffee at the office. Damn stale coffee. He hated the stuff at the office but had no choice. He left the house with his briefcase and laptop and made his way to the car.

From his gated community, he could see the sun's reflection on the many high-rise apartment buildings that housed Denver's citizens. Out in these closed-off suburbs lived only politicians, lawyers and city workers who chose to distance themselves from reality.

On his way in for 9 a.m. session, he got nothing but phone calls. How can we increase jobs in the agricultural sector? Colorado was on its way to becoming the next drought state, and so many S-Corp food labs and Centralized Animal Feeding Operations thrived here. That was where the jobs were. Unfortunately, only immigrants would work those jobs.

Immigration. Another issue that got under his skin.

He pulled up to the capital building parking lot. He waved his head in an up-and-down motion to trigger the screen image on his forearm again, just above the implant. There, he scrolled through his vitals. Everything was good. His A1C levels were a bit high at 5.9. His doctor had told him he was pre-diabetic, but he wasn't planning to do much about it.

After session, he quickly stumbled back to his office on the capital building's third floor. Inside, a pair of interns were tapping away at their laptops.

"Good morning, Senator Hoffman." One of them smiled.

"Please, you can call me Cole. Really," he said.

He shut himself in his office. His mahogany desk faced him, its back to a floor-to-ceiling panoramic window that looked out into downtown Denver. He considered scheduling a press conference. After that news story he would need to address the press. This story would blow up if anything more came of it. Though his family had long since been torn apart and distanced by Bray's mental illness and Dianna's efforts to control it, the media attention would end any chance he had of regaining trust with his daughter.

He plopped his briefcase down beside the desk and sat down. He needed to work on his campaign, but he couldn't focus right now. Opening his laptop, he turned on his music playlist. Music usually calmed him down, the likes of Coldplay, Spoon, Muse and Vampire Weekend, maybe some U2 every now and then.

An hour passed. Time for another meeting. He hated meetings, which often made him wonder why he chose to be a politician. The money was great, but he didn't go into it for the money. He really thought he'd change things. But lobbyists changed things, not politicians.

As he headed for the elevator, he wasn't sure whether he truly wanted to run for president. It was Dianna who had convinced him. As a Senator for Colorado for the past eight years, he knew he was fit for the job of president. But no one really knew him. He was a quiet man, not much for the spotlight. All of that would change if he ran for president.

The Agriculture and Water Committee meeting was in a conference room on the first floor. He was the last one to enter the room, letting the door glide shut behind him as a row of various representatives sat and waited.

"Sorry I'm late," Cole said. He caught his breath as he sat down. His heavy midsection was a sad reminder that he was no longer the strong man he had been back in his twenties. He was aging, and he resented every bit of it.

The Agriculture and Water Committee was designated to address the drought in the West, and to ensure that animal agriculture continued without risking state-wide drought. The only way to do that, Cole had proposed, was to bring S-Corp representatives to the committee. Never mind that his wife was S-Corp's Regional President. That was not his motive, and any representative that knew the nature of Cole's relationship with his wife knew he was telling the truth. S-Corp owned the nation's water, so they were the tie that could bind Colorado to safe drinking water for eternity.

The history of S-Corp dated back to 2024, the year of President-elect Francis Walker. Cole was twenty-five and in his last year of law school at the University of Colorado. He and Dianna were struggling to have more children after Bray was born, mostly because he feared he might be impotent. As a result, Dianna began to focus more heavily on her career with S-Corp.

The Sustainability Committee, later known
as S-Corp, was developed in 2025 under
Walker's administration. It had originally
been set up as a government committee whose
main mission was to reduce factory farming
by designing a more sustainable food system.
The Sustainability Corp included chemists,
farm directors, agribusinesses, politicians,
lobbyists, lawyers, pharmacologists,
biotechnologists, plant biologists,
geophysicists and government officials. Its
two primary goals were to develop a
genetically-modified, drought-resistant crop
to respond to the drought out west and to
design a system to increase access to water.

The genetically-modified crops proved
successful. S-Corp created a new gene that
provided these crops with rapid leaf pore
closure that had a reduced rate of water
loss. The crops were also modified with
reduced cell membrane damage and improved
photosynthesis. Since many S-Corp members
worked for the Environmental Protection
Agency, the crop was not tested and was

immediately planted out west. A new fertilizer, Genelife, was developed to aid in the growth of these GMDR crops. Industrial farms throughout the country began utilizing these crops and fertilizers by 2026.

Cole's arm itched, bringing him back to the matter at hand. He scratched it, tapping lightly against the area where the implant slept beneath his skin. It flashed a silent, red alarm along his forearm: TAKE BLOOD PRESSURE MEDICATION...BLOOD PRESSURE HIGH. After he had a mild heart attack four years ago, he tried to take his health more seriously.

He turned his arm over on the table, hiding the indicator light from the other members of the Agriculture and Water Committee. The medication would have to wait.

Chapter Twenty-One

Bertan

Two nights after Carmen's ultimatum, Bertan found himself standing outside the S-Corp facility. The somber security guard uniform stuck to his skin in the mucky night. It was hard to know how long he'd been standing there, but now that he'd snapped back from wherever he'd been, it was time to get back to work.

There was nothing from Carmen for two days. She should've arrived in San Pedro Sula yesterday. He called her three times last night, five more times tonight before his shift. The calls dropped. Not even a ring.

Something was wrong.

He began his security shift at the front offices and did his usual walk-through. Every night it was dark, muffled and cold on this side of the facility. He had been awaiting his paycheck, and today it arrived in his bank account. It was never enough money because S-Corp always skimped on his paychecks, along with everyone else's. He had to work two jobs just to make ends meet, and even so ends were still not met. Ever.

Shifting over to the Dirty Side, Bertan walked up to the security office to check video surveillance. He opened the door to the security office, a room small enough to be a closet, with one folding chair, a desk, two filing cabinets and a wall of televisions displaying surveillance video.

Sitting down at the desk, he noticed a blank, manilla folder hidden beneath one of the laptops. Bertan looked out into the silent Kill Floor on one of the video screens and then remembered there was no one else there. He lifted the laptop and pulled out the folder.

Bertan was always a curious one. It had made him the best security guard for Medina. His fingers pulled open the folder. Inside rested one single document. Bertan saw a

list of numbers, dollar signs, and at the
top, he recognized the words: MEDINA CORP.
As his eyes scrolled down the page, he was
transfixed.

"Medina," he read beneath his breath. His
heart stopped for a moment.

Bertan slammed the folder shut. His hands
shook and it fell onto the desk. Heat
suddenly filled his forehead. His heart
raced. Was S-Corp somehow working with
Medina? Or vice versa?

Bertan grabbed the folder and returned it
beneath the laptop. He stood up and paced
the floor. His phone vibrated.

"Hola?" he answered quickly. He prayed it
was Carmen.

"It's Alex. Have you heard from Carmen?"
It was Carmen's cousin, the one she and
Gabriella were supposed to go stay with in
San Pedro Sula.

"No," he said, stopping in his tracks.

"She's not here. She hasn't contacted
you?"

"Last we talked she was leaving for the

bus the next morning. That was two days ago."

Alex went silent. So did Bertan. It seemed they were both at an impasse.

"You have anyone in Bajo who can find her?" Alex asked.

Bertan traced his mind for people in Bajo Aguan. He'd been gone so long he didn't know anyone down there anymore. This was the scariest and saddest part about being so far from home. If something did happen, there was little he could do about it. Now he fully regretted not going ahead and committing to getting himself down there. And now he feared that was his only option.

"I need to get down there," Bertan said. "Can you send me money to help?"

"I used all my extra cash to get a bus ticket for Carmen and Gabriella," Alex replied.

Shit. Bertan ended the call. He needed to think up some fast way to get cash and get back home.

Bertan threw the phone across the room. It

hit the door and landed with a bounce on the ground. Thinking of Carmen, he ran over and grabbed the phone, checked it for damage. It wasn't cracked, luckily. That was his only connection to her, all he had left. He stood up and slid the phone into his pocket.

He heard a thump somewhere below his feet. Bertan froze, listened. Another thump. He ran downstairs, yanking his gun from its holster. If Medina was here to get him, he'd get them first. He'd shot and killed plenty of men, right between the eyes, in complete darkness. He was prepared to do it again.

Another thump, louder this time. It came from the Cooler. Bertan approached the Cooler door. He pulled out his keycard. His adrenaline rose. He was ready to kill.

He slid his keycard through the door's security lock, and the door clicked open. With one hand holding the gun near his face, he used his free hand to open the door to a crack. It was pitch black inside. He pulled the door open, slowly.

"Who the fuck is in there?" he yelled

through the crack.

Silence.

"I've got a gun, you asshole. Come out."

Still nothing.

Bertan slowly pulled the door open. He stepped into the Cooler, allowing the door to shut behind him. Placing one foot in front of the other, he followed the wall along the inside of the Cooler. Another thump. Bertan ducked on instinct. Another thump, near the Fabrication Department door. He ran over to that door and ran his keycard through again, yanking the door open. His eyes widened and his adrenaline took over.

Entering the room, he let the door close behind him. He pulled a flashlight attached to his holster and flipped it on. He pressed along the left wall, touching the cold steel of the hand-held knives and saws that hung there as he passed.

The energy in the room shifted. It felt...tighter. Was someone watching him? He turned and quickly pointed his flashlight. Its beam jumped along the far walls and in

between the disjointed body parts of beefs.
Nothing. He gulped. The hairs on his arms
stood on end. Short glimpses of his breath
pushed out like smoke into the cool air. He
stepped forward, one foot in front of the
other, his heart pounding. Everything was
quiet, but he knew he was not alone.

His eyes followed the glow of the
flashlight. It streamed slowly along the
concrete walls. Something stood in the back
corner. He squinted. It was a silhouette or
a shadow or something. His flashlight was no
match for the mysterious image. He tried
pointing the light into the corner, but he
saw nothing. He removed the light, and then
the shadow reappeared.

Frozen, Bertan dropped the flashlight to
his side.

"Who-who's there?" He forced the words
out. Now he was getting scared.

Silence.

Bertan held out his gun. The shadow rolled
and elongated. Its shape melded into a

translucent, smoky form. The head of a young girl came into formation. She had long, wet black hair. It stuck to one side of her face and crawled along her shoulders. One half of the top of her head was missing. Instead of an eye, he saw a hole where he could see through to the wall. Blood and bone and skin and brain all mixed together and crowded the hole like a pack of hungry dogs fighting over the dead.

She'd been shot.

The girl's body continued to form, but not into a human. Her head remained as it was and the rest of her body transformed into that of a beef. Bertan's hands shook. He struggled to slip his gun back into his holster so he wouldn't drop it on the floor. He held his breath. The girl turned and glared at him. A fierce wind spun around the room, pushing the heavy carcasses to one side and causing sharp instruments of death to drop to the floor.

"Run. Run goddamnit, run," he whispered to himself, but his legs would not move. Knives rose in midair and turned. One of them pointed itself at Bertan. Before he could respond, it flew toward him, just missing his leg.

Running for the door, he grabbed for his keycard with a shaky hand. The wind pushed him up against the hard steel barrier with a thump. He triggered the door to open and kept running without looking back.

But then he stopped cold in the Clean Side hallway. There, standing idle in a corner, was another ghostly image. Bertan's body went cold. His skin raised with goose flesh from his neck down to his lower back. He shivered.

It was a little boy, maybe four years old. He was naked with a distended belly. His skin was the color of Bertan's. Bertan recognized him instantly. The boy just stood there, hands down to his sides, and stared at Bertan. Bertan shivered, turned, and ran.

Once outside, he tripped against the hard earth and fell, his hands sliding into the dirt and burning with pain. He remained on the ground, his head down, while he caught his breath. Afraid to make any sudden movements, he slowly lifted his head and surveyed the area. Everything was dark and quiet.

The dark landscape was a comfort. No ghosts out here. Sitting up, he felt instantly dizzy. He lay down on his back and glared up at the stars. That little boy and girl would never stop haunting him. At first they had just appeared in his nightmares, but now they'd come to haunt him at work. Where would they follow him next? He deserved it, after what he'd done to them.

The stars began to spin in circles above him. They felt so close but were so far away, just like Carmen and Gabriella. And time was only passing while he was no closer to finding them.

The world closed in on him then, and he passed out in the grass.

#

Bertan's eyes shot open. A blank ceiling stared down at him. He sat up. The sight of bunk beds gave way to the realization that he was in his bed.

He didn't remember coming home.

He turned in bed, and his feet landed on the floor. He was wearing his underwear and nothing else. His security guard clothes were strewn all over the floor.

"Rough night?" Merced, one of his roommates, asked. He wore a pair of washed-out jeans and a black t-shirt. Merced was also from Honduras, so Bertan trusted him a bit more than the others.

"Yeah," Bertan responded.

He stood up and walked over to a side table where Styrofoam cups and a coffee maker waited for him. He poured himself a cup of coffee. He hated it, as it was nothing like the coffee back home.

"You hungover?" Merced asked, stepping up beside him. "Got some alcohol I don't know about?"

"No..." Bertan turned to him, whispered low, "You know that plant is haunted?"

Just then, Axel, a six-foot-tall Mexican with broad shoulders and a bald head, stepped out of the bathroom. Axel was new, had just started at S-Corp about a week ago. He was quiet and had hardly spoken a word since moving in. He had yet to say anything to Bertan.

"Haunted? You believe in ghosts, man?" Merced replied.

Axel walked past them, saying nothing. He glanced down at Bertan, his eyes catching the tattoo on Bertan's back. Bertan ignored him as Axel strolled over to the bunk next to Merced's and began dressing. Bertan took Merced by the arm and pulled him near the bathroom door. He turned his back to Axel so that Axel wouldn't overhear.

"I saw two, last night. One was a little girl with the body of a beef," he whispered.

"No way, man," Merced said with a laugh. "You sure you weren't seeing things?"

Bertan glared at Merced.

"Bertan says he saw a ghost last night," Merced yelled over to Axel.

Bertan shot his eyes at Merced, brought his finger up to his lips to keep Merced quiet.

"Where? At the plant?" Axel asked. He wore a pair of sweatpants and a hoodie over his t-shirt. He approached the two of them and crossed his arms.

"Yep," Merced replied.

"You sure you're not sick, man?" Axel asked, touching Bertan's shoulder. Bertan pulled away, turned to face him, on guard.

"No. I saw it," he replied.

Merced and Axel stared at him blankly. To avoid coming across as crazy, he changed the subject.

"My family's missing," he said. He wasn't sure he really wanted anyone to know, but it was too late now.

"Shit," Merced replied. "What are you going to do?"

"I need to get down there, find them."

"How?" Merced asked.

"Take a bus down to Texas, then I guess just cross on foot from there."

"You can't do that without Marshals getting you at a state checkpoint. You might be able to use an S-Corp paycheck to get through, but they don't like us leaving and traveling home. You'll lose your job."

"If they deport me, then that would be best."

"No way, man. You'll be held by ICE for months while they process you. I've heard of some guys trying to get deported and it took six months or longer before they got home. Some never did. You don't want that."

"Then what do I do?" Bertan asked. He was losing hope.

"I know a guy who's got many connections in Central America. I bet he can track down your family, make sure they're safe."

Bertan nodded but said nothing. He'd already said too much in front of Axel. He didn't know why, but there was something about the guy he didn't like. Something about his energy felt "off." Bertan liked to believe he was a good judge of character.

"So what's with the tat?" Axel asked him, nodding at Bertan's back.

Merced walked over to his bed and sat down, began putting on his shoes.

"Uh, it's nothing."

"Hmm," Axel replied. He stepped to Bertan's side, unfolded his arms. He pointed at the tattoo, which spanned across Bertan's upper back, and read it:

"Bajo Aguan. That in Honduras?"

"Yes," Bertan said, rolling his eyes.

"Where? And what's with the rifles?"

"It's none of your business," Bertan said. Frustrated, he turned away and quickly walked over to his bed. He grabbed a shirt from the floor and put it on. Now that he was awake, he needed to decide what he was going to do.

He stood and waited for Axel and Merced to leave for work. He'd go in on his own. Turning to check the door and then browsing the room to find the place was empty, he bent down and reached under his bed. He pulled out the lockbox and opened it.

The $500 was still there. It was all he had until his next paycheck, which wouldn't be for another week. It was all he had to get himself home. But then he thought about what Merced had said. Maybe the money would be best spent on finding his family after all, then he could hurry up and get himself to the border. His body cringed at the idea, remembering what it was like to travel on *La Bestia*. Neither option was good. Either one could result in death, or worse.

Bertan left the cash untouched, closed the box, locked it and slid it back under the bed. Standing up, he finished his coffee and headed out the door for work.

Chapter Twenty-Two

Kage

It took one full day, and into the night. Kage had remained down in the subway, and slept there the first night. He missed his bed. He missed waking up to the scents of fruit, toast, maple syrup. And how he would work in the garden with Ethan the first few hours of the day.

He spent the entire next day pacing around the corner of West Lincolnway and Pioneer, waiting. He'd watch people walk and drive by. This was his first exposure to city life in twelve years, and it was unsettling. No sign of live trees or flowers. Everything was artificial, maybe even the people. The lie was that nothing could survive grown on soil, but Kage knew that wasn't true.

Kage knew a lot, and he was beginning to wonder if it was enough power to do some damage to S-Corp, as leverage for finding out what happened to his parents.

That's when, as he sat on a bus stop bench, he saw her. The woman from the jail cell approached just as night two had fallen. She was wearing sunglasses, a green mask, and breathable, cotton, black pants that waved as she moved. A thin, long-sleeved, black shirt clung to her upper body. She walked up to Kage, silently motioning her head back as if to ask Kage to walk with her. Kage stood up and followed.

"Stay behind me a couple feet," Tori whispered. "No talking."

Kage obliged and started following Tori away from the city, toward I-80. He couldn't believe this had actually worked, that she got his message and even came out here to find him. If it was a trap, Kage would be ready. He remained on edge, keeping his senses alert.

Tori approached the edge of the street. Just then a navy blue Honda pulled up. Tori pulled open the back door, motioned Kage inside with her hand.

He stopped and looked into the car. The back seats were empty. He stepped closer, peered at the driver. It was that beautiful woman he had seen at the Justice Center.

"Come on, get in. We didn't come all the way out here to kidnap you," Tori said.

"I don't know that," Kage said.

Tori huffed, shut the door.

"Look," she said, "I told you we were like you. Get it? You reached out to us. Either get in now, or we leave." Tori glared up at the darkening sky.

Kage looked into her brown eyes. He didn't see anything questionable. Just plain, dark eyes. Unassuming, truthful.

"Okay," Kage said. He opened the back door, got in, and shut it.

Tori got into the front seat and they drove off. He watched her remove her mask by looking at her in the side mirror. Then he shifted his gaze over to the woman driving.

Kage felt immediately nervous at the sight of the beautiful woman. In the dark he could see the shape of her eyes, how they fell down sharp at the edges. Her hair was long, flowing down to her shoulders in a way that left Kage feeling safe. He wished he could see the rest of her face, but he supposed he would soon enough.

"What's your name?" she asked. Her eyes flashed at him in the rearview mirror. He gulped.

"Kage," he said. He really didn't want to tell them his name, but it slipped out faster than he could stop it.

"I'm Lana. What landed you in jail?"

"Trespassing," he replied, regretting again how he just let the words slip. Lana's looks were too distracting. He tried changing the subject. "So who are you guys?"

"We ask the questions, for now," Lana replied. "Trespassing where?"

"For people who say you're like me, you sure don't act like it," Kage said. He was nervous. His palms were sweating.

"If you're one of us then you'll understand why we're questioning you," Lana said back.

Kage was impressed. He liked how she
pushed back, didn't give in. She was quick,
smart. Already he could tell he'd have zero
chance with someone like her if he tried. He
took a deep breath and answered.

"Salt Lake City."

"Utah?" Tori asked. "What were you doing
in Utah?"

The car moved swiftly north, exiting the
highway and turning onto less-traveled
paths. They must've been accustomed to
avoiding the checkpoints.

Kage really didn't want to answer that
question, at least not truthfully. He tried
coming up with other ideas, but he kept
drawing blanks. His attraction to Lana kept
throwing him off. He never got to see
attractive women, so now he found himself
losing his usual quick wit. But maybe
telling some form of the truth would help
him get closer to her.

"I used to live there," he replied. "Years
ago, before the 2030 Migration. I just
wanted to go back, see what was left."

"Did you know someone there?" Tori asked as she looked out the window at the open Wyoming land. Her voice sounded far away, as if maybe she'd lost someone, too.

"I did," Kage admitted, letting his guard down at the thought of his parents. "But they're gone now."

The car went silent. Out the window, the stars and moonlight blanketed the prairies, exposing deep and black mountain ranges in the night. Kage watched the ebb and flow of the land, how it shifted from plain to hill and back again, and wished for that movement, for some kind of momentum, in having discovered something about his parents by now.

Having found nothing made him feel even more alone.

Lana shifted onward down the empty road, now so dark only the headlight beams could be seen. She slowed the car to a stop. She turned slightly, and looked back at him. Her face rounded beneath her hair. Her eyes on him made him feel exposed. He went flush.

For a second he feared this was where they were going to murder him.

"Where do you live?" she asked.

"Wyoming," he said, sweating. "So now what, you going to kill me out here?"

"Ha!" Lana let out a laugh. "Of course not. We just need to know more about you before we go any farther."

"Farther? What's farther?"

"That depends on what you tell us."

"What do you want to know?" he asked. Truth be told he wanted out of this dark, strange place they'd brought him to.

"Just tell us your story. As much as you can."

Kage didn't know what he could say. He was afraid to open up. But he figured these two couldn't be undercover. Tori had been in jail, and she clearly came to get him out. At least, that was how it appeared. Kage knew a lot about appearances.

"I'm sorry, but how am I supposed to trust the two of you? You've got me out here in the middle of nowhere," he said.

Lana glanced over at Tori, then back at Kage.

"You know Tori picked you out because of that emblem on your jacket. That's the Animal Rights Movement emblem. These days, not even Marshals recognize it. S-Corp would, but that's all. And by now we could have you tied up and blindfolded, doing nasty things to you. So what does that leave?" she asked.

She was right. At this point, they clearly were not a threat. And even if he gave them some vague semblance of who he was, so long as he didn't give away his home in Meeteetse, none of it was really going to do him any harm.

"My parents were animal rights activists," he said. "This was my mom's jacket. They disappeared twelve years ago, from our home in Salt Lake. They were supposed to come meet my uncle and me in hiding, but never did."

"Man," Tori said. Lana looked at Tori, raised her eyebrows.

"I went back because I wanted to see if I could find something. A clue as to what happened. Unless I go back again, I have nothing. I'm sure it was S-Corp who did it."

"How do you know that?" Lana asked.

"I just know," he replied, turning to look back out the window.

"They must've been important," Tori said.

"They were," Kage replied, thinking back to the days he used to help his dad save animals from S-Corp facilities.

Kage stopped there. That was enough information. He and Lana met eyes. She sighed, and then turned to face the windshield.

"Well," she said. "You're welcome to join us. We're activists, too. I'm a lawyer. We're trying to build a case against S-Corp. We could use more help."

"A case?" Kage asked.

"Yes. Proof of their practices, to sue them."

"Sue them for what?"

"Animal cruelty, for starters," Lana

replied.

"Right," Kage laughed. Suing S-Corp wasn't going to stop them from using and hurting animals.

Lana glanced at Kage pointedly.

"You have some better idea?" she asked.

Kage didn't answer. The way to stop S-Corp was through their pockets. Destroying their facilities, taking the animals back. But he knew this wasn't possible like it was back when his parents were alive. So much had changed—stopped—since then. This made him feel regret, not so much for himself, but for all the activists who disappeared before him, and the billions of animals who had died and continue to die under S-Corp's practices. So he looked up at Lana and simply shook his head.

"We should probably get back," Tori said to Lana.

"Agreed," Lana replied. "If you're coming with us, you need to put this on." She opened the compartment between herself and

Tori. She pulled out a black face cover and tossed it back to Kage.

Kage caught it in his hand, then looked out the window. He wasn't sure how well he'd work with others, considering he didn't do too well back home, but it was worth one try until he could figure out his own plan. If he got out of the car here, or anywhere, he'd never see these activists again. His mouth was wet with curiosity. Maybe working with them would get him closer to finding his parents, or at least finding who knew about his parents.

Kage eyed Lana, then pulled the mask on over his head. Everything went dark. The car moved on down the road.

Chapter Twenty-Three

Bray

Morning had arrived. Bray watched the sun stretch along the horizon. It was so far away, yet right there. Three more days and Alice would be sent to slaughter. The recurring nightmare she'd had last night was a confirmation. A promise that just as this new day approached, so did the end.

Sitting up, she glanced over at Elliott. He was still asleep on his side, his back facing her. The horses still had not moved on. They slept, their bodies circling Bray and Elliott as if for protection.

Elliott turned and lay on his back beside her. He reached for his backpack and pulled out another protein bar.

"You really should eat something," he said. His hands delved into the backpack and he pulled out a bag and tossed it to Bray. "Here, trail mix. Surely you can eat that."

Bray opened the bag and studied the contents.

"Just not the chocolates," she replied, grabbing a handful of nuts and raisins. She picked out the chocolates, handed them to Elliott, and then began eating.

"When we're done eating, we should get going," Elliott said.

"Yeah, you're probably right," Bray replied, chomping on a mouthful of nuts.

If she was going to try to find Alice, then she would have to get moving. A part of her didn't want to, wanted to stay here, where she could already communicate with Alice, until time was up. But she couldn't give up on her friend like that. Alice deserved better.

Elliott finished his protein bar and tossed the wrapper into his backpack. He stood up and threw the pack on over his shoulders. Bray shivered, suddenly realizing how cold it was out there, and came to stand beside him. He shifted the backpack over to one side and unzipped it, pulling out a sweater.

"Here," he said. "Wear this."

Smiling, Bray took the sweater and slid it on over her. It came down to her thighs, and hung a bit heavy in the arms, but it was cozy. It was Elliott. She wondered how she might get his help without telling him the truth. He'd never believe her anyway.

"We need to get back to the highway. Why don't you ask your horsey friends for some help?" Elliott said, smirking.

"Whatever," she said, feeling a sting in her chest. Sometimes he was a complete jerk.

But he was right. They had no idea where they were. They wouldn't be able to find their way back to the highway without help. Begrudgingly, she closed her eyes. The horses lifted their heads in unison.

"Whoa," Elliott said.

Then, a pair of them stood and approached Bray and Elliott.

"I was half-joking when I said that, and now you're just freaking me out," he said.

"You were being a jerk," she replied, opening her eyes and glaring at him.

It was coming back to Bray's memory how love/hate her friendship with Elliott really was. Maybe love and hate were closer emotions than she thought. He constantly challenged her thinking, leaving her feeling insecure about the things she didn't yet know. She reminded herself that he had nearly five years of age on her and a ton more experience. Having spent much of her life in the psych ward, she avoided formal education as much as she could.

They each got onto the back of a horse. The rest of the horses remained where they were, watching Bray and Elliott as they started for the highway with their horses in a slow trot.

Approaching a set of wind turbines just in view of the highway, the horses stopped and let them off. Bray thanked them, and they disappeared in the direction from where they had come. Bray watched their bodies dart deep into the remaining semi-darkness. She tried wrapping her head around the fact that they'd helped Elliott and her twice, without condition.

She turned to Elliott but he was gone. Her eyes shot around in the coming dawn. The sound of running water came from one of the turbines. At a closer glance, she could see Elliott peeing on the turbine.

"Gross!" she shouted.

"Just look away if you don't like it," he shouted back and stuck out his tongue.

Bray rolled her eyes and turned away. The morning felt more crisp and raw as time passed. Bray's breath spat out of her mouth in quick clouds.

"I'm hoping we get to Cheyenne by lunch," Elliott said as he returned to her side. He glanced up the highway.

"What's in Cheyenne?"

"It's the nearest city. From there I plan on hitching a bus up to Red Lodge."

"What about me?" she asked.

Once afternoon arrived, she'd only have
two days to find Alice. Without his help,
she didn't think she could do it. Then
again, if she were going to die, did she
really want Elliott there?

"I wasn't planning to stay in
Cheyenne," she said.

"You do whatever you want, kiddo," he
said, and began walking along the side of
the road.

"I want to go with you," she said,
catching up to him.

"I already told you, you can't go with
me to Montana."

"I know. I just want to get farther
north." Since she had no idea where Alice
was, she just needed to buy some time.

"But there are no cities up north,
other than Red Lodge."

"I don't want to be in a city."

"Where the hell do you think you're
going to go then? We're in the middle of
nowhere."

"Can't I just come with you to Red Lodge? I can find my own place and I'll leave you to do your thing."

"You're seventeen. No one's going to just rent a place to you."

"I'll find a roommate."

"Ugh," Elliott said, putting his hands on his head. "I don't know."

"Fine. When we get to Cheyenne just give me some cash and I'll go my own way. Is that what you want?" she said. She was getting fed up with his rigidness.

"Are you mad?"

"A little, yes. I thought you were going to help me."

"Help you with what, Bray? You just keep saying you need to get up north. Why north? I know when you're keeping things from me, and right now you're hiding something. If I'm going to keep helping you, then at least I deserve to know what's going on."

This was always the frustrating part—

trying to get people to understand what she felt inside, instinctively. If she told him about Alice now, she ran the risk of him finding it completely ridiculous and walking away.

"I'm just getting a feeling is all."

"You mean your abilities are telling you to go north?"

"Something like that, yes."

"I thought you could only feel what was happening with animals. Now you have some kind of psychic ability, too?"

"It's not that simple. I'm sorry, I'm not ready to tell you what's going on. If you can just help me get past the city. I promise I'll tell you what's going on. Then you can do whatever you want. Please? I really need your help."

"I'll see how far I can get you, but I'm not promising you anything," he said, resuming his walk parallel to the highway. "This wasn't supposed to be the plan."

And that was that. The talking just stopped. She was glad for that. She just needed some peace and quiet for a while. She'd never spent this much time with another person other than her parents. It was beginning to weigh on her, his uncomfortable energy. She got the sense he was on edge, stressed. And reasonably so.

But then her senses crossed. There was something else present, and it wasn't just Elliott. Something was coming at them. Bray squinted up at the sky. Her feet quickened their pace so that now she was walking right next to Elliott. A humming sound approached her ears from behind. There was something coming near, something dreadful.

Bray stopped.

Chapter Twenty-Four

The Knocker

Time was less than a construct when the Knocker was in his zone. It was nothing, it was death. He could count the beefs he knocked as a way to measure time, but there were too many to track. Or there was the reggaeton music, today the hard and fast pace of Punta Cara in his ears. The length of the songs, their beginnings and endings, he paid little attention as each one streamed into the next.

The only way time became real was when he was given his fifteen-minute break. His knees were weak from standing all day, but he was used to this. Blisters developed along the inside of his thumb where he held the knock gun day after day for years. Often the blisters would break open. If he wasn't wearing gloves, they'd probably get infected.

This job made his joints feel old.

The Knocker found himself in the Fabrication Department, where men stood against metal tables in an organized conveyor system, passing down parts of beef, packaging them, dropping them in boxes to be shipped out to Boise. There was a general scent of shit and urine and metal that permeated throughout the Kill Floor. He could never tell if it was coming from the workers or the beefs. Probably both. In the Fabrication Department the smell hung in the cold air and cooled his nostrils.

Merced was working in the middle of the room, wrapping each package of beef that came to him, seamlessly as if he did it in his sleep. The Knocker leaned against the wall behind him, watching Merced with an impressed grin on his face. He'd never seen Merced at work, and it was like watching something as natural as rainfall. It nearly put him to sleep.

A buzzer sounded. The Knocker stood to. Merced finished one last package and turned around.

"Bertan!" he shouted, yanking off his goggles and mask.

"Don't call me that here. Call me Knocker."

"Uh, okay. What's up, *Knocker*?" he asked, starting for the hallway.

"You said you know someone who can find my family?" the Knocker whispered as he followed Merced out into the hallway toward a staircase.

"Oh. Yeah man, no problem. You want his info?"

The Knocker thought of the time he'd spent here in the US. It was no festival. Life here was hard, and there was no hope for citizenship. Once an illegal, always an illegal. And the work was torture. He had attempted to request S-Corp to allow his family to come to the states, but the days of the H-4 immigration status for families of agricultural workers were long since over. Since the 2020s, immigration laws had tightened, and getting into the United

States was like trying to get that camel into an eye of a needle.

"Yes," he replied.

Merced pulled his phone from his pocket.

"His name's Julian. He lives in Juarez. Here's his number." Merced pulled a notepad from his pocket, ripped off a piece of paper, and wrote the number on it. "If you can get your family to Juarez, he can do the rest."

The Knocker glanced down at the paper. He knew more than he cared to about the men of Juarez. Most of the men that worked at the plant were from there. The city had fallen into a dead zone after decades of street wars, violence and decay. It had devolved into the "City by the Desert" after the 2030 Migration. Though Juarez was located directly on the border of Mexico and Texas, it housed the lost souls of the world. That was what the Knocker believed.

#

His shift ended abruptly. It always ended that way, but these days things seemed to just stop and start without him ever remembering how. The Knocker stood outside the plant in the parking lot. The sun hid behind a set of clouds that hung over the horizon. It was beginning to set, but the clouds paid it no mind. He dialed Julian.

"Yes?" a voice answered on the first ring.

"Is this Julian?"

A pause, and then a response, "who is this?"

"My name is..." he stopped. Shit, he couldn't remember. What the fuck was his name?

"I don't have time for this," the man replied quickly.

"I got your number from Merced. I need help finding my family."

"Names?"

"Carmen García Duarte and my daughter,

Gabriella García Duarte," the Knocker said confidently.

"Okay. Give me a couple days," Julian said. "It costs 500 US dollars up front, then another $500 when I find your family."

The Knocker gulped. This would take the remaining savings he had left, and then some.

"Okay," he said.

"Send it to this account." The man provided a six-digit account number and the Knocker wrote it down.

Eyeing Merced and Axel as they neared him, he hung up the phone and stepped over to his car. He drove them back to the hostel as he did most days. Once inside, he waited for everyone to go to sleep. Then, he slid the lockbox out from beneath his bunk. The chain Gabriella made for him hung from his neck and he yanked it out from under his sweat-soaked shirt. He wrapped his fingers around the cross, brought it to his lips, and kissed it. A tear approached his eye and he pushed it away by quickly opening the lockbox.

Inside, the $500 waited for him. He took out the cash and hid it under his shirt. He grabbed his security uniform pants and tie and scurried over to the door, leaving the empty lockbox behind.

Back outside, the Knocker threw the uniform and bag of cash into the front seat. He checked his phone. Two hours until his security shift started. He could stop to eat, but he wasn't hungry.

Starting the car, he sped to Total Mart. Darkness covered the sky and edged along the road. He pulled into the half-empty parking lot and jogged inside.

Approaching the front desk, he saw that a white lady stood there alone. He smiled at her and pulled two money order forms from a plastic bin beside the desk.

As he began to fill them out, his pen froze on the NAME line. Why was he blanking on his name?

"Name," he whispered.

The lady glanced over at him, her curly

gray hair hanging down over her ears.

He looked away, in deep recollection. Over near an end cap, another woman stood with her back to him. She had stringy, black hair that stopped mid-back. She was shorter than he, with broad shoulders. Carmen was the only woman he knew with shoulders that broad. He turned toward her, stepping away from the desk. She turned a corner. When she did so, her profile revealed a nose with a longer bridge and a wide base, kind of flat. Just like Carmen. He swore it was her. His heart jumped. He quickly walked over to the woman. She turned toward him, revealing a face he'd never seen before.

"Sorry," he said to her, and he returned to the front desk.

The Knocker pulled his phone out of his pocket and filled in the amount, Julian's full name, account number and address. He double-checked everything, then checked it again. Still, it happened again.

Name?

He closed his eyes and imagined the

uniform in his car.

H scribbled *Bertan Duarte* on two sheets
and handed them to the lady.

The lady rolled her eyes and turned to a
computer behind the desk. The transaction
went through smoothly, to his relief.

When he exited the store, he wandered the
parking lot, looking for his car. Couldn't
quite remember what it looked like. Feeling
slightly confused, mostly annoyed at his
lack of memory these days, he peered into
every car until he found one with a crumpled
uniform in the front seat. Had to be his.

He tried the driver's side lock with his
key and it opened. He took a deep breath and
got inside.

Next he swerved out of the parking lot,
raced down the road and pulled into the
plant's empty parking lot with five minutes
to spare.

He was sweating as he buttoned up his gray
shirt, tightened his tie, slid his pants on
and pulled a black belt tight around his
waist. This was the first time he'd noticed

himself getting thinner.

As he walked the property, he tried Carmen's phone again. He'd gotten used to the calls dropping. When it happened again, his heart closed off. It was a way to protect himself from the inevitable.

But he went ahead and sent a text to Julian:

MONEY SENT.

LET ME KNOW WHEN YOU RECEIVE.

He felt a bit off, like something inside himself was fractured the way a bone fractures when someone comes down on it with a heavy weapon. It felt as though it had been fractured for quite some time, and now he'd finally noticed. Like that time he'd broken his toe and walked on it for weeks before he realized anything was wrong.

And so this fractured feeling did not scare him. It was more of a strange yet welcomed revelation, an opening to a piece of himself he thought he'd closed off.

That part of himself that had fractured knew this wasn't going to work, knew there were no more options, and went ahead with sending the money anyway. Like how the Knocker went ahead with knocking beefs, how a killer goes ahead with killing innocent people, knowing it's a life he's taking and, on most levels, he finds he doesn't really care. He tries to, but he can't. He wants to care, but not today, not when he figures his family is gone. When he knows from history and home that probably his family is dead, he just accepts that this is life and sometimes life has a way of surprising him, but most likely it would just do what it was going to do.

Chapter Twenty-Five

Kage

Kage nodded off in the back seat. He hadn't slept much in days, and he missed his bed.

When the car came to a stop, Kage's body was pulled forward into wakefulness. He coughed through the mask.

"You can take that off now," Lana spoke.

Kage pulled the mask off and static attacked his hair. He saw that Lana's face mask was off, too. She grinned at him. He quickly flattened the long strands of his hair, wishing he could just cut it all off.

He exited the Honda. Before him was another car, and two cabins stood side by side. They were about 2,000 square feet each. The outer walls were coffee-colored logs, and each had a porch and two windows that looked out at Kage.

Following Tori and Lana up to the porch of

one cabin, he got a better look at Lana. She was a few inches shorter than him and had a fuller figure. He was always skin and bone. Beneath the amber light of the porch, he noticed Lana's eyes were a light hazel, almost green. Full.

Lana unlocked the cabin door and entered. Kage followed behind. The place was dark, empty. Two navy blue couches sat over in the living room. Behind them, where the dining room should be, was a long, rectangular table full of laptops and various electronic equipment Kage did not recognize. A filing cabinet occupied the far corner behind the table.

He stood there in the kitchen, taking it all in. The kitchen was clean, with a high-tech dishwasher and a few plants on the counters, which he figured had to be fake.

"How'd you end up here?" Kage asked, bewildered that the place even existed. Of course, if they knew about his home in Meeteetse, they'd be shocked, too.

"Maybe we'll tell you in the morning,"

Tori replied. "It's time for bed."

She walked over to the door and readied herself to leave. Meanwhile, Lana walked over to the laptops, checking to see they'd been turned off. She double-checked that the filing cabinet was locked. Kage didn't blame her.

"You can sleep on the couch," Lana said. "The guys all sleep over in the next cabin."

"I'm actually not a female, if that's what you're assuming," he replied, though he wished he hadn't said anything. He'd much prefer staying in the same cabin as Lana.

"Right," she replied, blushing. "Then go with Tori."

"Tori?" he asked, wondering if maybe Tori was also trans since she was staying in the guys' cabin.

"Andy's my partner. You'll meet him tomorrow," Tori replied, smiling.

Kage's shoulders slumped. He'd have to wait until morning to see Lana again.

He left with Tori and crossed over to the next cabin.

"You wouldn't happen to have some hair clippers, would you?" Kage asked.

"I think Andy does," she replied, letting Kage into the cabin.

"How many of you are there?" Kage asked as he walked inside. This cabin was identical to the other, and just as clean.

"There are five of us," Tori replied, removing her shoes by the door. She glanced over at Kage, and Kage took the hint. He pulled off his boots. They clumped down onto the floor.

"Those things have seen better days," Tori commented.

"Yeah, they got covered in dust when I was in Utah."

"Right. Well, the clippers should be in the bathroom, just down the hall. Help yourself to a shower. There's food in the fridge. Take the couch and I'll see you in the morning."

Kage watched Tori disappear into a room down the hall. He heard the door close and lock. He found the bathroom and closed himself inside. When he flipped on the light, he took a look at himself in the mirror. His eyes were heavy, dry. His skin needed a good clean. He felt embarrassed, wished Lana hadn't seen him this way on their first encounter. But once he found the clippers beneath the sink, his chest rose.

She'll see a whole new me tomorrow, he thought, and he plugged in the clippers.

Kage's hair used to be short, back when he was a teen. That was his preference, so people wouldn't mistake him for a girl. He had never felt like a girl. And he had been scheduled to get top surgery just a few weeks after he had to go into hiding. Once that happened, he let his hair grow back out like a sad shroud to hide his grief. He thought if he cut his hair, he'd be too exposed, and he wasn't ready.

Not until now.

Now, he was on his own. Not fully a man but definitely no woman, and starting his own life. Needing a new look to be unrecognizable to Marshals now that they'd gotten his mug shot. And, he'd met Lana. Who knew what she felt about him, but he got some vibes from her and he was fairly confident. He'd be even more so once he cut off this damn hair.

He pulled off his jacket and t-shirt. He removed his chest wrap and stared at his breasts. They were small, a size A, and he was grateful for that. He'd have them removed if he could.

Refocusing his attention on his hair, he raised the clippers to his scalp. The hair, which had grown down to near his waist, fell heavily to the floor. He cut along the sides of his head and then the back, leaving hair on the top. As he watched himself in the mirror, he felt more and more liberated. More and more himself.

Once the hair was gone from the sides and back, he cut away at the blonde length on the top. He cut and cut at it until it held against his ear, so that when he played with it, it fell to either side of his shaved head in a voluminous, sexy pile.

Meow, he thought, smiling at himself in the mirror.

He then removed the rest of his clothes and started a hot shower. Once morning arrived, he'd feel very new indeed. And he hoped Lana would notice.

#

Morning lifted quickly through the blackout shades on the window behind the couch. As soon as Kage sensed it was morning, his eyes opened. He sat up, his head clear. He hadn't gotten much sleep, but it was enough for him to feel recharged and ready.

The place was still dark. He stood up and stretched. Back home he'd start his mornings in yoga poses with Emily, but he was far too hungry for that now. He walked over to the refrigerator. There, a note hung from a single black magnet.

We're next door. Come eat.

Kage read the note aloud. A tingling sensation rose in his stomach as he thought of Lana. He took a deep breath to calm himself. He ran into the bathroom and rinsed his face in cold water. The clothes he'd been wearing stunk of perspiration, but what could he do? He returned to the living room and slid on his jacket and boots and headed out.

When he arrived at the next cabin, he heard voices laughing and talking. He froze on the porch, nervous. He hadn't been around people outside his own crew in ages, and he wondered how awkward he was going to be.

The door popped open. There stood a scrawny, bald guy with a black mustache.

"I'm Ben," he said, putting out his hand for a shake.

Kage shook his hand firmly. He couldn't take his eyes off the mustache. It looked silly to him. He'd look like Hitler if he put on an SS uniform. Kage tried not to laugh.

Kage entered. The place was lit with overhead lights. On the countertop stove stood a pot of oatmeal. The stove was something high-tech Kage had never seen before. It was sleek, black, with six square ranges. There were no knobs to turn them on. There was a screen on the stove showing a recipe, and beneath the pot a blue light was lit to keep it warm. Must've been electric. Steam lifted from the pot and quickly disappeared in the breeze from the ceiling fan that kept the kitchen cool.

"Have a seat," Tori said, motioning to a chair across from Lana.

Kage sat down at the fold-out table.

"Did you shave your head?" Lana asked, half smiling at him.

"Yep," he replied, looking around at the others at the table.

Tori sat down beside Lana, and Ben had just walked over and set a bowl of oatmeal in front of Kage. Ben sat down on the other side of Lana and started eating.

Kage looked down at the oatmeal. He was starving, but way more interested in these activists and what they were doing.

"So where you from, Kage?" Ben asked

before Kage could get a word in.

"Salt Lake," he replied, and stopped there. He didn't feel comfortable telling this whole group who he was.

"Lana tells us your parents were activists?" Ben asked.

"That's right," Kage said, thinking simultaneously how this guy asked way too many questions. He began stuffing his mouth with oatmeal in the hopes it would stop the questions.

"I thought you said you lived in Wyoming," Lana said.

"He asked where I was from," Kage replied, shrugging with a mouth full of food. He gulped it down and grinned at Lana.

"So what exactly do you guys do?" Kage asked, looking at Lana.

"Mostly undercover work," Lana replied. She was wearing a forest green jacket over a pink blouse. Her skin along her neck line and collarbone was smooth, the color of sand. She appeared to be of Asian descent, and Kage wanted to know more.

"And how do you suppose I can help?" he asked. He wanted to know how he could get inside S-Corp, find out about his parents.

"I'm not sure yet," Lana said, finishing up her bowl and standing up. "I'll give it some thought today and we can talk about it later. For today I suggest you lie low. You're already in enough trouble with the Marshals."

Lana walked her bowl over to the sink and washed it. Kage sat and looked at her, desiring to have this conversation with her later. Maybe they could be alone, where he could get to know her more personally.

"When's your court date, by the way?" Tori asked.

Shit. The court date. Kage had completely forgotten, thrown out that letter the lawyer had given him.

"Sometime next month," he replied, shrugging. He stuffed the last spoonful of oatmeal in his mouth and washed it down with the cup of water before him.

"When, exactly?" Lana asked, turning from

the sink and returning to the table.

Kage sat there, chewing the remains of the oatmeal that clung to his teeth. Lana dropped her hands to her sides, waiting. He continued to stall, now running his tongue along his teeth and wishing for a toothbrush.

"You don't know, do you?" she asked.

Kage grinned innocently.

"I'll find out when I go into the office today," she replied, walking over to the door and slipping on a pair of flat, black shoes. "What's your last name?"

"Zair," he replied. "But I'm not going to any court hearing."

"If you want to work with us, you are," she replied.

"But they're going to stick me with one of those implants," he argued back.

"We know how to remove those, so don't worry about that. You've got to get your name cleared."

Kage felt another tingle inside. He liked it when she told him what to do, but it didn't change the fact he wasn't going to any court hearing. Working with this bunch of activists was only to serve his need to find out about his parents. Deep down he always wanted to do activist work, but not this undercover shit. He wanted to do what his dad did. His dad saved animals from factory farms... a true animal rights activist, he was. And Kage couldn't do that until he first found out what had happened to his parents. And any time someone told him what to do, if it wasn't going to get him closer to finding out what he wanted to know, it only made him want to revolt further.

Kage raised his eyebrows at Lana, but said nothing. He watched her leave, then turned back to the others. They all got up, moved to the back table with the laptops.

"Let's get set up for tomorrow," Tori said as she sat down with the other activists.

"Come on, help me clean up," Ben said to Kage. Kage stood up and started clearing the table where they had just eaten.

283

"What are they talking about in there?" Kage asked. He carried empty bowls over to the sink.

"Tomorrow night? They're going to one of the facilities. Two of them got jobs as sanitation workers. They start tomorrow. They're going to get surveillance while they're in there."

"And you really think this is going to stop S-Corp?" Kage asked as he watched Ben take down the fold-out table. As was his nature back home, Kage turned to the sink and found himself washing the dishes with a hot rag.

"It's not going to stop them," Ben replied from behind. He closed up the six folding chairs and set them in the corner beside the refrigerator. "But it could convince the public to reconsider S-Corp, to reconsider how animals are being used."

"And what difference will that make?" Kage asked as the steam from the hot water warmed his face. He thought of the Animal Rights Movement, how countless activists had worked to get laws changed and factory farms shut down. It didn't seem likely that these five people would make an etching into S-Corp's dominion any time soon. Once Kage found what he was looking for, he'd get to work stopping S-Corp himself.

"Who knows," Ben said, leaning against the counter beside Kage. "But we have to try. Surely with your background you can appreciate that." He glanced at the ARM insignia on Kage's jacket.

Kage finished washing the dishes. He put them away in the cabinets. When he pulled open the drawers to put away the silverware, he noticed a set of keys to one of the cars. He took note of them and finished up, then sat and watched the activists work. They had video cameras the size of a fingernail that they attached to the clothes they planned on wearing. They talked through scenario after scenario so as not to get caught by other workers. They spent time editing a video of male chicks being tossed onto a conveyer belt and quickly pulled into a machine that ground them to pieces.

In another video, workers at an S-Corp facility were picking up calves by their hind legs and throwing them against the wall. One of the workers slammed a calf into the wall over and over and over again. Blood splattered against the wall in circles. Kage wanted to turn away but willed himself not to. It was what the whole world did: turned away so they could go on eating animals.

He'd seen it all as a teenager, but that was years ago. Seeing it today made his full belly turn. He felt light-headed. He got up and quickly walked to the bathroom, shut himself inside. Throwing some water on his face, he bent over and took a few breaths.

He needed to do something to find his parents. He couldn't just sit here and wait for some person he'd just met to tell him what he could and couldn't do. If that was all they had for him, he might as well just return home.

Tomorrow night he'd take one of their extra cars, follow the two activists out to the S-Corp facility. He'd sneak in behind them, see if he could get into some offices, find any info.

Then he would know what to do next.

Chapter Twenty-Six

Bray

"Something's coming," Bray said. She sensed something moving quickly toward them from the north.

Whatever it was, it wasn't galloping like the horses. It was running. More than one...three. They were coming fast.

But then there was something else. Not an animal. Bray closed her eyes.

"What's going on?" Elliott asked.

"Sh," she said, waving him off.

Her senses heightened. This time, every sound was amplified. A bat's wings as it crossed the sky. Coyote howls. Humming, like a car. Crickets sounded like vibrating, high-pitched glass breaking. It was overwhelming, but Bray sensed it wasn't good and so she kept on concentrating.

Whatever they were, the three were coming at them from the northeast. Running from something and chasing Bray and Elliott's scents.

From the south, a humming engine noise grew into a loud rumbling. It overtook the sound of crickets. Bray tried making it out in her mind and could not. It was no animal.

Bray opened her eyes. She turned to face the south. There, a set of headlights dotted the road. Bray thought maybe it was just some random vehicle, but then in the early morning light, the shape of sirens atop the car came into view.

"Marshal!" she yelled. "Run!"

They turned and ran just as the Marshal vehicle pulled off to the side of the road, its lights silently flashing.

Perpendicular to the highway, a small hill of rocks lifted out of the ground. Elliott ran faster than Bray, and dropped behind it. Bray came around and knelt down beside him. Out in the open, they had been completely exposed. The Marshal had clearly spotted them or he wouldn't have stopped. They had no time.

Bray closed her eyes again. The three that were coming their way raced toward them along the highway. They were alive and well, running, hearts racing. She felt a mouth-watering sensation and she drooled.

But then, from around the hill walked the Marshal. As soon as he saw them, he stopped, pointed his gun.

"Freeze. Don't move!" he shouted. "Hands up, now!"

Elliott's hands rose slowly into the air. Bray hesitated. If she allowed the Marshal to take her, she'd be back in the psych ward by morning, no doubt. While trying to think up a way to escape, she closed her eyes and raised her hands.

Suddenly, she could see down on top of herself from above. It was like she was in the sky watching herself in a movie. The three energies running this way came into view. Dogs. All of them black, full of muscle, teeth shining as their lips flapped through the air. Maybe they could help her like the horses had. She called to them, but their intention was automatic. They were coming despite being called. There was something they wanted here, something—or someone—they needed.

"Identify yourselves, now," the Marshal said from behind his gun.

One of the dogs came running from behind the hill. As it leapt, Bray looked up. The dog's body rolled across the sky above her, its front and hind legs fully extended, its mouth opening to reveal its teeth.

The dog took the Marshal down to the ground. The gun shot into the air. Bray and Elliott flinched. The dog bit into the Marshal's throat. The Marshal shrieked and then gurgled. A tattered collar hung from the dog's neck. Bray's arms, still in the air from the Marshal's command, were getting tired. She dropped them to her sides. She froze. She couldn't stop watching.

Now that she had connected with the dogs, she could feel them. Mad hunger, like the rage after having been denied a basic need all one's life.

"Shit, shit, shit," Elliott whispered. "They're eating him."

A second dog came around and grabbed the man's leg with its mouth and shook it, growling. The sound of crunching bones made Bray nearly puke. Its hunger mixed with her own, became her own. She grew queasy. Her heart pounded against her chest. Pain pressed into her teeth from the biting. Then, she felt...almost...excited. It burned in her pelvic area, and some kind of odd pleasure was beating at her heart.

She'd never experienced this before.

Dropping her head into her hands, she tried shaking off the connection. It wouldn't let her go. It was nearly impossible to focus, to maintain a hold on who she was. Between Elliott's cold fear and the dogs' rumbling and their absent hearts, she was losing herself.

A third dog appeared. Now all of them were ripping apart what was left of the Marshal's body. The rest of him was long gone.

One of the dogs shifted its body and eyed Bray. The dog kept watching her while it bit into the man's face and shook it. More bones snapped.

Elliott stood up and fled. Bray wanted to, but the dog held her in its gaze. Suddenly a series of memories flipped through her brain like the pages of a book. Dog fights, chains, whips. The dog was pushing itself into her mind. She nearly cried. *Get up, get up, get up*, she yelled at herself. She forced herself up from the ground and ran around the rocks. Ahead of her Elliott ran for the Marshal car.

As she ran, she felt the dog behind her. She didn't have to turn around to know it had broken away and was chasing after her. It edged closer to her feet. A panting sound beat in her heart. She couldn't tell if it was her or the dog.

In those moments as she ran, the thought of death occurred to her. A painful, ripped-apart, violent death. Slit open by sharp objects. Punctured. Bleeding out. Eaten.

And then she thought of Alice. That would be her death in a matter of days.

The Marshal vehicle was just up ahead. It felt too far away. The dog's feet beat into the ground behind her. There was no outrunning a feral dog. There was no outrunning death. It would come, whether in a few days or another sixty or eighty years.

Bray glanced behind her and wished she hadn't. All three dogs were behind her. Tears fell from the corners of her eyes. Her heart jumped into her throat. She could barely breathe.

If this is it, then what of Alice? she thought.

Elliott made it to the car and jumped into the driver's seat, which faced Bray. He slammed the door, searched around for keys.

"C'mon!" he yelled through the open window.

When Bray neared the car, the hood caught her attention. She jumped up onto it, belly first, and slid-then fell-over on the other side. Her hands met the concrete. She managed to stop her head from meeting it, too.

A dog slammed into the car from the other side and whimpered. It fell backwards, as if dizzied, and turned away.

Bray stood up, reached for the passenger door. Her sweating hand pulled at the door handle and fell back. It was locked.

"Unlock the door!" she shouted at Elliott.

Elliott looked over at her. He pressed the door lock button. It clicked. The head of a dog rose into the open window. Its snout reached in, grabbed hold of Elliott's forearm.

Elliott looked down at his arm and screamed. The dog's teeth ripped into Elliott's skin. It growled. Elliott tried using his free hand to pull the dog's teeth away, but then he screamed even more.

The third dog came around and growled at Bray. It hunched back onto its hind legs, ready to attack. Bray made eye contact with it. With the fear that Elliott might be

losing his life, and then her life being
next, she instinctively growled back at the
dog. She even surprised herself by jumping
at it. The dog flinched and ran off.

Everything started spinning. Inside the
car Bray spotted a holster mounted beneath
the glove box. There was a gun inside. Bray
yanked at the door and it opened. The sound
of ripping flesh made her lightheaded.
Elliott had fainted.

Bray grabbed the gun and pointed it at the
dog's head. Cringing, not wanting to shoot
the dog, she aimed it at the sky above the
dog's head. She pulled the trigger. A hole
popped open in the dog's eye. The dog
screeched and then went limp. Blood poured
out from the wound, and the dog's teeth
slowly loosened from Elliott's arm. The dog
fell to the ground with a thud.

Suddenly a splitting pain shot through
Bray's head, just above her eye. The gun
fell from her hand. Her head dropped. She
fell unconscious in the passenger seat.

Chapter Twenty-Seven

Bertan

Now Bertan found himself in Ruben's office, prior to the start of his day knocking beefs. He hadn't realized that another week had already passed and somehow he was still here and hadn't left for Honduras. What the hell was going on? He could have been down there by now. This habitual losing track of time was becoming worrisome.

"You okay? You look...ill," Ruben started. He was sitting across the desk from Bertan.

"I'm fine," Bertan said, shrugging and crossing his arms. "Just didn't sleep well."

Ruben looked at him but said nothing. This made Bertan feel uneasy, naked, like he was being interrogated by the police.

"How's your family?"

"I don't know."

"You don't know?"

Bertan squeezed his upper arms with his hands. An air conditioner whirred from the wall behind Ruben's head. Bertan's eyes burned as he stared at it. There was some kind of ticking noise coming from somewhere in the office. Bertan glanced around for it.

"Something wrong?" Ruben asked.

"What's that noise?"

"Uh, what noise?"

"It's like, a ticking."

"That's probably the air conditioner, sorry," Ruben replied, grimacing.

Bertan went quiet. The ticking went on several more times before Ruben said something.

"So, I do have some work to do. You want to tell me why you're here?"

Bertan thought for a moment, then asked, "You ever here at night?"

"Sometimes."

"You ever see ghosts?"

"Can't say I have. Why? Have you?"

"Last night. Or a couple nights ago,"

Bertan admitted. He couldn't remember how many nights had passed since he'd seen the ghost.

"What did you see?"

"A little girl. Except her body was a beef."

Ruben nodded. He jotted something on a notepad. Bertan glanced down at it, curious.

"Where did you see it?" Ruben asked.

"In the Fabrication Department."

"And did you recognize the girl?"

Bertan went flush, then felt cold all of a sudden. Should he lie or tell the truth? *Tell him the truth*, a voice whispered, *see how this goes. See if you can freak him out.*

"Yes," he said, "I killed her."

Ruben stopped writing, looked up at Bertan.

"Yeah?"

"She was the daughter of...of someone I was sent to kill. I thought I was killing him, and I shot her by mistake."

"Oh. When was this?"

"I was twenty-three."

"And this was for Medina?"

"Yes."

"How old was the girl?"

"I don't know. Maybe twelve or so."

"Hmm. Same as Gabriella."

Bertan shot a look at Ruben, right in the eye.

"What's your point?" he asked. This wasn't going the way he had expected.

"No point, just making an observation."

"Then what's your observation?" Bertan leaned forward, now feeling heated.

"You said earlier you don't know how your family is doing. Usually when you talk about them, your face lights up. Now you seem...lost. I just wondered if there was a connection."

"Connection?" Bertan asked, but he knew what Ruben was implying.

"Did something happen with your family?"

Then Bertan suddenly remembered why he came here.

"I'm not sure. Haven't heard from them in days. They were supposed to go to San Pedro

Sula. Their lives were in danger," Bertan said, the words falling out of his mouth with ease. "I need to leave."

"To go find them?"

"Yes," he replied. And then he remembered something else: that Medina was working with S-Corp. Or maybe they were S-Corp. And if they found out he was headed home, they'd track him down.

"You're not going to tell anyone, are you?"

"They'll find out. You'll lose your jobs."

Bertan looked at Ruben. Losing jobs versus losing his family. That's what it had come down to.

"What's going on, bud?" Ruben asked. "You can tell me."

"Can I? I don't know. Medina finds out, then I'm screwed and my family might as well be dead."

"What are you talking about?"

Bertan thought about that file folder he found. The one that proved S-Corp and Medina were working together. He wondered if Ruben already knew. If he did, then there was a chance he was one of them, and that he'd rat Bertan out in a heartbeat.

"What do you know about Medina?" Bertan suddenly asked. He had to know if Ruben could be trusted. Despite they'd worked together the last five years, it didn't mean Ruben wasn't hiding things. This was the place where all things remained well hidden.

"Nothing. You're the first person to tell me about them. Why? What's going on?"

Bertan looked into Ruben's eyes. He read no lies in the man's face. As far as Bertan could tell, Ruben was being honest. But just to be safe, he decided to keep his mouth shut about the folder, for now.

"I need to go down there, find my family."

"If you leave, it'll be very hard not to be tracked down and placed in deportation. You really don't want that."

"I know, I heard. But what choice do I have?"

Ruben did not reply. He sat there and looked at Bertan, almost as if he agreed.

"So what happened with the little girl?" Ruben asked, changing the subject.

"What little girl?"

"The one you killed."

Telling someone how he killed people was difficult. Bertan didn't feel good about the things he had done. But if Ruben knew about the work he'd done for Medina, maybe this would scare him into leaving Bertan well enough alone.

"There was this guy named Chino. He was a campesino. He was on my death squad list."

"You had a list?"

"Yep. Medina wanted these campesinos dead, or at least dead enough inside that they'd stop, so we could get their land."

"I can see why they make you nervous."

"Yes," Bertan said.

"And the little girl?" Ruben asked again.

"She was Chino's daughter. I went to their home late one night. I thought they'd all be sleeping. I broke in, saw a light on in the bathroom. I figured maybe it was Chino. So I quietly stepped up to the bathroom door. I had my gun out in one hand and pressed the door slowly open with the other. I had to be quick. A silencer was on the gun so the family wouldn't hear. I was supposed to be in and out."

Bertan spoke matter-of-factly. As he told the story, there was only a slight twinge building inside him. Not knowing what it was, he went on.

"As soon as I opened the door, I pulled the trigger. I didn't wait to make sure. You never wait. You just shoot. And then I saw the girl fall into the bathtub. Blood all over the walls. Next thing I know the mom is running down the hall, screaming. Don't know how she heard me. So I had to shoot her, too."

"And then Chino?"

"Yes. We got into a fight, then I grabbed his head and slammed it into the bathroom sink and he fell unconscious. Then I shot him. Just to be sure."

The room fell silent.

The twinge that had started deep in

Bertan's chest expanded out to his lungs and his ribs. He held his breath, wondering what Ruben was thinking right about now.

"Does it ever haunt you?" Ruben asked.

"What?"

"Killing the little girl, and the mom."

She just haunted me the other night, Bertan thought.

The little girl came to him always. Always it was the same bloody face, a hole where her right eye used to be, and red mixed with black in the background. She would whisper something, but he could never hear what she said, and then he'd wake up.

"Not really," Bertan said with a shrug.

"Do you feel bad, for what you did?"

Bertan leaned back in his chair. Did he feel bad? His arms were crossed and now he crossed them even tighter. Sweat permeated his underarms. The twinge in his chest chimed along with the ticking noise, which grew ever more intense in his ears.

"Why are you so curious about the girl when I just told you I was leaving?"

"I don't think you should leave, Bertan,"
Ruben replied. "I've got resources. I can
help track down your family for you."

"For what?" Bertan asked, suddenly not
trusting Ruben.

"What do you mean, for what?"

"At what cost?" Bertan said flatly.

"None. I consider you a friend. I just
want to help."

Bertan went quiet. He wasn't sure what to
think now. Ruben didn't appear to be lying.
As part of his work with Medina, Bertan had
been trained to catch liars. But from what
he felt inside, Ruben was still telling the
truth.

But it still made no sense.

"I'm worried about you, Bertan."

"Why?"

"Have you noticed any other, strange
things lately?"

"Like?"

"Like, visions."

"No," Bertan said, letting out a laugh.

"Have you been feeling more anxious

lately?"

"Only about my family," he admitted.

"That makes sense."

"What are you trying to say, that I'm mentally unstable or something?"

"Well, we do have to be sure our workers are in a good state of mind. Especially for knocking cows. But that's not what this is about."

The room suddenly shrank, walls came closer to Bertan's skin, nearly touching it. He glanced around at them, shook it off.

"You okay? You look pale," Ruben said.

"I need to go," Bertan said, scratching his skin.

"What are you going to do?"

"I don't know."

"Get back to work and try to focus on something else for a while. Just let me know if you want me to help find Carmen," Ruben replied.

Bertan stepped out of the office and shut the door behind him. He closed his eyes. Feeling shaky, not remembering when he last ate, he opened his eyes and hurried to the cafeteria locker room. As soon as he pulled his smock on over his clothes and hung his goggles around his neck, he felt different, better. Switching over to the Knocker was as seamless as falling into a dreamlike state in his sleep.

Chapter Twenty-Eight

Kage

A knock softly clapped against the front door of the cabin. Kage sat up on his elbows. It was night and so it seemed unlikely that someone would knock this late. He had been lying on the couch, wandering through his brain for a way into S-Corp once he followed Sara and Andy to the facility tomorrow.

The door opened.

It was Lana.

She was wearing a pair of yoga pants and a long-sleeved, black shirt.

"Hello," Kage said, surprised. "To what do I owe this pleasure?"

"I couldn't find any info on your court date," she replied, sitting down on the couch across from him.

"Not sure why. They gave me one. I just

tossed the paper in the recycle bin."

"I guess there's nothing we can do about it now. They'll put a warrant out for your arrest, so now you really have to lie low."

"I'm good at that," he said, winking.

Lana blushed and shook her head, but said nothing.

Kage looked her over. He didn't want to come across as a creeper, so he turned and looked into the kitchen. Otherwise, he couldn't keep his eyes off her.

"Let's go for a drive," she said. "I need your help with something."

Kage's heart leapt. To have an opportunity to be alone with Lana was something he wanted almost as much as he wanted to find his parents.

"Okay," he said, holding back his excitement.

Kage pulled on his jacket and boots. He followed Lana out to the Honda. Across the way, a red Prius Prime sat beneath a pine tree. It was in decent shape, too. He wondered how they funded their lives here.

He and Lana got into the Honda and she drove. It was cold out, maybe only fifty degrees. As with most nights, the sky was clear and full of every star in the universe. They brightened his desire for Lana, for a chance to know her on other levels other than just the surface.

"Where we going?" he asked.

"There's a dam at Boysen Reservoir we've been keeping our eyes on. Although the Parks Service gave S-Corp a permit to extract the water, we're pretty sure they're doing some illegal things."

"Like what?"

"Well, the dam, for one thing. It's harming the natural environment, and they're only supposed to be extracting water on a monthly basis. We have proof they're extracting every day."

"No shit," Kage said. He shook his head.

Wyoming was one of the last states in the west—along with Oregon and Washington—that had managed to keep S-Corp from coming in and extracting more water than what they were allowed. That they were doing it illegally did not come as much surprise to Kage.

The Honda continued along WY-487 North. There was nothing much to see outside the window. Layers of forest and then rolling hills of rock. That was about it.

It was 7:30 p.m. The road was empty. From his teen years, Kage remembered full roads and highways in the evenings. Back then he had friends, and a lot of them. There was a time he had missed his friends. He used to wonder if they ever thought of him after he disappeared.

"When did it start?" he asked, forcing himself back into the present.

"About three years ago. We've been taking video and getting proof. We plan to take it to court in the next year, once the evidence is substantial enough. Tonight I need you to look out for me while I get more photos. They complete the illegal extractions at night."

"I'm all for it," he said, his chest now pounding with aliveness.

#

Three hours later, Lana pulled the Honda into a field across from the Reserve.

"It'll be a mile hike in," she said, exiting the car.

Kage got out and looked around. From here, all he could see was an empty parking lot that faced two small hills of rock. He assumed the reservoir was somewhere beyond it.

Lana pulled on a backpack from the back seat and started for the parking lot.

"Cute," Kage said, smiling. "You look all ready for school."

"Shut up," she replied. "I used to get bullied a lot for being short."

"Aw, really?" he asked, now regretting what he'd said.

"I was also overweight as a kid, so I got made fun of a lot."

"Where'd you grow up?" he asked.

They passed through the parking lot and entered a hiking trail that led them through the rocky hills on either side.

"Hawaii."

"Oh, nice. Is it true what they say, that activists fled to Hawaii after the 2030 Migration?"

"Yes."

"I thought Hawaii was under some state of emergency...because of the rising sea levels and whatnot?" he asked.

"That was years ago. The climate isn't what it used to be, but now that most residents have resettled inland, the state is doing okay."

Kage nodded. Having lived in hiding all these years, it was easy to forget that he had had no way to keep up with the times.

"Then where do the activists hide now?" he asked.

"We fled into the mountains where it's safe. S-Corp will never find the activists there."

"Do you still have family there?"

"Yep. My mom and dad, and little brother, Jacob."

"Do you miss them?" he asked, thinking about his own parents, and about Trevor and Ethan. His heart stung for a moment and then calmed.

"Yes, every day," Lana replied.

They went quiet after that. Admittedly Kage didn't know what to say once his mind got carried away with thoughts of his parents.

They were supposed to come. That was the thought. He used to have it every hour of every day, in the beginning. Now the thought loomed in the back of his mind and came front and center like a nightmare at any mention of family.

Kage was looking down at the ground and following the dirt path up and up and around one of the hillsides. He had fallen a few feet behind Lana, immersed in himself, when she suddenly stopped.

"Here we are," she said.

Kage stopped and looked up. The land

opened out and down below them, exposing a
forty-foot-tall dam that cut off the Wind
River. It was like an arm cut off from the
rest of its body. He remembered Trevor
saying that dams were bad for the
environment, unnatural. And now as Kage
looked down at this tall, concrete structure
and how the water just stopped, he had to
agree.

"Unreal," Kage said.

Lana nodded silently. She stepped down the
hill to an open section of gravel, like
another parking lot.

Off to the left stood a small building. An
S-Corp vehicle sat beside it. Kage had never
been so close to S-Corp in his life. It felt
surreal, like it wasn't even really
happening.

They stopped beside a set of sage bushes
along the edge of the gravel lot.

"Stay here. I just need you to watch that
truck. If a driver gets in, or you see any
movement, call me," Lana said. She slipped
the backpack off and pulled out a palm-sized

device. It was shaped like a mini smartphone but had a circular indent in the bottom half. Lana handed it to him.

"What's this?" he asked.

Lana looked at him. She appeared shocked.

"It's a walkie."

"Right."

"You really have lived in a cave. Explains a lot," she said. "Just sit tight and speak into it if you see anything."

Lana pulled her phone out of the backpack and strode off toward the dam.

Kage watched from afar. Her body was a small dot below that enormous dam. She was taking photos of the extraction site where a thick, dark brown hose attached itself to the dam.

He turned and kept an eye on the S-Corp truck. His mouth watered at the fantasy of stealing whatever was inside, or using it to get closer to finding what happened to his parents. Or maybe he could sneak into that building. Obviously nothing here would lead to his parents, but anything linked to S-

Corp would be a step closer.

Kage glanced back over toward the dam but didn't see Lana. His heart rate picked up. His eyes darted around the place.

"Where is she?" he whispered.

He lifted the walkie to his lips and spoke into it.

"Lana. Where are you?" he whispered.

Nothing came back. He checked the device but couldn't figure out if it was on, or if he was using it correctly. He looked around for her. The stars had shed a glaze of light down onto the ground, like a dim white haze. But it wasn't enough for him to see where she'd gone. The S-Corp truck hadn't moved. He saw no one around it. He had to trust that she knew what she was doing.

And then a twig snapped behind him.

"Boo," a voice followed.

Kage jumped. His chest tightened.

He flipped around. It was Lana. She laughed.

"Ha. I got you," she said.

"Jesus. You suck," he replied back,

nervous and smiling.

"Come on, let's get out of here."

Kage caught his breath while she packed the walkie back into her backpack. They headed back up the hill for the parking lot.

At the top, Kage stopped and turned back. He felt sickened by what S-Corp was doing here. If they went at Wyoming's water the way they had that of other states, Wyoming would become a desert, too. And then what about Meeteetse? What about the family he did have left? He got a sudden sense they were running out of time.

"Did you get what you needed?" he asked, turning back to Lana.

"I did. Thanks for your help."

They continued their hike through the hills.

"And you said it's going to take a year before you go after them for this?"

"Probably. These things take time."

"What if we don't have that kind of time?" he replied, growing concerned.

"Why do you say that?" she asked.

"What happened in Utah. And Nevada, and so on and so forth."

"Yes, but it would take them another decade at least to do that kind of damage here. And what happened in those states had more to do with the 'terrorist attack,'" she said, using her hands to quote in the air.

"You make a decade sound like a long time."

Lana stopped and looked at him.

"What's this really about?" she asked.

"Just...my family lives in this state. If we lose Wyoming, we have nowhere to go."

"You and I both, Kage. Do you think I just want them to take Wyoming?" she asked. Her voice grew strained. She turned away and started down toward the parking lot.

Kage's parents entered his mind again. Yes, they were supposed to come. They were supposed to be right behind him, moments behind, maybe a day at most. But a day turned into a week. And then a month. Then a year, two years, five. Now Kage blinked and he stood here, twelve years later, and his parents were still gone. He might've waited too long to get out and find them. If that was the case, he'd only have himself to blame. There'd always be that regret, what could've been. And Lana said it'd be a year before they even started a case against S-Corp. All the while S-Corp would continue extracting water and causing so many animals to suffer and die. Ten years would pass and then Wyoming would be a goner, and maybe animal activism would be too far gone, too.

"Are you okay?" Lana asked, turning to him. They'd arrived at the parking lot and he'd hardly noticed.

"Yeah, why?"

"You just got real quiet. Did something I said upset you?"

"I'm not sure you'd understand," he replied. He walked past her and toward the Honda.

"Try me," she said, walking up beside him.

Kage approached the car and then turned to her.

"My parents," he said. "They were supposed

to come, and they never did. Twelve years passed and I waited so long that now I might never find them. It might be too late," he said. Suddenly he began to cry.

Lana walked up to him and wrapped her arms around him. Her head came to his chest and pressed into it. He felt the heat between them. He felt the chemistry, the energy, and the deep sadness of realizing that everything might be too late.

"I'm sorry," she said. She pulled back and looked up at him. "You know this isn't the same situation. I can't imagine how hard it must be to not know where your parents are. But we are all committed to stopping S-Corp as fast as we can."

Kage nodded, but he still wasn't sure. He pulled back and cleared the tears from his face. He didn't quite believe that Lana's methods of going after S-Corp in court were going to work. It was a gamble.

He turned and got into the car. She followed behind, sliding the backpack onto the back seat. Kage remained silent on the drive back. His head was full and processing. If he sat and waited for Lana and her team to make things happen, even if he chose to stay and help them, he'd be wasting time. Just like he did back in Meeteetse.

Lana would hate it, but he had to take things into his own hands. He had to get into S-Corp, find who had the answers, and get to them. He just couldn't afford to waste any more time.

Chapter Twenty-Nine

Bray

Bray...

*Bray wake...*a voice whispered into Bray's mind. It came first like a soft breeze, so relaxing Bray didn't wish to wake.

Bray. This time the voice was firm, simple. Immediate.

Bray's eyes opened. Her head was pressed against a car window. It was light out. Not knowing where she was, she sat up. She was inside a car. From the looks of the electronics, the random gun on the floor, a Marshal car.

When she turned her head, she jumped. Elliott was passed out. Blood everywhere. She screamed.

"Elliott, Elliott!" She shook him.

Nothing.

She picked up Elliott's hand and placed her fingers on the veins in his wrist. They beat into the tips of her fingers. Tears of relief fell out of her eyes. But he'd lost a lot of blood.

Panicked, she got out of the car and ran around to the driver's side. There, the dead dog. More blood on the ground, dark and black. Suddenly nauseous, Bray threw up onto the side of the car. She opened the driver's side door. Elliott's bitten arm fell to his side and hung toward the ground.

The arm needed wrapping. She popped the trunk. Inside, there were more weapons, stuff for fixing the car, and a first aid kit. Bray grabbed the large case and pulled it over to the ground beside Elliott's driver's-side door. Popping it open, she ripped open the alcohol swabs, one at a time, and rubbed the blood off his arm. The punctures where the dog had bitten him were deep, black holes. More blood coursed from them. Lightheaded, Bray turned away, took a deep breath, and then continued.

She squeezed all the gauze around his arm as tightly as she could, hoping that would be enough to stop the bleeding. But why wasn't he waking up? She checked the pulse in his neck, and it was beating. Surely he was still alive. Not dead, no, no, no, no. Not dead. Alive, yes.

She stood up and opened the car's back door. She slid the first aid kit to the floor behind the passenger seat. Returning to Elliott, she looked at his body. He was a big guy, so moving him would not be easy. And she didn't want to hurt his arm. But they had to get moving, couldn't stay here like sitting ducks.

Elliott's backpack sat crushed between his body and the driver's seat. For some reason, she feared touching him, like any amount of pressure or movement might kill him instantly. She shook it off. Gently placing her hands on each of his shoulders, she pulled his body forward and pulled off the backpack. She tossed it onto the back seat. Stepping out of the car to take a breath, she looked up. The rocky hill in the distance caught her eye. The Marshal's dead body was there. For a second, she thought to go check on it, but any moment now perps or Marshals would be on their way. Sudden flashes of being chased by the dogs froze her in trepidation.

Reaching into the car, she wrapped her arms around Elliott's torso, and pulled. His body came out of the car, and its heaviness pushed the both of them hard onto the concrete. She began to cry, scared and furious at herself for potentially hurting him even worse.

Bray gathered herself. She stood up and slid her arms beneath his arm pits and dragged him onto the back seat. She lay him down inside the car and shut the door. When Bray returned to the driver's seat, she saw it was covered in dried blood. She nearly gagged. There was nothing left in her stomach to throw up. She sat down and pulled the seat forward so she could see over the wheel. Not having learned to drive a car, she would have to wing it.

Starting the engine, she searched for the

lights and switched them on. The stick down
near her right thigh had letters near it: P,
D, N, etc., etc. Currently it was on P,
which she knew meant park. She pulled it
down to the D, and the car started rolling
forward.

Pressing her foot down on the peddle, Bray
sent the car screeching forward.

"Whoa, too fast," she said, slamming down
on the brake.

But they had to get moving.

The sun was climbing into the middle of
the sky. Time passed too swiftly. What was
happening to Elliott? Was he dying? Should
she take him to a hospital?

Probably.

But for now, she just kept driving. Not
knowing where she was, she didn't know what
else to do but move forward. Her stomach
growled. She tried remembering the last time
she ate. Glancing into the rearview mirror,
she angled it down to see Elliott, still
passed out on the back seat. The gauze was
turning red, but only where the wound was.

She would have to keep checking to see how long it took for the gauze to fill.

When she shifted the rearview mirror to see out the back of the car, her eyes caught an image of the gun she'd used to kill that dog. It sat there on the floor below the passenger seat. She hadn't meant to kill the dog. It was an accident. A pain seized her heart. The yelp it had made echoed in her mind. She felt sick, and a cold sweat wrapped around her neck. She wanted to roll up the driver's side window, but she was afraid of any blood—or other things—she might see if she did so.

She must've passed out earlier after she had connected to that dog. It made sense, considering how the dog was able to penetrate her mind, to send her those memories. Nothing like that had ever happened to her before. How she nearly lost herself in that dog, how she nearly felt herself wanting the way the dog wanted her. It frightened her, how this gift she had seemed to be getting stronger. She wasn't so sure she wanted to be able to connect with animals anymore, not if it was going to turn out like this.

The fact that she'd passed out would not escape her. Her connection to that dog was still mild in comparison to her close, intimate link with Alice. Now Alice could sense her, could sense her physical proximity. Bray's mind revisited the probability that if Alice died, she might die, too.

She shivered.

And then she thought about what Elliott said, about how she was just as bad for using animals for her own benefit. Here she was, worrying more about what would happen to her if Alice died, than worrying about Alice losing her life—and to a very violent end. Maybe Elliott was right about her.

Elliott.

She looked back at him again. The arm still hadn't completely reddened. Some color was returning to his face. She told herself he'd wake when he was ready. But then what? Would he be mad at her? Because of her, he nearly died—if he made it out of this, that was. Because of her, a Marshal was dead, a dog was dead.

And now all she could think to do was reach out to Alice. She didn't like that she had to. For the first time in her life she felt bad about reaching out, because she knew deep down inside she was using Alice. Perhaps it was true that Alice needed her, too, but she wondered if she needed Alice more. She began to hate herself for this.

But she did it anyway.

"Alice," she whispered to herself. "Alice, I'm afraid."

She felt Alice's presence. Like being in a room by yourself and you think you're alone but actually someone else is in there, you just can't see them. It was a comforting presence, maybe the kind of presence that religious types meant when they said they felt the presence of God.

"What's happening?" Alice replied.

"Elliott's injured. We were chased by dogs. One of them bit Elliott in the arm. I killed the dog."

"It's a good thing you did," Alice said.

Shocked, Bray almost didn't reply.

"What?" she asked.

"If you hadn't killed the dog perhaps it would've killed you."

Bray stopped and thought about it. No, that wasn't the case. The dog didn't even kill Elliott, though nearly. And, of course, Elliott wasn't yet out of the woods. But Bray was okay. They were in the car and safe. They could've just driven off. She could've yelled to Elliott to just start the car and go. There was no reason to pick up the gun. She just panicked.

"Sometimes these things have to happen," Alice said.

"But I don't believe in killing animals," Bray replied, still shocked.

"Why not? Nature does."

"That's not the same thing," Bray said, unwilling to accept what Alice was saying. For a second she considered telling Alice that she was on her way to death—

"We are all on our way to death," Alice broke in.

Suddenly, Elliott moaned from the back seat. Bray pulled herself away from Alice and looked over her shoulder. His eyes blinked open. They glanced around the car. Then his head turned and he saw his arm.

"Fuck!" he shouted, sitting up. "I thought I had a nightmare. That was real?" he asked, looking up at Bray.

"Unfortunately."

"Where are we?"

"Headed north, I think."

"You gotta get me to a hospital," he said. His voice shook. Sweat shone along his forehead and nose.

Bray didn't know what to say. He wasn't wrong. Clearly he had a serious injury that needed to be checked. But if they went to the hospital, they'd both be caught and that would be serious, too. They had gotten a Marshal killed, and no one would know it wasn't them who had done it. And they were driving a stolen Marshal vehicle. They were on so much borrowed time that Bray's heart picked up with every anxious thought passing through her mind.

"But if we go to the hospital, we'll be put away next. We're in a stolen Marshal car and that Marshal back there is dead," she replied.

"None of that'll matter if I'm dead," he replied.

She knew he was right. How could she not take her best friend to the hospital? Yes, she had another friend in need of help, too. Two best friends, both suffering and in need of help. If something happened to Elliott, she'd never forgive herself, and she'd be devastated. If she lost Alice, she risked losing herself, not to mention their friendship.

Just then, she noticed a group of old

houses dotting the hills up ahead. Beyond them, a small town. The houses had fenced-in yards, and people were sitting out on one of the porches. Bray couldn't believe her eyes, seeing as rural living was a thing of the past. At least so she had been taught.

As they approached a small road on the left that led to the houses, Bray slowed down. She turned onto the road. In the back yard sat three dogs. Suddenly Bray felt an unease, not unique from that she had sensed when she had first noticed the feral dogs.

"Maybe they can help us," Elliott said, sitting up in the back seat.

As much as she wanted to turn around, she couldn't. Elliott did need help, and now. She pulled the car up beside the house. The man and woman sitting on the porch stood up and stared down at them. They looked to be in their thirties, with long hair and dirty clothes.

"We need help," Bray called out the window, placing the car in park.

The man looked into the back of the car at

Elliott, said nothing.

"What do you need, sweetheart?" the woman asked, stepping down into the grass and stopping. She wore a long dress with pockets, her hands pushed into them.

"My friend's arm is injured."

"Well come on out, let's take a look."

Bray and Elliott stepped out of the car. Bray looked up at the man, who remained still on the porch. He eyed her as he took a few steps back and stood by the door.

"I hope we're not imposing," Bray said.

"Not at all, we just don't get much passersby through here is all," the woman replied. "Now let's take a look at that arm."

Elliott allowed the woman to lift his arm and carefully inspect it. Bray walked over and stood beside him, wanting to stay close.

"What happened to you, darlin'?" the woman asked.

"I was bit," he replied, wincing.

From where she stood, Bray could see into the back yard, at least halfway. The dogs had approached the fence and were looking at her. They were all black, the same kind of dogs as the ones that attacked them before.

"Bit by what?" the man suddenly blurted out.

Bray and Elliott both looked up at him. Bray felt hesitant to answer, and Elliott also remained silent.

"Wouldn't happen to be dogs, would it?" the man asked, stepping up to the edge of the porch.

"How'd you guess?" Elliott asked.

The woman let go of Elliott's arm, stepped back.

Bray glanced into the back yard again. The dogs were emaciated, despondent. They reminded her of how she often felt when she connected with Alice.

"A few of our dogs got away last night, been missing. You happen to see them?" the man asked.

Bray's face went flush. She didn't know what to say. The man kept his eyes on her. He slowly came down the porch steps. When he reached the grass, he stopped. His eyes shifted over to the driver's side of the car.

"That's a lot of blood on that...Marshal car," the man said slowly.

"That was from my arm," Elliott replied.

"Is that right?" the man said, approaching the vehicle and leaning down.

Now they could no longer see him. Bray grew anxious. She looked back at the dogs again. This time she could see bite scars on their necks and legs.

The man quickly stood, opened the car door. He glanced around inside.

"How'd you end up with this nice Marshal vehicle? And where's the Marshal?"

The woman turned away, stepped back up onto the porch. Meanwhile, the man leapt into the passenger seat and a moment later came out with a gun. The same gun Bray used to kill that dog.

"Look what we got here," he said, twirling it around and then pointing it at Bray and Elliott.

Bray's legs shook. She felt Elliott shivering behind her.

"You two have lots of explaining to do," the man said, and he slid his finger in and onto the trigger.

Chapter Thirty

Cole

Cole sat silently in the back of a private room, contemplating divorce. He tapped his fingers against the door handle. His scheduled press conference approached. He closed his eyes and thought. Maybe that could be his way out. Get elected and divorce her. There would be less hope for re-election. If he was going to do it, he would have to do it now. And even now, with the presidential election less than four years away, it could be too late. It would be seen as political, convenient. Dianna had all the power over him, and he knew it.

The implant in his forearm buzzed again. A notification in bold, capital letters: TAKE BLOOD PRESSURE MEDICATIONS. His medications were back at the office. He checked his vitals: 180/120. *Shit*. It would have to wait until after the press conference. There was no time.

The press conference was held on the first floor of the capital building. A set of reporters from each news station, along with journalists from The Denver Post, Denver Daily News, and The Denver Times, were all present. Cole gulped down a cup of room-temperature water and peeked out into the crowd from behind a curtain. The reporters were all mumbling amongst one another. Sweat built up on his palms and he rubbed his hands together. He eyed the podium and the microphone that was attached. He'd rather be doing a presentation to Congress than be subject to the press.

His cell phone vibrated. He stepped into a side hallway and took the call.

"Yes?" he asked.

"It's Thom, you called?"

"I did," Cole said, relieved. Thom an old friend from law school who had changed careers and gone into a private criminal justice sector. He knew of people who knew of other people. If anyone could find Bray and bring her back home before Dianna could, it was Thom.

"What's up man? Haven't heard from you in forever."

"I know. And I don't have a lot of time now. About to go into a press conference."

"What's going on?"

"I need your help. Bray escaped the psych ward."

"Jesus."

"Yeah. She's somewhere in Wyoming. She's with her best friend, Elliott, a Black guy about twenty-two years old. I need help finding her and bringing her back home before Dianna gets to her."

"Okay."

"Can you please help? I don't want Marshals involved at all."

"Yeah, man. Let me see what I can do."

"They're ready for you," a spokeswoman said from around the corner, waving Cole toward the conference room.

Cole hung up and turned off his phone. His breath was short. He stopped right outside the door and took a few deep breaths, then entered the room.

Cole stepped out into an array of flashing lights. He stopped at the podium and faced the crowd. He counted twenty people. He hadn't thought this news about his daughter would be such a big deal. His mind went blank. He looked down at his shoes. Took a deep breath. This was his tactic with each speech he gave. Lifting his head to the mic, he spoke.

"Good morning, everyone. Thank you for being here today. As you have heard, my daughter, Bray Hoffman, disappeared from the Denver Health Adolescent Psychiatric Unit two days ago," Cole said. Dianna wanted him to tell the press that Elliott kidnapped Bray, but he knew in his heart this was not true. He knew how much Bray hated that place and would've sought a way out with the first opportunity. Elliott was her opportunity, that was all.

"What do you mean, she disappeared?" one of the reporters started.

Here we go, Cole said to himself. His skin grew clammy. His head spun and he shook it off.

"She escaped the hospital and fled with her friend, Elliott Bansfield," he replied.

"We received word that she was kidnapped. Is that true?" another reporter's voice boomed. Cole's jaw began to ache.

"I'm not sure she was kidnapped," he said. The pain in his jaw moved to the space in between his shoulder blades. He couldn't focus.

"Why was your daughter in the psychiatric unit?"

"She has schizophrenia. She was there to be treated," he said, pushing the words out of his mouth.

"Do you have any idea where she is now, or if she's even safe?"

If she's even safe? The words repeated in his head over and over again. Was she safe? Anything could have happened in three days. Starvation. Dehydration. Out in the wilderness, dangerous animals. Elliott. No, wait. Elliott was her friend.

"Sir, are you okay?" he heard someone ask.

Cole cleared his throat.

"Authorities have tracked her in Wyoming. Please," he looked into the cameras, "if anyone sees her or knows of her whereabouts, please contact my office at..." Cole dashed off a series of numbers and the camera lights blinked furiously in his face. "And Bray, if you are watching this now, I just want you home safe. That's all. At least give me a sign that you're safe out there."

His heart palpitated and he broke down right there at the podium. In between his sobs, the pain moved to his chest and clenched it, squeezing and draining his heart of blood. Bray's name flashed through his mind, and everything went black.

Chapter Thirty-One

Bertan

Two days passed with aching, sleepless nights. Mostly Bertan dreamt of *La Bestia*. Memories of people falling asleep and then their bodies falling off the train would not let him rest. He tried to save them, but every time he got close, he'd wake up.

He feared returning home and hoped he wouldn't have to. He hoped and prayed that Julian would find them in San Pedro Sula, safe and sound. But it had been two days and he'd heard nothing.

Something felt off.

Bertan shook himself back to present. His limbs were heavy and begged for sleep. He didn't want to lie down. He couldn't stand another dream about *La Bestia*. His eyes had remained peeled open for days, and crevices of shadows hung beneath them, waiting.

Currently, he sat in the security office, his eyes fixed on the videos. His phone sat silently on the desk. He ran his hand busily through his hair. It had grown down past his ears. A haircut was not in his future now that he was out of money. His growing beard itched, and he scratched at his chin and cheeks. Over and over again he wondered if his family had been kidnapped, if he'd made a mistake in hiring Julian.

Finally he yanked his phone from the desk and dialed Julian. There was no dial tone. The call dropped. He tried again. Nothing. A third, fourth and fifth time produced the same result. Cringing and squeezing the phone in his hands, resisting the urge to throw it at the wall and listen to it break into a million pieces, he let out a scream.

Then a snap came from outside the office. Bertan froze, held his breath. Slowly, he turned in his chair and faced the office door, which opened out into the dim Kill Floor. Setting the phone down on the desk without a sound, he stood up. He pulled the

GLOCK from its holster and stepped out onto
the steel deck overlooking the Floor.
Scanning the facility, he waited, gun out
and ready to shoot.

"Hello?" His voice echoed across the
floor.

After a few moments of silence, he
returned the GLOCK to its holster and turned
back to the office. He picked up the phone
again and texted Julian:

DID YOU FIND MY FAMILY?

THIS IS BERTAN DUARTE

He hit *Send* and slid the phone into his
back pocket. Downstairs, he paced the Kill
Floor. He stayed away from the beef pens,
where most of them slept and those that did
not sat with their shiny eyes peering into
the darkness. No matter how their eyes tried
to pull him over to them, he resisted the
urge and turned away.

He entered the Clean Side, paced the
halls. Checking the phone became a game. Get
to one end of the hall, check again. Get to
the opposite end, check again. Over and over

again to pass the time that was left.

The hours that passed until morning were not like the hours that passed at his knock job. These hours were like the ones he'd spent as a Medina guard, waiting all night for his target to fall into place so he could complete his assassination.

When morning arrived, the air outside was stifling, unmoving, yet like a warm, comforting blanket wrapping around Bertan's body with the familiarity of home.

Home. That was a far-away concept now. There would be no going back there now. No matter what happened with his family, there'd be no going back.

On his way out to his car, he checked his phone for the hundredth time. Julian had not responded. This was the third time that he'd tried Julian and gotten no response.

In just a few hours, he'd be returning for his knock job. The ignition of his car turned with force. His foot pressed hard down on the gas pedal, down as far as it could go, an image of Merced burning in his mind. Merced was the one who had connected him with Julian. He would know something. He would have to know something.

Pulling into the hostel, the car jerked to a stop and Bertan jumped out. He entered the room where Merced was dressing for work. Coffee sat out on the table but he didn't need it. He felt plenty awake.

Bertan forwent a shower. No sense in getting clean only to get dirty again. And the dirtiness felt good, like an extra layer of protection over his skin.

Standing beside his bunk, he unbuttoned his shirt, loosened his belt and let his pants fall to his feet. He kicked off his shoes and the pants. He glanced over at Merced, kept his gaze there as he stood in his underwear.

"You all right, man?" Merced asked, meeting Bertan's eyes from across the room.

Bertan said nothing. His hands reached for a clean, white t-shirt beneath his mattress. He slid it on with a pair of blue jeans. Then his mind flipped the way a beef flips upside down after it gets through the knock box.

The Knocker stood there, waiting for Merced to exit the hostel. The Knocker grabbed his keys and stepped out behind him.

"Merced," he spoke, waving him over. "Let's talk."

"Sure." Merced shrugged, following the Knocker around the corner to the back of the hostel.

There, they stood on a concrete walkway across from a set of bushes that had long ago dried out from lack of rain. Above them the hostel rose forty feet to the roof. Windows covered in shut blinds dotted the building. The Knocker took note of all of this and then, squeezing his keys into his pocket, eyed Merced.

"How come I haven't been able to reach Julian?" the Knocker asked.

"Uh, I don't know," Merced replied, his arms dangling by his sides.

"I think you do. It's been days since I've heard from my wife. Did you set me up?"

"Set you up?" Merced laughed. "No man, I didn't set you up. Maybe something happened to your family—"

The Knocker reached out and grabbed Merced by the neck. His boot kicked Merced in the knee. Merced's leg gave, and the Knocker dropped him to the ground.

"C'mon man." Merced spat, his arms flailing.

The Knocker came to his knees over Merced. He released one hand and softened his grip on Merced's neck. Raising a fist in the air, he squeezed Merced's neck firmly.

"Where's my family?" he whispered.

Merced dropped his arms. His face changed. His lips curled into a closed smile. His eyes lit up. A laugh rose out of his teeth.

"Fucking son-of-a-bitch," the Knocker yelled. His fist came down on Merced's eye, and then the other. He wanted, needed to shut the light out of Merced's eyes. The eyes were forced shut by impact, bruised, wrinkles stretching out of them as Merced continued smiling. A heat rose from within the Knocker's belly and he came down hard on Merced's nose and mouth.

Merced started laughing.

The Knocker released his grip on Merced's neck. Both fists closed, his mind now free of thought, he went at Merced's face like he was tenderizing a piece of meat. It was nothing to him now but a bloodied, hot, wet mass of bone and flesh. Blood splattered onto his face. No different than knocking a beef. *Now I'll knock you and we'll see who walks away laughing.*

He forced two more blows to Merced's mouth. Teeth snapped off. Blood spilled out. Merced had gone unconscious at some point, but just to be sure, the Knocker gripped Merced by the hair and slammed his head onto the concrete.

Standing up, he glared down at the motionless body. He caught his breath as he wiped sweat and blood away from his face with his forearm. He wiped the blood from his hands onto his jeans to dry them off.

Bending down, he checked that Merced still had a pulse, and then he stood.

That would teach him not to mess with the Knocker again.

Chapter Thirty-Two

Kage

The next night came very slowly for Kage. Lana had not yet returned from her lawyer job, which was probably for the best. She wasn't going to be happy with him stealing a car and following the other activists, but he had to get answers. He'd deal with the consequences later.

The two activists, Sara and Andy, had geared up and left the cabin after everyone else had gone to sleep. Kage pretended to sleep on the couch. The door clicked shut and he shot up. He ran to the window and watched them get into a Honda Clarity.

Kage grabbed the keys to the red Prius from the kitchen drawer, quietly pulled on his boots and took an extra ski mask from the back table. Slipping quietly out the door, he ran for the car, unlocked it, and got into the driver's seat. He hadn't driven a car since Trevor took him out in the Jeep a few years ago. He thought about the motorcycle, hoped Trevor got home with it safely.

Kage started the car. Leaving the lights off, he started down the narrow drive. Just a half mile ahead, the Toyota was crawling along the path in front of him. It stopped at the main road and turned right.

Kage held back, turned right, and remained behind them with the lights off. As he passed the sign for Medicine Bow Mountains, he couldn't believe these activists had been living here, only 300 miles from Meeteetse. All this time and another set of activists was right under his nose. Could this mean there might be more?

Kage shook the notion out of his mind. No good to get his hopes up in a world like this. Hope had expired the year his parents disappeared.

The Clarity headed southwest. Out here in the dark of night, Kage guessed it would be rare to see another vehicle. Maybe some trucks, or Marshals. Probably drones circling the skies. Kage thought suddenly about Trevor, how he had said this world was no longer safe for people like them. Of course Trevor was right, but that didn't mean giving up. Like Ben said, they had to try. When more ecoterrorism laws were put into effect in 2029, any "stealing" of S-Corp property, like saving animals, became illegal. Smaller acts such as protesting, leafletting and the like were never illegal, but that didn't stop Marshals from putting a watch on people who did too much of it. Leafletting and protesting were to the ecoterrorism bill what people said marijuana was to other drugs: a gateway to even more "criminal" acts. And so over time, as Ethan had told him, more and more activists were arrested preemptively, to prevent worse "crimes" from ever happening. Most activists didn't have money for decent legal representation, so they'd end up in prison or with citations on their records, making it challenging to find work. S-Corp knew how to hit activists where it hurt, just like activists had nearly done to them.

And S-Corp had won.

Kage followed the Clarity along the Wyoming landscape. He'd never realized how alone it felt out here. Back home he would go outside at night and stand beneath the stars. They'd hang so low it was like they were lights hanging from the ceiling. And the stars bundled up like firm, clear pieces of a larger puzzle, that when put together made up everything. And because they always stood alone, yet so close together, they provided a sense of wholeness while being apart. Like how his mom used to say everyone was connected though you couldn't see it. And standing there beneath them made him feel separate but still a part of the puzzle, and so he never felt alone.

But out here, as he drove deeper into places he'd never been, he could see the stars now as deep holes where inside there was emptiness, and to connect them together now would only lead to one enormous question. One massive, white space where answers were supposed to be. He thought about his mom, and he teared up. His hands rubbed at the steering wheel. He pulled one away and pushed the tears from his eyes.

Then, a mile up, the Clarity turned. Kage shifted his attention back to the present and turned behind them. The Clarity slowed, as did he. About a quarter of a mile ahead, a line of orange dots poked out of the dark. Kage came to a stop. Upon a closer look, his eyes made out the lines of a single-level building.

"S-Corp," he whispered.

The Clarity disappeared into a field of grass. Kage backed the Prius into the same field, but one hundred yards from the Clarity. He shut off the engine. Sara and Andy got out of their car and started up the road.

Kage slid the black ski mask over his head. Now only his eyes could be seen through a rectangular slit. He stepped out of the car, bent down, and slowly shut the

door. He crawled away from the car and
neared the road. Ahead, Andy and Sara
continued walking.

Kage stayed in the grass. Its blades came
only to his calves, but if he needed to hide
he could do so more easily here than beside
the road.

Bending down, he started walking. He
followed behind until he neared the S-Corp
facility just across the street. A large
sign stood outside the fence, the S-Corp
insignia painted on it. He had heard the
activists say it was a chicken processing
plant. No sign called it what it really was.

Andy and Sara walked up to the front of
the building and stopped at the doors, spoke
their names into an intercom. If Kage was
going to get in, he'd have to be quick. He
made a run for the parking lot, where two
cars sat side by side. Kage ran up and hid
behind one. Andy and Sara disappeared into
the building. He wanted in, but how?

Above him, a light shown down on the cars.
He wondered if S-Corp had security cameras

out there but had no way of knowing. He hoped not.

As Kage slid around to the side of the car, he peeked around the bumper. The building was quiet. He had no idea what went on inside, but he could guess from all the stories he'd been told. This was the closest he'd ever come to S-Corp. Goose flesh ran up his arms. He went cold despite the night air being pleasant.

A sound came from the other side of the car. A kind of crunching, like boots on gravel. Kage gulped, and slowly lifted his head over the hood of the car. A guard caught his eyes. He quickly ducked his head.

Crap. He thought. *Now what?*

The guard drew closer. He could sense it. If he didn't make a run for the Prius in the field, he'd be caught.

And so he crawled away from the cars in the parking lot. Once he was out of the light's gleam, he stood up and ran for his life.

Chapter Thirty-Three

Bray

A warm, running sensation melted down Bray's lower back. It moistened her pants, slipped inside her underwear and down her legs like a slow-moving stream of blood. As it coursed downward, a piercing pain stung her back.

The blister from her burn wound had burst. The pain made her want to scream, but a gun was pointed at her chest, so she clamped her jaw together to stop any noise from getting out.

"Look sir," Elliott said. "If that was your dog that bit me, we had no idea. We were chased by a couple of them. The Marshal car was just sitting there on the highway. We ran, got in it, and one of the dogs caught my arm through the window."

"Then what?" the man asked, one eye closed while he aimed point-blank at

Elliott.

Bray heard rustling coming from the
back of the house. Clinking sounds followed
by huffing. She wanted to turn her head and
look at the dogs, but she dared not move. If
she did, the gun would surely go off. The
dogs barked and she jumped. A little urine
came out and leaked onto her underwear. She
thought to close her eyes and get a sense of
the dogs, but she was too afraid to even do
that. What if the dogs were just as feral
and nasty as the others? Reaching out to
them might not be a good idea.

"We drove off," Bray said, lying. "That
was it. We saw your houses and were just
coming for help. He's going to lose his arm
if it's not treated."

"Well, ain't that too bad," the man
said, unwavering.

Clearly these people were not going to
help. The woman was now standing on the
porch with her arms crossed. Bray had to do
something. Elliott needed help, and this guy
wasn't going to give it to him.

Without closing her eyes, Bray tried focusing her attention on the dogs. Elliott and the man exchanged words, and Bray ignored them. She sensed the animals were in a state of unrest, but not because they wanted to harm Bray or Elliott. They were starved, abused. Suddenly an image of a dog chained up in the yard popped into her mind. Its leg was in the mouth of another dog—a dog whose face she recognized as the one she shot.

She attempted to communicate with the dogs: *maybe we can help each other out of this*. She waited. What she received was some strange feedback loop—like the fuzz from a far-off radio station—and then a series of flashbacks. The dogs were sending her memories. Memories of fighting, being whipped into shape by this man who held a gun on her and Elliott.

Her eyes turned to the man, who still stood with the gun on them. In her mind she called for the dogs to jump the fence, make a run for it. One of them was still chained up, but the other two were not. For now, Bray would have to set aside the concern that she was using animals to her own advantage. She instead encouraged them to get out, then maybe it would be enough of a distraction for her and Elliott to get away, too.

"Let's help each other," she repeated in her mind.

More shuffling from the backyard. The woman turned from her spot on the porch. The gun remained steady on Elliott. One of the dogs yelped.

"Shut up, Merl," the woman yelled back to them. She grabbed a broom from the corner of the porch and shook it at them. "Don't make me come back there."

They growled in response. Bray's heart raced. She hoped they weren't growling at her. They disappeared from her view. More shuffling. The chain clattered.

And then she saw them. They leapt the fence. As their back legs cleared the top of it, she remembered seeing that first dog jump clear over her head, down onto the Marshal. She and Elliott turned in unison. The two dogs ran at them. Bray shook in fear.

Not again, she thought.

Then the dogs turned the corner of the house, running past Bray and Elliott. Their bodies shuffled around the car. They jumped the man. The gun went off. Bray and Elliott jumped in response.

"Run," she shouted to Elliott.

They turned and ran away from the house.

"God damn it," the man yelled from behind.

Elliott fell behind Bray as she ran faster. She ran as fast as she could, feeling the wound pound at her back. Looking back past Elliott, Bray saw the dogs running in the opposite direction. She slowed, feeling encouraged, and grabbed Elliott's hand. They ran together.

Soon they were a good distance away

from the houses. They slowed to a stop. She turned and saw the houses as small specks. The highway remained close beside them like a good friend. She caught her breath and came down to her knees.

Looking back at the houses, she watched the dogs continue toward a set of hills. They were black ants dotting the prairie. Probably they'd be okay out in the wild. Better than being chained up and beaten, forced to fight until death.

She thought of Alice. If Alice could be free, even if she was near death, she could die in peace. In nature. Free.

"My backpack," Elliott said, coming up behind her.

"What about it?" she asked, staring at the small town in the distance. Her thoughts on the dogs, on Alice, switched back to Elliott.

"Most of my money was in there."

"Most?"

"I've got some on me, but yes. I took out all my cash from the bank, to disappear."

"Why?" she asked, looking up at him.

"You know why," he said, holding his arm.

Bray thought a moment. Back in Denver, Elliott had a well-paying job with Embedicare. He made lots of money. So why would he leave? She glanced at his arm, now worried he wasn't going to make it much longer. If Elliott died, she wouldn't be able to fathom such a loss. She'd never be able to forgive herself. Already she wasn't sure she could, for all that had happened to him since she joined him. She'd always wonder how much different his life could be right now, and their friendship, had none of this ever happened.

And that's when it hit her. His parents. He believed S-Corp was responsible for their deaths. Maybe he was a conspiracy theorist, or maybe he was right. He'd spent years online, trying to find truths. But truth was never found online. This Bray knew, even at her inexperienced age. Truth was only found out here, away from technology. That's another reason she had to get out. And maybe Elliott had to get out, too. To find his own truth.

"Come on," she said, standing up and looking at the town just ahead. It appeared both ominous and quaint. The fact that she was even considering taking Elliott there made her question herself, but her instincts were strong. When she turned to face the town, they grew stronger. It wasn't something she'd ever experienced before. "Let's get you some help, for real this time."

"I couldn't agree more," he said, shivering.

Chapter Thirty-Four

Kage

A gunshot pierced the air. Kage jumped but kept running. He glanced back. The guard was chasing, catching up.

This dude's fast, he thought, picking up his pace.

Kage wasn't a runner. His exercise consisted of pulling weeds, pushing wheelbarrows, lifting heavy rocks. This level of cardio was new for him, and it was starting to show. His breath was heavy. His heart pounded through his rib cage.

The guard approached, gun pointed. The Prius came into view. Kage laughed with relief. He pulled the keys from his pocket. He gripped them, ran to the car and opened the door.

Another gunshot. The windshield cracked. Shaking, Kage jumped inside the car. The door slammed closed. The guard stopped just past the bumper. He pointed the gun at Kage.

"I've got your ass," the guard yelled.

Kage ducked down. He pushed the key into the ignition and turned the engine on. He revved the engine, hoping it would scare the guy off.

The guard didn't move.

Kage didn't want to injure the man, but if the guy didn't move, then this was on him.

Kage put the car in drive. He slammed down on the gas, ducking as low as possible. He could just see the man over the dashboard.

The car jutted forward. The guard jumped out of the way, landing in the grass. Kage sat up and looked back. The guy stood up, shot the car's brake light out.

"Damn it!" Kage screamed.

He sped past Andy's car and kept going. He had no idea how to get back to Medicine Bow. He turned on the screen beside the steering wheel. Had to be a GPS installed in this thing.

"What can I help you with today?" a man's voice spoke.

"Uh, get me to Medicine Bow Mountains, please," Kage yelled.

"Medicine Bow Mountains, Wyoming," the voice replied. A map popped up on the screen. The voice began directing him back to the cabins.

"Thank the unicorns!" Kage said, taking a deep breath.

Now to figure out how he would explain himself once he returned with a damaged car that wasn't even his.

#

When Kage pulled up the driveway to the cabins, he shut off the headlights. His heart pounded. He hoped everyone was asleep. Maybe he could play dumb, act like it wasn't him who got the windshield and brake light shot up.

Kage parked the car in the exact spot it he'd found it. The cabins were dark. Lana's car was parked closest to the porch. He wasn't someone who prayed, but right now he prayed she'd never find out.

Before stepping up onto the porch, he pulled off his boots. He carried them in his hand while walking up to the cabin door. Gripping the door handle, he turned it. He sighed with relief that it was still unlocked. As he tiptoed in, he pressed the door closed behind him, and waited.

Nothing. All dark, quiet. Everyone asleep. Kage set his boots down by the door. He started for the couch.

"Hello?" Tori's voice came from down the hall.

Kage quickly pulled off his jacket and threw it on the floor.

"Just me," he called back, sitting down on the couch.

Tori appeared in the kitchen. She looked over at Kage, then flipped on the light.

"Where you been?" she asked, rubbing her eyes.

"Me? Nowhere," Kage replied, sitting back on the couch. "I just grabbed a snack."

"No, you were gone. I know you took the Prius." Tori placed her hands on her hips.

Uh-oh.

Kage froze, tried to think up something.

"I get alerts on my phone anytime one of our cars starts," she said.

Well shit, Kage thought.

"So...where did you go?"

There was no denying it any longer.

"I followed Sara and Andy out to the S-Corp facility."

"And why?" Tori asked. She walked over to the kitchen cabinet, reached for a cup. She poured herself a cup of water from a filtered pitcher that sat lonely on the counter.

"I thought maybe I could get some info, on my parents."

"I see." Tori nodded, gulping down the entire glass of water and setting it beside the sink. "Well, we'll talk about this with Lana. For now, I can tell you, you're in deep shit."

Tori disappeared down the hall. Kage

looked over at the door. He could make a run for it, but he had nowhere to go. He'd have to face Lana, see if he could make her understand.

Tori retuned to the kitchen, cell phone out. She lifted it to her ear.

"Yeah, he's back," Tori said. "You wanna come over?"

A moment later, she hung up, walked over to the couch and sat down across from Kage.

"We helped you out. This is how you repay us?" Tori said.

Before Kage could apologize, the front door opened. There, Lana stood in her pajamas, staring down at Kage.

"What the hell?" she said, her voice sharp. "The windshield and brake light look like they've been shot."

"Yeah, I'm really sorr-"

"Sorry doesn't cut it," Lana interrupted. She shut the door and walked over to the couches.

Kage remained silent. She was upset, and

she had every right to be.

"I can't believe you took one of our cars without telling us, and then you followed our people and nearly got yourself killed," Lana said, raising her voice.

"Can I tell you why I did it?" Kage asked.

"It doesn't matter. We helped you out, brought you here, fed you and gave you a place to stay," she replied, then stopped. She turned away.

Kage sensed she was getting emotional. He stood up and walked over to her.

"Look, I'm really sorry," he replied. He reached for her arm. She pushed his hand away.

"I messed up. If there's any way I can make up for it, please tell me."

"You can leave," Tori said, grimacing at Kage from the couch.

Kage's shoulders slumped. He turned to Lana, tried looking into her eyes but she was still turned away.

"Is that what you want?" he asked Lana.

She nodded silently, then turned back to

him. She crossed her arms.

"I have nowhere to go," he answered. He thought to go back home, but that would just be another dead end. He still needed to find out about his parents.

"You should've thought of that before you went out on your little adventure," Lana said coldly.

"You're right. I admit I can be impulsive," Kage replied.

"I'll take you down to Cheyenne in the morning, drop you off," Tori said, standing up and walking back to the room she shared with Andy.

"I really thought you were something, Kage. With your background, having lost your parents. Of all people, you should know how dangerous it is to go out there alone. They could've traced you back here, and then what? You put all our lives at risk tonight, and you've really disappointed me," Lana said, stepping back from him.

Kage felt a deep pit sink from his heart into his stomach. The last thing he wanted was to mess up any chance he had with Lana, and now that ship had sailed. He stood there quietly, knowing there was nothing he could say to make this better. What was done, was done.

Lana walked over to the back table and picked up a card. She walked over to Kage and held it out to him.

"Here's my email. You can stay in touch through that. I do care about you, and I want you to stay safe out there. We just can't have people like you working with us."

People like me? he asked himself.

Kage took the card and slid it into his pocket. He watched Lana exit the cabin. Standing there alone in the kitchen, he felt a sense of regret. Not about going out there, but he wished he hadn't gone behind her back, hurting Tori and Lana like he did.

He lay down on the couch and tried to sleep but only looked up at the ceiling, playing the conversation with Lana over and over in his head. If he ever saw her again, he'd be shocked.

All that was left for him now was what he'd come out here for in the first place: to find his parents. He'd been sidetracked by Lana's beauty, enamored with her, and now he had hurt her. He should never have come here. He was better off alone—and they were better off without him anyway.

Chapter Thirty-Five

Bray

Elliott's body shook with fever. Sweat drenched his clothes. They walked along an open prairie of sage brush, now only a mile or so from the town. His shivering grew into a kind of shake as they walked. Bray stopped. She pulled off the sweater he had given her and pulled it on over him.

She wrapped her arm around his torso to help him along. It was clear his wound had become infected. The sun was dropping fast, as was the temperature.

It was becoming more and more apparent to Bray that, if she listened to her instinct, she could be guided. Not only could she link with Alice and connect with other animals, but now that she had been fully off of medications for a couple of days, she found that she had an internal compass that led her, if she really paid attention.

The thing she knew about infections was that they could, eventually, kill a person if left untreated. She didn't know how much time Elliott had or how long it would take to get him help.

She closed her eyes.

Please, her thoughts begged. *Whatever you are, whoever you are, that's guiding me. Please help us find safety. Please.*

Bray suddenly noticed how hungry she was. And thirsty. It wasn't her stomach that told her. It was the light-headedness. The sudden and immense clarity. Lightness. She squeezed Elliott's side.

"Just a little farther to go," she said, trying to reassure the both of them.

He looked at her, but in his eyes he was somewhere else.

Bray continued toward the town. With her arm around him, they both wobbled back and forth, nearly fell. His weight on hers was substantial. Eventually, she regained some balance and he began to walk with her.

In plain afternoon, she could hear

nothing but the occasional whistle of the wind, a bird flapping through the sky. The sun hovered like a watchful eye behind her. It was strange, how the town had no sign of life. No people walking around, no traffic. Nothing. A complete ghost town. There were cars by the sides of the roads, but they were decades old and clearly hadn't been moved in that long. The buildings were quiet, empty, some of them boarded up.

She gulped, but kept on.

Questioning every step as she trembled from the quiet and from fear, she couldn't resist the call. It felt like a warm hand closed around her heart, firmly pulled. The pull was so strong that she felt if she stopped walking, her heart might be pulled right from her chest.

Soon they came upon a dry river bed. Its width could easily hold three or four cars. She wanted to get closer, see how far down the empty bed went, but it was far too eerie to get any closer. She shivered as the river bed guided her along into a suburb of houses.

"Elliott, look," she said quietly.

Elliott raised his head and nodded at the houses.

Continuing on, she allowed herself to be led along the streets. There were no cars. Still no lights. No real or artificial grass. Everything was dry and dead. The houses were intact, but she got the sense there were no people in them. Her heart stopped beating a moment. She held her breath.

The pull inside of her grew stronger. It was intense, like being inside a moving car and being driven somewhere. The walking happened automatically. Something else had taken over and was guiding her along.

Then, she was halted. The instinct just withered away. There they were, standing in the middle of the road in this strange suburb, something she'd only seen in history books. She turned to face one of the houses. Nothing. She felt something behind her. With Elliott hanging on beside her, she turned again. His sweat permeated her clothing.

The instinct returned.

"There," a voice said.

"What?" she whispered to herself.

It was just a house. Empty driveway. Closed windows. Yellow siding. A white garage door. Dead tree in the front yard.

And then Elliott dropped to the ground. Bray came down to her knees, the wound in her back stinging from the weight of Elliott's fall.

"Elliott!" she yelled.

He was unresponsive.

Chapter Thirty-Six

Dianna

Dianna stood quietly at her desk, a white L-shape with a glass top. She had a corner office with ceiling-to-floor windows looking out over the city of Denver. She had been working since 6 a.m. on a budget for the Wyoming Extraction Project. They would need to hire more workers for distillation, filtration and a variety of other jobs. The undocumented workers were the best, and cheapest.

A chat box blinked in the lower right of her laptop's screen. It was Carl Florez, S-Corp's Regional Midwest President. Dianna's equal, her counterpart. Carl was fifty years old but didn't look a day over thirty-five. He was of Hispanic descent and came from a family of migrant workers who all worked for S-Corp, so it was only natural that he'd follow suit and end up in leadership. He had been doing this work much longer than Dianna, and he had taken her under his wing as a mentee.

She went to answer a question he had about the budget spreadsheet when her phone vibrated beside her. She picked it up from its place atop the clear desk and glared at it. S-Corp Security had texted her a series of images: aerial views of some ecoterrorist nearly getting caught by a guard at their Hanna facility.

The text read:

CHECK YOUR EMAIL

Dianna switched over to her email app on the phone. Maybe she should've felt nervous that an activist could get this close to their facility, but instead, her heart lifted. Finally, they could put a name to at least one of them.

The email from Security contained a video. She pressed play. Her mouth dropped open as she watched. Drones had followed a Prius Prime into the Medicine Bow Mountains.

There, the activist entered one of two cabins.

"What's this?" Dianna whispered.

She exited the email and called Dan.

"What are these images I'm seeing?" she asked.

"We're still looking into it, but I think we found the activists' hideout."

"Brilliant," Dianna replied. A smile grew on her face.

It wasn't that she had something against activists. Everyone really should have the right to speak their truth. But truth was subjective, different for everyone. Every day she passed protesters right outside the building, but she just ignored them. They were harmless.

It was when people started directly attacking S-Corp, going after them economically, that was when things got serious. S-Corp was the nation's only food and water industry. Dianna didn't see anyone else out there trying to solve the nation's food crisis. These damn ecoterrorists didn't understand the harm they were causing.

"Can you find out their identities?" she asked.

"On it," Dan replied.

"And find the exact location of those cabins."

"Sure thing. Let me get off here so we can do some digging."

Dianna hung up. She walked over to a pair of geometrically-shaped lounge chairs and sat down in one of them. Across from them rested a lounge couch that doubled as a bed. That was where she slept most nights.

Twelve years ago, when Walker was assassinated and all the ecoterrorists lost their power, Dianna was thirty-three. She'd been coming up in S-Corp as the Regional West Director of Future Initiatives. She didn't know then what she knew now. Sometimes knowledge was a curse. Dianna believed its absence kept the country safe. Citizens didn't want "truth." They thought they did, but it would only get in the way of what they thought the truth really was.

So people like her, people in positions of power, made up truths.

The cell phone vibrated. This time it was ringing. Dianna rolled her eyes and stood up. Returning to the desk, she saw it was the Denver Marshals.

"Yes?" she answered.

"Mrs. Hoffman, this is Chief Thomas. I have an update."

"Go ahead." She felt a sudden dread, that maybe something had happened to Bray.

"One of our Marshals is dead. Appears to have been a dog attack. Bray and Elliott got away, stole the Marshal's vehicle."

"Jesus. Her meds must be wearing off," Dianna said quietly.

"What's that?"

"Nothing. Go ahead."

"We were able to track the vehicle to Douglas, but it was left at some outlander's house. Outlanders were arrested but Bray and Elliott were nowhere to be found."

"What? Again? How do you keep losing my daughter?" She grew irate.

"Listen, Mrs. Hoffman. With all due respect, we just lost one of our men out there."

"Of course, I'm sorry," she said, pausing. "Is there anything else you can do?"

"We've got drones tracking them. They've made a stop in Casper."

"They're getting farther and farther away," Dianna said.

"Well, now that we know where they've stopped, I can send Marshals out to get them."

"No," Dianna said. She remembered how ineffective the Marshals were back at the checkpoint. If Bray and Elliott could get past all those drones and Marshals, and then somehow cause another Marshal to lose his life, who knew what they were—no, what Elliott was—capable of.

"Just keep tracking them. I want you sending me their location coordinates every hour on the hour," Dianna demanded.

"Yes ma'am," Marshal Thomas said, and

ended the call.

Dianna was disturbed by what she heard about the Marshal's death. Had to be Elliott. Bray was only a danger to herself. She wasn't capable of harming anyone. Dianna always found her daughter to be quite gentle, almost weak and in constant need of reassurance.

She took after Cole.

Dianna flipped back over to her texts. Cole had sent one an hour ago and she hadn't responded. Something about how he'd found out Bray was in Wyoming. *No shit, Sherlock,* she said to herself. Apparently he'd also hired men to go looking for her, which meant she had to hurry up and get to Bray before he did. If he had his way, Bray would be at home and not in a facility. She often thought of divorcing Cole so she could get full custody of Bray. Cole couldn't prove to a judge that he'd be around enough to care for Bray. Too busy with his political life.

She moved over to the windows and looked down at the protesters by the building's entrance. She called Dan.

"I want you to keep on those activists," she said. "But I also need a couple security men pulled. I need them to take me to Bray, help me get her home."

"That's not official S-Corp business, though," Dan replied.

"Then I'll pay out of pocket for it."

"Okay. What are we talking here?"

"I'm not sure exactly. The Marshals tracked Bray and Elliott to Casper. I need to get up there as soon as possible. I can't trust the Marshals."

"Helicopter would be fastest," Dan replied.

"When can we leave out?"

"I have to see what we've got available. Where can we pick you up? Needs to be a discreet location," Dan said.

"I know just the place. I'll send you coordinates."

Dianna hung up. She pulled up the exact coordinates of the S-Corp facility in Fort Collins. She held onto the phone and turned back to the window. The Rocky Mountains hung around the horizon like an unknown yet familiar presence. *Like when you know something is coming,* she thought, *but you don't know what. And you don't know if you're supposed to be afraid or excited.*

Dianna chose to feel determined, confident. A feeling that she was right about Bray and would soon have her back in Denver. She returned to her desk and sent a chat to Carl:

I HAVE A FAMILY EMERGENCY-IT'S BRAY.

I'LL NEED A FEW DAYS OFF. CAN YOU COVER ON THIS END FOR ME?

Carl: YES OF COURSE. I'M IN KANSAS THIS WEEK SO I CAN HOP OVER IF NEED BE.

Dianna took a deep breath of relief. She shut off the laptop, exited the office, and headed out to be bombarded by pointless protestors.

Chapter Thirty-Seven

The Knocker

The lunch bell rang, taking the Knocker by surprise. Six hours had disappeared. He didn't know what had happened to the time, didn't really care. His mind was set on finding his family, and now he would stop at nothing to do it.

He dismantled his goggles, smock and gloves. Outside, he stood with Serpentine, holding a plate of food he didn't remember ordering from the food truck. He tried eating but wasn't interested. Wasting no time, he turned to Serpentine.

"I need to make fast cash," he whispered.

"Okay. This about your family?" Serpentine asked, biting into a blackened sausage.

"Yes. I need to get home."

"Hm," Serpentine said, looking the Knocker over, "maybe you can help me out."

Yes, like when I worked for Medina, he

said to himself. *Did I ever stop working for them?*

Confused, the Knocker glanced around the lot. Men stood in groups beside the food truck. Some of them kept looking at him, giving him cold stares. They whispered amongst themselves. It was about him, how he beat Merced to near death.

"You okay, buddy?" Serpentine asked.

Suddenly it felt like days had passed, like he was losing time and soon he'd run out altogether, and then his family would be lost for good.

"How long we been out here?" he asked, nervous.

"Just a few minutes. What's wrong with you? You're so on edge lately. Wait." Serpentine grinned. "I know. I bet you haven't fucked in ages. You just need to get yourself off, man. How 'bout later I bring out one of the ladies? They're already on all fours." He laughed.

"Fuck you, man. Just tell me what to do and I'll do it."

Serpentine walked over to the food truck and returned with a pen and a piece of paper.

"I got some guys that owe me money," he said, jotting something down. "They all work here." He handed the paper to the Knocker.

The Knocker studied the five names. He knew three of them from the Kill Floor. Serpentine's handwriting caused him pause for a moment. It was tiny, scratchy, barely legible. And it was all in caps.

"You get each of them to give you $1,000 and I'll give you half," Serpentine said. "I need to leave town for a week, so you can get it all for me while I'm away."

"Write that down," the Knocker replied. He'd done things like this enough times to know you always get the agreement in writing.

Serpentine rolled his eyes, took the paper, and scribbled on it, adding his signature.

"There, you happy?" he said, handing the paper back.

Then the Knocker saw it. As Serpentine handed him the piece of paper, a tattoo ran across his knuckles. The word FALCON, all in caps. Just like the tattoo The Knocker had on his arm.

Only men who worked for Medina got that tattoo. But then again, Serpentine *did* work for the cartel. It was possible he was a falcon for the cartel and not for Medina.

The Knocker shrugged it off, and spoke. "Perfect. I'll have the money to you when you return."

#

More hours disappeared. The beefs moved through, same as always. The ease and familiarity of this job allowed the Knocker's mind to go...to blank and to get completely lost in the loud music between his ears. His head was so immersed in the job that it took a moment to realize the line had stopped.

The Knocker looked up at the empty knock box, wondering where the next beef was. He turned to the serpentine. Down at the far

end, a beef held up the line. It whimpered
and heaved. The Knocker stepped back and
lifted his goggles for a better view.

The beef came down onto its two front
legs, its knees pressing against the
concrete floor. Serpentine held a metal pole
with a metal rope attached at the other end.
He forced the rope around the beef's neck
and tightened it, holding the beef down
against the ground. Its hind legs were up to
standing, and they trembled.

Two other men kicked at the beef's side.

"Come on fucking cunt," one of them
yelled. He kicked the beef in the mouth and
then laughed. He kicked again. The beef let
out a deep howl in response, but did not
move.

Within a matter of seconds, red liquid,
maybe blood, fell out of the beef's back
end, followed by the slimy body of a baby
calf. The damn thing was pregnant.

The Knocker's hands dropped. He stood
there in disbelief, his heart going still
beneath his ribs. One of the pen workers

pulled the calf away by its leg and lifted it into the air, swinging it around, showing it to everyone on the floor. The calf screamed, covered in blood and birth. The beef called back in response, the rope squeezing more tightly around her neck.

No. Its neck. It's a beef, nothing more.

The beef lifted itself up on all fours. The worker disappeared outside with the calf. There by the back door, which stood slightly ajar, the bright, blinding sun peering into the death of day, that little naked boy reappeared.

The Knocker, stunned, stared at the little boy, who was peeking out the door. The Knocker wanted to run after him, but he couldn't move.

The beef mooed and it stirred his ears. It whaled back and forth. Serpentine pulled violently on the metal stick. The beef fell to the ground in response, her head on its side on the concrete.

Its head.

The Knocker tried to move, but his feet

stuck to the bloody, sticky floor beneath him. The Knocker felt himself beside the boy —yet he hadn't moved. A gunshot rang outside and the boy jumped back, startled. He fell to the ground, crying.

Then the Knocker felt something inside, but he couldn't recognize it. It was sickening and harsh and wounded, and he evaded the sensation by turning away from the boy and setting his eyes the beef, who now lay still on the ground, its tongue hanging from its mouth. Its body was dragged out of the facility by a lift driver and that was the end of it.

The Knocker turned back to his job, awaiting the next beef. Out of the corner of his eye he saw the boy had disappeared. He swallowed hard, forcing down the ache in his chest. Clenching his jaw, he eased back into knocking beefs.

The last time he saw that little boy, he was in Bajo Aguan, on an abandoned palm oil plantation. The place was abandoned because he'd made it so. The boy was all that was left. His life was spared because he was innocent and would always remember what happened.

That was the last thing the Knocker thought about before time disappeared again.

Chapter Thirty-Eight

Kage

The drive south to Cheyenne was uncomfortably quiet. At times Kage attempted to talk to Tori, asking her questions about herself, but mostly he got one-word answers. He could tell the woman did not want to converse.

And so, when Tori pulled up at the exact location they'd first met, he expected that the goodbye would be brief, if there was any goodbye at all.

"I hate to ask this," Kage said. "But I have no money. Can you at least give me something to grab food?"

"Man, you about ruined one of our cars, to say the least," Tori replied.

"Technically it was the guard that did that," Kage said, trying to be amusing.

Tori looked at him, then at the passenger door.

"Okay. Well, it really was nice to meet you. And I really am sorry," Kage said, opening the door.

Tori did not reply. Kage got out and shut the door. He watched her drive off.

Kage stepped up onto the sidewalk and glanced around the city. It was mid-afternoon and the sun was hiding behind a white sky. The scent of rain touched his nose. It must've just rained. People passed by him wearing their masks, many holding umbrellas above their heads.

Somehow he would need to get a job. Something under the table. He turned and started up Bent Avenue, passing storefronts and a line of apartment buildings. There was nothing in a place like this for Kage. He felt suffocated, almost a bit claustrophobic, with all these people and buildings bearing down on him. He needed to make some money quick and get the fuck out of there.

He crossed the street and passed a street musician sitting on an egg crate. He was playing a set of Djembes. Behind him, a parking garage took cars in from the street— which gave Kage an idea.

"Excuse me," he asked the drummer. "Do you know where the nearest mechanic shop is?"

"Mechanic shop?" the man replied. His face was worn, either sunburnt or wind, Kage couldn't tell.

"A place I can get my car fixed."

"Oh. Up on Lincolnway, about three blocks down."

"All righty, thank you," Kage said. "Sorry I can't give you anything. I'm homeless."

The man only nodded, then turned his attention to the drums.

Kage walked three blocks through the city and found the auto repair shop on the corner of West Lincolnway. He stepped into its lot and observed the place.

It looked a bit shady, but maybe this was what all car repair places looked like. Hell if he knew. It was fenced in, and the red brick building housed two open garages.

Inside, one car was on a lift, holding steady ten feet off the ground. A pair of mechanics stood under it, surveying its exposed parts. If Kage were that car he'd feel extremely violated right about now.

Kage shook off the thought and approached the office door. He stepped inside. At the counter across from him sat an overweight woman, probably in her mid-sixties, staring at a computer screen. To his left stood a mechanic, a tall, toothpick of a man with curly black hair.

"Can we help you?" the woman said, peering over at Kage.

"Yes," Kage said, smiling and approaching the desk. "I'm looking for a job."

"Ha," the man spat out a laugh.

Kage stopped and glared at him.

"Brian, be nice," the woman said and stood up. "We're not hiring right now sweetie, I'm sorry."

"Not even for manual labor? Cleaning? I'll do anything. And I'm really good at fixing cars."

"Hmm," Brian responded flatly. He looked Kage over and said, "Sorry kid, but like she said, we're not hiring."

Kage's shoulders slumped. He exited the building and stopped to watch the mechanics in the garage. The skeleton of a motorcycle hung in the back of the garage. Looked to be one that had been totaled in a wreck and was being put back together.

Kage admired the bike for a moment and then returned his attention to the mechanics. They were working on a Chevy Tahoe. It was still up on a lift. The men were checking the tires. One of the mechanics was rubbing his chin and said something about the front tires binding when the owner turned the steering wheel.

Kage walked up to the mechanic and spoke.

"Have you checked the actuator?" he asked.

"Huh? Who are you?" the mechanic replied, looking Kage up and down.

"Just a person looking for a job. I know a thing or two about cars and thought maybe you looked perplexed."

"She may be right," another mechanic replied from beneath the car. Kage cringed, but said nothing. He figured they assumed he was a woman by the sound of his voice.

The mechanics lowered the Chevy to the ground. One of them got in the driver's side, checked around beneath the dash, and got back out.

"Yep. I think that's it," he replied.

Brian entered the garage from a side door that led from the office.

"Is there a reason you're still here?" he asked, looking at Kage.

"She helped us fix the Chevy," one of the men said.

Kage cringed again. He thought to correct the man's misgendering, but if he wasn't going to work here or see them again, there was no point. It still stung and burned in his chest, but he just swallowed and said nothing.

Kage turned to Brian and looked him in the eye.

"You sure you're not hiring?" he asked.

"I suppose we could find some work for you," Brian said.

"It's the least we can do," the other mechanic added.

"What's your name?" Brian asked.

Kage paused and rummaged through names in his head. His dead name was Alexa, so he just made a quick change.

"Alex," Kage replied. "I'm just looking for something under the table. You can pay me cash, just a few hours a week, whatever you need."

Brian looked Kage over again. His eyebrows shifted. "All right, but if you try to rob us, I'll hunt you down like there's no tomorrow."

"Deal," he said, smiling, and offered his hand.

Brian shook his hand, the sweat from Brian's palm transferring to his and causing him temporary disgust.

#

Three days passed. Kage was given his first $400 payment. Not enough to get a room, which was why he ended up sleeping behind the shop every night. But he managed to get a few cans of food and some water. The rest he used to purchase a tablet and a wi-fi drive.

He sat now in the breakroom at work. He'd sent a message to Lana two days ago, saying he'd found work and was okay. There was no reply. The screen stared back at him with an empty box below his message where Lana should've written something. There was no denying he had feelings for her, which only deepened the sting when she didn't respond.

Closing out of the social media account he'd created to connect with her, he brought up Quest. There he'd saved the website for S-Corp's regional office, located 120 miles away in Denver. He'd researched the site for the last couple days. His plan was to go down there, see about this Dianna Hoffman, the regional president. If anyone could get him the information he sought, it would be her. All he needed was a way there and he'd improvise the rest. Maybe if he somehow got to Dianna and found what he was looking for, he could impress Lana with the accomplishment.

The clock on the tablet flipped to 3 p.m. Break time was over. He locked the tablet in his locker and ran down a set of stairs. He opened a steel door that led into the garage.

In the garage, the wide doors opened out to the parking lot and a dry day. One Chevy EV Pickup sat on a raised platform. Two of the mechanics, Tim and Ray, were messing around beneath it. Kage thought he wouldn't want to be that car right about now.

"Alex," Tim shouted over. "Come check this out."

Kage heard the name called. It took him a second to respond. He was glad he'd given them another name. It had become essential to hide as much about himself as possible.

He even left his jacket out behind the shop where he slept, so no one would ask questions about the insignia.

"What's that?" Kage replied, walking past a work desk and station full of tools and flat tires and random car parts. He stopped beside the Chevy and looked at Tim.

"Over here," Tim said, walking to the back of the shop.

Kage followed him to a Hybrid Honda Racer.

"Wow. That's a nice bike," Kage said, missing his own.

"Thought you might like her. Maybe you can get those soft hands on that tight body, find out why she won't run right."

"What'd they say was wrong?"

"She shakes at high speeds." He paused, smiling, as if about to crack a joke. "Anywho, it's a simple fix, but I thought I'd give it to you."

"I'd love to give it a try," Kage said.

"I'll leave you two alone," Tim said, winking and walking away.

Kage knew a lot about motorcycles, learned

everything about them from his dad. Some
fathers took their sons out sporting, but
Kage and Todd bonded over bikes. They'd
spent hours at a time fixing up and
detailing bikes. Kage had wanted to start a
side business building his own, a way to
make money while doing animal activism.

Then everything in his world went to shit.

With that memory, the idea came to him: he
could get this bike up and running, use it
to sneak out and check that S-Corp office in
Denver. Of course, he'd have to be more
careful this time, but he'd learned enough
from messing up with Lana to not make the
same mistake twice.

It only took Kage one hour to figure out
that a front wheel bearing needed to be
replaced. It would only take another hour or
so to fix, with a new part. But he didn't
want the guys knowing that: When the bike
was fixed, it would be returned to the
owner. And a bike would be much easier to
sneak out with than a car.

He returned to Tim, pretending to be

frustrated.

"Any luck?" Tim asked as they began closing down for the night.

"Yeah, I need to order a part for it tomorrow. I'm pretty sure it's the wheel bearing. I just need a bit more time."

"That's what they all say," Tim said, smiling and slapping Kage on the shoulder.

As the other two mechanics closed the garage and left for the night, Kage slid the motorcycle key into his pocket.

"Is everything a sexual reference with you?" Kage asked Tim. The two of them shut off the lights. Kage watched Tim set the alarm, and they exited. He repeated the code over and over in his mind while he watched Tim get in his car and leave.

Then, Kage walked to the back of the shop and sat down beneath the overhang of the building's roof. That morning he had wrapped up his jacket in a bundle and hidden it beneath a set of concrete blocks. Now, he pulled it out and put it on. Returning to the garage, he unlocked the front door and entered Tim's code to stop the alarm.

He knew there were security cameras
everywhere. The computer that controlled
them was down the far hallway in the office.
He ran in and checked the computer. It
requested a passcode.

"Shoot," Kage whispered.

He searched the room. Getting down on his
knees, he found the power plug to the
computer. He yanked it from the wall.
Sitting up, he saw the computer screen go
blank. He stepped out into the hall,
approached the front office. A camera poked
out from the corner opposite him. Its red
light was off. That meant the cameras were,
too.

Kage entered the garage. Walking the bike
over to the garage door, he gave it a once-
over. He bent down and fixed the wheel back
in place.

Then, he gleefully ran upstairs. He
grabbed the tablet from his locker. He had
saved the directions to the S-Corp office in
Denver. It would take two hours to get

there, so he had to be quick if he was going to get back in time for work the next morning.

Kage ran back downstairs. He rolled the bike out the front door, set the alarm again, and left. The bike hummed awake. Kage read over the directions again and then returned the tablet to his secret stash behind the garage.

He started down I-25 on the Honda. He picked up speed and noticed no shaking. Impressed with himself, he took that as a sign he could make it in this world, regardless of what Trevor said. He would find this Dianna Hoffman, and he'd get answers. No stopping until he had answers.

Chapter Thirty-Nine

Bray

"Elliott!" she shouted.

Bray reached over and checked his pulse. He was still alive, but barely. For some reason beyond her own understanding, she was supposed to bring him inside that house. It was dark, formidable. She didn't want to go in there, but it wasn't about her anymore.

She lifted Elliott up to sitting. From behind, she brought her arms under his and tugged him up so that his head fell back against her chest. She pulled. His legs scraped against the concrete. As fast as she could, she dragged him up to the yard just outside the front door and carefully laid him there.

Running up to the front door, she yanked open the glass storm door and tried the knob of the front door. It was unlocked.

The door pushed slightly open when she touched it. Bray's eyes widened. She waited for someone to scream or to come out at her.

Nothing happened.

"Hello?" she called in.

She froze in the silence. She waited another moment and then returned for Elliott. Picking him up as before, she lifted him up the one concrete step and sat him down. Pulling the door open and holding it open with her side, she hauled Elliott in. She laid him down on the front room carpet and looked around.

Dirt lines in the form of squares covered one of the walls where framed pictures used to be. A large window looked out onto the front yard. There, a baby swing hung from a dead tree branch. Bray felt sick to her stomach.

"What happened here?" she whispered.

Elliott groaned.

Bray looked down at him, afraid, and walked into the kitchen. She tried flipping on the lights, but of course there was no electricity. The kitchen was void of dishes, of trash. It was as though the people left for vacation and never returned. Except everyone in this whole town seemed to have done that.

"Br-r-r-uhhhhhh," Elliott mumbled from the living room.

Bray ran out to him and stared at his sweating body.

"You...you..."

"Yes?" she asked, coming down to sit beside him.

"Cut...off my arm," he whispered. The words came out quick, effortlessly, and then he went unconscious again.

"No," she said, jumping up to standing.

There had to be another way. She was guided here. Surely it wasn't so she could cut his arm off. No way, not happening. She closed her eyes, begged for some more guidance. The waiting was tremendous. But she had to get quiet, clear. The silence helped.

The clarity forced her eyes open. She

was looking at a set of kitchen cabinets. She walked over to them and pulled the cabinet doors open.

Jars of raw honey sat stacked on two shelves. They were covered in dust. Bray's heart sank and her shoulders slumped. Honey? What was that supposed to do? She grabbed one of the jars. On it, a sticker with a cartoon bee smiling and waving to her made her cringe. Honey bees were another thing of the past, just another sad use of intelligent beings so humans could enjoy something tasty.

She pushed the jar back into the cabinet. It slammed into another jar, causing it to fall down onto the counter before her. It rolled to the edge, then stopped. The back label looked up at Bray. Her eyes met it, read the words:

Sweet, delicious taste. Great in teas, on crackers, for colds and building immunity! Homemade, medical-grade antiseptic.

Antiseptic?

Bray's eyes widened. This was it. Had to be. Why else would she be guided all the way here, to this empty house, this full cabinet of Manuka honey?

"Okay," she said to herself, trying not to doubt what was happening.

Bray grabbed two jars of the honey and rummaged through drawers until she found a large spoon. She ran over and set them down beside Elliott. A series of stairs led up to the second floor. She approached them and looked up. At the top, an empty wall looked down at her. A table with dust-covered candles stood against it. It was unsettling, how void of life this place was.

She slowly stepped upstairs. Once she arrived at the second to last step, she stopped.

"Hello?" she called out.

The nothingness that called back made her hair stand on end.

She stepped up into the hall, stopped again. She peered into the rooms on either side of her. They still had furniture in them, but no pictures on the walls. No toys, sentimental items. Just a house for show, not for living in.

When Bray found the bathroom, she checked the medicine cabinet, found some acetaminophen and took the bottle. She reached down into the cabinet beneath the sink. There, she found a first aid kit and some soy candles. Taking everything she could carry, she walked back downstairs.

Sitting down beside Elliott's bad arm, she took a deep breath. Her fingers picked at the old, red bandage. She lifted his arm and began pulling off the bandage. She threw it off to the side. No reason to be clean in a place no one would ever live again.

The bite marks were dark holes of blood so black she could hardly make them out in the dark room. Elliott's veins rose and coursed through his forearm in red rivers. Bray picked up one of the jars and looked at it. She hesitated, not wanting to use honey taken from bees. But this honey had been here for years, most likely since before the

2030 Migration.

Bray grabbed the lid and twisted it.
Even with all her strength, it would not
open. She stood up and ran into the kitchen.
She slammed the jar against the corner of
the kitchen table. It fell to the ground,
cracked open. She grabbed a spoonful of the
sticky substance and ran over to Elliott.
She smoothed it over his wound. She repeated
this action several times until his wound
was covered with almost all the honey from
that jar.

"God, I hope this works," she said.

Opening the first aid kit, she pulled
out an unused roll of gauze. She wrapped it
around Elliott's arm and taped it. Now she
just needed to get his fever down. Then
maybe he would come out of it, arm intact.

Bray grabbed a cup from the kitchen and
turned on the faucet. Nothing came out. Of
course not. Bray checked the refrigerator,
but it was empty. She shrugged, beginning
to grow discouraged.

Turning, her eyes caught the door to

the garage. She ran over and opened it. The garage was chilly, the air stuck from years of non-movement. It smelled of gasoline and other hard, mechanical things. The room was dark. As she held the door open, a subtle light crawled in from the kitchen. She followed the light in until her eyes adjusted.

In the far corner, a pack of bottled water and cans of soda sat on the concrete floor.

"Yes," she said, smiling. She walked through the empty garage to a row of storage shelves. There, engine oil, tools and random car parts collected dust. So did the bottles of water. Bray pulled out as many bottles as she could hold, nearly dropping them when she saw the words *SpringOne Water* all over them.

But there was no time to think about S-Corp or her mother right now. She turned and ran back into the house. She dropped the bottles onto the living room floor. Sitting down, she twisted one open. She brought

Elliott's head up onto her leg. He moaned.

"Come on," she said. "I need you to take this."

She opened the bottle of acetaminophen. Dropping three pills into her palm, she took one between her finger and·thumb and held it up to his mouth.

"Open your mouth," she said.

But he didn't. She separated his lips with her fingers, then his teeth. While holding the tips of her fingers between his teeth to keep them open, she dropped the pills onto his tongue. She sat him up and slowly poured the water into his mouth.

Suddenly he gagged, then awoke. His Adam's apple moved up and down. He'd gulped down the medicine, nearly spitting out the rest of the water. Elliott's eyes opened slightly.

"What's going on?" he whispered.

"Lie back down," she said, helping him down to the floor. "I gave you some medicine for the fever."

"Why is my arm sticky? It smells

like...sweet," he said, his eyes closed.

"It's honey. Apparently it helps heal wounds. I had no idea."

But Elliott did not respond. He went quiet. She looked down at his face. He at least seemed peaceful. All she could do now was let him be, and wait.

She got up and pulled a blanket down from the nearby couch. She placed it over his body and walked back into the kitchen, using the remaining honey to smooth over the burn wound on her back. Maybe it could heal that, too.

There was nothing left to do for Elliott. She watched him lying on the floor, quietly asleep. Beside him, the candles called to her. She went over and picked them up, set them on a chocolate painted coffee table. From the kitchen, she took out a matchbox, hoping the matches would light.

Back in the living room, she sat down, pretzel style, beside Elliott. The candles sat before her on the coffee table. She struck a few matches before she got one to light. Soon the three candles lit up the walls in dancing light.

Bray closed her eyes, took a few deep breaths. She was hungry, but she needed the hunger to keep her clear. It was time to find out exactly where Alice was.

The darkness behind her eyes gave way to the view of metal bars. The view expanded outward to reveal concrete floors, vats covered in excrement and blood. Above, fluorescent, painful white lighting bore down on gestation crates like the pain of sunlight after being in a dark room.

The view rose a few inches from the floor and turned. Somehow Bray had linked to Alice's view of the facility. For some reason, Alice had something she wanted Bray to see.

Workers began opening the crates, one at a time. At the first crate, the workers whistled at and called for the sow to move. She remained still. Three workers surrounded the crate and pushed at her, raising their voices. Still nothing. She just sat there, her eyes heavy and sunken. Suddenly one of the workers grabbed a nearby electric prod and stuck it into her backside. Jumping up, she squealed. The workers laughed. She was hit three more times with the prod, all in her backside and belly. Finally, she ran out of the crate.

This process was repeated with every sow until they had all exited their crates. Bray watched as the sows were forced into single file, marched down a concrete isle toward an open door. Outside that door, a transport truck sat open, waiting.

"This can't be right," Bray whispered. "You still have two days left."

"I don't know what that means," Alice replied.

"I thought we had more time," Bray answered, goosebumps running down her arms.

Chapter Forty

The Knocker

Ruben had a sit-down talk with the Knocker
that same day, and it went something like
this:

"What's going on with you?" Ruben asked.

The Knocker glanced at him and grinned. He
leaned back in the folding chair, his legs
spread and his boots pressed hard into the
floor. His hands rested, palms down, on his
thighs.

"Nothing," he replied. Ruben hadn't gotten
him a raise or said anything more about
helping him find his family, so he decided
the man could not be trusted. He was Medina,
too.

"What are the red marks on your knuckles?"
Ruben asked, his eyes set on the Knocker's
hands.

"That's not your territory, man."

"Not my territory?"

"No. You stay on your side and I'll stay on mine. That way no one gets hurt."

"Can you say more? Sorry, I'm just confused," Ruben said.

"In Medina we have this thing. If you see another Medina squad member out and about and you've got to keep your cover, you just mind your own business and they do the same. Unwritten rule."

"I see."

There was a pause. Ruben jotted down some notes. The Knocker looked up at the ceiling.

"Heard anything from Carmen?" Ruben asked.

"No," The Knocker said, sitting up. "I'll find them myself."

"So you are leaving?"

"As soon as I can, yes. Going to get the man who said he'd find them."

"Who's that?" Ruben asked. He'd crossed his arms at some point.

"Some guy in Mexico who was supposed to find out about my family. Maybe you know him. He's from Jaurez. Name is Julian."

"Never heard of him. You planning to hurt

him?"

"I ain't answering that. I'm going to look for him, and he better give me my family."

"Or?"

The Knocker stopped, looked Ruben in the eye. Then he scanned Ruben's desk for photos, for some indication that he had a family.

"You have kids?" the Knocker asked.

"No."

"I can't believe that beef out there popped out a calf, right there on the floor."

"Happens a lot," Ruben replied. "More than I'd like to admit."

Then Ruben's eyes shot down to the floor. He appeared sullen, almost sad.

"What's wrong man, you have a thing for those beefs?"

"They're cows, Bertan," Ruben replied. His eyes shot up, looked directly at the Knocker. When the Knocker heard that name, he was confused—and angry.

"They ain't cows, they're beefs."

"I'm afraid to ask, but what did they do with the calf?"

"Wouldn't you know?" the Knocker asked.

"Uh, well, it usually depends," Ruben replied. "What did they do...this time?"

And then he knew Ruben was lying.

The Knocker made the shape of a gun with two fingers and pointed it at his head. "Pow," he said.

Ruben nodded silently. The Knocker looked him over and smiled. Why was this man lying? The Knocker got to thinking about it. Ruben had worked here five years, however, he wasn't in the office much. And when he was, he seemed to be checking over videos. Whenever the Knocker would come in to say hello, Ruben was quick to hide whatever he was working on.

Like maybe that folder he'd found on Medina, the one that was under the computer.

"You work for Medina, too?" he asked finally.

"I'm sorry?" Ruben asked. His eyes

narrowed.

"You're lying about something. I bet you're the one who had that folder of Medina bank info. Do you work for them?"

"No, I don't."

"Well, I don't believe you," the Knocker said, his hands dropping to his thighs, making a slapping sound against his knees.

"You don't have to believe me. Sounds like the work you did for them was quite...traumatizing."

"What are you talking about? I never stopped working for them."

"I don't think I understand," Ruben said.

"You don't stop working for them. You die, but you don't stop." The Knocker was thinking about the job he had to do tonight.

"Can I ask you a question?" Ruben said.

The Knocker nodded.

"How old are you?"

"Twenty-three. You know that."

"And what's your name?"

"You know that too, man."

"Just humor me for a moment."

"The Knocker, dumb ass," the Knocker said, chuckling.

"And do you know what you're doing here?"

"Sometimes when I knock a beef," he whispered, leaning forward with his elbows on his knees and his hands clasped, "I get hard." He was smiling.

"You do?" Ruben replied.

"Yep."

"So the beefs are just things, yet when you knock them, you get hard?"

"So?"

"So don't you see how that's confusing?"

"No," the Knocker said, sitting back again. His chest was elevated, his heart rate increased.

"What else makes you hard?"

"Carmen. Sometimes, killing a man."

"Hmm. So is it the knocking that turns you on or the fact that the beef is female?"

"Fuck you, man," the Knocker shouted, standing up quickly and pacing the floor.

"Sorry. That was out of line. You can sit down, if you want."

"I know what I can do." He glared down at Ruben. "I can do whatever I want." He sat down, smiled again.

A bell rang. The sound seemed to snap him in half. He sat up, took a deep breath. He couldn't remember coming to Ruben's office, but he was used to being confused these days.

"You better get back to work," Ruben said. He appeared frustrated.

"What? I just got here," Bertan said, confused again. "I need to know if you can get me some extra money."

Ruben slowly leaned forward and looked him in the eye.

"Bertan?" he asked.

"Uh, yes. Who else would I be?" Bertan said.

"You don't remember what just happened?"

"The bell rang. Means break is starting."

"No, Bertan. I'm afraid break is over."

"What?" Bertan said. He needed this time to talk to Ruben about leaving, about options.

"You don't remember anything from the last fifteen minutes?"

"No, I don't," Bertan admitted. The last thing he remembered...shit...what was the last thing he remembered? He thought over the last few days. Blank, black spaces where memories used to be.

Total-Mart. He went to Total-Mart and sent money. And now it was morning.

"But it's morning," he said.

"I'm sorry, but it's 4 p.m. Time to finish up work."

"It's 4 p.m.?" Bertan asked. He suddenly felt nauseous.

"Yes," Ruben said, frozen in his chair. "You can look at the clock, if you don't believe me."

Bertan turned and glanced down at the laptop. It read 4:03 p.m.

Lightheaded, he shakily returned to his chair and sat down.

"What's the last thing you remember?"

"I-I don't know anymore. Working, I guess."

"So you don't remember knocking beefs today?"

"No," he said, shaking his head and looking down at the floor. He crossed his arms and slouched.

"You don't remember the pregnant cow?"

Bertan slowly shook his head. He continued to stare at the floor, started zoning out.

"Bertan?"

"Yeah?" he said, pulling his eyes up to look at Ruben.

"Come by in the morning. We really need to talk."

"Okay." Bertan nodded, standing up.

When he exited the room, the office door clicked. The click snapped something inside him. Suddenly he remembered: he had a job to do tonight for Serpentine.

He probably could do this for another twenty years. Find Julian, get his family back, and make money with Medina. Leave this fucking knock job and have a mansion in Texas. Raise Gabriella, become a jefe, make more money than anyone knew what to do with.

Enough money to protect him and his for life.

Chapter Forty-One

Kage

The S-Corp regional office was a tall, four-story structure. Nothing but a square covered in tinted windows that hid everything that went on inside. It was surrounded by an empty parking lot, save two cars. Security, Kage surmised. He sat in the grass just across the road from the building. The motorcycle lay on its side beside him. He'd used the last of his cash to charge the bike, which would give him an additional 350 miles of riding.

Kage eyed the S-Corp building. Inside were secrets, he was sure. He knew many of them, and he wondered if the things he knew would be enough to blackmail the people inside for info on his parents.

There was only one way to find out. He'd watched the building for the last couple of hours. Soon, it would be morning. He wouldn't make it back to the shop in time for work. And once they found the bike missing, and him missing, they'd know.

There was no going back there, and no reason to. Kage didn't leave home to find another home for himself. He thought of Trevor, how he was probably worried sick about him. One day when it was safe, he'd return for a visit. For now, it was time to get what he'd come for.

Kage lifted the bike to standing. When he rested on it, he came alive in a way. The feel of the firm seat between his legs made him feel strong, confident.

He started the engine and proceeded over to the building. He pulled into the lot and rolled to a stop beside one of the vehicles, a white Tesla Model S. Teslas like this one were not cheap. Not something a security person could afford, unless the country had flipped upside down in the past twelve years. This had to be an executive's car, someone high up. Someone he'd want to know.

Kage drove around behind a nearby
dumpster. He parked the bike. He took off
his jacket and set it on the seat. He stood
at the corner of the dumpster where he could
keep an eye on the Tesla and waited.

\#

Morning came. Cars streamed into the lot.
Kage had fallen asleep against the dumpster.
He was jolted awake by the sudden warming of
the sun. The Tesla was still there.

A group of protesters marched up to the
building from across the street. They
carried signs with S-Corp crossed out. One
said: S-CORP LEADS TO DEATH'S DOOR. Kage
stood up, fascinated. Those were bold
people, small in number and yelling and
shouting right outside the building. A
security guard stood between them and the
front doors, but he did nothing to stop
them. Kage figured protesting must still be
legal. At least so it seemed.

Then, a woman in a suit exited the front
doors. She stood about 5'9", thin,
attractive. Her brown hair was up in a

ponytail. As she exited, the protestors approached and followed her to the Model S. She simply ignored them.

Kage recognized her face from the S-Corp website. It was *the* Dianna Hoffman, stepping into her car. Kage threw on his jacket. He jumped onto the bike, neared the edge of the dumpster, and peered out. The Tesla pulled out of the lot, and he followed. Wherever she was headed, he wouldn't be far behind.

#

There was no absence of sun this day. Even in April it was heavy and landed on Kage's back as he rode. Its warmth was inviting and left him smiling.

But not for long.

The Tesla exited the highway sixty-five miles north, in Fort Collins. The place didn't mean anything to Kage since he'd never been to Colorado, but the bold-looking building they approached gave him pause.

It had no windows, and its walls were concrete, beige. It lacked character. The sign outside the parking lot read:

S-CORP CENTER FOR TRANSGENIC ENGINEERING

Kage gulped. He slowed the bike along the road just as the Tesla turned into the parking lot. Kage was surprised there was no fence protecting the place. Seemed pretty scientific and private.

Kage slid off the bike. He rolled it down an embankment in the field beside the road. There was nothing else out here but dry earth. The Rocky Mountains spanned the horizon behind the building, their gray color leaving a dull shroud of mystery.

The Tesla pulled into a parking spot. Dianna Hoffman got out of the car and used a key to enter a small door.

Kage set the bike down on its side. He scanned the sky for drones. He was sure they were up there, hiding above layers of atmosphere. If he was going to get inside this building, he either had to wait till nightfall or be very swift.

He was incapable of waiting.

Kage walked across the road. He didn't want to appear suspicious to drones, so he cordially walked up to the Tesla, as if this were where he was supposed to be.

He glanced at the building. A charcoal-colored steel door stood in the dead center of the building. It made him think of an odd contemporary painting. He walked toward it, and as he got closer he could see the place did have windows, but they'd been boarded up and painted over.

"What is this place?" he whispered to himself.

He started for the back of the building. There had to be another way in. Every twenty feet he encountered square ventilation systems. Hot air streamed out of them and hit him in the face. He turned the building's corner and stopped at the next one. He'd never seen anything like this before, not that he ever would have. He knelt down and, keeping his head turned away from the hot air, looked inside.

All he could see was darkness. Why were there ventilation systems in the ground and not attached to the building itself?

Kage stood up quickly. He ran around to
the back of the building. The sound of
trickling water itched at his ear. It was
coming from the field beside the building.
Kage followed the sound to the edge of the
parking lot where the asphalt stopped and
dirt ground took over. There, a PVC pipe the
size of a basketball poked out from the
ground. Brown water fell out of it and onto
the ground, leaving a grayish residue. Kage
didn't dare touch it. Instead, he stood up
and backed away. It reminded him of a story
Trevor told him about Oxygen 11, how it got
into the water and ground soil, how it
killed all those people. It was S-Corp,
Trevor had said, that developed a new
transgenic fertilizer to help curb drought
in the west. It was rushed through trials
and tested in California. The
biotechnologist who'd worked on the
fertilizer had accidentally created a new
type of Oxygen 11 that, when interacting
with ground soil, created devastating
poison. But S-Corp hid it, and the

government provided cover by labeling the incident a terrorist attack.

Trevor knew these things because he had been a lobbyist for President Walker. He knew many things, but he usually chose not to speak about them.

Well, today Kage was here to get some answers. He walked up to the edge of the building and glanced out at the S-Corp sign.

"Transgenics," he read aloud and returned to the building. There had to be a way into this place. He couldn't see any security cameras, not that that meant anything. There wasn't even a security guard, which left him feeling even more uneasy.

But the back of the building was just as empty as the front. There was no way up to the roof. No back door. He turned and scanned the surroundings. One hundred yards from the building, a square toll-booth-type building stood. A few cars were parked on the dirt beside it. Kage looked back in the direction of the bike. Out past where it was parked, across the road, stood another, duplicate, booth building. Both had glass windows. Kage ran toward the one with cars parked beside it. As he approached, he saw it was empty. It was indeed a toll booth. It was like they'd just taken two toll booths and dropped them out here.

"So weird," he said.

He stepped up to the door and tested the knob. The door popped open. Kage jumped back, expecting something to happen. But the door just sat ajar, the place empty. Kage realized then that he'd stopped breathing. He took a breath and entered the booth. Leaving the door open behind him, he stood and stared down. There below him, a set of concrete stairs led down to a steel door.

"Aha, now we're talking," Kage said.

He stepped down to the door and stopped. A box of numbers with a red light hung in the center of the door. Some kind of pass code was needed to get inside. No surprise. He'd have to wait for someone to show up. He walked back up into the booth and curled up in a corner, closing his eyes.

A sudden thought came to him: *get some rest now, you're going to need it*. It stung at his chest, gave him a strange sense of doom. He swallowed it down and closed his eyes.

Chapter Forty-Two

The Knocker

He sat outside in the car, in the dark. The engine was off, windows rolled up despite the arid night.

Carmen used to be his home.

"Nope. Stay present," the Knocker said to his reflection in the rearview mirror. It was a black hole in the indigo sky.

Turning, he scanned the hostel that was home to the man he'd come to see. Marques Arollo. The Knocker had looked up his address after everyone left the plant. He'd stolen a black face mask and goggles from work and slid them onto his face.

Stepping out of the car, he pulled up on the door handle and shut the door carefully. He unlocked the trunk and pulled the gun from his security uniform, then quietly shut the trunk.

The Knocker ran up to the hostel and

pressed his back against the wall. He slid along the wall, approached the door. He pulled his identification card from his wallet and slid it between the door and its frame. He grabbed the door knob, slid the card down until it pushed the lock away and the door opened.

Inside, he turned and shut the door. He stood against it in the dark, waiting. His eyes barely adjusted to the room. The goggles didn't help. He came down on all fours and crawled to the nearest bunk. A man slept there, near snoring. The Knocker put his hand over the man's mouth and pressed the gun into his throat. The man jumped, mumbled.

"Sh," the Knocker whispered. "Marques Arollo."

The man's arm lifted, shaking, and he pointed to the other side of the room.

"Don't do anything or I'll shoot you."

The man nodded and turned away, facing the wall. The scent of hot urine filled the air.

"Son of a bitch," the Knocker whispered,

standing up.

He approached the bunk the man had pointed to. There, a body lay still, except for its chest rising and falling.

The Knocker pulled out his phone and tapped on the flashlight. The man's wallet sat on the floor atop a pair of pants. He opened it and checked the ID card. *Marques Arollo. Bingo.*

The Knocker came down on his knees. He bent down over Marques's body. Unblocking the safety on the gun, he pressed it into Marques's temple. He brought his forearm down against Marques's throat, and Marques struggled to breathe. The Knocker pointed the flashlight at the man's face as his eyes shot open.

"Are you Marques Arollo?" the Knocker whispered.

"Who's asking?" Marques spat through his teeth, struggling against the Knocker's forearm as it pressed deeper against his throat.

"Don't be stupid. You owe Serpentine some

money, don't you?"

The man's eyes met the Knocker's goggles, but he said nothing.

"Five hundred dollars, now," the Knocker whispered into Marques's ear.

"Fuck you."

Angered, his face sweating beneath the mask, the Knocker dropped his phone and set the gun on the ground. He grabbed Marques by the throat. He yanked him down onto the floor, and his head slammed onto the concrete.

Marques reached for the gun. The Knocker squeezed the man's neck while taking his knee and pushing it into his stomach. Marques grabbed frantically for his throat, his hands pulling at the Knocker's fingers as they squeezed tightly.

The Knocker freed one hand and grabbed the gun. Marques's hand pulled at the Knocker's mask. The Knocker lifted Marques's head into the air and slammed it onto the concrete. Marques began laughing.

"You look like a bitch in those goggles,"

he said, laughing more.

The Knocker pressed the gun into Marques's genitals.

"Hey! Fuck, man, c'mon."

The Knocker took his free hand and pressed it into Marques's face, forcing it to one side and coming down on it with all of his weight.

"Aah," Marques groaned.

"I'll fucking blast your dick off if you don't give me $500. If I have to ask one more time, I won't even bother ending you. I'll shoot off everything down here and just keep you alive for Serpentine to deal with. I'll make you wish you died."

"All right man, all right."

The Knocker lifted the gun up to Marques's head. He released his hand from Marques's face. Marques sat up, one side of his head bleeding. He pulled his wallet from under his back and handed cash to the Knocker.

"This is only $300," the Knocker said, keeping the gun pressed against his temple.

"I know. The rest is in my car."

The Knocker grabbed his phone from Marques's bed and followed the man outside, the gun pressed between Marques's legs.

Marques unlocked the door to a rusted Honda. He opened the door. The Knocker pushed him over against the back door and leaned into him from behind.

"Where's the money?" he asked.

"In the glove box."

The Knocker grabbed Marques by his t-shirt and dragged him around the car to the passenger side. He held the gun up to Marques's face.

"Open the door, get in and sit on the floor."

Marques opened the door. He bent down and squeezed his body onto the floor in front of the passenger seat.

The Knocker sat down on the seat. He held the gun up to Marques's eye. The glove box dropped open and hit Marques in the head.

"Ow, son of a bitch."

"I'll show you a son of a bitch if you don't shut up."

The Knocker reached in and found an
envelope of cash. With one hand he counted
through it. Another $500. The more money,
the faster he could hunt down Julian.

Sliding the envelope down into his jeans,
he shut the glove box.

"Asshole! Don't take all my money,"
Marques spat.

The Knocker leaned down and glared at
Marques from behind the black goggles.

"Dude, you look like a fucking idiot,"
Marques said, laughing again.

The Knocker, running the gun down and into
the side of Marques's throat, sat back.

"You know if you shoot a man here, he
won't actually die, unless he bleeds to
death. No, as long as someone finds you in
time, you'll just lose your vocal cords. You
won't be able to eat."

Marques said nothing. He gulped, sweat
rolling down the sides of his face.

The Knocker reached up and pulled down on
the neck of his own t-shirt, exposing the
tattoo along his chest.

"You see this?" he asked.

"Yes," Marques replied.

"You know what it means?"

"Yes."

"Good. You call me Sicario, all right? You know what that means?"

"Yes." Marques's voice quivered.

"Great." The Knocker smiled, though he doubted Marques could tell. "Then we're done here."

The Knocker stepped out of the car, keeping the gun pointed at Marques.

"You stay there, got it?"

Marques nodded.

"If I see you move, I'll blow your head off."

The Knocker slammed the door. He walked backwards, slowly, the gun pointed at the car door. Once he got to the road, he turned and ran for his car.

Inside the car, he dropped the gun onto the passenger seat and started the engine. He backed the car down the road, turned around in the dirt, and sped home, laughing

while pulling the mask and goggles off his
face.

Chapter Forty-Three

Bray

Alice had only two more days. Maybe that was all Bray had, too. If the honey didn't work, then time was short for Elliott, too. Bray was concerned least of all for herself. She found herself unable to worry about such an unknown as the end of her life. With all that had happened to her and Elliott, it just didn't seem to matter. Losing Elliott and Alice, however, was beyond all comprehension.

How could she prioritize one life over the other? Wasn't that just the way of things in this world? Someone was made more important than someone else? Animals less than humans. Humans were animals, too, but that didn't seem to make any difference. Even if she could find Alice, then what? It wasn't like Bray could do anything about it. She was powerless.

Shadows danced across the walls of the house. The flickering light from the candles invited these shadows in. She'd only just sat down, it seemed, and already everything around her had become hazy. The shadows on the walls took the form of animals. Heat gradually replaced all thoughts in her mind with emptiness. Everything was clear. The shadows drew into the shape of sows, their bodies shaking back and forth in movement.

The transport truck.

Bray's eyes fully closed. In the darkness there was a dance of dim light. She sat there and called for Alice. The response came with ease.

"Something happened to you," Alice said.

"Yes, but I'm okay," Bray replied, thinking of the dogs and Elliott's arm.

"And your friend?"

"He's okay, too. I think."

Everything remained dark and dim as they spoke. Images of Alice's throat being sliced open with a boning knife encroached on her mind and would not leave.

"Alice, I want to find you, but I need to know exactly where you are."

"Yes, go ahead," Alice said.

They both went silent. Complete darkness rolled in over any dim light that remained. The sound of an engine hummed in Bray's ears. Bitter wind hit her on her face and the sides of her body. The feeling of hard metal pressed into her bare feet. She felt herself pushed into other bodies around her. The image of round bodies, other sows, could be made out in the dark. She was inside a metal box with slits in the sides where fresh air came in.

Her legs were numb from a lifetime of standing. The scent of ammonia and shit and other harsh smells stung her nostrils. They burned. Some of the sows had not made it. Their bodies were motionless, soulless bags of bones and organs lying on the truck bed's surface.

Bray turned and looked out one of the slats, but she could see nothing with clarity. Pulling back, she lifted up and

rose above the truck. From this vantage
point she could see it traveling down the
highway. As she followed the truck, flying
above it, she came upon a highway sign: I-25
North.

Then the image faded. Everything turned
black. The heat deepened her breathing,
extended it into exhales so long it felt she
wasn't breathing at all. The heat pulled
everything from her mind. It took away mind,
made it absent and irrelevant. Her senses
heightened. She felt light-headed, and it
felt good. Like a natural high.

The heat drew her back, back in time,
where she found herself sitting outside,
surrounded by newly-born piglets. She was
thirteen. It was that time her mom had taken
her to visit an S-Corp facility for "Bring
Your Daughter to Work Day."

The sky was white and absent of sun. It
was hot. As she sat down to meet the
piglets, her arm slid along some fencing
beside her and ripped open a slice of skin.
Bray wiped the blood off with her shirt and

then became instantly distracted by one
piglet that was playing with her
shoestrings. It pushed its snout into her
hand as if to demand a pet. She laughed.

Then it was in her lap. And then it licked
her bleeding arm. In that instant, while the
piglet's saliva and scratchy tongue slid
along the line of the cut, Bray felt
something awaken in her. The heat pulled at
her. DNA strands danced around in her mind.
The clear liquids of the piglet's tongue
mixed and danced with Bray's blood like
dancing flames of a fire, flames coming
together, in union, as one.

Bray's eyes popped open. They shot around
the room. Her breathing stopped, froze in
exhale. So that was it. Alice had licked her
cut. She hadn't remembered that until just
now. It made sense, explained how she linked
with Alice unlike with any other animal
she'd ever met.

Now she knew how it was all so real, how
she linked with Alice all those years ago.
They were indeed in union. Which meant it

was very possible she could die with Alice. She invited it in, to her mind, her heart. But it didn't seem to matter. Death felt more real for Alice than it did for her. If Bray died, that would just be it. If Alice died the way it was planned, by violent slaughter, enslaved, separated from nature, it would all be wrong. Backwards. A win for S-Corp, a loss for nature. A loss for all good things of the world. Because in union all things were connected, contained life. The loss of one would affect the rest. Like a body losing a limb. Like Alice losing her children. Life was precious and no one saw it.

And then Elliott woke up, screaming.

Chapter Forty-Four

Cole

When faced with mortality it was only natural that a person would need time alone. Such was the case for Cole. It had been two days since the heart attack. He'd been home ever since. He didn't want to be anywhere else. The thought of never seeing Bray again brought constant tears to his eyes. Now that the heart attack had taken from him a certain amount of concentration, he'd lost count of the days since she'd left.

That was how he saw it. She had definitely left. It was a choice. There seemed no results from the press conference. Most likely, she was not in a place where she had access to the news. Cole was familiar with Wyoming from all the trips he used to take to Yellowstone as a kid, before the Migration of 2030. His parents had often taken him there. They were very active, always close, died only within years of one another. And when he'd met and married Dianna, he'd hoped for the same. He had really believed they'd be together forever. They'd raise a family, never struggle with money, and give their kids the freedom to do as they pleased. But now he realized that was not at all what Dianna wanted. She wanted Bray to be like her, and Bray was the opposite. She was more like Cole.

He stood up from the desk in his home office. He'd been working from home, but not really working. Just answering emails. After a while he'd get tired and take long naps into the evening. Sometimes he took naps just to get away from the thoughts about Bray, the flashing memories of his pleasant childhood, how normal and easy it was, and about his marriage to Dianna and how wrong it had all gone.

In the bedroom, a soft light from the sun cast yellow markings on the bed. It hadn't been made. The sheets were waves of fabric in an ocean he dipped into for escape. The

way the sun entered the room made him feel
lonely. Everything was so quiet. He turned
and glanced down the hall. Bray's bedroom
door was closed. He thought to go in, but he
didn't want to be that parent. Leaving it
alone, he turned back to the bed. A feeling
of regret overcame him. All those years he
had hurried off to DC for work, never asking
if she might want to come with him or spend
time together. He assumed she'd be
disinterested, and he would leave it at
that.

Shutting off the sensor to his implant, he
sat down on his bed. His phone stuck out
from the pocket of his sweatpants. He pulled
it out and set it on the table beside the
bed. He stared at it. Maybe if he stared
long enough, it would ring.

Every day, several times a day, he stared
at his phone. When it did ring, he jumped
for it, his heart racing. But always they
were calls from his campaign manager, an
intern, or someone else at the office. He
was supposed to be working on campaign

plans, but he really didn't want to. It didn't take long to realize that the campaign dream was Dianna's, not his. The heart attack had put this into perspective.

Cole lay down on the bed. His heart ached. Staring up at the ceiling, he thought about his life. This wasn't how he imagined it would turn out. Bray being sick—or maybe not sick, but clearly with something very wrong. Dianna being a total bitch right now while he just wanted a divorce. And then there was himself, a person he no longer took any time to get to know, because he wasn't sure he would like the man he'd become.

After a while, the fatigue set in. His eyes closed, heavy. The whole world so quiet, both outside and in. Only moments later he was out.

#

Ringing edged into Cole's mind. At first he thought it was an alarm. He grabbed the phone to shut it off. He felt so tired he could sleep another several hours. Feeling it vibrate in his hand, he turned his blurry eyes back to read the screen. It was Thom.

Cole shot up from the bed.

"Hey man," he answered, his heart hoping for some good news.

"Hey, how's it going?" Thom replied.

"Don't ask."

"Well, we found Bray."

"Where," Cole said, standing up. He got dizzy and slowly sat back down on the bed.

"She's in Wyoming, still. Casper, to be exact."

"Were you able to see her?"

"Yep."

"Is she okay?"

"From what we can see, yes. Friend is pretty injured, though."

"How?"

"Hard to tell. She carried him into an abandoned house. He was unconscious, but not bleeding. His arm was bandaged."

"Text me exact coordinates," Cole replied,

his heart racing.

"Sure."

"And keep close. I don't want to lose her if she decides to leave. I doubt they will stay in one place for long."

"Yep, will do."

"Thanks, this really means a lot," Cole said, a sudden rush of relief warming his shoulders and chest.

"Any time."

Cole hung up the phone. He turned the volume up as loud as he could so he wouldn't miss Thom's text when it came through.

So he'd found her. Dianna might be aware of Bray's location too, so he'd have to be quick. And he sure as hell wasn't going to call her and tell her what he knew. He needed to get to Bray, hopefully before Dianna did. For tonight, he'd rest up, get all the sleep he could. Once he got the coordinates, he'd plan on leaving out in the morning. Finally, he'd get to Bray and he'd listen.

Maybe now he could get his daughter back.

Chapter Forty-Five

Kage

Kage was bored out of his mind. There was nothing here for him, save whatever might be hiding underground. He sat with his head against the wood walls of the toll booth. His butt felt like a hard mass of steel, he'd been sitting so long. He wanted to sleep but was able to stay awake. Mostly he thought about Trevor and Ethan, wondered what they were doing right about now. From the looks of the darkness unfolding outside the walls of windows encasing the booth, they'd be sitting down for dinner. His mouth was dry. It watered for Virgil's fresh apple cider.

Suddenly, a click came from down the stairs. Kage jumped to his feet. The darkness of the staircase and lack of outside light would help him with the element of surprise. He tiptoed down a few

steps. The door clicked again. Someone was
on the other side. He stepped down until it
was so dark he couldn't see his own hands.
The door slowly opened. Kage pressed himself
up against the wall adjacent to the door.
The door opened and a faint light touched
his boots. He turned for the door. A hand
came out into the darkness, followed by an
arm, then a shoulder. Kage raised his leg
and kicked the door back as hard as he
could. The man inside fell backward. Kage
pulled the door open. There was just enough
light for him to see that the man's head and
back had hit a wall behind him. Kage entered
and kneed the man in the stomach.

"He—" the man tried to scream.

Kage grabbed the man's mouth with his
hand, shutting him up. The man turned into
him and jabbed him in the side with his
elbow. Kage took the hit, then pulled the
man back until both their bodies slammed
into the door, shutting it.

Now Kage was inside. He pulled the knife

from his jacket and then yanked himself away. He faced the man, pointing at him with the knife.

"Sh," Kage said. "I won't hesitate to stab you a couple times, leave you here bleeding," he whispered.

The man, similar height to Kage but more stalky, wearing jeans and a button-up white shirt, went pale. Kage could see his face even in the dull, yellow light that came from down the hall.

"You're going to help me get to Dianna Hoffman," Kage said.

"Hell no," the man replied.

Kage ran at the man. The man panicked, curled up against the wall. Kage jabbed the knife just up to the man's eyeball and froze there. The man shook, his eyes wide.

"Please," the man said. He sounded like he might cry.

"Tell me where she is, and I'll let you go home. How's that?"

The man nodded his head slowly.

"Where?" Kage whispered, still holding the

knife to the man's eye.

"Follow the hall. It's like a maze. Follow the red lines on the ground. You'll get to a set of white doors. Then, security. Dianna will be just past those doors."

Kage pulled the knife back from the man's eye.

"What is this place?" he asked.

"You'll find out soon enough. Now will you please just let me go?"

Kage looked at the man. His eyes dropped down to the button-up shirt, where a badge hung from the left pocket. Kage took the badge and put it in his jacket pocket.

"How much security?" Kage asked.

"Two guards."

"You're lying," Kage replied, watching the man's eyes.

The man shook his head.

Kage would have to believe him. He stepped away.

The man, now shaking, entered a series of numbers on the door. Kage watched: 327985. He committed the numbers to memory.

The door opened and the man ran up the stairs. He'd probably alert them that Kage was here, so he'd have to find Dianna quickly.

Kage ran down the long hall. The walls on either side of him were only a few feet apart. It was claustrophobic. Dark, with a faint yellow light edging closer. There were indeed red lines along the floor, like hallway markers. It made sense this place was underground. That ugly, beige building was probably just a facade to hide what was really going on.

S-Corp was a master at that.

Kage continued running. Off-shoots of hallways passed by, dark, unknown places. A constant humming filled the air. Above, Kage noticed vents that led to the outside.

The hallway turned a corner. Kage stopped before the turn. He approached the corner and peeked around. There, he found the source of the yellow light. The two white doors the man had mentioned stood there closed beneath one single yellow light. But

there were no guards. Cut into each door
were wide squares like windows, but instead
of being see-through, they were mirrored.

Kage's hairs stood on end. He sensed the
guards were standing on the other side,
maybe awaiting him. And he wouldn't know
because all he'd see when he neared the
doors would be himself.

Before turning the corner, Kage slid his
knife into his jacket pocket. He crouched
down and slowly approached the doors. As he
got closer, he pressed himself up against
one of the doors and listened. The humming
noise was preventing him from hearing
anything. He figured that was on purpose.

Surely he couldn't just open the doors.
There had to be some kind of security
clearance. He pulled out the badge he'd
taken from the worker. The man's picture was
on the front, a QR code printed on the back.
He searched the area for a code box but
found nothing. Then the mirrors caught his
attention. There could be anything inside
those mirrors, or behind them. Security

cameras, most likely. For him, this was a dead end.

Kage turned around, remaining low to the ground, and ran back to the turn in the hall. He stood up against the wall.

Opposite him was another hall, dark and without the red lines. He slowly followed it. Everything got very dark. He gulped, pulled out the knife, and continued, one foot in front of the other. The hallway turned and he turned with it. At the end, another door. A white light shone down on it. On the wall beside the door, he saw a key code box. He stepped up to it and pressed the badge's QR code up to the screen on the box. The door clicked. Kage pushed at it with two fingers. It was heavy, reinforced steel. He pushed it with more force, and it opened. The room was dark, aside from a dim red light that shone down from a series of fluorescent bulbs along the ceiling.

In that red light Kage could see rows of gray, steel tables. Some held laptops, graduated cylinders, pipettes, microscopes.

But it was what he saw lining the walls that really disturbed him, stopped him in his tracks. Along one wall, caged chickens, heavily breathing. He approached them and peered more closely. Each chicken was large enough to fit inside one eight-by-eight-inch cage. Too large. The chickens were tall, their legs standing at twice their natural height. And they had no beaks.

"What the..." Kage started, but then trailed off.

At closer glance, he saw their talons were also gone, replaced with softer, rounder toes that looked just like human toes. Then, he saw they had no eyes. Just grown-in sockets where eyes should be. And through their chests Kage could see frantic beating, like their hearts were racing. Their mouths were strange, pointed, difficult for Kage's brain to understand. They were being genetically bred, maybe to make it simpler for humans to farm them for food.

Kage stepped back, in shock, to the back

of the room. A glowing, aquarium-like rectangular structure stood nearly ten feet long. Inside, strange little things floated in thick liquid. Kage came closer, his heart now beating out of his chest.

"Fucking shit," he said as the blood slowly drew away from his face.

Hundreds of embryos hung from long, pink cords. Like umbilical cords. Fucking human embryos.

Kage followed the aquarium over to a hose and a series of wires that led to another enclosure just feet away. He froze. His legs shook. His stomach went hard and nauseous.

Inside the second glass enclosure were two sows. They were both lying on their sides, one behind the other. Their backs faced him. He stepped closer. His eyes could see a slow rise and fall of their stomachs. They were adult-size pigs, healthy. Bolted to their heads were complicated apparatuses with wires flowing out from them.

Kage walked around the other side of the glass enclosure. Their eyes were wide open,

large, unblinking. He jumped back,
frightened.

"What the fuck?" he said, pacing back and
forth. He clenched his fists. His breath was
fast, his heart pounding, lungs squeezing
inside his chest.

Kage ran back over to the embryo aquarium.
He stood behind it. With all his anger and
strength, he pushed at it. It didn't move.
He turned and pushed his side into it.
Nothing. He pushed again, still no movement.

Soon he was crying in anger and
frustration. He kicked and pushed and kicked
at it, trying to knock it over. Everything
in this place had to be destroyed, then he'd
find Dianna Hoffman. He paced the room,
searching the equipment for something sharp.

Suddenly, the overhead lights rolled on.
Kage turned. Two guards stood at the door,
guns pointed.

Chapter Forty-Six

Bray

The scream started as a gurgle, then a quick rise, as a flame from a once-still candle wick. Hot, shaky, waking the walls of the house. Bray opened her eyes. She turned to Elliott. He was lying on his back, his arm raised in the air.

"It burns!" he shouted. His body shot up to sitting. He looked down at his arm again.

"What did you do?"

"I put honey on it," she replied, in sudden shock at what was happening.

"Jesus it stings," he said. "Get it off."

Bray sat up and reached for the bandage. She quickly worked to pull it off, round and round until the gauze came apart, sticky in her hands. Elliott stood up and ran into the kitchen. He turned the tap, but nothing happened.

"There's no water," Bray said, standing up. She grabbed a bottle of water and ran over to him.

Elliott held his arm over the sink and she poured the water over the honey-covered wound.

"Ah," he said. "Shit!"

"Sorry. It said it was antibacterial," she replied, near crying.

"Find something to wipe it off!" he shouted.

Bray dropped the empty bottle in the sink. Startled by his anger, she turned away and ran upstairs. She found a closet full of linens and pulled out a sheet. When she returned to Elliott, he was keeled over on the floor, shaking back and forth, holding his arm. Bray handed him the sheet and then took a step back.

Elliott slowly wiped the honey away from the wound. As the honey disappeared, it exposed his arm. The thick, dark red blood vessels had relaxed and settled back down under his skin. The wound had even cleared up. Now it didn't look so black.

"It worked," she said, wanting to smile but holding back.

"Yeah, but I must be allergic. See if you can find some actual hydrogen peroxide, to clean the rest."

Bray returned a moment later with a half-empty hydrogen peroxide bottle. Elliott took it and dabbed it into the wound with a cotton pad from the first aid kit. Bray sat and looked into his face, noticing that the fever had also broken.

"You're not sweating like a cold can of soda anymore," she said.

"True. I do feel better," he said, focusing his attention on the wound.

Bray waited for a thank you, but received none. She thought maybe he'd be relieved that she didn't have to cut off his arm. Instead, he wrapped his arm in a clean bandage, walked over to the couch, and lay down, his back facing her.

Bray just stood there in the kitchen,

looking in at him. The candles grew dim,
losing most of the wax they had left. Soon
they'd wither and darkness would come again.
Then she would just be alone in it.

Why was he so mad? He barely even spoke
to her. It was like she wasn't even there.
Like she wasn't important. And then she
thought back to his apartment in Denver, how
she begged Elliott to take her with him
across the border, getting mad at him when
she found out he was going to take her only
as far as Cheyenne. She heard desperation,
greed, selfishness. Not his, but her own. A
complete lack of consideration for the
other. She heard the sounds of separation,
the pulling apart of friendships, of lives,
of hearts at the benefit of someone else.
And suddenly she realized she was the one
who had both done the biting and, then
afterword, nearly done the cutting. The
taking apart of Elliott's desires just to
serve her own. She had done it. Bray had
gotten Elliott to this very point. If not
for her, he'd be halfway to Montana. Not

that he wasn't an adult who'd made his own choices, but once they were stopped at the border, he had had few.

When Bray was fourteen, she witnessed Alice lose her first litter of piglets to factory farming. She was there when Alice was impregnated, a frightening image burned into her mind that never really left. She was there to see the piglets stuck beneath the gestation crate vats, trying to reach their mother but never quite getting close enough.

Then, several days later, the piglets were taken away. Bray felt the whole experience in her chest, her bones. A thousand-pound weight of grief pushed down on her chest. It was a demon that sucked the air from her lungs, stole the tears from her eyes so she couldn't cry. But the crying was there. Like the ever-present thunder that comes with every storm, the crying was there. Bray felt it inside, a loss of something as though it were a part of her, an extension of her that she would never get back, and therefore she could never fully be herself again. There'd always be something missing. That was the cry she felt from Alice so many years ago.

It was the same cry she experienced right here, coming from Elliott as he lay on the couch. He'd nearly lost his arm, then awoke in such severe and unexplained pain. Now she felt like crying, but not because she needed to. The crying was all Elliott. On some level, she'd connected with him, too. Her body shivered. She felt sick again. But was it Elliott feeling sick, or her? She didn't know.

Her powers were growing stronger, and it frightened her.

Chapter Forty-Seven

Bertan

Bertan stood facing his locker for what might've been hours. It felt like hours. It also felt like time had broken apart and become nothing. It had no meaning anymore. He was stunned, unable to bring himself to move.

He'd come in here to...what? Now he couldn't remember. He just stood there, staring into his locker at the photo leaning against a pair of goggles. It stared at him the way a beef's eye did right as it was about to be knocked.

It was a photo of Carmen and Gabriella. Their hands were bound in rope, resting in their laps. Cloth wrapped around their heads and covered their eyes. There was blood on Carmen's face. A note was stapled to her shirt. It read in all caps...tiny letters...scratchy:

YOU CAN NEVER LEAVE.

NOT NOW THAT WE HAVE THEM.

Stapled to Gabriella's shirt was the next message:

YOU OWE US.

WE WANT YOU, NOT YOUR MONEY.

RETURN TO MEDINA AND YOUR

FAMILY WILL BE FREE.

Bertan felt himself dropping away. He grabbed the photo and slammed the locker shut. Pushing the photo into his pocket, he managed to get out into the hallway before going lightheaded. He pressed his back against the wall and closed his eyes. It felt as though his eyes were darting around and around inside his head. He felt he might throw up. Kneeling over, he took a few breaths, and then he cried.

And then he stood up and walked himself into the Kill Floor.

#

The door to the plant manager's office stood cracked open. A yellow light seeped out of it and created a glow along the dark hallway floor. Bertan stepped up to the door and lifted his hand to knock, then heard Ruben talking softly.

"I know, I'm working on it," he whispered. "I need more time with him."

Bertan's ears lifted.

"Lana, I can't just ask him. It doesn't work like that. Hold on, I think someone's at the door. Hello?" Ruben called, his voice rising.

Bertan pressed the door open and stood there in the hall. He wondered if Ruben was talking about him. Ruben hung up the cell phone and set it on the desk.

"Come in, have a seat," Ruben said, grabbing a notepad and a manilla folder, then sitting down.

"Who was that?" Bertan asked, remaining in the hall. He figured it was his business if it was about him.

"Just another plant manager. We check in with each other every now and then."

"You talk about me?"

"Yes. I talk about a lot of the

workers."

"Okay," Bertan said, not sure if he believed Ruben.

"Look, anything personal you tell me, I keep to myself. I was trying to get you some extra money, but it didn't work," Ruben said, stopping. He eyed Bertan, and Bertan noticed a stern look in the man's face.

What if it was *him*? What if it was Ruben...who had his family kidnapped? It had to be someone who knew the combination to his locker. The only person he could remember giving it to was Serpentine. There was no way Ruben could've done it...

"We've got something we need to talk about," Ruben said. "Please, have a seat."

Okay, maybe he did do it, Bertan thought. He could feel himself falling down into the Knocker. He brought himself back, just to hear what Ruben had to say.

"Like what?" Bertan asked, shutting the door and sitting down across from Ruben. He crossed his arms and waited.

"Do you remember anything from

yesterday?"

"No. We only talked five minutes."

"Well," Ruben said, biting his lower lip. "You were actually here the entire break time."

"No I wasn't." Bertan sat up, feeling unsettled.

"I think you may not remember what happened."

"What are you talking about?"

"Bertan, can I ask you a few questions?"

"Sure." Bertan shrugged.

"Have you been losing track of time?"

Bertan leaned forward, gulped. "Yes," he said.

"Have you been feeling...like you're not yourself lately?"

"Yes," Bertan admitted.

"Are you blacking out?"

"What?" Bertan asked, confused.

"Are you missing long blocks of time, like you wake up or end up in places and you don't remember how you got there?"

Bertan's eyes shot up at the ceiling. A cold sweat developed along his forehead. He ran his fingers through his beard and nodded.

"How about any urges to hurt yourself, or others?" Ruben asked.

"No," Bertan lied, swallowing a hard knot in his throat.

"Okay," Ruben replied.

"Are you some kind of therapist or something?"

Ruben glanced up at Bertan.

"Okay," he said, pausing. "You've been honest with me, so maybe now it's time I'm honest with you. You just have to swear to me you won't share this with anyone."

"Depends what it is," Bertan said frankly.

"It's not about Medina, if that's what you're thinking."

Bertan looked into Ruben's eyes. He searched in there for the little dances that eyes make when they're lying. But they looked back at Bertan straight, clear, unmoving. This time, Ruben *was* telling the truth. Bertan hoped the man was about to give him proof that he was not the one who had his family kidnapped. Anyone in this facility could've done it.

"Okay, go ahead."

"I'm a social worker. I work undercover here."

"What do you mean, undercover?"

"I am a plant manager, but I'm also something else."

"What?" Bertan said, wishing the man would spit it out already.

"I'm a...an animal activist."

"What?" Bertan asked, nearly laughing. He sat up in the chair.

"I am working undercover to shut down S-Corp for their abusive labor practices and for how they treat the animals."

Bertan grinned. He believed Ruben, he just didn't *like* what the man was saying. This whole thing about how the animals were treated. They were just beefs. How else were they supposed to be *treated*?

"Please, don't tell anyone. If they find out, I could be put in prison for the rest of my life."

Bertan understood that. Same as if S-Corp found out—or anyone found out—that he was trying to get home, he'd be detained. Same thing. Now he *really* had to find a way back home to get his family back and kill whoever took them.

"I won't say anything," Bertan replied. "So you think there's something wrong with me?" he asked. It took effort to get back to the subject at hand.

"No, not at all. I think you may be responding to the trauma you've experienced, and that it was triggered by the disappearance of your family."

"I don't understand," Bertan said. He was beginning to think he might be mentally ill.

"When we experience trauma, like when you worked for Medina and you killed people —"

"But that never bothered me," Bertan interrupted.

"You may *think* it didn't bother you. Our minds are not designed to handle that level of trauma. All those years of killing, of violence-and whether you agree with me or not, even knocking cows. Trauma can cause the mind to...shut down."

"So when my mind shuts down, I black out?"

"You become like someone else."

"Someone else?" Bertan chuckled. He leaned back in the chair, smiling. "You're starting to sound wacko, Ruben."

"As a social worker who's worked with this kind of thing, I'm just telling you what I see. Yesterday you sat in that very chair, but as someone else."

"Oh yeah? Who?"

"The Knocker."

The Knocker. The words echoed in Bertan's mind. An image of the gun against a man's head, in a car, cash, flashed through his head. When he woke up this morning, an envelope of $500 hung from his jeans. And in this very moment, when he was trying so hard to stay present and not fall, maybe this is what Ruben meant...that he *fell* into the Knocker but was not aware of it until now.

Sweat dripped from his beard.

"Here," Ruben said, handing him a handkerchief.

Bertan took it and wiped his face and beard and went to hand it back.

"It's yours." Ruben smiled.

"I sweat a lot when I'm nervous," Bertan said.

"Are you nervous right now?"

"Of course, man. You're scaring the shit out of me."

"I'm sorry. That was not my intent. It's important that you understand what's happening, so you can make it better, if you want."

"Make it better? How?" Bertan said. He wasn't sure he believed all of this, yet it was also beginning to make sense.

"There are some types of therapies we can try, but it will take an open mind and a lot of practice."

Bertan thought for a moment. His back and chest were soaked with sweat. He shivered. He thought over things. This all definitely started when his family went missing. And the times he could no longer remember were the times he was at his knock job. Suddenly, he realized that all he could remember was his security job, putting on his smock for knocking and then taking it off again. He was losing track of entire days.

Shit, he said to himself, feeling a bit light-headed, frightened.

"So you said even knocking cows—beefs— is bad for the head?" Bertan asked.

"I believe so, yes. And plenty of studies show that."

"Then why would they let people do it?"

"Because, like you said, people love their steaks."

"Blackouts, losing time, all this started when my family disappeared," Bertan admitted.

"Yeah. That's why I think we can help you manage it."

Bertan looked away, down at the floor. He remembered all the nightmares and flashbacks he used to have when he was in Honduras and still with Medina. He remembered how he almost hit Carmen, and that was the last straw. Leave Medina or I will leave you, she had said.

"Bertan?" Ruben asked. "You okay?"

"No," he replied. Now it was time to say out loud what he really, really didn't want to be true.

"What's going on?"

"My family," Bertan answered, and then stopped.

The room got quiet. Bertan looked away from Ruben, at the wall behind him. The room closed in around him. Maybe, if he said it aloud, he wouldn't practically pass out this time.

"They've been kidnapped."

When he spoke it into being, his head throbbed. A hardness grew between his ribs and heart, like a protective wall. Although he'd said it, he couldn't *feel* it. The belief of it still was not there. The cross necklace Gabriella had made for him burned against his skin. The word kidnapped echoed in his mind.

"I'm so sorry," Ruben said, drawing near and pulling Bertan into his arms.

Bertan went cold. The pain was too much. It was Medina, they did this. He pulled away, looked at Ruben. He backed away and stood up.

He knew the Knocker was coming, and now he allowed it.

Bertan went for the door and threw it open.

Stepping out onto the Kill Floor, he stood beneath a bright, blinding light and stared. There to the right, a sanitation worker was scraping blood off the floor.

The Knocker reached into his pocket and

pulled out a piece of paper. On it was the name of the next man on Serpentine's list. One of the sanitation workers, perhaps the one there on the floor.

The Knocker slid the piece of paper back into his pocket and disappeared down the hall toward the locker room. It was time to get to work. He needed money to track down Medina and find his family.

Chapter Forty-Eight

Bray

Alice was alive but unconscious. That was always how it began. An electric gun ripped open a hole between her eyes. The pain shot back into her brain. Her life was split in two. A warmth rolled down her nose. It was soft, slow, like a whole life gone by without living. Head heavy, it dropped. Her body was pushed out and then flipped upside down. Suddenly the view changed and Bray was seeing everything from above. The knife came so quickly Bray couldn't even see it. The slit was a clear line against Alice's throat, and then blood spat out like angry seas in a hurricane. The pain was a stinging, opening and shattering scream...ripping apart carotid arteries and killing whatever life remained.

Bray shot up in bed. Her eyes wide, she looked around at the bare walls. Her throat hurt again and, for the first time, her head ached between her eyes. She panicked. Sweat covered her body as she tried catching up with a long-gone breath. How did she end up back here? Surely her parents didn't find her. How could they?

Through the haze, a natural light appeared. It came from her left. She glanced up. Beside her, a window looked down, morning coming in to remind her where she was.

Across from her stood a dresser, a chair and a door. An open door. She wasn't in the psych ward after all. She must've come in to this room last night and passed out in the bed.

She took a deep breath, stood up, and went downstairs. There, Elliott was in the kitchen, eating out of a can of beans.

"Hey. You look how I feel," he said, "Here's some beans. Surely you can eat those."

"How are you feeling?" she asked, taking the open can and peering inside. The beans were runny, unappealing. She took a fork that had been sitting out on the counter and started eating.

"Like I almost lost an arm."

"Yeah." She smiled, though regretfully.

They stood quietly while they ate.

"Oh, almost forgot," he said. "Check this out."

Elliott handed her an old, yellowed newspaper. Its bottom pages fell apart in her hand, landed like leaves on the tile floor. It was dated June 19, 2029. On the front cover, a photo of the town of Casper with a flowing river beside it. The front page read:

"As Water Shortages Loom, Casper Migrates South."

Bray set the beans back down. She pulled the paper up to her face, reading the article. Something about S-Corp using the water from the North Platte River.

She didn't need to read any further. She dropped the paper on the counter.

"Of course," she said. "They took the

water. That's why everyone left."

"Yep. It's what I figured," Elliott
replied, walking over and picking up the
paper. "I need this, for proof."

"Proof?"

"It matches my theory about S-Corp. I know
they had something to do with the water
crisis, maybe even with that terrorist
attack."

"And your parents?" she asked.

"Yes. It's why I need to head up to Red
Lodge."

"But why Red Lodge?"

"I have friends up there. They can help me
get settled, start over. They've got some
resources."

It all made sense. Bray watched Elliott
place the newspaper in a plastic bag and
carefully wrap it like a Christmas gift.

"Listen, about that," she said. "I owe you
an apology."

His eyes darted over to hers.

"I'm sorry I expected you to help me get
out here. I know you had your own plans to

get to Montana, and I feel like I derailed them for my own interests—"

"Bray," he interrupted. "We're friends."

"I know. But let me finish."

Elliott took a breath, but said nothing.

"I haven't told you the truth, not since the beginning. That wasn't fair to you."

"What truth?" he asked.

"About four years ago, I linked up with this pig. Her name is Alice."

"She has a name?"

"I gave it to her. After my grandma."

"Okay."

"I've been communicating with her ever since. Right before I escaped the psych ward, I got injured."

"You mean that burn on your back?"

"Yes. Alice had gotten shocked on her back by an electric prod, and then I ended up with this wound."

Elliott looked at her.

"Are you sure you're not mentally unstable? Maybe we do need to take you back to that psych ward."

"Shut up," she said. "Seriously. I can get injured when she gets injured. We're linked."

"You've got superpowers," he said jokingly.

"What is with you?" she asked.

"I'm a bit loopy, from the meds."

"Right, sorry. Anyway, I found out she's being transported to slaughter. Today."

"And you're afraid something might happen to you if she dies?"

"Yes. But that's not as important as trying to save her."

Elliott nodded. He tossed the can into the empty trash bin, shrugged his shoulders.

"What I'm really trying to say is that I lied to you, because I thought you wouldn't believe me. I was afraid you'd make fun of me. I got so wrapped up in my own stuff that I just didn't acknowledge your own needs to get where you were going."

Elliott nodded, looked her in the eye.

"I'm really sorry. I feel like this whole

thing is because of me," she said, starting to cry.

Elliott reached out to her with his other hand.

"I'm okay," she said, composing herself. "I just want you to know that I realized some things last night. I need to go, now. You can stay back. I'm asking you to stay, get rested, so you can go to Montana and find out about your parents. I don't want you to delay that for me. You've already done so much, more than I can ever repay—"

"It is true I've done a lot for you," he said. "And I do need to rest a bit longer."

Bray nodded. She felt afraid to go on without him, but she knew it was right. Finally, she knew what to do to help both her friends.

"I'm not sure I'll ever truly believe this whole linking with animals thing, but I do support you at least getting as far away from your parents as possible, if nothing else."

"Thanks," she said. "And I hope you find out what happened to yours. I can't imagine how hard it is, not knowing."

Elliott stood there quietly. Bray walked over and hugged him. His good arm came around her back as his hand rested on her waist. Bray loved Elliott's hugs. Safe, warm, whole. As they embraced, she thought how he really was the closest person in her life. Her only family outside of Alice, whom she couldn't guarantee she could find.

Bray ran back upstairs. In the room where she'd slept the night before, she pulled open the dresser drawers. They were empty. No chance for a change of clothes. Over in the closet she found a few shoe boxes on the floor. She opened each one until she found a pair of sandals and put them on. They were one size too large. She remembered seeing some duct tape down in the garage.

Bray walked downstairs and into the garage. She found the duct tape and Elliott helped her tape the sandals to her feet. When they returned to the kitchen, a bag of canned goods sat on the counter.

"Those are for you...Beans. Perfectly vegan," he said, smiling.

Bray took the bag and smiled back, a feeling of sadness approaching her heart.

"I found something for you," he said. "Come outside."

Bray followed Elliott out into the sunlit morning. There on the driveway stood a bike.

"Thought you could use this. To get where you're going a little faster."

"Perfect." She smiled.

Bray turned to Elliott and looked at him. There was really no reason to delay. She had to find Alice, and the longer she stood there, the more she missed Elliott.

"I love you, Elliott," she said.

"Yep. Same, same. Take care out there," he said, grinning.

Bray turned and got on the bike. She pulled the bag on over her back. Elliott stepped back up to the front door and turned to her.

"Hey kiddo," he called.

She glanced back at him.

"Be sure to come to Red Lodge, look me up."

Bray smiled, nodded in agreement, and lifted the kickstand with her foot. Knowing this could be the last time, in possibly all of her life, that she'd ever see him, she got a glimpse of him one last time before he went inside. He waved to her and smiled.

Looking out into the light of morning, she felt pulled open. Like a vast and empty desert full of the unknown. A place cleared inside of her, expanded, grew. She felt so many things at once. Her guidance system was fully intact, ready to show her the way.

Now she would go alone. She reached down into her pants pocket and pulled out the worry stone. On it, she read the carved quote: Love ALL beings equally.

It was the only way she knew how to love Elliott now, by letting him go.

Chapter Forty-Nine

Kage

Kage was taken quickly. He couldn't fight them, as they had him cuffed and were dragging him down the hall.

"I want to see Dianna Hoffman!" he yelled, hoping still to blackmail the woman for the info he so desperately needed.

The guards remained silent. They were both wearing civilian clothing, yet their faces were covered by their masks and dark blue sunglasses. This was how he knew they were S-Corp and not Marshals, which meant they probably weren't able to arrest him. Most likely, he was being taken somewhere worse.

This place certainly was a giant maze. The guards each had him by an arm. They walked urgently, twisting deeper and deeper down hallways. Kage would never find his way out of this place. Soon they approached what appeared to be a dead end: a gray wall just

like all the rest. But then one of the
guards pressed into the wall beside him and
the wall slid open. It was an elevator.

The guards pulled Kage inside. The door
shut.

"Either of you mind telling me what the
hell's up with those embryos?" Kage asked.

"Shut up," one of them said and jabbed him
in the stomach with his elbow. Kage felt the
wind temporarily knocked out of him.

When the elevator door slid open, what
Kage saw gave him pause, again. The large,
open room, the size of an entire floor,
spanned out before him. The ceilings hung
low, with plenty of fluorescent lights
shining down on a tile floor. Looked to be
an old office building but without desks or
people.

Well, there was just one person. A man in
a gray blazer and pink shirt. He was
Hispanic and looked to be about forty years
old. He had on transitional blue glasses.
Beside him sat an empty folding chair, which
Kage knew was for him. He was disappointed

he wasn't going to meet Dianna Hoffman.

The guards yanked Kage out of the elevator. They led him to the chair and sat him down. One of them cuffed his wrist to the chair's back leg. The other walked back over to the wall by the elevator, turned, stood and stared at Kage.

"Who are you and what the hell are you doing on our property?" the man asked, glaring down at Kage.

Kage found the man instantly creepy. Maybe it was the glasses or the musky scent that wafted from his body.

"I can ask the same of you," Kage replied.

"Ha," the man let out a laugh. "Okay, sure. My name is Carl. I'm S-Corp's Regional Midwest President. Now, your turn."

Kage shook his head and turned away. The other guard, who stood over at the far end of the room, was positioned in front of the only exit. When Kage recognized the tall windows that had been boarded up, he knew where he was.

"I'll just cut to the chase," Kage

replied. "I saw all those embryos down there. And the pigs, the chickens. Whatever you're doing here doesn't appear to be ethical, apparent by this large building you're using to hide your underground lab."

"And your point?" Carl asked, seemingly unaffected by his words.

"I know things. Lots of things. About your past, about the Oxygen 11 fiasco," Kage said. He felt his heart beat through his ribs. "And if you give me some info, I'll keep my mouth shut."

"Ha!" Carl laughed. "You are cuffed to a chair. You trespassed on our property. You're in no position to blackmail me."

Carl nodded at the guard by the elevator.

"Keep him here till morning. I've got just the punishment," he said, smiling.

Carl turned and walked up to the door. He stopped beside the guard.

"You want us to do anything with her?" the guard asked Carl.

"It's him," Kage yelled, his blood boiling.

"Just let him sit there. Bring him some water," Carl replied, opening the door.

Outside, Kage could see the dark night holding strong. He'd be here for hours.

#

Kage's arm went limp. It hung painfully down along the side of the chair where his wrist was cuffed to the chair leg. His neck and back throbbed. They'd brought him water but he kicked it away. *Mother fuckers*. As soon as morning came, he'd show these assholes.

No sooner did he think that than did the door open. A pair of men entered, both wearing white lab coats. Scientists, he assumed. One was bald but appeared not much older than Kage. The other was the same man he'd attacked in the hall when he broke in. He was carrying a black box. Kage stiffened. Perhaps they were going to give him some truth serum or torture him into talking.

But what he saw next scared him far

more than anything inside that box.

Through the door walked a man dressed in skinny jeans and a black polo shirt. He pulled with him a woman in pajamas. Her long, dark hair was mangled as if she'd been pulled out of bed. Kage recognized her eyes immediately.

It was Lana. He could tell she'd been crying.

Chapter Fifty

The Knocker

The Knocker found himself alone in the locker room, standing in his boxer shorts and undershirt. His clothes were scattered on the floor.

He opened his locker and pulled out his stained smock. There was also a gun in the locker. His eyes narrowed. Why would a gun be in his locker? It didn't matter, he needed it. Maybe God left it for him. He clicked on the safety and slid the gun down in his shorts, pulling the smock on over his body. A few pairs of goggles hung from the wall. He took a pair and unwrapped them from their package, slid them on to hide his eyes.

The Knocker marched out into the Clean Side. There, the sanitation worker was beside the entrance, his back to the Knocker as he lined a garbage can with a new garbage bag. The Knocker's eyes followed the hallway down into the offices. Everything was dark. Doors were closed. There seemed to be no one else around.

The Knocker ran quietly up to the worker and grabbed him around the neck from behind. The man, whom the Knocker knew only as Ramiro, was probably no older than eighteen. He grabbed at the Knocker's forearm, which was lodged against his throat. The garbage bag he held dropped to the floor.

"Shit," Ramiro said through clenched teeth.

"You owe Serpentine money. I've come to collect."

"Fuck you," Ramiro said.

Ramiro bit down on the Knocker's arm. The Knocker flinched. His grip loosened. Ramiro gripped his wrist with both hands. He somehow managed to flip the Knocker's arm around so that he was now behind the Knocker. The Knocker's arm twisted behind his back in a painful and unnatural way.

"Son of a bitch!" the Knocker screamed. He

yanked his foot backwards, the toe of his boot met Ramiro's calf. The Knocker flipped Ramiro over his foot. Ramiro landed hard on the ground with a crack. The Knocker came down onto his chest with his knee. Ramiro huffed, his eyes wincing.

"You owe Serpentine $1,000 and you're going to get it to me tonight," the Knocker said.

"I only owe him $500, asshole," Ramiro replied, his hands trying to push the Knocker's knee away from his chest.

The Knocker pulled out the gun that hid under his shorts. He pressed it into Ramiro's ear.

"Guns don't scare me," Ramiro said. "You can kill me if you want. I ain't got nothing to live for."

"Yeah? It's not the dying that should worry you. It's what I'm going to do to you instead."

Ramiro gulped but said nothing.

The Knocker grabbed Ramiro by his hair and pulled him out onto the Kill Floor. Ramiro whimpered. The Knocker yanked him over to the Knock Box and pressed a button. The chute opened.

"Get inside," the Knocker said.

"You're sick, man!" Ramiro cried. "I ain't getting in there."

That made the Knocker think about his family. Medina wanted him to trade his life for theirs. Surely Ramiro worked for Medina, so he had to know where the Knocker's family was.

Holding tightly to Ramiro's hair, the Knocker pulled him over to the hanging electric prods. He slid the gun back into his boxers and pulled a prod off the wall. He stuck the prod against Ramiro's neck and an electric shock jolted through the man's body. The Knocker lost his grip of Ramiro's hair and Ramiro fell to the ground, screaming. The Knocker pressed him in the lower back and shocked him a second time.

"Ahhh! Fuck!" Ramiro yelled.

"I said get in the box." The Knocker shocked him again.

Ramiro crawled into the box, and his head poked out the other side. The Knocker stepped over to his station and picked up the knock gun. He turned and pressed it into Ramiro's forehead.

"Now, if I place the knock gun right here and pull the trigger, it won't kill you. It'll knock you unconscious, but not without causing so much pain you'll bite off your own tongue. You want that?" the Knocker asked. "You want to walk around this world without a fucking tongue? You want to tell people you lost your tongue while sitting in a fucking knock box?"

"No!" Ramiro shouted.

"Then give me the goddamn money."

"Okay, okay!"

The Knocker hung the knock gun on the wall and opened the chute, allowing Ramiro back out. Ramiro fell out onto the ground, shaking and crying.

"Where's the money?" the Knocker said, pulling the gun back out.

"I got it, I got it," Ramiro said,

reaching for his wallet. He handed the Knocker a pile of bills that were soaked with sweat. The Knocker held them carefully in his fingers, counted the money, and put it in his pocket.

"You still owe $300 more."

"I'll bring it to Serpentine tomorrow."

The Knocker leaned down and pointed the gun at Ramiro.

"I know you ain't afraid of guns, but now I know what you are afraid of. If Serpentine doesn't get the money tomorrow, I'll come find you. I'll bring you back here and make sure you understand exactly how the Kill Floor works. Got it?"

Ramiro nodded.

"And one more thing." The Knocker leaned down and neared Ramiro's face.

"What man?"

"Where's my family?"

"What?"

"Where is my fucking family?"

"I don't know what you're talking about," Ramiro said, shaking.

The Knocker pressed the gun harder into Ramiro's skull.

"Medina has my family," the Knocker said, pulling out the photo and showing it to Ramiro.

"Oh shit, man. I swear I don't know. I only smuggle drugs for them, nothing else. I swear!"

The Knocker pulled the gun away and walked around the knock box, then turned and faced Ramiro. He looked the man in the eye.

"I'll ask one more time," the Knocker said in a gentle voice. "Where...is...my family?"

Ramiro's eyes darted around the room and then closed.

"I don't know, but I can ask around, find out."

The Knocker took a deep breath. It would've been a lot easier if Ramiro had known. Now he would have to keep searching, and he had no idea how much time he had. He assumed they'd leave him another message tomorrow as that's how things worked with Medina. They'd leave you a little nasty note

without all the information, then they'd
come back with the final punch after you
spent an entire day screaming in fear.

"Get the fuck out of here," the Knocker
said, sitting down on the cold concrete
floor.

Ramiro pulled himself up and ran down the
hall for the Clean Side, his shoes slapping
against the concrete as he went.

The Knocker leaned back against the wall.
He set the gun down on the floor. Closing
his eyes, he took a few deep breaths.
Removing the goggles, he opened his eyes and
looked out into the dark Kill Floor, the
only home he knew anymore.

Across from him, golden dust particles
gathered and rose from the floor. They
danced and twisted into an image of that
farm in Bajo Aguan. The little naked boy
quickly ran along the land and then
disappeared. The Knocker sat up, rubbed his
eyes. The image repeated itself. First an
empty farm and then that naked boy, stomach
distended, running and then disappearing. It

happened again and again as if the scene were some broken film stuck on one scene.

The Knocker stood up. The image disappeared. The hairs on his arms rose, goosebumps traveled up to his neck and along his back. He shivered. His eyes stared out into the dark, watering in fear. Bending down slowly, he grabbed the gun and held it out in the empty air. He stood there, frozen. He wanted the image to come back-and then he didn't. He wanted to run but couldn't. His heart stuck in his throat.

The decision to stay and wait for the image to return overcame him. Sitting back down, he set the gun beside his leg and gulped. He waited, his eyes growing heavy with exhaustion. When was the last time he'd slept? He forced his eyes back open, only to see more darkness. Finally the silence and exhaustion won and he passed out.

Chapter Fifty-One

Bertan

Something tapped against his knee. He felt it but didn't want to wake up. Sleep had come deep and full and void of nightmares, and he didn't want it to end.

Then he felt something brush against his arm. Again, and then again. Finally Bertan forced his eyes open and looked up.

A sanitation worker was pushing at him with a mop.

"What the hell you doing, man? Get up," the worker said.

"Huh?" Bertan said, confused. Looking down, his smock was wrapped around his body like a blanket. He looked down to see that he was wearing only an undershirt and his boxers. His boxers were wet, and beneath where he lay a puddle had formed.

Bertan was accustomed to peeing himself at night. It was those damn diapers. He'd worn them so often that when he didn't have one on, he couldn't control his bladder.

The sanitation worker laughed and moved on along the Kill Floor.

The Kill Floor? he asked himself. *What the fuck?*

He thought back to yesterday. The last thing he remembered was being in Ruben's office. *Gabriella!* Was that photo he found in his locker real? How could he know anymore what was real and what was...what was happening to him?

"Hey," Bertan shouted over to the sanitation worker, who was mopping beside the serpentine. "What time is it?"

"Four a.m.," the man replied.

That gave him about two hours to go home, change and get back to work. He hoped he wasn't supposed to work last night. These gaps of time between blackouts were getting shorter and shorter. He remembered less and less of his life.

One of the beefs called out from the holding pens. It wouldn't stop. Usually they

were pretty quiet. Bertan pulled his smock
from around himself and stood up. Inside one
of the pockets was a wad of cash. He wrapped
the smock in his arm to hide the cash. He
wanted to escape out back so as not to risk
being seen half-naked by any more workers,
but he'd have to pass the holding pens to
get there.

Bertan stepped up to the holding pens. The
crying beef was sitting in the center of one
of the pens, surrounded by other beefs. The
lights in the Kill Floor were dim, so Bertan
could not see that anything was wrong. For
once he could not help looking into the
beef's eyes. They popped out like shining
stars in some strange night sky. But then
the whites of them started to look so pale
they were too unsettling to be like stars.
They expanded. They reminded Bertan of all
the times he'd come home to Carmen and
Gabriella after days of doing squad work for
Medina. Always he came home in the dark of
night. Bajo Aguan was far from any city, so
when the stars were out, they were

spectacularly quiet, dancing on and off with perfect timing.

Bertan had accepted the promotion with Medina so he could support his family. Everything he did, he did for Carmen. He left home to get better work here—not only because home was dangerous, but also because he could do better for his family. He'd sacrificed everything so he wouldn't lose them, and he had lost them anyway.

As he stood there and stared into the beef's eye, he saw that the whites of them popped out in fear. The beefs knew what was coming to them.

Bertan stared at the beefs, and his hairs stood on end. A chill raced down his spine. He shivered. He could look at them no longer. He turned away and ran out to his car.

#

That day disappeared as if it had never happened. Bertan began to wonder if Ruben was right. Maybe he was mentally unstable.

He wasn't so sure it could be helped, though. He now sat in his guard uniform, in the office, staring blankly at the surveillance videos. His fingers rubbed at the wooden cross on his dog chain, the one Gabriella had made for him.

A bulkiness in his back pocket caused him to shift and pull out his wallet. Hundreds of dollars of cash were waiting for him to hide away in his lockbox. He couldn't remember working enough to make this much money, but...whatever.

In one of the surveillance videos, a transport truck pulled up to the front gates. Bertan closed the wallet and pressed it back into his pocket. He stood up. He leaned over and pressed a button on the far wall and the gates opened.

The transport truck jumped forward. Bertan left the office and jogged down to the back of the Kill Floor, past the now-empty holding pens. Stopping at a wide, metal door, he grabbed a walkie-talkie from the wall. He went to call for two sanitation workers to help bring in the beefs, but then forgot their names.

"Hey...I need two workers down here to bring in the beefs," he called. Returning the walkie-talkie to its place on the wall, he pressed a button beside the door and it rattled open, slowly.

Bertan stood there waiting as the door lifted to reveal the transport truck backing up to the ledge of the Kill Floor. The engine shut off. A white man in jeans and a black long-sleeved shirt jumped down and approached the back of the truck. Just as he began to open the trailer doors, the two sanitation workers arrived. One was already holding an electric prod.

The trailer was packed full of beefs. Bertan wondered how many. Probably a couple hundred. He would send them all to their deaths tomorrow, yet he couldn't remember the last time he knocked a beef.

"You gonna help me with these damn things or what?" the driver screamed back to the workers.

Bertan stepped back beside the empty pen and watched. As the security guard, he was tasked with ensuring all the beefs got inside without issue. But he wasn't about to help them do it.

The second sanitation worker reached for a cattle prod that hung against the wall. Meanwhile the truck driver let down a ramp from the trailer. Bertan stood tense, staring at the crowd of beefs as they stood before death.

The truck driver disappeared into the trailer. In all the darkness Bertan could only see the first five beefs, their heads poking out from the blackness of the trailer. A buzzing sound came from inside the trailer. The floor of the trailer slowly rose one foot, then two feet up, and the beefs slid toward the ramp. They mooed. The first beef slid down the ramp toward the first sanitation worker. He aided the second worker in pushing the beef up to standing. The workers both prodded it in the back and it shrieked as it was forced forward into the empty holding pen beside Bertan. They continued on like this, one beef after another.

The remaining five beefs were now sitting in the corner of the trailer. They refused to move. The workers prodded at them and used all their body weight to get one of the beefs to move, but nothing seemed to work. The truck driver grabbed a cattle prod from a worker and approached the beefs.

"C'mon motherfuckers," he screamed, hitting one in the back and then another. They cried out but still would not move.

The driver dropped the cattle prod and jumped down from the trailer, disappearing into the front cab. He returned a moment later with a rope. Both workers just stood there, watching him.

"Will y'all stop standing there and fucking help me?" The driver glared at the workers.

The workers followed him over to one of the beefs. Bertan froze as he watched the driver tie the rope around a beef's neck.

One worker stood behind the beef and
repeatedly shocked the beef with the cattle
prod. Bertan flinched in response. He
couldn't understand why, but this whole
thing was beginning to set him off. He had a
bad feeling about the driver.

The driver pulled at the rope, forcing the
beef to standing. He and the sanitation
workers pushed and pulled until the beef
walked down the ramp and into the holding
pen. Once they got the beef inside the pen,
the driver removed the rope and wiped sweat
from his face.

"Are you just going to stand there?" the
driver said as he stepped up to Bertan.

Bertan said nothing. He smelled alcohol on
the man's breath. He clenched his fists and
his jaw.

The driver rolled his eyes and ran back
into the trailer. He grabbed the cattle prod
that he'd dropped earlier and started
hitting the beefs with it. The workers stood
back. The cattle prod rose up into the air.
In the dark night it reminded Bertan of

another time. But then it came down madly onto the beefs and they screamed. Bertan turned his head, felt sick to his stomach.

Somewhere in it all there was laughter.

"This is gonna take all night," the driver said after he and the two workers pulled another beef into the pen. "Would go a lot faster if this pussy would help us." He laughed, pointing at Bertan.

"Oh, he ain't no pussy," one of the sanitation workers replied. "He's the Knocker."

"Well, I've had about enough of this," the driver said. He pulled a gun from behind his back and lifted it into the air. "I'm going to scare them and you push them into the pen, got it?" he said to the workers.

The Knocker? Bertan said to himself. *Am I, though?*

And then a gunshot echoed inside the trailer. The bullet grazed the metal roof and then escaped out into the sky.

Bertan was twenty-two. Two squad members had driven him to see a palm plantation. The campesino who owned the land was refusing to hand it over to Medina. They brought Bertan out on his first test, to see how he'd react.

The night was hotter than day. Lightening flashed across the sky and brought no sign of reprieve. It only served to light up the sky in violent, frightening mystery. It made Bertan nearly pee his pants.

They pulled up to a thirty-foot-tall fence just outside the plantation and shut off the car. Bertan and the two other squad men, Carlos and Juan, got out and broke down the fence within minutes. They stomped through the plantation, where thin, tall palm oil trees danced with the wind.

Bertan stood outside the campesino's house and waited. They brought the man out and dropped him to his knees, right in front of Bertan. The man was old, probably in his fifties. He certainly was not capable of defending himself.

Carlos stepped up to Bertan and held out a gun.

"You know what to do," the man said.

Bertan's eyes met the gun. It stared at him, waiting. He reached up and took it in his hand. It was heavy in his grip. He'd shot a gun before, but not at another person.

"C'mon Bertan. We ain't got all night," Juan said, crossing his arms. "Just close your eyes, point and shoot." The man pointed at Carlos with his finger and pretended to shoot. "Pow. Just like that. It'll happen so fast he won't feel a thing."

Won't feel a thing...won't feel a thing...

The words echoed in Bertan's mind. The plant manager had told him that on his hiring day, when Bertan asked whether the beefs would feel anything when he knocked them.

Bertan raised the gun to the campesino's head. Carlos used his free hand to pull the campesino's head up by his hair. Bertan pushed the gun in between the old man's eyes. The old man closed his eyes and whimpered and shook.

"I'm sorry," Bertan whispered, tears streaming down his face-tears that he didn't notice because he had detached from his body and was now looking down at himself from above.

He knew that if he waited, it would just get worse. So he pulled the trigger and that was it. He had changed after that. All he wanted as he watched them bury the old man's body in the vast open land for the birds to eat was to take all those squad workers and strangle them to death. He imagined himself running up to one of them, pushing him down and getting on top of him.

It felt so real, like he could feel the neck muscles and soft tissue beneath his thumbs. Hot energy burned through his arms and hands. Fingers reached up and grabbed at his nostrils. Bertan lifted the man's head up and slammed it down onto the metal flooring.

Beefs moaned.

Beefs?

Bertan shook off the noises and closed his eyes and squeezed. He'd show this asshole, for making him kill that old man.

"Sto—" The syllable spat from the man's mouth, and hands now slapped at Bertan's arms. He felt himself getting warmer.

"Sto-ooooooppppppp!"

Bertan opened his eyes and glared down. His eyes widened as he suddenly recognized the man struggling beneath his weight.

"Shit!" Bertan shouted. His heart raced as he pulled away from the truck driver and fell backwards until his back met steel behind him.

His face red as he massaged his throat, the transport truck driver sat up slowly and spit blood onto the bed of the trailer. A worker ran up and pressed a cattle prod against Bertan's chest to prevent him from moving.

"Fuck! What the fuck was that?" the driver screamed.

"I-I don't know," Bertan responded. He

shook his head and checked himself. He wasn't in Honduras. He wasn't twenty-two. There was no squad member. He was at the plant. The beefs were getting free from the transport truck. He raised his arms at the sanitation worker to show he was not going to further harm anyone. The other worker helped the truck driver to standing.

"I'm sorry. I thought you were someone else."

"Someone else? Who the fuck would I be?" The driver rejected Bertan's outstretched hand.

"Please," Bertan pleaded. "Don't tell management about this."

"Don't tell management? You almost killed me!" The driver's voice sounded strained as if he was about to cry.

"I know. I don't know what was happening. I was...it was like I was somewhere else."

"Whatever." The man wiped blood from his nose with his shirt.

"I'm sorry," Bertan said. "Please, I can't lose this job."

"You have cash on you?"

Bertan felt flush and sick to his stomach. The sanitation workers both eyed the driver, but said nothing. The one holding the prod against Bertan's chest turned and looked down into Bertan's eyes. He pulled the cattle prod away, allowing Bertan to stand up. As he did, Bertan pulled his wallet from his back pocket.

"Here, it's all I got," he said, handing it to the man.

"A thousand dollars? Damn, boy, you're rich," the driver said, smiling. And then his smile shut off like a light, shifting into a narrow frown.

He grabbed Bertan by his hair and pulled.

"Ah!" Bertan screamed.

"You two better get the rest of those beefs inside," the driver said to the workers. The both of them looked at the driver, to Bertan, and then to each other. A second later they ran out.

The driver yanked Bertan into the building. Bertan tried to resist. The man

pulled him into his chest and wrapped his
arm around Bertan's throat. Now Bertan was
stuck. His eyes darted around for the
workers, but they were nowhere in sight.

The driver pushed Bertan over past the
knock box and stopped at the row of chains
that hung down from the floor. Bertan
gripped and pulled at the man's arm, but to
no avail. The man tightened his grip. He let
go of Bertan's hair with his hand and
reached up. Pulling down a chain, he wrapped
it around Bertan's neck, removing his arm.
He let go of Bertan, and Bertan stood there,
near choking.

"Can you breathe?" the driver asked.

Bertan shook his head, pulling at the
chains.

The man loosened them and Bertan let out a
heavy exhale, nearly passing out. The driver
walked over to the wall nearest the trailer
and found another prod. He took it down from
the wall and returned to Bertan. He was
smiling. He pushed the electric prod into
Bertan's side. The shot ran through his

body, and his body shook. Bertan screamed
out, tried not to lose his footing for fear
of choking on the chains. The driver laughed
and shocked Bertan two more times, once in
the side and another in the groin. Bertan
screamed, now in anger, and spat toward the
driver.

"Ooh. Getting angry now, huh?" the driver
said. He looked up at his truck. The
sanitation workers had gotten all the beefs
inside the holding pens. "Well, consider
yourself lucky. All the cows are in and I
gotta go. You can see yourself out of those
chains."

The driver dropped the cattle prod and
looked at Bertan. Bertan stood and glared at
the man. They eyed each other for a moment.
If it wasn't for Bertan's immigration status
and desperate need for his job, this man
would be dead already. But that was not the
way things were. He was stuck in a vicious,
never-ending cycle, and now he'd lost all
the money he'd saved to find the coyotaje.
No matter which way he turned, he was

screwed. And what was more concerning to him in that moment than anything else was that he was most definitely losing his mind.

The driver laughed and disappeared out to the truck. One of the sanitation workers shut the back door. Bertan frantically pulled the chains off from around his neck. He fell to his knees. The workers ran over to him.

"You okay, man?" one of them asked, putting his hand on Bertan's shoulder.

"Yeah," Bertan replied.

The beefs called out from the holding pens. Bertan turned and glanced up at the pens. His side and groin burned from the electric prod. He pulled up his shirt and touched the red and brown burns. They stung. If this is what the beefs felt, then for once he could respect their pain, if it was true what Ruben said, that they could feel it.

Bertan stood up and walked over to the pens. The beefs stood like stone. The pen was too full for them to move much. Their eyes were wide. From his work in the squad, he could sense fear from a mile away. There was plenty of it in here tonight. It shook him and he walked away from it.

Chapter Fifty-Two

Bray

Bray struggled along the Wyoming terrain. Who knew how much time had passed since she left Elliott, but it felt like hours. She rode parallel to the highway, keeping far enough away that she wouldn't be seen by any passersby. Her feet pushed and pushed into the bike's pedals as it crawled and pushed through dried grass, dodged sage brush, and bounced off fist-sized rocks.

She was exhausted. Her arms burned and ached and tingled from grasping the bike handles. At least the burn wound had subsided with the aid of the honey.

After a while she grew so hungry and dizzy she had to stop. The bag of beans Elliott had given her was hanging from her shoulder. As Bray walked over and sat down on the ground, the highway half a mile away to her left, she pulled it off and looked inside. There were two cans, a knife and a fork.

"Good old Elliott," she whispered, smiling.

Using the knife to cut open one of the cans took all the arm strength she had, which wasn't much. Seeing the knife drove her mind to places no mind should go: death, loneliness, pain, cutting and chopping and slitting and whatever else Alice would succumb to. She hated how she used animals for her own benefit, and how she used Elliott. She wanted to reach out to Alice now, but feared it would only slow her down. The instinct inside her said she had hours yet to go. She wasn't sure her body could handle another second on that bike.

But what choice did she have? Walking? That would more than double her time. And when the transport truck passed this way, she wouldn't be able to stop it. How was she going to stop it?

She didn't know. She shook off the thought and started eating the black beans.

They were room temperature and tasted like
mushy cardboard. But she ate them anyway.
She put the empty can, fork and knife back
into the bag and got back on the bike. Now
that she had stopped for a break, her
muscles felt even more weak. She sat on the
bike and stared ahead. Miles and miles of
prairie, a few mesas popping up here and
there. Not much else.

Bray started moving again. Her leg
muscles ached as she pushed the pedals. It
felt like riding through molasses. At this
rate, the transport truck was sure to pass
her by. Yes, it would pass by, blow up dust
in its wake, and move on down the road with
no knowledge of Bray's existence.

The bike stopped. Bray planted her feet
on the ground. She stared at the highway.
Who was she to try to help Alice? Of course
their friendship meant the world to her, but
that didn't change the fact that Bray was
just some five-foot-three seventeen-year-old
who could link with animals. What was so
special about that?

Bray stepped off the bike, let it drop to the ground. As it lay there on its side, an image of Alice lying there flashed through her mind. What did it all matter?

She turned away, tears building in her eyes. Coming down to her knees, she cried into her hands. This was all too much. She was so tired her body could hardly move. She wasn't going to catch the transport truck. And even if she were able to catch it, she didn't think she could stop it.

She came down and lay on her side. Curling up in fetal position, she cried more. Maybe she should just say goodbye to Alice now, let it be. Then if she died out here alone, at least no one would have to see it. The crying slowed. Her eyes grew heavy. The exhaustion took over and pulled her into sleep.

#

Something nudged her face. It felt both

soft and prickly. Like fur. Bray's eyes slowly opened. A wet, black nose and tan snout sniffed her face. She jumped up.

There before her stood an entire stable of wild horses. The same ones that had helped her and Elliott.

"What are you doing out here alone?" they asked. She heard it as a thought but knew it was coming from them.

"I was trying to get somewhere," Bray said, rubbing the tiredness from her eyes. "But I must've fallen asleep."

"Do you need help?"

Bray looked at them. They stood around her intently. If she said yes, wouldn't she be taking advantage of them...again? She was tired of feeling like she was using everyone rather than doing the work on her own. It made her feel low.

"No," she replied. "I just needed a rest."

"We can get you where you're going much faster."

"I know, thank you. I just need to do this on my own."

"Very well then. Just don't give up. She needs you."

"What?" Bray said, looking into the eyes of the closest horse.

But they said nothing. One of them nodded to her, and off they went. The stable swiftly pranced off toward the horizon, away from the highway.

"How could they know about Alice?" she asked herself. "Makes no sense."

She stood and watched them. Their bodies shrank in the distance. *She needs you*. It continued to baffle her, what they'd said. But now the sun had traveled up higher in the sky. She was losing time.

Grabbing a few swigs of water from a bottle in the pack Elliott had given her, she set out again on the bike. She still wasn't confident she'd make any difference when she encountered the transport truck, but with more rest and energy, she decided to keep on anyway. She couldn't just stay where she was.

A couple more hours passed. The bike

slowed again. The tiredness and aching returned. The transport truck would have to be passing through eventually, unless her instincts were off.

She heard a strange sound behind her. A buzzing, and then another. It got louder: buzz-buzz, buzz-buzz. Bray glanced up in the sky.

Perps.

Bray pushed hard into the bike's pedals. As she pressed on through an increasing amount of rock formations, the perps drew closer. The wind picked up around her.

"No!" Bray screamed against the rising wind. She wouldn't let them stop her. Alice was too close now. She could feel it. Her heart pumped up into her chest, just below her neck. She leaned forward, riding faster.

The perps were right above her now. She couldn't hear anything but wind and buzzing. Rocks kicked up from the ground and hit her in the face. She squinted her eyes to protect them.

A buzzing sound approached. A perp dropped

down beside her face. Its speed matched hers. There was no outrunning it. She felt its air against her cheek. Lights flashed on its nose. Just like that time in the fake flower patch back in Denver. Disgusting, how close they got.

Something whizzed past her ear. The front tire was punctured. Her body was sent into the air. Her hands lifted, caught the ground. Her body slid onto the earth. Scrapes ripped skin open along her palms. They burned. Her chin hit a rock, jolted back, and then when her head fell forward, it landed on something hard.

The rock was the last thing she saw before blacking out.

#

As much as Bray wished to move quickly, her body was hit hard by the fall. She turned her head from side to side. She sat up and checked herself. Nothing seemed broken aside from the bike, its front tire now completely flat.

The perps continued to buzz around her. They just hovered above her head, as if waiting for something or someone. Surely the Marshals would be here any moment.

Bray's eyes watered from the reality around her. She sensed herself only miles from the transport truck, or perhaps the other way around.

"Shoot," she whispered. Of course she'd expect nothing less from S-Corp. She knew they had sent those perps.

Bray stood up suddenly. Up ahead, she saw some kind of bright, blinding sand dropping down into a canyon. The canyon was partially surrounded by a fence, opening out to the road. Maybe if perps couldn't track people near mountains, the same was true for canyons. It was her only shot, so she abandoned the bike and made a run for it.

The terrain transitioned into a set of hills. The perps followed behind in the air. It took only a few rises over the hills for

Bray to arrive at the canyon. It was surrounded by a fence that appeared about six feet high.

Bray looked up at the sky. The perps hovered just above the fence line. Bray stepped around the fence. She walked one hundred feet to the edge of the canyon. Stopping, she turned and looked up. The perps had not followed. She stood and watched as they eventually flew away.

Looking down, she saw that the canyon's floor was forty feet below or more. The rock walls that surrounded it were mixed in deep reds, browns, beige, white. The silence of it was enormous.

In the distance, Bray heard thumping. Thump-thump, thump-thump, and then thump-thump-thump, thump-thump-thump.

Coming in perpendicular to the highway, a helicopter approached.

Chapter Fifty-Three

Dianna

"I know where Bray is." Cole's voice spoke quickly through the phone.

"Good for you. I'm already on my way to her now, so there's not much you can do," Dianna replied. She was bouncing around inside an S-Corp-issued helicopter. "I've got this all under control."

"I'm on my way, too. I'm her father. I have a right to be involved."

"Funny how you say that only when it's convenient for you," she replied back. Dianna had been angry at Cole for years. Maybe it was because she was like him in that she rarely spent time with Bray and didn't want to admit it. But he was the one who hardly made an effort to see her.

"Whatever, Cole," she replied. "I guess I'll see you on the ground."

Dianna hung up and rolled her eyes. Truth

was, he didn't know that she had two S-Corp security men with her. Whatever Cole tried to do, he'd be outnumbered and unable to stop them from taking Bray.

This wasn't Dianna's first time in a helicopter. S-Corp used them frequently. Visits to facilities and offices throughout the west required it. Helicopters were easier to transition to electric power than jet engines, and in a time when the climate demanded the elimination of fossil fuels, S-Corp did all it could to rely on wind and electric power.

As the helicopter pushed through the Wyoming winds, Dianna sat between the two S-Corp security men, her eyes following the terrain below. She'd never been this far north. It was astounding, how much live grass and trees existed out here. And the space, so open and under-utilized. Miles and miles of fresh grass and liveliness. Her mind sifted through all the possibilities of this state's natural resources and how they could benefit the rest of the western states.

If only Wyoming didn't make the use of
their resources illegal to S-Corp. But that
would change some day. It was only a matter
of time.

"We're closing in on her." The pilot's
voice spoke crisply into Dianna's
headphones. "Only about a mile away."

"Thank God," Dianna whispered, sitting
back and closing her eyes. Finally she could
get Bray home and back on meds. Stable. And
then she could better focus on S-Corp.

That's when she remembered: Carl had
messaged her a while ago. One of the
ecoterrorists snuck into their Transgenics
facility in Fort Collins, and they'd been
caught. It was the same person who had led
them to the ecoterrorist hideout in Medicine
Bow. She opened the email on her phone.
There, Dan had left information on their
identity, along with images of the Medicine
Bow cabins and the Prius Prime.

Perfect.

She opened a new chat with Carl:

HERE'S THE INFO FROM DAN:

NAME: KAGE ZAIR

PARENTS TODD & VALERIE ZAIR

DISAPPEARED—TELL THEM

PARENTS ARE DEAD...

Dianna stopped and glanced out the pilot's windshield. Darting along a growing hill of rock formations was a small body.

Bray. She had on the same clothes Dianna had seen a few days ago. From this distance she was just a minuscule thing crawling along the rocks on some kind of bike. Now they'd found her and there was no way she'd get out of this one. A sense of relief came over Dianna. She hadn't realized how stressed she was about this whole thing until now.

"That's her!" she yelled into the intercom. The helicopter began its descent. Dianna quickly finished her message to Carl:

TELL KAGE THANK YOU

FOR LEADING US TO THE

OTHERS—THEN SHOW HER THESE

Dianna forwarded the images of the Prius and cabins to Carl and pushed the phone into her pocket. She smiled as she did it. Her heart pounded with a sense of righteousness. Finally, she was not only getting Bray back but now she was also getting at those damn ecoterrorists. Things were going her way.

The wind pushed back at the helicopter. The helicopter fell backwards in the air. Dianna and the two security men bounced around in the back. For a moment Dianna's stomach flipped and she thought she might puke. Then, the pilot pushed the throttle forward. The helicopter slowly landed just beside a huge, desolate canyon. It was enormous, seemed to spread for miles. The sun was bright and the sand-colored canyon walls blinded her as she stepped out and bent down beneath the copter's blades. The canyon was not like anything she'd ever seen before, but right now Dianna had more important things to focus on.

It was time to get her daughter back home.

Chapter Fifty-Four

Kage

Kage locked eyes with Lana. The skinny jeans man pulled her into the room by her arm. The man forced her over toward the guard who'd been standing near the elevator. She was handed off like some animal. The man in skinny jeans turned and exited through the door from where he'd came.

In Lana's eyes Kage saw confusion, then a change to either fear or sadness, he couldn't tell. He wished he knew her well enough to tell the difference.

As they brought in another chair from outside and forced Lana down into it, Kage looked over to her and suddenly wished he hadn't messed things up. Now he had to figure a way out—not just for himself, but for the both of them.

Carl paced back and forth in front of Kage and Lana. One guard remained by the

elevator wall. Another at the door. The last
stood behind Kage. The two scientists stood
on either side of Carl.

"The two of you seem to know one
another. Isn't that right, Kage?" Carl said,
stopping cold in front of Kage, his arms
crossed.

Kage glared up at him but said nothing.

Carl pulled a smartphone from his
pocket and unlocked it with a quick glance
of his dark eyes.

"Take a look," he said, bringing the
phone's screen down to Kage's face.

There, a video of Kage jumping a ride
on the volocopter way back in Cheyenne.
Followed by an image of him using the
volocopter's internet, typing in Tori's
email address.

Kage's face went flush, then the blood
returned with a sharp anger. Trevor hadn't
been kidding when he said Kage would have to
be careful out here. He hadn't been careful
enough.

"I see a reaction. Is that anger,

maybe?" Carl asked.

The image flipped to a video of Kage driving the Prius Prime to the S-Corp facility. Then a video of Andy and Sara arrested by Marshals.

Kage stiffened again. It took everything inside for him not to react, not to show he recognized anyone.

"I don't understand what you're showing me," he said.

"Lie all you want, but your ecoterrorist friends have been arrested, thanks to you for showing us their location," he replied, waving his hand over at Lana.

Kage gave Lana a quick glance. In her eyes now he saw tears welling up. He turned away, kicking at the chair leg in anger at himself for being such an idiot.

"There's more," Carl said, showing him the phone again.

Now there was a video of Kage driving into Medicine Bow in the Prius. It was an aerial view of the car, but because Kage knew cars the way doctors knew bodies, he couldn't deny it. It was him, leading a drone right to Lana's camp after having stolen one of their cars.

"We've been watching you for quite some time. I know you followed Dianna here. She was sorry she couldn't stay, but she had an...emergency. You just missed her. I know you harmed one of our workers to break in," he said, pointing at the scientist Kage threatened the night before. "You've broken plenty of laws at this point. And all to find out about your parents. Todd and Valerie Zair, right?" he said, then suddenly stopped as if expecting a response.

Kage wanted to scream. And cry. And throw this chair at him, break his skull. He was mostly angry at himself—more and more as the minutes went by.

"I can tell you about your parents. It's quite simple. They're dead. They've been deceased for years. Died of natural causes. Prison was just too much for them, I gather. You animal rights folk, when it comes right down to it, are quite weak."

Kage stopped listening after that. All he could hear was his mind, telling him over and over what an asshole this person was. Worse than that—he was actually quite composed, unemotional, calculating. Kage had never met anyone who could purposefully pull at and then break another human's heart. Because that's how it felt just then.

Carl was still talking, waving the two scientists over. Kage's eyes remained set on Carl while the two scientists knelt down in front of Kage. One of them set a small black box down on the floor. Kage watched him open the box. In his mind all he heard was Carl's voice:

Prison was just too much for them. You animal rights folk...are quite weak.

As Carl's voice droned on, Kage observed the contents of the box. A syringe. A small, brown bottle of liquid, which he assumed was anesthesia. And a very tiny implant, the size of a fingernail. His ears then honed in to Carl's voice.

"And then we'll be able to track you, wherever you go. Grateful that you've led us to Lana and her team, and now you can lead us to so much more, I'm sure."

But Kage wasn't about to lead them anywhere. He sat, cleared his head while they inserted the implant into the syringe of clear liquid, and waited.

.

Chapter Fifty-Five

Bertan

Bertan made sure the morning came to him by staying awake, his eyes peeled on the videos in the surveillance office. He'd received the second note from Medina, this time a text to his phone:

YOU HAVE THREE DAYS.

GET TO BAJO AGUAN OR FAMILY IS DEAD.

Three days. That was impossible. He'd have to leave now to get down to Texas, then get across the border, and then there was *La Bestia* to tame all over again. Having lost all his money—and now his sanity—he was beginning to see that Ruben would be the only one to help. So he waited hours for Ruben to arrive.

Around 6 a.m., he changed out of his uniform. He'd lost his smock the day before so he stole a clean one from an unlocked locker. Bertan entered the Kill Floor and

started up the stairs to the manager's
office when he heard Ruben's voice.

"Good morning," Ruben said.

Bertan stopped at the top of the stairs
and turned to look. Ruben approached him
wearing gray slacks and a black short-
sleeved shirt. "To what do I owe this
pleasure?"

"I need to talk," Bertan responded. He
felt on edge, uptight, like something inside
him might burst. He felt moments away from
hurting someone else if he didn't get help
for his family.

Ruben unlocked the office door and they
both stepped inside. Ruben closed the door
behind them. The lights flipped on. Bertan
winced at the brightness and sat down. Ruben
sat down across from him.

"So, what's going on?" Ruben asked.

"Medina wants me to go back to work for
them or they'll kill my family," Bertan
said. He pulled out his phone and showed the
text to Ruben.

"Jesus," Ruben replied.

"Well, he can't help me now, but maybe you can? I need money to get down there."

"I don't have that kind of money. Three days means we'd have to get you on a plane to give you enough time. I only have a couple hundred dollars until I get paid, which isn't till next week."

Bertan shrank back in the chair. His hand opened and the phone fell on the floor. He'd never felt more cornered in his life, which said a lot for the life he'd lived. All he wanted was to create a safe life for his family, and now it seemed as though they were going to be killed, and he was helpless. His shoulders slumped and he just sat there, staring down at the floor.

"I know another way, I think," Ruben said.

Bertan's ears lifted. He looked at Ruben, but he had little faith.

"I've got some connections in Mexico. I used to do some social work down there with undocumented immigrants all the time. Maybe I can help find your family."

"Yeah? And how would you get them away

from Medina? They want me, not money. Nothing else."

"It doesn't change the fact that kidnapping is illegal. If I can make a copy of that photo, and the text they sent you as proof, I know some clean officers who can help."

Bertan didn't believe in this plan one bit, but he went ahead and gave the photo and his phone over to Ruben. Ruben took photos of them with his phone. When he handed the photo back to Bertan, Bertan's eyes focused in on the handwriting on the notes. Suddenly he recognized that handwriting from...somewhere. Where, exactly? He couldn't place it.

"You okay?" Ruben interrupted his thoughts.

Bertan closed his eyes. Picturing Carmen and Gabriella trapped in some dungy room, surrounded by Medina workers—by men who killed just the way he did—hurt him deep, deep down. His eyes flashed open.

"I deserve this," Bertan said, the words trickling out of his mouth without him being one hundred percent aware of what he was saying.

"Deserve what?"

"My family's kidnapping. That's what I get for killing all those people...for leaving my family and coming here to work in this shithole, thinking this place would somehow be my ticket to giving my family a good life. I came here to stop killing, and the killing only followed me...because that's who I am."

"You're lying to yourself if you think that," Ruben said. He pulled his chair closer to Bertan. "Medina is what really killed those people, not you."

"No!" he shouted at Ruben, but the anger was pointed inward, aiming for his heart. He stood up and paced the floor. "I pulled the trigger."

"Yes," Ruben said, standing up and coming eye-to-eye with Bertan. "You did pull the trigger. But it was Medina that made you do it. You were so young. You didn't have many other choices," Ruben said, placing his hand on Bertan's shoulder.

Bertan felt Ruben's warm hand on him and his heart squeezed in fear. The man was getting too close.

"No," Bertan said. He pulled away and sat back down. He began rocking back and forth in the chair. "I've killed a lot of people."

"Yes, you have," Ruben agreed, sitting down. "Take a deep breath, Bertan."

Bertan did as he was told, feeling the air move from his chest up and out of his mouth. It didn't do much good but at least he stopped rocking back and forth.

"Can I ask you a question?" Ruben continued.

Bertan nodded silently. It took everything he had to stay present when all he wanted was to hide away...to disappear.

"Why did you go to work for Medina?"

Bertan closed his eyes for a moment. He remembered back to his childhood, to his father. For a few more moments he was able to focus on what Ruben asked.

"My dad went to help my grandparents with their plantation in Bajo Aguan. He worked for Medina, too. But then he learned that Medina was trying to force my grandparents off the farm, so he tried to get away. He was murdered." Bertan continued on. He talked about how he admired his father, respected him for the work he did. His father had taught him how to read and introduced him to the revolutionary life of Che Guevara. His father got into countless labor fights with Medina, which led his mother to divorce. She took Bertan and left his father, and Bertan never forgave his mother for it. When he was sixteen, his father was murdered. Bertan never wanted to believe it was Medina, despite that being what his mother believed. He didn't want to believe her because Medina had offered him a very good job.

"Medina was my ticket out," Bertan said. That's when he realized his own shame. He chose to trust Medina over his own deceased father. The father he loved and adored.

"Exactly. You came from a place where there's virtually no way out. Can you see how it's not your fault where you came from?" Ruben added.

Bertan did not respond. Instead, his head went hot with anger. He looked down at the photo in his hand. His eyes studied the handwriting as Ruben's words sifted into his ears and tried latching on to his heart.

"I'm not saying that what you did was okay. I'm just trying to get you to entertain the possibility that if you hadn't grown up there, if you had lived somewhere else, maybe you wouldn't have gotten involved with Medina."

"What's your point?" Bertan asked. He was beginning to grow impatient. His pulse raced with the need to figure out who the hell knew where his family was.

"That you, by nature, are not a killer. It was just how you were raised...conditioned. Can you see the bigger picture here?"

Bertan sat up. He looked Ruben in the eye.

Medina had been controlling much of Honduras for nearly thirty years. He had never seen it that way, until now.

"I guess I can see what you're saying," he replied.

"It doesn't change the fact that you're an adult now and you can make different choices. But you may just want to consider letting go of this false reality that you're some horrible human being, because you're not."

Bertan nodded. As much as he wanted Ruben's words to sink in, there were more important things at stake. His eyes were drawn back to the photo. He needed to tap in and remember where he had seen that handwriting. It was the key to saving his family. Once he found out who wrote that note, he knew what he needed to do.

He would have to kill again. There was no other choice. It was the only thing he knew to do when he felt powerless. Killing gave him control over something, over another being's life when his life was out of control. Yes, he was a killer.

Yes...I am a killer, the thought played on repeat in his mind.

"I happen to believe you're an okay guy," Ruben said, grinning.

"Hm," Bertan replied. "The only thing is-you say I'm an adult and I can make different choices now, but I'm still just as trapped."

"We all are, my friend. Most of the available jobs for undocumented people are with S-Corp. And all these jobs involve the very dirty work of killing animals for food. There's a reason for that."

Bertan remembered the file he saw in the office, the one showing S-Corp in cahoots with Medina. With nothing to lose at this point, he mentioned the folder.

"And S-Corp works with Medina," Bertan added.

"What? How did you know that?" Ruben asked.

"I saw some papers in your office. Bank

statements. Money exchanged between S-Corp and Medina."

"Ah, yes. That folder was mine. I just found this out myself."

"You mean you've been working here five years and you didn't know?" Bertan asked, skeptical now.

"I really didn't. They don't give me a lot of access to their information. I've had to be very covert about finding information on S-Corp. It took years to find that proof of their connection with Medina."

"How did you find it?" Bertan asked. Now he wasn't so sure he could believe Ruben.

"On the laptop. I asked another plant manager for the password to get into some locked files. I lied, told him I needed to look up some workers' information. Nice thing is, most people around here are pretty trusting, so they gave it to me, no questions asked."

Bertan looked Ruben in the eye. Ruben was right. The workers around here developed trust easily, unless they sold drugs under the table, as Serpentine did. Because everyone here was an immigrant, everyone was in the same boat, so to speak. So there was always an unspoken amount of trust that no one would rat another worker out.

A bell rang, startling Bertan into sudden transition. The anger he felt at Medina turned him back into the Knocker as instantly as flipping a light switch. He stood up, feeling the photo in his hand. He brought it up to his eyes and examined the handwriting one more time. His mind flashed back to the time he'd begged Serpentine for work. Serpentine had given him that list of men who owed him money. He'd have to check the list in his locker, but he was almost certain the handwriting was the same.

"Got to get to work," the Knocker said. "But one more thing."

"Yes?"

"I'm pretty sure I know who kidnapped my family."

"Uh, dare I ask?"

"You know I can't answer that," he

replied, showing no emotion either way.

"Okay. Come by tomorrow?" Ruben asked. "We have some more things to go over."

The Knocker nodded, turning for the door. He was sure that might not happen-not now that he had to go find Serpentine.

"And Bertan?"

The Knocker froze at the unfamiliar name. He remained with his back to Ruben, not letting his confusion show.

"There are other choices. I promise."

The Knocker was the only choice when he had dirty work to do.

Chapter Fifty-Six

Bray

The helicopter approached and hovered just above the highway. The wind picked up around her.

Bray hoped it would land on the highway, helping to block the oncoming transport truck. But it came slightly forward and began its landing on the ground, just between the highway and Bray. Now it stood between her and Alice.

The helicopter's blades swiped through the air, its wind pushing Bray to the very edge of the canyon. She was trapped. In Bray's stomach came a strange urge. A feeling of certainty that pushed at her heart and chest. The transport truck was only miles away, coming from the south.

"Alice, I don't know what to do," Bray said to herself. "I'm trapped."

"Sounds like we are both in the same

place," Alice responded.

The helicopter touched ground. Its blades slowed.

There was nothing else to do but call for help.

She closed her eyes. She remembered what Elliott had said about using animals to her advantage. Her uncertainty around the ethics of calling out for help caused her eyes to dart open. How could she do it now, after all she had learned? Her mind grew over with vines of thoughts, all crowding her to the point of doubt.

Out of the helicopter climbed two tall men. They wore black fatigues and holsters lined with ammunition, bobby clubs and handcuffs. Black masks covered their faces, revealing only eyes and mouths. In their hands they carried M16 rifles.

These were no Marshals.

The men approached, stood in front of the helicopter.

But then a third body stepped out of the back of the helicopter. Dressed in her usual business suit, Dianna stood beside the armed men.

Dianna yelled above the copter's blades, "You're coming back with me."

Bray froze.

#

She stood there, staring at her mother.

She didn't know what to do. In all the times in the past when she got caught running away, or her mom discovered she wasn't taking her medication and had her readmitted to the psych ward, Bray would simply shut down. She didn't know how to stand up to her mom. How was she supposed to stand up to the one who made her? The one who was supposed to love her, to have her back, no matter what?

Then her senses caught onto something big and dark. In her chest, she felt like a solid rock had formed. When the dark thing came into view from afar, the feeling made sense. Coming in like a black cloud, a murder of ravens floated into view. As they neared, she counted well over twenty of them.

Bray hadn't seen anything like it. All her life she had seen few birds. With half of her time being spent locked away behind four walls, the only way she learned about nature was from the books she was given. These birds looked nothing like the ones she'd seen in books. Their ink-black feathers were so shiny they reflected the light of the sun. And their beaks, also black, curved away from their heads like a cat's nail.

"Do you need help?" they called down to her. It was so strange. It was as though they were speaking as one singular unit. One mass consciousness, like the horses.

"Yes!" her mind responded automatically. *But only if you want to,* she then thought, reluctant to take advantage of them.

"When one needs help, they need only

ask. Nature does the rest," the murder of ravens replied.

Before Bray could respond, a handful of the ravens dropped down from the sky as the rest landed on the helicopter's blades. They screeched and flapped their wings at the men. There were so many of them they hovered over the men like dark clouds.

Bray ran for her mother.

"Mom!" she yelled over the ravens. They flew around her, their talons scraping into the men's clothing and gear as the men shielded themselves with their hands over their heads.

Bray grabbed her mom's hand, pulled her away.

"What are you doing?" Dianna screamed. "You're coming with me!"

"No, I'm not!" Bray yelled back. She pulled Dianna out near the highway, away from the helicopter, and faced her.

"You need to listen to me," Bray said, catching her breath. "Do you see those ravens?"

"Of course," Dianna said. She pulled her hand away from Bray.

"Why do you think they're here, attacking those men?"

"I don't know, but I need to stop them," Dianna said, turning to start for the helicopter.

"No," Bray said, and closed her eyes. She took a risk in asking the ravens to pull back for a moment.

They did. And Dianna saw it.

"Shoot them!" Dianna yelled.

"No!" Bray shouted.

Suddenly the men lifted their rifles and pointed into the sky at the ravens. Shots pelted the birds. They hit skin and bone. Several ravens dropped, made thudding sounds when they hit the ground.

"No!" Bray screamed again, now crying. She started for the birds—or the men. She was so angry she wasn't sure what she was doing. But she had to do something.

A hand squeezed around her wrist,

pulling her back. It was her mother.

"Get off me," Bray snarled, yanking herself away.

But then Dianna ran after her and grabbed her around the chest, her forearms pressing into Bray's shoulders. Dianna was too tall for Bray to get leverage over her.

"You're coming back with me!" Dianna yelled.

Bray struggled against her mom. The men continued shooting at the ravens. Those that survived managed to escape and fly off.

She couldn't let this happen to herself again. Her body was being pushed toward the helicopter. Sensing a rolling movement inside, she knew the transport truck was now only a mile away.

Dianna's arms wrapped tightly around Bray's chest and upper arms. Bray pulled and struggled against Dianna. Dianna only squeezed tighter. Bray couldn't believe how strong her mother was.

Bray was being forced closer and closer toward the helicopter. Her insides squeezed with fear. The more she tried fighting, the worse it got, like being in the grip of a bulldog.

So Bray stopped cold. Her feet planted into the ground like tree roots. She then let her feet fall from under her. As she fell, her body slid from Dianna's grip. She used her hands to push Dianna's arms up and away. When her butt hit the ground, her head fell back against Dianna's legs. She turned to one side and grabbed Dianna's calves.

"Bray!" Dianna shouted.

Bray yanked at Dianna. Dianna fell backwards and onto the dusty ground. Her elbows stopped her fall.

Then Bray turned and stood up. She looked down at her mother. Her mother quickly sat up, wiping dirt off her now-tarnished clothing.

"What's the matter with you?" Dianna said.

"I'm afraid *you* are what's the matter with me," Bray replied calmly.

Then two clicks sounded behind her. She

turned her head to see the barrel of a gun pointed at her back. Turning the other way, she saw a second.

"Don't move," one of the men said.

Bray gulped. Her shoulders slumped. Now that the birds were gone, half of them dead, what could she do?

In the distance, a car approached. Also from the south. It looked familiar. An electric BMW, black and blue. The only person she knew who owned such a car was...her dad?

Suddenly the BMW veered off the highway, just past Bray. It stopped just before hitting the helicopter. Her dad jumped out of the car.

"What the fuck is going on here?" he screamed.

Then, a glare popped up from where Cole had just come. Approaching, along the highway, a tiny speck grew slowly into the commanding frame of a semi.

The transport truck came into view.

Chapter Fifty-Seven

The Knocker

The Knocker went to the locker room for his goggles. On his way, he inspected the photo of Carmen and Gabriella. They were set in chairs, and behind them was a plain, concrete wall. There was nothing else to see, no way to know where they were. But since he'd worked for Medina, they were still in Honduras and most likely never made it out of Bajo Aguan.

In the locker room, Serpentine stood alone beside the bathroom door. His frown was deep, his eyes narrowed as he glared at the Knocker. He must've returned from his "work trip." Convenient. Right after his family went missing.

The Knocker opened his locker and noticed the list Serpentine had given him. He quickly glanced back at the photo. Something nudged him in the chest. He matched the note with the handwriting in the photo. It *was* Serpentine's handwriting.

"So you're back," the Knocker said, shutting his locker.

"Yes," Serpentine replied, approaching the Knocker and coming within inches of his face. "And you owe me money," he whispered.

"Money?" the Knocker asked. He tried remembering what had happened the last couple of days, but it was all a blur.

"You asked for a job, to help you pay to find that *coyotaje*. I was being generous, you dick. Now I'm out hundreds of dollars and Medina is coming for me. You have $1,500 for me by the end of our shift or you're a dead man. Your family can join you in hell because I'll make sure they do," he hissed.

"Medina? So you *do* work for them," the Knocker replied.

This gave the Knocker an idea.

"I do, you son of a bitch, so you'd better get me my money. You, of all men, should know what happens when you cross men like me," Serpentine replied.

The Knocker slid on his smock and goggles. As he did, he placed the photo in the locker and stared at it, burning the image of Carmen and Gabriella into his mind.

And then he forced himself to cry.

#

The tears welled into his eyes. They were warm, like the nights in Bajo Aguan in the summer. One teardrop managed to roll halfway down the Knocker's face and then stop.

"Please," he started, his voice quivering, "I'll go back...just ask them to please let my family go."

"Go back where?" Serpentine asked. He was grinning like some dumb stray dog having just found food.

"Medina. I'll go back. I'll do whatever work they want. Just don't let them hurt my family. They're all I have left." The Knocker dropped his head and forced out a wail. He quickened his breathing and pumped his stomach as if to show he was having a panic attack. He came down onto his knees and rocked back and forth in a near fetal position.

"Okay, okay, man," Serpentine said. He bent down and reached his arm around the Knocker. "You're embarrassing yourself. Now get up."

The Knocker allowed Serpentine to help him up. He pressed himself into the lockers and closed his eyes.

"What do I need to do?" he asked, his eyes remaining closed.

"Give me my money, for starters. Then, we can talk about more work for Medina. I won't let anyone hurt your family."

And that was it. Serpentine did know where his family was. The Knocker opened his eyes. He ceased crying.

"Will you please call, at least let me hear their voices so I know they're alive?" the Knocker asked calmly.

"Sure." Serpentine smiled again. The Knocker was beginning to hate that grin of his.

Serpentine pulled a phone from his back pocket. He unlocked it with his fingerprint and then brought it up to his ear. The Knocker closed his eyes and pretended not to listen, but he was close enough to hear.

What he heard was nothing. Serpentine talked but there was no voice or noise from the other end.

"Yeah...Bertan says he's good for it. Coming back...can you put his wife on the phone? He wants to hear their voices," Serpentine spoke. There was a long pause. In that pause the Knocker thought of his next move.

"Sorry man," Serpentine said to Bertan, "they're sleeping."

Serpentine slid his phone back into his pocket.

The Knocker looked at him. Whatever tears he summoned earlier had shifted into a hard substance in his chest. Serpentine was lying. All the training the Knocker had received from Medina was paying off now.

"Right," the Knocker spoke. He opened his eyes and turned toward the exit. "We got to get to work. When our shift is over, I'll get you your money."

Serpentine smiled again. But what he
didn't know was that smile was about to be
ripped right off his face.

#

The Knocker welcomed the end of his shift.
He followed Serpentine quietly back to the
locker room. Serpentine's neck was wet with
sweat from the day's work. His hair hung in
a ponytail. The Knocker imagined using it to
pull Serpentine backwards.

"So, my money?" Serpentine asked. They
were standing in the locker room.

The rest of the day-shift workers had left
for the night. It would be another hour
before the sanitation workers arrived.

The Knocker was alone with Serpentine.

"I hid it inside the Knock Box," the
Knocker said.

"Smart man," Serpentine said, grinning.

Serpentine followed him back to the Kill
Floor. The overhead lights had been shut
off. The machines cast black shadows on the
silvered floors. The Knocker moved quickly

as he approached the Knock Box.

"Slow down, man," Serpentine said, rushing to keep up.

The Knocker remained silent. They passed the Gutting Stand.

"Man, what's up with you? You're like, so wound up," Serpentine said, his voice light. "You need to get off, or something?" Serpentine laughed.

The Knocker turned and punched Serpentine in the mouth. *There goes that smug smile, you son-of-a-bitch*, he thought.

"Ah!" Serpentine shouted as blood rolled down from his mouth. He jumped at the Knocker. He grabbed the Knocker around the waist and pulled him down to the ground. Serpentine stood up. He came down on the Knocker, punched him in the nose, and then again in the lip. His steel-toed boot rammed into the Knocker's stomach repeatedly. The Knocker keeled over from the pain. Serpentine turned and went for one of the cattle prods. Suddenly the Knocker remembered the truck driver...*wait, no...but*

was that him? He remembered being attacked
with electric shock. As his head rested
against the concrete, blood dripping from a
cut below his eye, he tried to remember.
Something didn't make sense just then. He
shook off the memory and sat up. Serpentine
grabbed a prod off the wall past the Knock
Box. The Knocker's head cleared once again,
and he pressed his back against the wall and
used it to hoist himself up to standing.

Serpentine ran at him with the prod and
the Knocker grabbed onto the shaft.
Serpentine pushed it toward the Knocker's
face. The Knocker held it, his grip slipping
from his sweaty hands. He pushed at the prod
as hard as he could. It came within an inch
of his eye. Finally he yanked his head away.
The prod hit the wall. Serpentine fell
forward. The Knocker grabbed Serpentine's
head and thrust it into the wall. Serpentine
fell back, his head circling from the
impact, and nearly fell. The prod fell to
the ground. The Knocker picked it up and
stabbed Serpentine in the back.

"Ah!" Serpentine screamed.

The Knocker grabbed him by the neck and dragged him over to the Bleed Pit area. Serpentine tried to run. The Knocker leapt forward and came down on Serpentine's back with the cattle prod. The electrodes pinched Serpentine's lower back. The Knocker pushed it hard against his skin. Serpentine screamed and dropped to the ground. The Knocker stabbed Serpentine in the leg with the prod and shocked him again to ensure he couldn't run. Serpentine screamed out again.

He grabbed Serpentine's legs with his hands and pulled the man's body over to the Knock Box. There were already plenty of blood stains and brain matter smudged along the box. No one would be able to tell the difference.

"Please, Bertan, don't do this!" Serpentine yelled.

The Knocker froze. For a moment everything stopped. He looked around the room, trying to figure out who he was, what he was doing. From above, he could see himself holding

Serpentine's legs. And then he remembered
and returned to himself again. He was the
Knocker.

"Don't ever call me that again," he said.

Nearing the Knock Box, he dragged
Serpentine up to it and pulled it open from
the back, right where the beefs got pushed
in every day. He let go of one of
Serpentine's legs and reached into
Serpentine's back pocket, pulling out his
phone. He slid the phone into his own pocket
and grasped both of Serpentine's ankles
firmly so he couldn't try to run.

"Now, we can do this the easy way, or I
can knock you out and toss you in there. I'd
rather you be awake, though."

"Please, man," Serpentine said, beginning
to cry. "I got a family, too. I got to take
care of them. Please!"

"You didn't think about my family though,
did you?"

"Everyone here works for Medina, man. You
know that," Serpentine said, laughing
uneasily. "It wasn't me who kidnapped them."

"But you sure know where they are, don't you...making a fake phone call to Medina and then lying to my face."

Serpentine stopped crying. His eyes widened. The look in his eyes confirmed he was lying. Shaking his head at Serpentine, the Knocker dropped Serpentine's legs to the floor. He walked over and grabbed the knock gun from the wall. He used the back of it to whack Serpentine in the head.

Serpentine went unconscious.

Chapter Fifty-Eight

Kage

Kage had a knack for timing. He'd gained it from his experiences gardening with Ethan. If they planted something too early or too late, they wouldn't be rewarded. They'd end up with nothing. And in a place where the food they relied upon came largely from the ground, their lives were dependent on timing.

It was all about instinct, a strength he acquired from his mother. And today, as he sat cuffed to this chair in some strange sci-fi-esque S-Corp building, fearing he'd be next on the frightening lab rat list, he listened to his instinct.

The lab coat Jonny knelt before him. Across the way, Lana was watching. She wasn't cuffed to her chair like he was.

Lab coat Jonny lifted the syringe toward Kage. Lab coat Jonny #2 came up to him and began rolling up the sleeve of Kage's arm. Kage didn't like the stranger touching his jacket. His mom's jacket.

And then, he felt it.

The instinct.

It always felt like a burning, hard rock in his chest. Something concrete, known.

Timing.

Kage gripped the chair leg with his cuffed hand. Jonny #2 was distracted while pulling up Kage's sleeve to reveal his bare skin. Jonny #1 brought the syringe of brown liquid closer to Kage's forearm.

In one swing, Kage pulled the chair out from under himself. He swung it at Jonny #2. The chair hit Jonny #2 in the face, knocked him clear to the floor. Jonny #1 came at Kage, dropping the syringe. Kage swung the chair backwards, knocking Jonny #1 in the jaw.

"Ah!" Jonny #1 screamed.

Carl came running at Kage. The chair fell heavily to the ground. His wrist snapped. A sharp pain shot up his arm and he winced.

Lana jumped from her seat. She grabbed Carl around the neck. Carl jabbed her with his elbow. Lana fell backward, hit the floor. The guard standing by the elevator ran for Kage. Kage reached for the syringe. The guard grabbed Kage by the neck. Kage's free hand stretched for the syringe again. His fingers just grazed it. The guard squeezed his forearm around Kage's neck. His knee was on the chair, which was lying on the ground. Kage's cuffed hand was pulled back, nearly behind him. The pain was hot. The guard began choking him.

Off to the side, Lana and Carl were fighting. Carl's phone slipped out of his hand and bounced onto the floor. The two Jonnys had gotten up but were keeping their distance. The other guard approached Carl and Lana.

There wasn't much time at all.

Kage strained for the syringe. He rolled it into his palm. His eyes began to water from the pain in his arm. He yanked the syringe up and stabbed the guard in the eye.

"Fuck!" the guard screamed, falling back onto the chair.

Kage yanked and yanked at the cuff. His wrist went purple. The cuff slit a deep cut into his wrist. He could see a bone protruding unnaturally out of his skin. If he looked too closely, he'd pass out.

Now the other guard was coming for Kage. Carl had Lana kneed down on the floor. The fallen guard was bleeding profusely from his eye. The syringe had landed several feet away.

The other guard went for Kage's torso from behind. They both fell forward. The swift, fast movement of their fall yanked the handcuff chain and broke it. Kage landed on his broken wrist and screamed in pain. The guard was on top of him on the floor. Beside him, inside the black box, was a bottle of brown liquid. One word from the label jumped out at Kage: anesthetic. If he

could free his good hand, he could reach it.
But the guard had him pinned down with his
knee. And with his wrist crushed beneath his
weight, the pain made him nearly pass out.

Then he heard Carl laugh.

"You two put up a good fight," he said.

His shoes clapped near Kage's ear. Kage
looked over past the black box. Carl stood
beside him, holding Lana by her neck.

They were only feet from the door, but
more trapped than ever.

The syringe rested on the floor, just
past Kage's head. No one had noticed it,
yet. The bleeding guard had passed out. Kage
hoped he hadn't killed the guy. He already
felt bad enough for leading these dick faces
to Lana and her friends. He had to get her
out of this, and away from them.

Carl continued talking. Kage didn't
bother listening to the bullshit. He let
Carl talk while the guard had him pinned
down. The two Jonny's remained in the
background, aloof and unmoving. Maybe even
scared.

Kage's good arm was lying by his side. If he simply went for the syringe, he was close enough to stab Carl in the ankle.

Again, it was all about timing.

So he waited.

He turned his head up to Lana. Their eyes met. He moved his eyes from hers over to the syringe, then back again. He did it a second time. Her eyes lit up. She looked down at her feet. Slowly, while Carl was looking up and talking, she slid the syringe over to Kage with her foot.

"Hey!" the guard shouted. He must have noticed the syringe move.

Time was up.

Kage went for the syringe. The guard went for his hand. But Kage had already stabbed Carl before the guard could reach him. He got Carl in the calf, then pulled the syringe out. Carl screamed. Lana got loose.

"Run!" Kage shouted, looking at the door.

Then, the guard's hand caught his. Kage

gripped the syringe tightly. He fought to turn onto his side. The guard had his hand around his good wrist.

Behind the guard, Kage saw Lana escape outside. He smiled, gained a new sense of purpose and strength. His bleeding wrist was in so much pain he couldn't feel it anymore. So he pushed back against the guard, the syringe in his hand, pointed toward the guard's neck.

The two of them pushed at each other. The guard pressed his forearm into Kage's neck. Kage shifted under him while using his long legs to wrap around the unconscious guard's leg to pull his body closer. He allowed the guard to come down on his hand. But then the guard's arm pressed down hard onto his neck. Things around him went black. His sight filled with little black dots, closer and closer in. He was losing consciousness.

From above the guard's head, Kage saw a chair raised into the air. It came down hard on the guard's head. The guard's face went expressionless, and then he fell over onto the unconscious guard.

There stood Lana, holding the chair and crying. Kage pushed the guard off and dropped the syringe. Lana helped him up, and he hugged her.

"You okay?" he asked.

She nodded silently.

Then, Kage noticed the scientists running for the elevator wall. Carl was on the ground, bleeding.

"God damn fuckers. I'm calling the Marshals," Carl yelled, crawling his way over to his phone.

Kage ran over and grabbed the phone. He threw it at the wall. It bounced off, landed flat on the ground.

"Let's get out of here," he yelled to Lana.

"You'll never get away with this," Carl yelled. "I'll have you both arrested for attempted murder."

Kage looked back at Carl, lying there on the floor. His face was sweaty, his hair

still near perfect. In Carl's eyes Kage saw
a dark cavern where many things lay hidden,
things far worse than what he had seen down
in that lab. Kage had to get Lana away, far
away.

There was only one place to go.

Now to get her there without being
followed.

Chapter Fifty-Nine

Bray

The transport truck was coming. Bray was going to miss it. One of the armed men had his rifle pointed at Cole, who now stood against the BMW with his hands lifted meekly in the air. Bray could feel that the other gun was still pointed at her back.

"Don't make me force you into the helicopter," Dianna said to Bray.

"I bet you'd love that," Bray said, tears rising up from her chest, remaining steady in her throat. She swallowed them down. She couldn't let her mom see her cry.

The transport truck came into full view. A long, painful, cold and moving prison of steel. Inside, she felt Alice. Felt closeness. Felt no longer just as herself, but like two selves. Two selves that were really just one part—two parts—of something much larger. She thought back to her first night in Wyoming with Elliott, surrounded by a billion stars. How he said she was just as bad for using animals to help her. That was true, yet other things were also true.

Bray watched the transport truck as it passed. Its body roared by, just on the other side of Dianna. As it did, one of the men came around and dropped the rifle to his side.

"Put out your hands," he said.

Bray met his eyes. Though the eyes were all she could see of his fully-covered face, she saw everything she needed to see. She saw that he didn't really want to cuff her. Didn't see the necessity of it. When her eyes met his, there was a connection.

She lifted her arms, turning her wrists out, and allowed him to cuff her. But she did it in complete revolt. She did it to show how ridiculous this was, to have two armed men out here stopping a seventeen-year-old from—from what, exactly? Separating her from the world outside the psych ward. Breaking her away, locking her up. The separation of her and Elliott. Her parents' beliefs about her versus what she knew to be true of herself. The distance between her and Alice as the back of the transport truck began to wither away toward the horizon.

Distance. Separation. Misunderstanding. That was true, yet other things were also true. Something she sensed deep inside.

The handcuffs snapped closed around her wrists. She dropped them in front of her. She chose not to fight because she realized something also true. It grew even more deep and certain inside.

She realized that Elliott was wrong when he'd said she was a hypocrite for using animals to save herself. Her parents were wrong about her schizophrenia diagnosis. None of these people really knew her abilities, how strong they were.

As she walked with the armed man over to the helicopter, she turned and glanced at her dad. He shrugged, worded, "I'm sorry."

Just as always.

She closed her eyes. In the darkness she imagined the horses. They weren't far, last she had seen them.

Stopping at the helicopter, Bray felt something in her chest. Something was coming. Tha-dump, tha-dump. Then, very suddenly, tha-du-du-dump, tha-du-du-dump.

Turning to the south, she saw them. All hundred horses leaping and galloping this way. No one else seemed to notice.

"She needs you," they called.

This she trusted.

And there was also something more she trusted.

They came so fast it caught the others by surprise. A wind pushed through along with the horses, blowing and hitting at the armed men. The horses ran through, crowding the area with a blur of brown confusion. Still handcuffed, Bray stepped back from the helicopter, stepped into the frenzy of the galloping horses.

As she stood there quietly, like a stone,

they all came out and around from behind
her. They ran at the armed men. The men
dropped their weapons and ran. A few of the
horses broke off, chased them toward the
canyon. Their bodies disappeared down into
the canyon.

"Bray, look out," Cole screamed. He was on
the ground, his hands over his head.

Maybe now they'll believe me, she thought
for a fleeting second.

Then a horse stopped beside her, knelt
down onto the knots in its legs.

"Get on," it said.

Bray sat down on it, turned and pulled her
left leg over so she was stable. She
stretched her cuffed arms over its head.
Crossing her arms around its neck to ensure
she wouldn't strangle it with the cuffs, she
held on tightly.

The horse stood. She felt it between her
legs.

"But how did you know?" she asked. "I
didn't even call for help."

"You didn't need to. We sensed you were in

danger."

And that's when she knew what was also true:

It went both ways. The animals could sense her, too. They had intricate design of intelligence, emotion, connection. All the things humans prided themselves for. It was not unique. All animals had it, and so long as they were not confined, taken by force or subjected to slavery by humans, they had certain freedoms. Certain choices. The horses could have chosen to walk away. The ravens could have chosen the same, and did so when they were in danger. Bray deserved that choice.

And so did Alice and the sows.

"Go!" Bray yelled to the horse.

It picked up and ran off for the highway. The others continued running north, along the highway behind Bray.

Soon the transport truck came back into view as they gained on it. Bray's heart thumped with the hooves of the horse. Her inner thighs burned with pain and passion.

The horse picked up speed. The others fell back slightly.

They reached the back of the truck. The horse and Bray worked together as one unit. It ran alongside the truck. Bray saw into the slats, met quick eyes with a sow, wondered if it was Alice.

"I know you're here," Alice spoke. "Don't give up now."

Bray heard Alice's words and her heart lifted. It was all the confirmation she needed to see herself actually follow through...to believe she could save Alice and the other sows.

But she could feel the horses' energy wane. Any moment the driver would catch on. As the horse neared the side of the truck, Bray brought her cuffed hands over its head. Now she sat up, her hands ready. All she had to do was grab onto the truck and jump.

They were moving at the speed of the truck. One wrong jump would land Bray under the truck, crunched by tires, a violent death. But it was this or nothing, and perhaps she would die anyway.

The horse drew close to the metal side.
Bray lifted both hands. Her fingers clenched
and squeezed tightly into a slat above her
head. Now her feet dangled at the sides of
the horse as it kept up beneath her. Her
heart racing—this could be it, just do it—
she closed her eyes. Taking a breath, she
lifted her legs away from the horse. It
slowed, fell back and stopped on the
highway.

Shi-i-i-i-it.

Bray quickly pulled her feet in. She tried
pressing them onto a slat below but they
slipped back out. The wind pulled them out
into the air. Her fingers slipped. The fact
that they were sweating did not help.
Frantic, she closed her eyes, pulled her
feet into the truck with all her strength.
They barely touched a pair of slats down
below. She pushed the front of her shoes in
as far as they would go.

Now she was on the truck. She turned and

saw the driver in his side mirror. He was slowing the truck, his face red while he stared at her in the mirror. She held on tight until the truck came to a complete stop.

The driver jumped out of the truck.

"What the hell?" he yelled.

And then the horse came running.

Bray watched the driver's face. His eyes bulged wide, mouth agape. He turned and started running. The horse ran behind and around him until the driver ran off the highway, chased by a couple of horses who pressured him until he jumped into sage brush some distance away.

Some of the horses came and surrounded the truck. Bray didn't know how to get down. If she jumped, she'd surely injure herself. It looked like a ten-foot drop.

One of the horses came up and stood beneath her. It looked up at her. She nodded, gently placed her foot on its back. Gaining balance, she placed her other foot down on it, too, afraid she was hurting the horse. She stood there while bringing her hands down, one slat at a time, together because of the cuffs.

Finally she fell onto the horse. She held onto either side of its neck as it turned and walked her over to the grass beside the highway. It sat down and she slid off.

"I can't believe that just happened," she said, laughing.

"It was supposed to. Now help your friend," the horse responded.

Bray looked up at the horse as it turned and ran off with the remaining horses.

"Thank you," she yelled to them, but they just kept on.

Bray turned back to the truck and saw that the BMW was coming near. It slowed and parked behind the transport truck. Bray stood debating whether to run and hide.

The BMW slowed to a stop. Her dad stepped out of the car.

Chapter Sixty

The Knocker

It took a lot of exertion to get Serpentine's body into the Knock Box so that his head would hang out the other side. It would have been easier if he'd not been unconscious, but at least this way there'd be no screaming or noises and the Knocker could be swift and done.

Once he had Serpentine's head in place, he stepped around to his spot beside the Knock Box. He pulled down the knock gun and held it in his hands. He thought about the beefs, how this was the beginning of the end for them. Probably the beginning of the end for him, too. Strangely this thought did not concern him. He knew his time was coming. Medina would catch up with him some day, but until then, he was already on his way to his own kind of hell. He didn't have to die to already be there.

None of that mattered now. The Knocker
was back in his element, had Serpentine
where he wanted him. He pressed the knock
gun into the spot between Serpentine's eyes
and held it there for a moment. This would
be the best time for Serpentine to wake up.
He needed for Serpentine to see this, or it
wouldn't have the same effect.

But first he set the gun atop the knock
box and grabbed Serpentine's phone from his
pocket. He brought the phone up to
Serpentine's hand and used his thumb to
press into the screen. The phone unlocked.
The Knocker scrolled through Serpentine's
photos and found an image of Serpentine with
what he assumed was his wife and child. He
left the screen open there.

The Knocker turned and picked up a
cattle prod. Opening the Knock Box from the
back, he stuck the prod inside. He pushed it
into Serpentine's side. The man's body
jolted. His feet kicked against the metal.
His head shot up and he screamed.

"What the fuck?" Serpentine yelled.

The Knocker stepped around to the front of the box. He leaned in and smiled at Serpentine. He grabbed the knock gun and pulled it down, pressing it in-between Serpentine's eyes.

"Please Bertan, what are you doing, man?" Serpentine pleaded.

"That's not my name," the Knocker whispered.

With his free hand, he held Serpentine's phone up to his face.

"See this? This your wife?" the Knocker asked.

Serpentine let out a scream. He tried pushing himself forward in the Knock Box as if to come at the Knocker. Now it was the Knocker who grinned.

"You know what it's like to knock beefs, right? You've done it a few times yourself," the Knocker said, staring absently into the dark Knock Box. "You know how this gun only makes them unconscious, but it's not till they bleed out and get cut to pieces that they really die. You think they can feel all that shit?"

Serpentine did not respond. He only shivered.

"We can find out right now," the Knocker said, "or...you call Medina right now, get them on speaker, and fucking tell them to free my wife and child." The Knocker screamed the last part into Serpentine's ear.

The room went quiet. A trickling sound came from inside the Knock Box.

"Hope you're wearing a diaper today...cause I'm pretty sure you just pissed on yourself."

Serpentine remained silent. He reached up to the phone, still in the Knocker's hand. The Knocker watched as he scrolled through his contacts and pulled up a name. He hit the call button. The Knocker pressed the speaker symbol, and waited.

"Alo?" a man answered.

"Let the woman and girl go," Serpentine said quickly.

"What?"

"I said fucking let them go...now!" Serpentine screamed.

"And why should I do that?" the man asked.

The Knocker neared the phone and spoke.

"Because if you don't...I'll kill Serpentine, I'll come for his family, and then I'll come for you. You know the kind of work I did for Medina? Whoever the hell you are, you better know what I'm capable of before you decide to hurt my family. I'm a trained killer. I was trained to hunt down men like you. I've got Serpentine's phone and I got your number. I'll have your head in a Knock Box next."

"Do it," Serpentine yelled into the phone.

They heard a few muffled voices in the background, followed by some rustling.

"You send me a photo of my family freed and in a hostel with the address so I can find them...send it to Serpentine's phone...and we'll call it even. But until then, Serpentine sits here with me, on borrowed time. Otherwise, I'll save your phone number and address and I'll be sure you're paid a visit. If not by me, then someone else," the Knocker said.

Holding the knock gun in place, the Knocker copied the image of the man's contact information and texted it to his own cell phone. He tossed Serpentine's cell phone against the wall, let it drop to the floor and then closed his eyes. Too bad he'd forgotten his goggles back in the locker room. This was about to get messy if they didn't send him that photo.

"Bertan?" Serpentine spoke, but the Knocker did not respond.

Who is Bertan? he asked himself. Maybe Serpentine was delirious and confused him with someone else.

The Knocker's eyes shot open.

"Please," Serpentine cried, the tears falling down onto the ground, "you got what you wanted, so let me go."

"Not yet I didn't. They send me the photo and address for me to verify and then you'll be free. Just be grateful I haven't knocked you yet. You're just like a beef...expendable until you're turned to meat, so be quiet."

The Knocker knew how to ignore these kinds of pleas. They weren't much different from those of the beefs, only the beefs couldn't speak. He rubbed the trigger again, getting another feel for its anticipation, and then the room went quiet.

#

The temperature dropped. The Knocker's breath shot out of his mouth in short clouds of air. He shivered. The prods along the walls began to shake. The chains hanging from the ceiling waved in the air as if moved by some breeze.

Serpentine remained quiet, or maybe he had passed out. The Knocker stood. His eyes roamed the room. Across from him, the image of Chino's daughter reappeared. His heart leapt. This time, she was not in the form of a beef. She was purely herself, absent of gun wound. Her face was whole. Her beady

black eyes looked gently over at him. He
gulped and then kept his eyes fixed on her.

Silently her body drifted over to him.
As it approached, it took on a more solid
form. His mouth dropped open. Surely he was
going insane. She placed her glowing hand on
the knock gun, nearly touching his own hand.
He jumped back.

"What do you want?" he whispered.

"Why do you do it?" she asked, her
voice echoing.

"Do what?"

"Kill."

The Knocker stared at her. Her eyes did
not blink. They looked into him, saw into
him as if he were the ghost. Lacking
substance, lacking direction, life. That was
why he did it: because he hated. He hated
himself, he hated this country, this job. He
hated what happened to Gabriella, to his
wife. What he had done to them. What Medina
had done to them. What he allowed, how much
blood he had taken from others when they
never deserved the loss.

Chino's daughter reached out and placed her hand on his. Somehow he felt it, like a cold breeze brushing his hand and fingers. It comforted him with an image of the times he'd read with his father before bed.

Then he saw himself sitting beneath a tin roof holding Gabriella. She was just a baby. The rainy season had come to stay with them, the sounds of it tapping gently against the roof as he sensed Carmen inside cooking tortillas. It was an image of the life he'd always wanted, and this strange ghost knew it and was giving it to him.

The pain grew in his heart and he pulled his hand away. She came closer, wrapped her arms around his torso. His mind screamed to push her away, to yell at her to leave, to disappear off. But nothing happened. He couldn't pull away from the stillness. Perhaps he didn't want to.

And as she embraced him, he looked down at her. He noticed the knock gun in his hand. He let go and it dropped to the floor. There was a wall in him somewhere, taller and more powerful than any wall along the Mexico border. The longer Chino's daughter held onto him, the more that wall softened into paper and then crumbled. His chest opened into a history of memories as they flooded into his mind. Gabriella, Carmen. All the stuff that made them a family. All the reasons why he'd come here in the first place. The loneliness he'd forgotten he'd been feeling all these years, how he felt so single despite being married. How he felt so disjointed, so separate from his home.

How he'd become a ghost.

And just like that paper wall that had now crumbled and was gone, so was Chino's daughter.

He stood there for a while, afraid to move. The beefs rustled around in the holding pens. They began to moo and huff. Soon it would be the end for them, and they had little choice.

He stepped back up to the Knock Box. Glancing over at the beefs, he remembered what Ruben said about there being other choices. He wasn't so sure that was true. It wasn't true for the beefs, that was for sure. And as he glared down at Serpentine's head in the Knock Box, he suddenly felt no desire for killing the man. Indifference came over him. The knock gun stared up at him from the floor, but he didn't pick it up.

Chapter Sixty-One

Bray

"What's up with her?" Bray said, pointing at her mom, who was motionless in the back seat of Cole's car.

"She's unconscious. She'll be fine," he replied.

Bray looked up at him and smiled. For once she was impressed that he had finally stood up to the woman. But then was he also here to stop her?

"What's up with your shoes?" he asked, pointing at her feet.

"Don't ask," she paused. "If you're here to stop me, just leave now."

"Bray, hold on now. Are you okay, first off?" he replied, rubbing her shoulder with his hand.

"Yes. I just need to get the sows out of here," she said, walking over to look at the transport truck.

"Wait," Cole said, stepping up to her.

Bray turned, and in his hands were a set of keys. Cole took her hands into his, unlocked the cuffs, and let them drop to the ground. He pulled her into his chest and wrapped his arms around her.

"I'm really sorry, for everything," he said.

"Really?" she said, pulling away. She glanced back at the BMW, saw her mother inside. The most she could say about her mom was that, at least, she was here. She hadn't just run off. And that was saying very little considering all she'd put Bray through. And here her dad was, for once trying to pick up pieces when he should've been here all along.

"How can you just show up here and then think things are going to be okay? You've never been here for me. Never."

"You're right. And I'm sorry for that. I've prioritized my career over you, and that's not something I can ever take back. I would like to make it up to you, somehow," he replied.

"Well, do you believe me now? About the animals?" she asked, crossing her arms.

"I did wonder how the hell you were riding a wild horse, unless I was seeing things."

"You weren't seeing things. I really can communicate with animals, dad."

"I don't know about all that, but I'm definitely not here to lock you away."

Bray glanced around for the men that came with Dianna.

"What happened to the men?"

"They won't be bothering us anymore," Cole said, looking back at the canyon.

Bray searched the area for the helicopter and didn't see it. Had it flown off while she was riding the horse? She wasn't going to ask.

She turned and pulled herself up onto the truck's rear bumper. Pulling the doors free, she jumped back down and watched them expand open.

"Where's the driver?" Cole asked.

"He ran off somewhere."

The air that hit her from inside the trailer was a smack of sweltering heat. It pushed out at her face. Scents of ammonia, iron and decay burned her nostrils. She turned away, nauseous, and took a deep breath.

When she turned back, she saw them. Dozens of sows stood there, eyes wide, staring at Bray. It was staggering, the sight of them. Some of the other bodies, long ago dead, had been lying on their sides, ravaged by flies, ripped with sores from the gestation crates.

Bray closed her eyes.

"Alice?" she called out.

"Yes. I am here."

Bray opened her eyes. The sows that stood at the door of the trailer began moving to one side. Slowly, a sow stepped forward, one hoof at a time, and stopped at the edge of the trailer.

The first thing Bray noticed was Alice's weight. It was overbearing, far too much for her legs to carry. And her hide, though a soft watermelon color, was scarred, deadened. One of her ears hung down. The other, cut at an angle, stood up as if to listen. And on her back, Bray could only just make out the red marking of the number four.

Then they met eyes. Bray recognized her immediately. It was as though they were two friends apart for centuries now come together, having lost nothing in their separation. Bray's heart grew heavy. She succumbed to tears. They rolled down her face, a long journey down to meet the earth—like the journey it had taken to get to this moment.

Bray jumped up onto the trailer, eager to touch her friend. Her hand reached out, felt along Alice's head, up and down her snout. Alice's eyes closed. Alice lifted her snout, licked Bray's hand. Bray smiled down at the sow, and then stood up. The ramp was on the truck's bed, beneath the sows.

"You are free to go," she said. "If you want. There are miles and miles of open land here, and—"

"Bray," her dad yelled, stepping up to the back of the truck. "I know you want to let them go, but if you do that, they'll die. Or S-Corp will come and get them."

"They're going to die anyway. And really, it's their choice. Some of them are dead already. And even if S-Corp does come for them, they at least deserve a few hours or days of open land, of freedom, of space to roam. Wouldn't you want that?" she asked.

Cole looked at her, but said nothing. In his eyes she could sense he knew she was right. She returned to Alice.

"If you want, I can help you down into the grass. You can be free, at least for a while."

"Please help us out," Alice said. The sows in the truck moved to either side of the ramp, giving Bray access to it.

With that, Bray pulled the trailer ramp

down. She walked up the ramp, and, one at a time, helped each sow walk down the ramp and into the grass.

When she returned to the truck, now empty save the deceased sows, she saw her dad walking over from afar, the truck driver walking beside him.

"What are you doing?" she asked.

"Letting him go," Cole replied. "Don't worry, he won't call the Marshals. Isn't that right, Mr.—"

"Philips," the driver replied in a hurry. "And if you can fairly compensate me, I'll go home and won't say a thing."

Cole pulled out his wallet. He reached in and grabbed all the bills inside and handed them to Philips. Philips nodded and took the money.

With that, Cole helped Philips unlatch the semi from the trailer. The man got into the semi. Bray watched him turn around and head back south, leaving the trailer and sows behind.

The sows that had disembarked slowly wobbled out into the open prairie and lay down. Each of them was horribly overweight, hide cut up or infected. They were all near the end of their lives, this Bray sensed. Without proper veterinary care or protection, they'd die in a matter of days-maybe sooner, if S-Corp didn't take them down first.

A few moments later, Cole came around the trailer. He stood beside Bray and looked out at the sows.

"Now what?" he asked, looking down at her.

"I'm going to sit here with them, until they die."

"You can't just stay out here in the middle of nowhere. You have no food, no water. Eventually drones will come circling the place looking for those two men your mother brought out here."

"One day you'll believe that I really can communicate with animals," she said,

looking away from him. She watched Alice lie
beside a group of sows on a hillside.

"But you won't survive out here," Cole
argued.

Bray turned and looked up at him. All
these years and he had never once stood up
for her. She was amazed he was even here,
that he wasn't trying to take her back home.
Even so, he owed her.

"Then bring me some food," she said.
"And how about this..." she continued.
"Bring *them* some food. Find someone to come
out here and protect them until they pass
on."

Cole looked at her. Then he looked at
the sows. He said nothing.

Bray thought about Alice dying. As she
looked over at her, lying there peacefully
in the grass, breathing in the fresh air for
perhaps the first time, and probably the
last time in her life, Bray's eyes teared
up. She couldn't save Alice, and now she
knew it. Something was going to happen to
her, too, as a result, but at least Alice

and the others weren't going to die violent, unnatural deaths. She was going to make sure of it. If she was going to die too, then she wasn't going to do it anywhere but out here. And she didn't want her dad to see. He'd be devastated, but none of this was up to him. Her life was no longer determined or decided by her parents.

It was hers now, and this was how she was going to live it.

"Okay," Cole spoke. "I'm going to take your mom back. I'll make sure she doesn't try anything. And I'll see what I can do to get you some help."

"Thanks," she said, holding back tears she really didn't want him to see.

He took her into his arms and hugged her, kissed her on the head. She welcomed it all. When he pulled back, his eyes were full of tears.

"Something tells me I'll never see you again," he said.

Bray looked at him. There was a chance he wouldn't see her again. And for a moment, she felt an inkling of sadness.

"I'll try not to be a stranger," she replied.

"Here," he said, pulling a small smartphone from his back pocket. "I got this all set up for you back in Denver."

"What, so you can track me with it?"

"All phones have tracking devices, but that's not the reason. I just want to know you're okay. Can you just send me an email every now and then, let me know you're alright?"

"No. I can't. I'm not taking that with me," she replied, unsure she'd be taking anything with her. "Why don't you write down your address. Let me know where you are. I'll send a letter."

"Okay, that's fair," he said. He walked back to the BMW, searched the glove box, and came out with a piece of paper and a pen. He scribbled something.

"I love you," he said, handing her the paper.

Bray nodded, smiling briefly.

Cole got into the BMW. Bray turned and watched him drive off, her mother's head motionless against the back window.

Chapter Sixty-Two

Dianna

When her eyes fluttered open, she saw a smoky gray ceiling. Things were blurry for a moment. She blinked a few more times. Turning, she recognized the white desk and the windows, through which she saw the sun was nearing the mountains. Over on one of the lounge chairs sat Cole.

"How the hell did I end up here?" Dianna asked. Last she remembered she was somewhere in Wyoming.

"I brought you," Cole replied.

"And Bray, where is she?" she asked. She sat up and composed herself. She didn't want Cole seeing her in any amount of weakness.

"She's fine," he replied, but said nothing more. He just sat there like a lump on a log. She couldn't believe she was attracted to him once.

"Where is she?"

"None of your business."

"Fuck if it isn't my business!" she shouted. She went to stand up and when she did, an ache pressed into her head. "What did you do to me?"

"You passed out, that's all. I've been keeping an eye on you to make sure you don't have a concussion."

"Oh, thanks," Dianna replied facetiously. "If you don't tell me where Bray is, I'll divorce you...and get full custody."

"We'll see about that," Cole replied. He stood up and walked over to the window, looked outside. It was evening. The sun had approached the horizon. It left a wave of peach color in the sky.

"Where's my phone?" She asked.

Cole reached into his jeans pocket and pulled out a small, red smartphone.

"Give it to me," she ordered, walking over to him. She grabbed for the phone and he yanked it away.

"I'll give it to you when you admit that Bray's not really sick."

"Excuse me?" she replied, aghast. He was being ridiculous. Again.

"I've been doing research on schizophrenia and I don't think she's sick. I think she's been misdiagnosed."

"Whatever, Cole," she said. Taking a step back, she crossed her arms. For him to say Bray wasn't schizophrenic was preposterous.

This was one of many reasons she couldn't stand Cole.

"I need to make some calls. Give me my phone," she said.

"Why? So you can try to find Bray again?"

"Absolutely. Someone has to take care of her, unlike you, being absent all these years."

"Hey," he replied, pointing a finger at her. "I realize I haven't been the best father. I'm trying to change that now. Here's your damn phone."

Cole tossed it on her desk and approached the door.

"You'll never find Bray. At least, not if I can help it. She's on her own now, and once she turns eighteen you won't be able to control her anymore."

"This isn't about control," she said, feeling uneasy in her chest. She picked up her phone and searched for Dan's number.

Cole did not respond. He only left, slamming the door behind him.

"Son of a bitch," she whispered, and called Dan.

He answered right away.

"What is it, Dianna?" he said. He sounded annoyed.

"I need your help again."

"Is it something for S-Corp?"

"No. Bray is still out there, missing."

Dan paused.

"I'm sorry, I can't," he replied. "I've got corporate handing me jobs right and left. I don't have the time, and really shouldn't be using S-Corp property for your personal issues."

Blood rushed to Dianna's forehead. She clenched her jaw. She wanted to throw the phone across the room. If she didn't find Bray, then Bray could be at risk of really harming herself, or worse. Especially being out there alone. The memory of the afternoon was returning to her. She hadn't seen Elliott with Bray. Maybe that was a good thing, but Dianna didn't like knowing that her daughter was out there by herself, at age seventeen, in a place where there was no civilization.

She closed her eyes. Her head filled with thoughts as to what kinds of things could happen to Bray, not to mention what could happen if the media eventually got ahold of this information. Surely there had to be a way to get Bray back.

"Fine," she said, taking a breath. "You know anyone else I can use?"

"I'll send you a couple contacts."

Dianna let go of the call and walked over to the couch, sat back down. She scrolled through missed emails and texts on her phone. She pulled up one from Carl:

GIVE ME A CALL ASAP.

KAGE & HER COUNTERPART ESCAPED.

"Christ's sake," Dianna said. Her head ached again. She lay back against the couch and rested her head. Closing her eyes, she let her mind flip through all the things she needed to do. The Wyoming project. Find Bray. Now, find Kage, because apparently no one else knew how.

Then, she remembered how Bray rode off on those horses—not once, but twice. Like they intentionally aided her in her escape from the checkpoint and then again in stopping that transport truck.

Which made no sense.

Dianna shook it all off and sat up. Her phone dinged with a set of texts from Dan. She'd find Bray soon enough. She couldn't have gotten too far. She would just have drones scan the radius for miles, then bring Bray back and put her in another hospital without Cole's knowledge.

Simple.

So long as Dianna was in charge, things always got done.

Period.

Chapter Sixty-Three

The Knocker

Pulling Serpentine's body out of the Knock Box was far easier than getting it in. When he had pulled it most of the way out, he held Serpentine's head and allowed the body to land on the floor, his head protected from hitting the concrete.

The Knocker ran upstairs and found some rope. Returning to Serpentine's body, he tied Serpentine's ankles and wrists together. Serpentine began to wake.

"Wha-what are you doing, man?" he asked, looking up at the Knocker.

"Be quiet. You're lucky I've spared your life," he replied, taping Serpentine's mouth.

The Knocker pulled Serpentine outside and over to his car. He unlocked and opened the back door. An unfamiliar, gray uniform sat bunched up on the seat. He stopped and

glared at it, confused. His chest rose.
Glancing around the property, his anxiety
building, he feared someone else was
watching. Medina was fucking with him by
putting some dead man's uniform in his car,
someone they'd offed to scare him.

"So be it," he said, yanking the
uniform out and tossing it on the ground.
Either Medina would fold to his request or
send someone to kill him. If he was going to
die after this, he was going to die.

Of course he couldn't just leave the
uniform on the ground. Then he'd be accused
of murder. He picked it up in his hands. A
memory of him standing in the uniform in the
surveillance office struck him suddenly. He
dropped the uniform and gripped his forehead
with his hands.

"No, no, no." He shook his head.

As he lifted Serpentine and pulled him
into the back seat, Serpentine moaned
through the tape on his mouth and struggled.
The Knocker just looked at him, shook his
head.

Glancing around, the place was empty. And he was parked too far away from the cameras for anything to be picked up on video.

With his forefinger and thumb, he carefully picked up the uniform and tossed it in on top of Serpentine's body. He slammed the car's back door shut and stepped into the driver's seat.

Veering out of the lot at eighty miles an hour, the Knocker drove thirty miles north. His hands shook as he drove. He ran them through his sweaty hair. His nerves raced in and out of his mind and chest. As the moon approached the top of the windshield, its fullness caught his eyes. Death would be still, like that moon, quiet. That wouldn't be so bad. For things to be quiet and dark sounded like a better life than this.

The Knocker pulled the car over to the side of the road along an embankment. He stepped out into the night air and took a deep breath. Yes, death wouldn't be so bad.

And if Medina or ICE or the police came for him, he'd off himself faster than they could catch him. That was the deal he made with himself.

#

The Knocker pulled Serpentine's body out of the car and dropped it into the dry grass. He ripped the tape off Serpentine's mouth, and Serpentine screamed. The Knocker took out a pocket knife and held it near Serpentine's face.

"Why did you have my family kidnapped?" he asked.

"They were becoming a threat to Medina. You know this. Carmen was involved with the coalition of campesinos that tried to stop Medina. Remember? I didn't really have a choice. You should know that too, since you worked for them yourself."

The Knocker pulled the knife away and sat back in the grass. He actually believed Serpentine. It made sense. Yes, now it all came together. He, the Knocker, *Bertan*, was a part of the intricate web of this corporate, disgusting agriculture system. Medina was S-Corp and S-Corp was Medina. Even as he thought he'd broken free all those years ago, it still had him. He'd been stuck in it and the delicate fibers wrapped around him so smoothly he did not notice, could not see.

But now, as he took a step back, he saw them all: Serpentine, Marcus, Ramiro, the list went on and on. Tiny ants climbing out of the web but getting nowhere. Those like himself who tried to get out only found themselves more deeply entangled. The others gave in, went along with the patterns rather than try to get away. They became the feed, and Bertan now saw the entire web as it stretched from Honduras, El Salvador, Nicaragua, Mexico, into the U.S. And now here, in Idaho.

Men like Serpentine weren't the problem. They were the bait.

Suddenly, his back pocket vibrated. The unexpected buzz against his buttocks jolted his memory. He was waiting on a text from

Medina. He quickly pulled the phone out.
Heart racing with anticipation, he saw a
photo text on his screen. He opened the
phone and then the text. Sure enough, it
wasn't an image, but a video. It showed a
car pull up to the side of the road
somewhere and push Carmen and Gabriella out
onto the sidewalk. The car veered off,
leaving them there, fully clothed and
without rope around their hands.

They were free. It wasn't exactly what
he'd asked for, but in that moment he
realized he didn't care. They were free, and
he now had to hurry up and find them.

"I'm going to let you go," Bertan said,
"but you better run, as far as you can. If I
ever see your face again, I will kill you.
You know I can."

Serpentine cried. He nodded his head,
tears pouring down his face.

"I'm getting away from all this, from
S-Corp, the plant, all of it. Maybe you
should, too," Bertan said.

Bertan cut the rope from Serpentine's

wrists and then his ankles. Serpentine stood up. Bertan stood and faced him.

"Get out of here."

And with that, Serpentine made a run for it. He ran toward the horizon where the sun was beginning to rise. There was nothing for miles and miles, so the likelihood of Serpentine surviving was slim. As far as Bertan was concerned, he'd spared the man's life, and that was enough.

Chapter Sixty-Four

Kage

Kage and Lana had made it back to Kage's bike across the road from the S-Corp facility. Night had arrived. It was cold. His breath racing, Kage pulled up the bike, started it. His wrist throbbed in pain. One of the carpal bones had popped out, and he was bleeding from it.

"I need something to wrap my wrist...stop the bleeding," he said.

Lana turned away from him. She reached up inside the back of her shirt and pulled out her bra. Turning, she wrapped his wrist with the bra. He winced in pain. For now, it would have to do.

He pulled himself onto the bike, and Lana got on behind him. She wrapped her arms around his torso. This gave him pause, to feel her arms wrapped around him. Despite his frantic need to get them both to safety, he couldn't help but take in how close she was to him.

"If you head for the Rockies, the mountains will block out the drones' search capabilities," Lana said, pointing northwest toward the etched-in gray mountains in the distance.

Kage revved the engine and drove off toward the mountains. Drones appeared as black dots in the sky, following them from above. Kage sped up to ninety miles per hour, crossing through the barren land, easing away from the highway and ever nearing the Rockies.

Thirty miles in, Kage came upon the edge of the mountains. The peaks crawled along the dark horizon like creepy, crawly creatures, which didn't give him much comfort. He turned the bike due north and bumped along the hillsides toward Wyoming.

Lana was right. Moments later the drones dropped away. He suspected Marshals would eventually be on their tail, so he continued on. The bike struggled along the

bumpy hillsides. The rough terrain slowed
their progress.

Then, Lana hit against his back with
her hand.

"Can we please stop?" she yelled.

Kage slowed the bike, approached a hill
of rocks that jolted out like broken teeth,
and stopped.

She jumped off the bike. She paced back
and forth. Kage could hear her breath
heightening.

"What's wrong?" he asked, stepping off
the bike.

"I just lost my whole team," she said,
stopping to glare at him.

"Yeah, I know," he replied. His
shoulders slumped. He knew it was his fault.

"You messed this whole thing up for us,
Kage."

"I know," he said. His heart sank. He
could tell she was disappointed in him.

"We're lucky they didn't take us, too.
Who knows what they've done with the others,
where they've locked them up," she said. She

stopped pacing and leaned against one of the two closest rocks, her back to Kage.

"Surely we can find out," he said, approaching her.

"No, we can't," she said, shooting back. She turned to him and her face was red, full of tears. "We can't just find them. Haven't you figured out by now who we're dealing with?"

"Of course I have," he said, stopping in his tracks. Now he felt offended. She knew what they did to his parents. He'd said from the beginning that S-Corp needed to be stopped, and she wouldn't listen. He was about to come back at her, but then he really saw her. He saw how shaken she was, her body visibly shook. Her eyes always had a light in them, and today it had gone out. And he was the one who had caused it to go out. Sure, S-Corp was responsible for that too. But she'd trusted him, opened her home, even a little bit of her heart, and he had hurt her. He was the reason they were standing here right now.

"I'm not going to waste your time with an apology," he spoke frankly. "I fucked up. And I can get us to safety, but we have to get moving. They'll catch up with us any moment now."

Kage looked back at the highway. It was empty, almost eerily so.

"How can I trust you when you got us all in this mess?" she said, wiping her tears away.

"That's completely fair. But where are you going to go from here?" he asked.

"I'll be just fine, I'm sure. You can drop me in Cheyenne."

Kage took a deep breath. He didn't know what to say. She was right, she had no reason to trust him. But if she knew about Meeteetse, maybe she could trust that.

"Look," he said. "I don't expect you to trust me. But you can trust where I'm taking you."

"And where's that?" she asked. She remained beside the rocks, only feet away, but the distance felt enormous.

"Meeteetse."

"Your home?"

"Yes. I'm sorry I didn't tell you earlier, because I was afraid to trust you. I lived there from the time I was sixteen, when my parents disappeared. My uncle Trevor, he worked for Walker's campaign. He was an activist, too. He came and got me and we fled. We'd heard from sources that Ethan Calter could house a few people at his sanctuary. Trevor convinced him to take us in."

"You mean *the* Ethan Calter?"

"Yes. We live there, at his sanctuary. There are no animals, of course. The government took them away. We've been hiding there ever since. It's completely off the grid. I can get us there, if you let me."

Lana looked at him quietly. As she did, his feelings for her came out of dormancy, lifted, and rose into his chest. Suddenly the pain of all that had happened, that asshole Carl, Lana handcuffed, crying, losing her friends to who knows what, all came up from a deep pit of guilt, and he cried.

Lana walked up to him, but he stepped back.

"I'm okay," he said, not allowing her to console him because of what he'd done. He needed to get her to safety, to redeem himself, partly, but mostly to just take care of her, because he loved her.

"We need to keep going, but I think you need to drive the rest of the way."

"But I don't know how," she said.

"I'll show you," he replied.

Chapter Sixty-Five

Bray

Pigs were such affable creatures. From the moment their feet touched the grass, the sows rubbed snouts, grunted as if greeting one another at a family reunion. Those who struggled to walk, such as Alice, leaned on the others for support. At one point they all stood together in a line, facing the mountains, and just quietly stared. It gave Bray shivers. It was a shame people never took the time to understand animals' capacity for friendship.

They all lay together in the grass until dusk. Bray sat beside Alice, exhausted. She had nearly fallen asleep when from the south came a line of three black pickup trucks, perfectly distanced from each other. Bray stood up.

Bray knew her mom all too well. By now

she could've woken up, taken control over her dad like she always did, and had S-Corp men out here in no time. The vehicles pulled into the grass beside the trailer.

One man stepped out dressed in jeans and a button-up shirt. He raised his hands in the air.

"We mean no harm," he yelled. "Your dad sent us."

Bray stood guard in front of the sows, watching as the men gathered around the trailer and pushed it off the highway and into the grass. The six men, all dressed in civilian clothing, donning their own rifles and shotguns, approached Bray.

"We came to protect them, as promised," the man said, pointing at the sows.

"Why?" Bray asked, not yet convinced.

"We owe your dad a favor. He's helped us all, a lot. It's the least we could do. My name's Rick. Here," he said, pulling a piece of paper from his pocket and handing it to her.

"He said you wouldn't believe me, so he

wrote you this note," Rick said.

Bray grabbed the note and stepped back. She read it, recognized her father's handwriting:

Bray — as promised, I'm trying to make up for it.

Please take the help. Rick's not here to hurt anyone.

It's the least I can do. I'm sorry.

Dad.

Bray took a deep breath, feeling a sense of protection from his words. Finally, he was doing something to help her. She folded up the letter and placed it in her pocket.

"We're not going to hurt anyone. You're welcome to stay with us, or our guy Tom over there can drive you back to Denver," Rick said.

"I'm not going back," Bray said, setting the rifle down.

"Well, your dad thought you might say that." Rick yelled, "Tom!" over to a younger man, maybe in his early twenties. Tom ran over to one of the trucks and pulled out a backpack and, returning, set it down in front of Bray.

"There's plenty of food, water. Your dad picked you out an extra pair of clothes. There's even a sleeping pad in the pack. That should hold you for a while."

Amazed, Bray went over and opened the bag. Sure enough, it was filled with food and water. He'd really come through for her this time. Better late than never, she supposed, and she smiled.

The men put up tents and started a fire. Bray stayed through the night to ensure they were doing what they promised— and also to rest for a fresh start in the morning. Bray's thoughts remained focused on Alice, who, though seemingly at peace, was growing tired along with the other sows. It wouldn't be long now, and Bray had no idea who she'd be, how she'd go on, if she survived this, without the constant companionship of Alice.

And that was the way of it with animals, wasn't it? That always humans thought of animals in relation to themselves, how humans would survive without them, not ever considering whether animals needed humans as much as humans needed them.

What was ironic to Bray in this moment was how they were all animals, and so, therefore, she was a part of it, thinking of not just animals but also other people only in relation to herself. How could she have done any of this without Elliott? He had lost so much, only to her own benefit, and it was wrong. It was the essential problem of separation, greed, that thing within each human that she couldn't quite put her finger on, or name. That thing that caused humans to thrive on the backs of others. It began with animals, with humans neglecting their own animalism.

Looking over at Alice, she thought it all quite sad. There wasn't much progress to be made if she herself could not look within and acknowledge that she, too, imprisoned the lives of others so she could be free. Because she was a part of it, she was responsible. In order to move on, she would have to see her own biases, her own shortcomings, how she took advantage of others.

How she was not much different from her mother.

Bray left the men sitting by the fire and disappeared into a tent. She lay down and nearly passed out from exhaustion. Before doing so, she called out for Alice. Alice wished very politely to be alone, just for tonight. Bray accepted, acknowledging Alice's right to say so. Only seconds later she fell asleep.

Chapter Sixty-Six

Bertan

Returning to the car, he saw again that uniform, staring out at him. He could not recollect why it was there. Hesitantly, he picked up the shirt and turned it over. The name badge on the chest read *Bertan*.

Bertan.

The name whispered in his ear, brushed his mind in a familiar, long-ago-heard masculine voice. It was as though he was being called, summoned.

"Bertan."

Bertan turned. There was no one around. The heavy moon continued staring down at him. Was it the moon?

No. That would be insane.

But wasn't *this* insane?

Could *he* be insane?

Probably.

"Bertan," a man's voice yelled out behind him.

He turned again, saw nothing but dry earth and a lonely sun edging up over the land. But then in the morning light, a shadow appeared. He froze. His heart opened by some outside force, something beyond his control.

"Bertan," the shadow spoke louder.

Bertan gazed at the shadow. It moved closer. He wanted to run but couldn't. The shadow took the shape of a man matching his height. The shadow came into fuller form. It stopped a hundred feet away. White hair flowed down to the shoulders and hung there. A soft, gray mustache lined his upper lip.

Bertan's father always had a mustache...and long, wavy brown hair.

The shadow stepped a few feet closer and stopped again.

Bertan's eyes winced. His heart raced with both fear and confusion, then began to open to a slim light of hope.

"Papá?" he called out, his mouth dry.

"Yes...it's me," the man replied.

Bertan's breath caught in his throat. Tears lifted from there and flowed from his eyes.

His father, whose name was Maynor, reached out his hand. Crying, not understanding—yet, not needing to—Bertan approached him. A wind lifted the dry dirt surrounding them. It circled Bertan's body, and the heaviness of it brought him to his knees.

Maynor stood out beyond the circling winds and could not be reached.

"Father, please," Bertan called out, "help me."

"I can't. I have to go," Papá said, his voice whispering in echoes.

"What? Where? Please, don't leave!" Bertan shouted, reaching out for his father.

The wind picked up. Bertan was pushed down onto his bottom. Sitting up best he could, his eyes locked onto Maynor.

"Your family is safe. Now end Medina,"

Maynor said, backing away.

"What?" Bertan screamed over the wind.

It sounded like he said to...end
Medina?

"How?" he screamed again, but Maynor
did not answer. Then, after a few moments,
he spoke.

"It's okay now, Bertan. Everything's
okay. Just come back, and it'll all be okay.
You do not have to use violence to end
violent things," Maynor said, his voice now
rising as he backed away farther. Beside
him, a second image appeared. That little
boy, the one Bertan had seen back in the
Kill Floor. Naked, protruding belly, about
four years old.

The boy he left to die.

Maynor took the little boy's hand in
his. Suddenly Bertan felt something in his
own hand. The sensation of tiny fingers
wrapped around his palm made his skin crawl.

Then, Maynor's body grew harder to see,
more transparent.

Bertan tried standing up. He pushed

against the force of the wind. It slammed him down to the ground.

"Just come back, just come back," Maynor said, repeating this over and over until his body disappeared.

Bertan's eyes flooded with tears. The wind calmed to a breeze and then stopped. Now there was nothing but the sky and the sun and the land and his car.

What did he mean, come back? Come back to where? Or from where?

The uniform.

He found it lying on the ground beside the car. Once again he looked at the name badge.

Come back.

How could he come back if he didn't know who or what to come back from? He was the Knocker. But then he glanced at the name Bertan, and slowly it came to him.

Bertan. His father had given him that name.

But that was not who he was. He was always someone else's. He was Medina's and then he was a slave for S-Corp. He was never his own except in those finite moments with Carmen and Gabriella.

Dropping the uniform into the dry grass, he lit a match. He watched the match as it fell, fully lit, onto the scrunched-up uniform. The tiny flame latched onto a piece of fabric and then doubled in size. It continued to spread. Bertan dropped the remaining matches into the pile. Slowly, the uniform went up in flames. He watched it burn. Something left his body and he felt lighter.

Maybe he did have choices.

#

Pulling out his phone, he called Ruben.

"Hello?" Ruben's voice answered.

"It's me...Bertan," he said, taking a moment to acknowledge the name.

"Where are you? You're supposed to be at work."

"I'm not going back to work. I'm done," Bertan said with finality, "and we need to talk...but not on the phone."

"Okay. There's a small trailer park in Clayton. Meet me there in an hour. Can you do that?"

"Yes."

Bertan hung up the phone. The uniform was now black ash, smoke rising into the sky. He couldn't go back to S-Corp. He thought of what his father said about ending Medina. He certainly wanted to end them, now more than ever.

But first, he had to get his family back.

Chapter Sixty-Seven

Kage

It had only taken a few hiccups in the road for Lana to learn how to maneuver the motorcycle. They got as far as the abandoned town of Casper when Kage noticed that the bra wrapped around his wrist was now soaked in his blood. They were still 140 miles from Meeteetse.

And Marshals were waiting at the gas station up ahead. Kage and Lana saw two of their shiny vehicles, lights off, in the station's lot as they approached. Lana stopped half a mile from the station, Kage shivering behind her.

"Why're you stopping?" he asked.

"You're losing a lot of blood. We need to get you medical help."

"But the Marshals," he said.

Lana slid off the bike and looked at Kage.

"Kage, you need help," she replied.

"But we're only a couple hours from home," he said, determined to keep going.

Lana looked back at the lot.

Kage tried to climb off the bike. Lightheaded, he fell forward, his head aiming for the concrete. Lana caught him in her arms and brought him down to sit on the earth.

He grew nauseous and lay on his side. He just wanted to go to sleep now. Everything around him spun. Through his eyes he saw Lana speaking down to him, but he couldn't hear her because he was so focused on not passing out.

He turned onto his good arm and faced the mountains from which they'd come. There beneath the morning's light he saw a pack of wolves or foxes trailing along. He thought of Lana and how he'd made a true mess of things. Trevor was right, maybe he should've never left home. He'd put everyone in danger.

And now here he was, lying helpless,

just beneath the nose of Marshals, with
Lana.

"Just go on," he called up to her.

"What?" she replied.

"Just—" he struggled to speak. "Just
go. I've already gotten you in this much
trouble. Just go into hiding, somewhere
outside of the city."

"No, Kage. We're in this together now.
You're the only teammate I've got left," she
said. Her voice was hollow. It sounded as
though they were talking under water.

His vision blurred. Lana knelt down
beside him and lifted him up. She removed
his jacket and used it to wrap his wrist.
Then he thought he saw her get back onto the
bike. His head fell to the ground and he
passed out.

Chapter Sixty-Eight

Bray

The next morning seemed to arrive in minutes. Bray woke feeling both rested and physically heavy. The heaviness she carried out into the daylight was not her own. Six of the remaining twenty sows had passed quietly in the night, and Alice had lost all ability to walk. Bray felt it in her thighs and feet. It was like walking with cement blocks. The six men sat around the fire, eating. She did not join them. She had no appetite. Soon she would need to move on, and there was still Alice to consider.

Bray walked slowly up to Alice.

"May I sit with you?" she asked.

"Yes," Alice replied.

Two sows sat on either side of Alice. Bray sat down facing Alice and looked at her eyes. They opened and glanced up at her with waiting.

Bray spent a moment just looking at Alice. This was the first time she had really seen her. The clipped ear, her eyes, her wet snout. The rosiness of her skin. The white spots on her back that were unique to her. She ran her hand along Alice's back where that red number four had damaged her beautiful skin. It was so surreal, sitting here now, seeing her friend like this.

What would she do without Alice?

"I want you to do something for me," Alice said.

"Anything," Bray replied.

"I want you to *live*. I want you to find your friends, find a home, and be happy. I want you to create a life for yourself."

"I'm not sure that'll be an option for me," Bray said, nearly crying. She wished so much that she could fulfill Alice's wishes. But what would happen to her physical body after Alice died?

"Will you die when I die?" Alice asked, lifting her head and looking at Bray.

"It's possible."

Alice scooted forward and rested her chin on Bray's knee. Bray teared up, afraid of the loss, of the not-knowing, of no longer having Alice to talk to. She brought her hand down and ran it along Alice's head and back, resting it there.

"I don't know how to say goodbye," Bray said.

"Life is continuation, never ending. We just go when it is our time, and we go alone because the journey is ours alone."

Bray nodded. "I'll miss you," she cried.

"Yes, indeed. As I will you. But we are a part of each other, as you said. You can take me with you, and I will take you with me."

Bray smiled, but there was no contentment in it. She used it as protection. She was going to lose Alice, and if she didn't die as a result, a part of her would die regardless.

"I hope you understand, now I need to be alone with the other sows. You must go, live, and be with others as you have been with me," Alice said. She raised her head and looked at Bray. "My suffering was made less because of you. Thank you."

Bray quietly nodded. While it saddened her down to the depths of her being that this was Alice's life from beginning to end, the only semblance of peace she could take from this moment was that, at the least, Alice would not be dying violently by the slit of a knife.

"I wish you safe travels, my friend," Bray said.

"Same to you, always. Always my friend," said Alice, and she pulled her head away and turned to lie on her side.

Bray stood up, feeling the weakness grow in her bones. *Like an old person*, she thought. She looked Alice over one last time. No one else would ever understand or know this friendship they had. That made her feel even more alone. But it was time to let it go, or at least just walk away.

Bray stepped through the grass, limping

as she went.

Suddenly she saw an electric motorcycle racing toward her through the prairie. Whoever it was had not been using the road and was approaching fast. Bray panicked and ran to hide behind the empty trailer.

The bike came to a stop behind the trailer. Footsteps trailed off to the side of the road. Bray moved around to the front of the trailer so she wouldn't be seen. She peeked around to view the bike. It wasn't a Marshal, just a plain bike. It could be S-Corp, though. She pulled back and begged for it to just be some strange, curious person. She worried about Alice and the sows.

"Can I help you?" she heard Rick's voice call out.

"I need help, please. My friend...he's injured. I left him back along the highway, too weak for me to carry him on the bike," a woman spoke. It sounded like she was crying.

Bray's heart opened. She sensed it was safe. She came out from behind the trailer. There standing across from her was a young woman, maybe in her early thirties, wearing sweat pants and a t-shirt. Not even a helmet. She looked exhausted and wired both.

"I'll come with you. We'll get him in the truck and bring him back here," Rick said. The woman followed Rick over to one of the trucks and got inside.

Bray watched the truck rush off and wondered who she might be.

Chapter Sixty-Nine

Bertan

Bertan drove twenty miles west. An abandoned trailer park came into view. He could tell it was abandoned by the damage of dust against the siding. On some houses the siding had completely slid off. Broken windows. No cars around save for Ruben's Volkswagen.

Bertan pulled up beside Ruben's car and got out. Now the day was warm, and Bertan felt at ease. Ruben was standing back between a row of trailers. Bertan approached him.

"Don't tell me you live here," Bertan said.

"No," Ruben said, smiling. "This is a good meeting spot, well hidden. I have to be quick though, so I can get back to the office."

"Okay. My family was released. They've been dropped in the streets...I think in Bajo Aguan. I need help finding them and getting them to safety," Bertan said, eager.

"What? How'd they get released?" Ruben asked, a look of surprise washing over his face.

"No time to go into that right now. Can you help me or not?"

"I'll try my best. I've got some people in San Pedro, old friends."

"Here," Bertan replied, pulling out his phone and texting Ruben the video of Carmen and Gabriella being pushed out onto the sidewalk.

Ruben reached for his phone and watched the video.

"I'll send this to everyone I know. It may take some time, but I'll do everything I can."

Bertan took a deep breath. He couldn't remember the last time he'd exhaled. He made one more call to Carmen's cousin Alex in San Pedro and begged him to go out and find his family. They weren't out from under the threat of Medina yet, but they were close.

#

Two days of excruciating time passed. Waiting, waiting. Checking his phone. Checking it again. Nothing. Bertan had taken all his belongings from the hostel in which he'd been living. He was now staying in Ruben's staff room in the S-Corp managers building. It made him extremely uncomfortable...sleeping so close to the very enemy he so wished to be rid of, but his choices were still limited.

It was night and Bertan lay on the floor staring out a square window, up into the empty sky. He hadn't spoken much to Ruben these last few days. He was frightened for his family and he could not keep his mind off their whereabouts.

The door lock clicked. He jumped. He wasn't expecting Ruben back for another hour.

Bertan ran into the bathroom and hid. He brought nothing with him to protect himself. Hadn't even considered it, for once.

The door opened.

"Bertan?" Ruben called out.

Bertan stepped out of the bathroom, looking down at his shorts, grateful he wasn't naked.

"You get off early?" Bertan asked.

"Well, not really. I just snuck away...when I saw this."

Ruben handed his cell phone to Bertan. On the phone's screen, a dark-skinned woman was lying in a hospital bed. The woman's face was drawn and pale. Was this Carmen? He zoomed in and saw the wrinkles in the woman's face. Bertan knew those wrinkles—from all the struggles they had been through together—well enough to know that this was his wife. A sudden feeling of elation, something he had not felt since the day his daughter was born, swelled within him, and he found himself weeping.

"Scroll to the next image," Ruben said

softly.

Bertan's finger swiped against the screen. There was an image of Carmen in the bed from a distance. Beside her...Gabriella.

"Where are they?" he asked.

"In a hospital in San Pedro Sula."

Bertan began to cry. It was relief and fear and some very odd sense of retribution. His family was safe, and alive.

"Thank you." Bertan lifted his head, rubbed the tears away from his face with the back of his hand.

"For what?" Ruben asked.

"For finding them."

"Well, it wasn't me, it was my coworker. But you are welcome."

"What coworker?" Bertan asked. His eyes met Ruben's.

"Just another social worker." Ruben cleared his throat. "We are working undercover together."

Bertan's face went white. An undercover cop had caught up with him.

"Don't worry." Ruben smiled. "You're

not in trouble. I'm not a cop, if that's
what you're thinking."

"Then what are you?"

"Social worker, remember?"

Bertan vaguely recollected past
conversations he had had with Ruben.

"I work for a grassroots animal rights
group. We have reason to believe that S-Corp
has been lying to the public about many
things. We've been building up a case
against them for quite some time now. And
that file you and I found confirms they are
connected with Medina," Ruben explained. "A
lot of the information we need we can't get
because we don't have the ability to access
S-Corp's system."

"Access?" Bertan asked. "Like to their
computer system?"

"Among other things, yes."

Bertan thought for a moment. He had
always hated working for S-Corp. They paid
next to nothing, sometimes didn't pay
workers at all, and there was nothing anyone
could do about it. They had complete control

over their workers because most were undocumented and had no legal rights.

Bertan also thought about that comment his father's ghost had made, about ending Medina.

"I may be able to get you in," he said at once.

"How? And why? This is your chance to be with your family."

"I'm more on the inside, even than you are. I'm one they can trust. All I need is to get the right passcode from a worker, and we're in. And I'm willing to get it in ways you are not."

"I'm not sure I like the sound of that."

"Trust me with this. If it helps take down Medina, that's a plus for me...and my family."

"Well, we can certainly keep Carmen and Gabriella in hiding. But are you sure? We could get you to them tomorrow, send you back home to be safe. All three of you will need to live in hiding."

Bertan thought again. His heart ached, cracked for Carmen and his daughter. And he knew Carmen wanted him to come home. She'd even said she'd leave him if he didn't. But he felt very strongly in his heart that first he needed to help this man, he needed to end Medina, to redeem himself.

"I'm sure."

"All right," Ruben said, smiling. "But there is one condition to you helping us."

"What?" Bertan asked, stiffening.

"I think you have what's called post-traumatic stress disorder. It basically means you were triggered, probably by the disappearance of your family, and it brought on a series of flashbacks, losing track of time, and anxiety. It may explain the split in your identities."

"What are you talking about? Split identities?" Bertan asked, trying to be open.

"Once, in my office, you presented as 'the Knocker.' You were like a whole other person."

Bertan's eyes widened. His mind drifted back to this morning. The fire. He held his security guard uniform in his hand, but he didn't quite recognize it. He remembered not wanting to be called Bertan anymore, not wanting to be called the Knocker.

"I remember now," he said, almost automatically.

"Remember what?"

"The other day. My father's ghost, he came to me," he said, staring at the wall behind Ruben's head. "He said come back."

"Come back?"

"Yes," Bertan said, his eyes meeting Ruben's. "Maybe he meant I need to come back to myself."

"That makes sense."

Bertan took a deep breath. "So what is the condition?"

"I want you to work with me, on the trauma. I can help you, if you feel ready to work on it."

Bertan glanced down at Ruben's phone, which was still in his hand. He pulled up

the photo of his family. Tears filled his
eyes completely. They really were alive.
Carmen would want a better life for him,
even more than he wanted it for himself.
That was how much she loved him. And the
only way he was going to get help with this
mental anguish he'd been through was to work
with Ruben. He was never going to be good
enough for his wife if he didn't get help.

"Okay, yes," he said, sniffling and
handing the phone back to Ruben.

"Great," Ruben said, taking the phone
and sliding it into his pocket. "The best
way to do this will be to have you
transferred to another plant, farther
north."

"Why?"

"My main office is there. I'll have
more time to work with you, and I think it's
best for you to retire from knocking cows,"
Ruben said, smiling.

"Right." Bertan nodded.

"I'll recommend you be relocated. I'll
request that you work in a security job

because of your trauma issues," Ruben said, and then stopped. "You sure you want to do this?"

"You just gave me my life back," Bertan said, glancing at the phone. "So, yes."

Ruben looked at Bertan.

"So...you never told me about the other day," Ruben said.

"The other day?"

"How your family got released in the first place?"

Bertan looked out the window into the night. He thought about Serpentine, wondered if the man was still alive. If he was serious about working with Ruben then he knew he'd have to tell the truth.

"I got into it with Serpentine. He had them kidnapped. I wanted to kill him. I had him in the Knock Box, ready to knock him. But then that ghost...Chino's daughter...she came to me. She asked me to stop killing."

"You mean her ghost?"

"Yes. And so, for whatever reason, I couldn't kill him. Instead, I threatened him until he called Medina and had my family released. I brought him all the way out here, let him go."

"Why'd you decide not to kill him?" Ruben asked.

Bertan turned to Ruben and looked him in the eye. For once, he could look a man in the eye and see him as himself, rather than someone he needed to kill or someone he couldn't trust. With a clean and firm resolution, he replied.

"Because I could."

Chapter Seventy

Kage

Kage felt himself being pulled up to his feet. He forced his eyes open. Lana helped him into a black truck. She got in the front seat, slamming the door. He heard gargled words, couldn't make sense of anything. He was lying on his back, looking out the window at the stars above.

They started moving. Crisp air from the driver's window touched his face. Its cool feeling brought some relief. He opened his eyes and saw the stars. They spun above him. Suddenly he was back at the age of thirteen, when his parents took him to the county fair to expose him to the way they treated their farm animals. He saw everything in those stars now, the mixing of the world and the animals, how if people would connect more to the stars maybe they'd see more clearly what was happening, what had happened years ago to his family. Though he was in a fevered hallucination, he saw so clearly now that the stars were calling him. Maybe it was his parents calling him. He did feel them in his heart just then, opening it and stepping in, echoing into his mind: we're still alive, come find us...

Then he grew nauseous. His head jolted forward and he turned it to the side as the truck slowed down onto the side of the road. He threw up on the floor, on his pants. He keeled over. The pain had turned into some strange ecstasy. Somehow he'd risen to some higher plane where nothing Lana said could reach him. He only saw himself being pulled out of the truck and carried over to a hillside. When they laid him down, he saw sows lying beside him.

And then he went unconscious.

\#

When Kage woke, everything was bright, new. He sat up on the hillside and glanced around. Beside him, a pair of sows lay quietly. His mouth dropped open from curiosity.

"What the hell?" he asked aloud.

Looking down at his wrist, he found that the bone had been set on either side with two pieces of metal and wrapped in layers of gauze. It was starting to hurt again.

Several feet down where the hill flattened out into a small field, there sat two tents. A man sat by a fire that was burning out. Lana was sitting there eating beside a teenage girl. Kage stood up, feeling queasy and hungry, and slowly walked over to them.

"You're up," Lana said, standing up and smiling.

Kage looked down at the man and the girl.

"Yeah," he replied, rubbing his head. "I feel like I'm going to be sick."

"You need to eat," the man said, lifting up a plate with baked beans on it.

"These vegan?" Kage asked without hesitating.

"Yep," the man said, handing him the plate and turning back to tend to the ending of the fire.

Kage sat down on a rock beside Lana. He looked over at the girl. She was wearing baggy, forest-green pants. They reminded him of Emily's yoga pants. Her short-sleeved shirt was dirty, and so was her face. Her flat, long, brown hair stuck to her shoulders the way wet leaves cling to the ground in the fall. She looked to be a teenager.

"Name's Kage," Kage said after gulping down a spoonful of beans.

"Bray," she replied. She turned and looked off at the sows.

"What's going on here?" he asked.

"You wouldn't believe it," Lana

replied. She was still smiling and seemed the most relaxed he'd ever seen her. "She stopped that transport truck. It was full of sows headed to slaughter."

Kage turned and looked over his shoulder. A transport trailer had been sitting by the side of the road. Three pickup trucks lined up in a row behind it. A group of men were sitting beside one of the trucks, talking.

"Who are the men?" Kage asked, a little on edge.

"Just some friends who came to watch the sows. Most of the sows have died off at this point," Lana said.

Kage looked over at Bray again. The girl was quiet, pensive. She kept her eyes on the sows and seemed to pay no mind to Kage or Lana.

"How long was I out?" he asked, still baffled by this whole situation.

"Just a couple hours."

He nodded and glanced over at Bray.

"So how in the world did you stop this

truck? Did these guys help?" he asked her.

But Bray only stood up and quietly wandered off toward the sows.

"That's the thing," Lana replied. "She did it with the help of some horses."

"What?" he asked. "Am I dead? Or dreaming?"

"No," Lana said, laughing. "Trust me, it's still sinking in for me, too. Apparently she has psychic ability. She can sense what's going on with animals."

"Huh?" Kage said. He'd never heard of such a thing. When he was a teenager, he'd met people who claimed to be mediums, spiritualists who could connect with a spirit world that he never believed in.

So he wasn't about to believe in this, either.

"We have a few of them in Hawaii," Lana continued. "They're called empaths. They can sense and, in her case, can even experience another's pain directly."

"What do you mean, experience their pain?" Kage asked.

"If something happens to them, it happens to her." Lana paused and looked out at Bray. Bray had gone over and sat down beside one of the sows. "I think she's experiencing their deaths, one at a time."

"Ha," Kage let out a laugh. "That's malarkey."

Kage finished off the beans and set the plate down on the ground beside him. He stood up, feeling fresh and like he'd slept for days. Curious about this strange teenager, he started over to her.

But then a voice lifted from somewhere within.

Stop, it said.

And it sounded young, feminine.

Like Bray.

Now even more puzzled, Kage was determined to go find out what the hell this person was all about.

No.

He stopped in his tracks. From here he could see Bray sitting beside one of the last remaining, living sows, running her hand along its belly. Suddenly Kage realized he was about to walk in on something private, so he kept back, and watched.

Chapter Seventy-One

Bray

With each moment she had left with Alice, Bray wanted to be fully present. But it scared her to be here, to be sitting beside her dying friend. Her heart pulled and ached like it was being stabbed with a very wide blade. She couldn't tell what scared her more: losing Alice, watching her die, or possibly dying herself.

Suddenly her body felt itself being stretched forward and back. Instinctively, without thought, Bray closed her eyes.

I'm ready now, Alice said, but the voice became Bray's own, in her mind. *Are you?*

I'm not, Bray thought. She felt tears reach up from her chest and roll out of her eyes. They were hot and, as they fell down her face, she noticed how her mind wished to resist what was happening. To push it away, to get up and turn away.

Bray opened her eyes. Her vision was blurred. Alice's eyes had shut to the world, never to open again. It was only a matter of time before Bray's vision would go, too. Her heart eased its beats. Rick and those new people seemed as though they were miles behind her. She could reach out to them for relief from the pain, but she knew this was where she was supposed to be.

She knew she had to experience it all.

Bray's motor skills dissipated. Her hand stopped touching Alice's belly and dropped to the ground. She felt her heartbeat through her entire body. It was all she could hear, thump...thump...thump...drawing down like sap from a tree. Down, down, getting darker. Her muscles released. Alice's name flashed through her mind.

Then, she released one lifted breath. A bright and coming shining star, like the sun but purple, and then a million rising stars

all around it, bright, white, blinking,
inviting, star dust. The thumping slowed
into a hum, a whispering hum, and then it
was gone.

Chapter Seventy-Two

Kage

Bray's body fell over onto the sow's belly. Her head landed there and remained, unmoving.

"Lana!" Kage screamed, looking back to Lana, and then he ran over to Bray.

He dropped to his knees beside her. She appeared unconscious. He shook her shoulder.

"Bray?" he called, but nothing. She just lay there, as if she'd passed out. He brought his fingers up to her neck to check her pulse. His heart raced and he took a deep breath, fearing that she'd somehow died.

"What happened?" Lana said, running up to him. She was out of breath.

"I don't know. She just...passed out," Kage said.

Suddenly he had the thought to check

the sow. He'd glanced over to her and saw that her stomach was not rising or falling. He placed his hand on her belly and, sure enough, she'd passed away. His eyes shifted back over to Bray. Just as he was making some connection in his head about the two of them, something in what Lana had said about Bray connecting to animals...

And then Rick approached and bent down beside them.

"You need to get her away from here," he said. "S-Corp is onto us. Just intercepted a radio call. Marshals are coming this way."

"Time to get to Meeteetse," Lana said, glancing over at Kage.

"Come on, you can take one of our trucks," Rick said, pulling Bray up to his chest and running off, carrying her.

Kage and Lana followed him over to the truck. Kage couldn't quite believe that these random men were really here to help, that they could be trusted. Clearly there were still people in this world who didn't side with S-Corp.

Rick slid Bray's body into the back seat of the truck.

"You'll have to drive," Kage said to Lana, pointing at his wrist and jumping into the passenger seat.

Rick shut the back door. He walked over to Lana and handed her a key.

"Why are you helping us?" she asked him. Kage was listening from inside the truck.

"No time to explain. You've got to go. Our scrambling equipment won't keep the drones at bay much longer."

Lana got into the driver's seat and slammed the door. When she started the engine, she immediately sped off, heading north.

"You lead the way," she said to Kage.

"Just keep north. About thirty miles up you'll take a left onto 120. I think if we appear as normal as possible we'll pass and won't be bothered."

Along the way, Kage climbed into the

back seat and tried waking Bray. She was out. Alive, but out. Her pulse was faint and sometimes went so low he could hardly tell if she was living or dying.

"She needs CPR," Lana shouted back to Kage.

"Uh...how?" he asked. He had never learned it. Not to mention his broken wrist.

"Lay her down as flat as possible," Lana said, keeping her eyes on the road. "Lift up her shirt and give her thirty chest compressions, right between her breasts."

Once Lana finished giving Kage direction, he carefully slid Bray's body down to lie flat on the back seat. He knelt down on the floor and looked at Bray. Her face was restful, at peace. For some reason he feared disturbing her.

He placed the broken wrist on top of her so that the splint pressed into her chest. He then placed his good hand overtop the splint. He took a deep breath and started the compressions. The pain made him cringe, but he kept going.

Then, he lifted her mouth open and pushed his breath in. It was strange to be this close to another human. Almost foreign to him. He detached from it emotionally, focused on the task at hand, and kept going.

But nothing changed.

Lana turned the truck onto 120 West.

"Now what?" she shouted back to him.

He was in the middle of compressions. He glanced out the window, tried remembering where they were. She'd just turned, which meant they were within fifty miles of home.

"Just keep driving," he replied.

Kage kept working on Bray. He'd pressed into her so many times he'd lost count. His wrist throbbed in agonizing pain. Eventually, he had no choice but to stop. Exhausted, he turned and looked at Lana.

"I can't," he said. The exhaustion was so much that he nearly cried.

"It's okay," she replied back. "Is she still breathing at least?"

"Yes."

"Just come up here and rest. There's

not much else we can do."

Kage pulled himself up into the front seat and sat back. He felt defeated. Though he didn't know the girl, he obviously didn't want her to die or end up with brain damage. Whatever happened back there confused him beyond anything, even beyond the confusion of what happened to his parents.

This was just some young girl that tried helping sows, that somehow stopped them from going to slaughter. Truth be told he was impressed, and he wanted desperately for her to live.

Lana reached over and grabbed his good hand, held it. She turned to him and smiled. He smiled back, but he was only feigning. There was so much going on in his head. Who was this girl? Why wouldn't she come to consciousness after all he'd done? And what were Trevor and Ethan and the others going to think when he returned with two strangers?

He closed his eyes and wanted to drift off.

"I need you awake," Lana said. "You have to show me the way."

Kage exhaled. He opened his eyes and nodded at her.

Soon they approached Meeteetse's abandoned downtown. Lana slowed the truck.

"Is it safe to drive through?" she asked.

"I don't know. Just keep going."

The both of them stared at the buildings as they passed. Old, concrete buildings that once housed cafes, inns, and banks. Then there were the houses, their siding falling off and windows broken or shuttered and sealed. Abandoned cars lined the two-lane street. These were cars that ran on gasoline and weren't even being made anymore. For Kage it felt like home, something familiar. He hadn't realized his shoulders were tense until the familiarity brought them down and calmed him.

"Wow," Lana said. "I feel like I'm in a time warp."

"And I feel like I'm home," Kage said,

smiling.

The town disappeared behind them. Everything opened to green valleys and prairies. The trees livened beneath a pleasant afternoon sun.

"Everything here is so...alive," she said.

"That's because S-Corp hasn't touched it yet."

And then Kage went quiet, as quiet as the land around them.

They turned onto a dirt road that had been created by years of Trevor and Kage passing through with their vehicles. Soon, the house would come into view. Soon he would know if Trevor made it back. Soon he would find out if they'd even agree to have him back.

When the corn crops popped up along the left, he sat up.

"Turn here."

"Where? Into the crops?" she asked.

"Yep," he said, his heart opening the closer they got to the house.

Lana turned the wheel. The truck
bounced and pushed through a narrow path
that cut through the crops. And then the
crops opened to reveal the front yard and
the house.

"My god," Lana said, parking the truck
and staring at the house.

"It's beautiful, isn't it?"

She nodded, as if speechless.

Kage got out and ran for help, praying
it wasn't too late for Bray.

#

There in the back gardens, Ethan sat
bent down, his back to Kage. Kage ran up to
him, hoping he wouldn't startle the old man.

"Ethan," he called out.

Ethan turned quickly. His confused face
swiftly changed into a warm smile. He stood
up, opened his arms. Kage walked up to him,
and they hugged. While in the firm embrace,
Kage broke down and cried.

"Are you okay?" Ethan asked,
immediately noticing Kage's wrist.

"We need help," Kage replied, pointing

back to Lana, who was attending to Bray in the back seat of the truck.

Ethan followed him to the truck.

"She's unconscious," Lana said, pulling away from Bray and looking at Ethan.

Ethan pulled Bray out of the truck and ran her into the house.

Kage walked up onto the porch, hesitant to enter. He was afraid to encounter Trevor, but after all that had happened, he knew he owed a huge apology, to say the least.

Kage opened the screen door for Lana. She stepped into the house. He entered behind her and stopped. There sitting at the dining room table was Trevor, reading some book, just as on any given day.

Trevor looked up and froze. Kage waved quietly to him.

Trevor jumped up and ran over to Kage. They hugged.

"Where the hell—" Trevor started, and then stopped with a heaving of tears.

"I'm sorry, uncle," Kage replied,

crying with deep regret.

"What happened?" Trevor asked, looking at his wrist and then up at Lana.

"I can explain everything. I just want to say how sorry I am. I really messed up. I hope you'll have me back home."

Trevor looked into his eyes.

"This is always your home, you know that," he said. "But who's this, and the girl upstairs?"

"This is Lana. She's an activist, and she needs to hide. S-Corp caught us, but we got away. And the girl, her name is Bray. Lana can explain better than I can, but apparently she saved a whole transport truck of sows from slaughter."

"She what?" Trevor asked. His eyes shifted from Kage up to the ceiling.

"She's an empath," Lana replied. "She has a gift."

Trevor said nothing. Instead, he looked back at Kage.

"Were you followed?" he asked.

"No," Lana spoke up. "Kage made sure of

that."

"You can stay for now," Trevor replied.
"But we've all got some talking to do. You
know having strangers in the house makes me
uneasy."

"I get it," Kage said. "But I made some
pretty big mistakes, caused Lana to lose her
entire team of activists."

"Don't give yourself so much credit,"
Lana said. "I think we can all agree that S-
Corp was the true culprit. You just led them
to us, is all," she said, touching his
shoulder.

"Right. Well I need to see Virgil about
my wrist," he said, eying the stairwell.

"Shit. Yes, sorry," Trevor replied,
stepping back so Kage could pass.

Kage walked up the wood staircase
toward Virgil's room. As he rose to the
second floor, he looked into his room. There
on the bed, Virgil was practicing Reiki on
Bray. Kage stopped at the doorway and
glanced in. He watched the young Bray, still
unconscious. His eyes glanced around the

room. All of a sudden, he felt inside a new
sense of knowing. All along he'd been
searching for his parents, yet his family
was here. It didn't mean he was done
searching for them. He knew they were out
there. But for today, he needed this family.
This was his *home*.

There was a place for him in this world
that needed protecting. A place that needed
him to step up and act on its behalf. A
place that, if he didn't act soon, might be
lost just the same as his parents.

He'd survived S-Corp, and he was still
here, intact. Nothing was going to break his
spirit. Living here all these years had
taught him what it was to be good, to stand
for something meaningful—even if the rest of
the world overlooked it.

As he sat and watched Virgil, Emily,
and Ethan gather around Bray's unconscious
body, he saw a gathering of something new.
He saw something coming. Maybe there was
more of a purpose to his life than only

seeking his parents.

Maybe this was only the beginning.

Chapter Seventy-Three

Cole

After he left Dianna's office, Cole returned home. Of course it was no home without Bray. He felt oddly alone. Empty. This because he knew Bray wouldn't come back. She couldn't, not with Dianna here. And that was the saddest thing of all. He had to let her go off and be herself without getting to see her do it. A heaviness hung in his chest. He was standing in the kitchen, staring at the family photos again.

He stepped over and pulled one off the wall, placing it on the table. Then, he just kept going. He took down all of them. He went out into the garage and found an empty box. There were several empty boxes sitting in the back corner. Suddenly he remembered how he'd accumulated them over the years, in case he ever needed them. He had known, on some level, that this marriage was not going to last.

What was more, he hated this house. Dianna had chosen it. It was stale and void of emotion and character. And it was too far away from the reality of Denver, of his constituents.

Throughout the evening, he busied himself by packing up all of his belongings. Upstairs he pulled all his clothes, suits, emptied the dresser. Dianna's belongings he did not touch, avoided them as if touching them might cause him certain death.

He called his lawyer and left a message. He wanted a divorce.

As the hours passed, he heard nothing from Dianna, and expected not to. By now she was surely finding new ways to track down Bray. And what of Elliott? He was nowhere to be seen when Cole found Bray. And he didn't even think to ask. That was his problem: never taking enough time to know Bray, anything about her life or this "gift" she claimed to have.

By night, the front room was filled with

boxes. His clothes, photos of Bray,
everything from her room that he would store
for her in hopes of seeing her again one
day. He looked over everything, saw his
whole life as just boxes of time that
passed, as if he wasn't there to experience
what was inside. Like the boxes were empty
and he avoided filling them. And now there
were fifty or so, to account for the number
of years he hadn't actually lived. And yet
the space around them was so vast, so open
and wide and uncharted.

A swirl of pain and sadness and hope
brought him down to the floor where he
cried. He cried until there was nothing
left. Until all that went unresolved inside
of him came to rise out and escape through
his tears.

And then he felt empty again. Empty but
resolved. There was nothing he could do now
but get up and move on, pick up the boxes
and leave. He thought about a vacation, to
go off into the mountains to reset for a
couple of weeks.

But he couldn't leave Bray. Though she was gone, he could still protect her from afar. He could keep an eye on Dianna, pull his resources to help her if she ever needed it, stay nearby to await the day she might contact him. For himself, he'd secure a suite on the top floor of one of those apartment buildings, get closer to the lives of his constituents. Use his senate position to consider things differently rather than be led by a chain he allowed Dianna to pull all these years. He was a grown fucking man and it was about time he lived his own life. For himself and for Bray.

He sat up on the rug, cleared the tears from his cheeks. He thought about Bray. She was so composed, brave, and with it, when he saw her. She'd been off meds for days, yet now that he thought of it, she didn't seem sick at all. She was more coherent and resolute than even Dianna. She kept her calm in the midst of a deadly situation. Didn't once lose her cool, even as he'd arrived and witnessed her handcuffed by Dianna's men.

How could it be that Bray was mentally ill? It was making less and less sense. Maybe she was a bit eccentric, with this whole thing about animals. But somehow she managed to free all of those sows, to know they'd be dying soon. If anything, it was Dianna who was mentally unstable.

Growing exhausted, Cole stood up. Not wanting to ever sleep in that bed upstairs again, he went in and lay down on the couch. Tomorrow he would call a moving company, put all these boxes in storage until he found a place to live. A place with a second bedroom for Bray, in case she ever needed it. A place to call his own. He'd divorce Dianna—she could have the damn house—and he'd continue on with his life. Maybe he'd run for president, maybe he wouldn't.

As much as he felt deeply sorry for allowing Bray to be carted in and out of that psych ward all these years like some animal, he didn't know then what he clearly believed now. Thanks to what he saw yesterday, the veil had been lifted from his eyes and he was beginning to *see* his daughter.

Epilogue

The scent of herbs touched her nose. She opened her eyes. Everything blurred. Blinking, she made out a white ceiling. Distant voices and rumblings caused her to turn. There, a closed door. She was in someone's bedroom.

"Bray?" said a vaguely familiar voice.

She looked over and saw someone sitting in a chair. It took a moment for her to realize it was Kage, the person she'd met back by the transport truck. He looked much cleaner now, and his wrist was wrapped tightly in some kind of makeshift cast.

"Where am I?" she asked, struggling to speak.

"It's a sanctuary, in Meeteetse. You passed out and we brought you here."

"Passed out?"

"Yep. Right when that sow died," he replied.

Alice?

Bray closed her eyes. She felt an odd, unfamiliar, almost frightening silence inside of her.

Alice? she called out.

Nothing.

Bray remained with her eyes closed, waiting. As she waited, she searched herself. She'd been accustomed to feeling the presence of Alice inside of her at all times. That feeling was only evident to her now that it was gone.

"I was scared to death you might never wake up," Kage said, interrupting her thoughts. She opened her eyes and looked at him.

She sat up.

"Careful," he said, helping her up to sitting. "I'll get you something to eat."

Kage left the room. The open fields outside the window caught her eye. From the bed she raised her head and looked out at them. A sudden flash of the open prairie and the sows slipped in and out of her mind. Were they still alive? She wasn't ready to accept that Alice was gone.

She sat back against the bed's headboard and closed her eyes again. For a second time, she called out to Alice. She listened, and listened, and listened. But there was simply nothing. There was just an empty space where another soul used to be. Like being in a house alone after someone had just left it. She shook with trepidation. This feeling, though peaceful, was also entirely unsettling. She didn't know how to feel so singular, so...herself. Alone.

Kage entered the room carrying a bowl of soup. He sat down gently on the side of the bed.

"Here you go," he said, handing her the bowl. "And you'll be pleased to know it's vegan."

"What?"

"Yep. We're all vegans here."

Bray looked down at the soup. It felt warm between her hands. She wished Alice were here.

"What's wrong?" Kage asked.

She hesitated. For a second she thought Kage might not understand. But she was here alone, and Elliott was long gone. If she was going to make new friends, she decided she'd better start out telling the truth.

"I'm not sure how much you know about me, or my abilities," Bray started.

"I was told you're an empath," Kage replied.

"Well, I think I experienced Alice's death," she explained. "I wasn't supposed to live after that."

Kage looked at her with narrow eyes, as if confused.

"Alice was one of the sows."

"The one I found you passed out beside?" Kage asked.

"Yes. She was...my friend. She was the one who led me to that transport truck."

"Huh," Kage blurted out. He looked over at the wall.

"You don't believe me, do you?" Bray asked. Once again, here were more people who might think she was mentally ill.

"Not really. But does it matter whether I believe you or not?"

And then Bray teared up. For whatever reason, that was exactly what she needed to hear.

"Hey now," he said, pulling her in and hugging her. "You gave those pigs a chance to die in peace."

"But I just wanted to save them," she responded, sobbing.

"I'm sure you did. I'm sorry," he said, pulling back.

Kage stood up suddenly.

"I'm going to leave you to it, let you rest," he said.

"Thank you, Kage."

"Sure thing," he said, winking and closing the door.

Bray set the bowl of soup on the table beside the bed. She went over to the window and looked outside. Corn crops separated the yard from the road. It made for good protection, safety. She heard voices downstairs, some laughter, carrying on. She didn't know anything about the people here but sensed the level of connection and relationship, even from upstairs.

Relationship. Connection. *That was it*, she thought. The thing she couldn't quite place her finger on before, when her mom nearly had her in that helicopter. That's what was missing from the world: the kind of friendship she had with Alice, *oh Alice*. How she missed her. And Elliott. Gone—but not really. The bond between animals, the bond that made everyone very much the same. Heck, if the bond between her and her dad could even be improved, then surely there had to be a way to help heal the bond between animal and human.

Now that Bray had seen herself save Alice with her own abilities, she began to wonder if there was more she could do. Maybe if people knew what she knew about animals, things could change. Maybe she could show them.

A slow knock tapped at the door. Bray's shoulders tensed. She turned.

"Yes?" she said, hesitating.

The door slowly opened. There stood a bald man, over six feet tall, toothpick thin.

"May I come in?" he asked.

Bray nodded, still uncertain.

The man walked in, left the door open. He stopped at the foot of the bed and looked at her. On the top of his head she saw the edges of a tattoo, what looked like a chicken talon. It was kind of strange.

"My name is Ethan," he said, smiling.

"Bray," she replied.

"Nice to meet you." He nodded to her, slid his hands into the pockets of his pants. "I hear you're a bit of an animal aficionado." He paused and sat down on the edge of the bed. "Tell me more."

THE END

ACKNOWLEDGEMENTS

Thanks to my patrons: Debbie, Raeann, Aurora and Sandy.

Thank you to my Higher Power, family and friends for giving me the space, creative energy and support to complete this long-awaited project. To all the fans and people that have supported Sentient from the very beginning, there are too many to list. Thank you for who you are and for how you believed in something when no one else would. You are why I write.

And thank you to my Editor Susan and my Book Marketer, Rachel. The both of you helped me believe in Sentient's worth.

To my long time Writing Coach, Robin: Your unbending encouragement and support have not gone unnoticed. You helped me see and believe in my own worth as an author. I will never forget you were the one that pushed me to finish this book.

Lastly, I cannot walk away from this novel without acknowledging the countless animal rights activists who silently and anonymously get out there every single day and do whatever they can to save animals. Thank you to those that have helped me along this journey, who have provided research, offered time for interviews, and have been there to ensure this book was as accurate as possible, regardless of its fictionality. I hope it does your work some justice.

Thank you.

ALSO BY JAY VANLANDINGHAM:

The Animalist Code Mini Series:

Finally, a dystopian fiction series addressing the dire effects of climate change as a result of animal agriculture!

It is the year 2035…

Emerson Howell is a transgender social worker who desires to end animal agriculture. When he develops special powers that cause him to experience horrific visions and voices of animal cruelty at a nearby factory farm, he creates a plan to save them. But these special powers become as much a curse as a blessing when he loses himself in the hidden world of animal agriculture. Will he be able to save these animals, or will he *disappear* like so many animal activists of the past?

To learn more and connect with Jay, visit: www.jayvanlandingham.com